"*Of Darkest Valor* is an ambitious first offering with excellent potential for a new fantasy action series! Highly recommended."

-The Columbia Review.

"Dotted with magical surprises and streaks of blood [Of Darkest Valor] provides a swift journey through a land of kings, warriors, and a populace struggling to make sense of it all."

-Kirkus Review

"This fantasy epic created by author Tom Cifichiello, is marvelously constructed and detailed, action-packed, and rivals *Game of Thrones* and *The Hobbit* trilogy. Excellent first outing! I look forward to reading more of Cifichiello's work."

-Roger Reece, author of
*Ascended: The Omega Nexus*.

# Tom Cifichiello

# Of Darkest Valor

To Jack & Tommy,

"Of Darkest Valor" began as nothing
more than a dream and now it is a
published novel. Never stop pursuing your
dreams and never stop reaching over the
horizon. Enjoy!

Regards,

Tom Cifichiello

PAGE PUBLISHING, INC.
New York, NY

First originally published by Page Publishing, Inc. 2014

ISBN 978-1-63417-131-1 (pbk)
ISBN 978-1-63417-132-8 (digital)

Printed in the United States of America

# DEDICATIONS AND ACKNOWLEDGMENTS

*Of Darkest Valor* is dedicated with love and affection to the memory of my grandfather, Paul Braun. You inspired me at a young age to dare to dream, to follow my heart, and helped shape me into the man I am today. I hope you're smiling up in heaven, Poppy. This one is for you.

# Acknowledgments

I want to convey a special thanks to my test readers, Jeff Cifichiello, who inspired me in a time when I needed inspiring; Shantel Taylor, who listened to my constant ramblings about plot twists and character threads and never once complained; Kai-Yen Cheung, who I could not write fast enough for; and Joanne Braun, the greatest godmother a godson could ask for. My thanks, as always, goes out to my parents and siblings, who supported me from beginning to completion. I wouldn't be standing where I am today if it wasn't for all of you. I also want to thank my editors, Sam Severn and Sally Reboul, as well as my illustrator, Kip Ayers, also known as the Clairvoyant Illustrator. Lastly; I would like to thank Noel Jones and Stephen Matthews over at Page Publishing for giving me a chance when so many others wouldn't. Each and every one of you has my gratitude.

# PROLOGUE

minous clouds obscured the crescent moon overhead as Lord Randell wound his way through the warren of back alleyways that made up the eastern port city of Sura. A bitter wind blew through the narrow passageway, forcing the stocky lord to wrap his fur-trimmed cloak tightly around his frame. *The last remnants of winter making its presence known*, thought Randell. Muttering a curse, he increased his pace.

Cutting left out of the alleyway, he glanced up. The sharp wind was causing an overhanging sign to clatter against its establishment. The sign showed the name of the tavern he was traveling to: The Triumphant Lion. Approaching the entrance, Randell blew warmth into his callused hands, rubbing them together. Winter weather did not agree with him, and he was looking forward to the warmer temperament of spring. Coming to the tavern door, he gave two quick rasps, paused, and then gave two long knocks. He stamped his feet impatiently as the locking bar of the door lifted.

As the door swung inward, Randell was met with the darkest eyes he had ever seen. Lord Drogos, the ruler of the eastern city-state of Yursa, met Randell's steady gaze. "Lord Randell, we have been expecting you. Please enter, my dear friend."

Randell merely nodded, brushing past his fellow eastern lord into the warmth of the tavern beyond. Drogos peered into the darkness, making sure Randell was not followed. Satisfied, he shut the door once more, setting the locking bar back into place. Randell shook off his fleeced-line hood, scratching at his thick red beard while he took in his surroundings. Other than the two men seated at a round table of pitted oak, the tavern was utterly empty. He took his place at one of the vacant chairs, greeting each man there with a nod of his head.

Here at this table sat the four lords of the city-states of the mountainous terrain of the east. Very rarely did all four gather together for banquets or other social gatherings. It was even rarer for them to meet in privacy, for none of them were close friends. Never before had they met in such secrecy. Each lord had gone through painstaking efforts to make sure their presence wouldn't be noticed in Sura tonight, for each man at the table knew what this meeting would be about.

War.

Lord Drogos took his seat, flashing a smile to the other eastern lords. The smile reminded Randell of white tombstones. Everything about Drogos oozed a slimy falseness and deceit. His skin was pasty white, his black hair waxed back over his ears. Even his apparel spoke of his character, a black doublet with serpents expertly sewed along the lengths of the sleeves and dark gray leggings. Randell despised the man though he was wise enough to keep his thoughts to himself. Those that fell out of favor with Drogos did not see the end of the week. Rumors began to circulate around the east that Drogos had personally funded the building of an assassin's guild in his own city-state. Randell had covertly sent agents into Yursa to find out the truth of the matter. Only one man returned of the three he had sent, reporting of a brotherhood of assassins calling themselves the Sons of Vikundo. Vikundo was the

God of War, and Randell did not need to guess as to the nature of this *brotherhood*. It appeared the rumors were true, and he feared that he had sent the other two agents to their deaths.

It was Drogos who addressed the other lords. "My lords and friends, I greet each of you as a brother. Our careful years of planning have finally come to fruition. The rich, fertile lands of Varkuvia are in turmoil, and through our careful maneuvering, the greatest fighting force in known history has been disbanded. The five kings look at one another with wary eyes, each more skeptical than the next. The reaving Argarians of the Storm Islands have joined our cause as have the barbaric tribes of the Northern Woods. Come spring, we must mobilize our forces and crush these arrogant kings," finished Drogos, leaning back in his chair, studying the other lords' reactions.

Randell found himself leaning back as well, allowing the words to sink in. Varkuvia, more commonly known as the Realms of the Five Kings. The continent was to the west of the city-states and was, without a doubt, the richest of the known lands. The very thought of the name was like sweetened honey on the tongue. Lord Dorian cleared his throat, causing Randell to glance his way. Dorian was the lord of Sura, the port city in which the meeting was being held. Sura was the closest city-state to Varkuvia, resting in the Gulf of Ramel, just to the south of King Stefanos's realm, the Horse Realm, and much of the information they received went through the port city first. The man was borderline obese, his eyes close set, and his nose short. He reminded Randell of a pig.

"We are sure that the Order of Acrium will not be a concern of ours?" Dorian asked. His voice was shrill and spoke of a coward.

A momentary flash of annoyance crossed Drogos's face. It was immediately hidden behind the prominent smile that was a weapon in his arsenal of deceit. "My lords, the Order of Acrium was disbanded over six months ago. We were able to accomplish this through our many agents stationed throughout Varkuvia. Not only were we able to convince the Five Kings that the Order was no longer needed, but that given time, they would rise up and rebel against them." Lord Drogos laughed softly, the hollow sound sending a shiver up Randell's spine. "How easily the fools were deceived. Only King Markos, ruler of the

Stone Realm, argued on behalf of the Order. His protests were heated and went long into the night, but he was finally overruled by the other kings. The Order is no longer a factor. Trust me."

Randell allowed the words to soak in. Every person in the known world understood the reputation of the Order of Acrium. They had been formed close to three centuries ago when Varkuvia had been all but overrun by barbarians and named after the ancient city in which the Order was formed. The kings of the time had banded together the last remnants of their forces and were able to drive the savage invaders from their lands. The cost had been appalling, Varkuvia all but in ruins, and the death toll catastrophic. That's when the Order of Acrium had been formed with one sole purpose in mind: to defend against foreign invasion. It was also around this time that a prophet predicted a coming evil, the likes of which these lands had never seen before. The kings of old also kept this in mind and knew the Order would be needed not only for themselves, but for the well-being of future generations. Since that time, they had established themselves as a deadly and formidable fighting force.

Only one out every hundred applicants was admitted into their ranks. Both nobles and peasants alike were allowed to join from all over Varkuvia with no distinction being made between birthrights. Sons of powerful lords and even kings had been turned away before. Only the best were allowed to don the cloaks of the Order of Acrium. Their fighting force always numbered three thousand, and each man practiced daily in the art of war. More importantly, since the Order had been formed, they had not lost a single battle.

In the last decade, the Order had become increasingly useless. With the peace treaties signed with the eastern city-states, the Order's only foes remained in the north. The tribesmen of the vast Northern Woods were broken up into close to thirty different tribes, each with their own customs and values. The tribes were constantly at war with one another, and only the most foolish of tribal chieftains would attempt a full-scale invasion on the Realms of the Five Kings. The last chieftain to make such an attempt had been close to five years ago, and the Order had crushed him in one decisive battle.

Then there were the Argarians who lived on the Storm Islands, just off the coast of King Eryk's realm, the Wood Realm, which jutted out into the frigid Okhelm Sea. Even here, there was no immediate threat, for the Argarians under the reign of King Ragnar's leadership rarely landed with a force large enough to be a threat. The last large raiding force had been almost three years ago, and the Order wasn't even needed. The raiders had been devastated by the deadly prowess of King Eryk's famed long bowmen. This only added to the ineptness of the Order, the Five Kings proving they could protect themselves easily enough without them.

Even though no one at the table would voice their opinions aloud, each feared that once an invasion began, the Order would reform. Randell glanced across the table at Lord Nikolaos. Lord Nikolaos controlled the southernmost Eastern city-state of Seren and had a consistent tan due to the warm weather year-round. Of the eastern lords, Randell liked Nikolaos the most. The lord of Seren's somber brown eyes met Randell's arctic blue gaze, the slightest of smiles crossing his tanned face.

When Nikolaos spoke, his voice rang with power. "My lords, it would seem that regardless of the Order, we are in far too deep to turn back. How long do any of you think it will be before one of the Five Kings realizes all of the scheming we have been doing behind their backs? Then we will have a united Varkuvia knocking on our doorsteps." He shook his head. "This I will not allow. As things stand, King Lucan, the most powerful and westernmost king, is looking at his neighboring kings with hungry eyes. Through Lord Drogos's agents, as well as my own, we have learned some interesting things about King Lucan. The esteemed king's father passed away a decade ago, leaving Prince Lucan the throne at the young age of nineteen. Now, almost thirty, the man is the youngest of the Five Kings and extremely ambitious. He dreams of ruling a united Varkuvia, one that does not include the other four kings. At the moment, he is not nearly powerful enough to move against the combined forces of the other rulers. It is my belief, along with Lord Drogos, that Lucan will sit in the shadows during the beginning stages of the war, hoping for us to eliminate some of the other kings, if not all of them. By the time Lucan realizes his folly, it will be too late. Then we will crush him, with an iron fist, along with any of the other kings remaining." Nikolaos slammed his fist into the table for emphasis.

As Nikolaos finished his speech, Randell noted the gleam in Dorian's eyes. The fat lord's doubts had vanished like morning mist before the rising sun. Lord Drogos noticed it as well and pounced upon it as a lion would a gazelle. "It would seem that we are all in agreement. And have no fear, My lords, we still have our man amongst the Order should they reform. Now with all of us in agreement, let us plan a war."

The talks went long into the night, and throughout the discussions, a persistent wind made the wooden structure of the tavern creak and groan. Randell found himself detesting the thought of going back outside once more. Much of the talk focused around supplies. The eastern lords and their allies to the north would be mustering an army the likes of which this world had not seen in well over a century. This would require a constant supply line. No matter how valiant an army was, if they weren't properly fed, the battle would be lost before it began. As Randell's late father always used to say, "A starved army is a lost army." Randell also made sure that a large supply of grain for the horses would be available, for he would be providing the majority of the horses, not only for the cavalry, but also to pull the supply wagons. Lord Randell took personal pride in the fact that his city-state of Cabalo was famed for its horses.

Cabalo's verdant pastures up in the high mountains raised some of the finest horses in the eastern lands, and Randell spent much of his free time there. He maintained that his joy for raising horses was passed down by his ancestors, along with his extensive knowledge; for Lord Randell was by birth and by right a king of Varkuvia. That birthright had been stripped from him by the ancestors of King Stefanos. King Stefanos's ancestors were lords in service of Randell's forefathers yet rebelled against them, claiming the throne for themselves. Randell had sworn several oaths upon the various altars of the gods, vowing he would have King Stefanos's head on a pike for his ancestor's betrayal. It was common knowledge that King Stefanos raised some of the best horses in the world, and Randell looked forward to meeting him on the field of battle.

The other lords each had their own roles to play. Lord Dorian, despite his grotesque appearance, was quite adept at making money. His port city exported some of the finest textiles, silks, and spices. Traders from the Northern Woods traveled to Sura with fur pelts from timber wolves, red foxes, and even the rare white bears. Merchants from all over the east migrated to Sura in the hopes of becoming wealthy, and most did, for there was always plenty of coin to be found for those ambitious enough. Dorian would be funding most of the venture. Already his granaries were overflowing with purchased food, and hired mercenaries prowled the streets of his city.

Nikolaos and Drogos would be providing the bulk of the infantry. The eastern lords' tribal allies to the north would consist of mostly infantry as well. However, the tribesmen relied on ferocity and sheer weight of numbers to overwhelm their enemies, lacking any sense of the word discipline. Nikolaos's infantry was well disciplined, well trained, and far better equipped than their allies in the north. They would be much more suited to sieges and pitched battles while the tribesmen would devastate the surrounding countryside, bringing havoc and fear to the populace.

Drogos would be providing the cream of the eastern fighting force. The Legion of the Rising Sun was modeled around the Order of Acrium. Whereas the Order was famed for its codes of honor, the Legion was known for its utter brutality. Knowing the man who formed the Legion, Randell did not doubt that for a second. The Legion had its uses though. Their fighting force, unlike the Order, always numbered five thousand. It would be the Legion that would be brought in to break an army's spirits and turn the tide of battle if it was going sour.

Lord Drogos's other qualities didn't need to be voiced at the table, for each man there was well aware of what else he brought to this venture: sabotage, espionage, and assassination. Randell had seen the gleam that appeared in Drogos's eyes when he spoke of the Order no longer being a factor. Randell knew with certainty that the lord of Yursa had already taken steps to ensure this was true. The man was dangerous, and each lord of the east knew it.

The mountainous terrain of the eastern lands prevented the city-states from uniting into one cohesive nation. To the east of Randell's city-state lay miles upon miles of swamplands while to the south of Nikolaos's city-state lay nothing but inhospitable rocky terrain. Beyond this rocky terrain, a desert stretched as far as the eye could see. They called it the Eternal Desert, for any that were foolish enough to wander into the desert dunes did not return. There was no hope of conquest these ways. To the west lay rich deposits of ore, multiple gold and silver mines, fertile lands for farming, some of the finest timber, and high quality stone quarries. Drogos maintained that once Varkuvia was taken and the tyrants were overthrown, they would form a leading council for the people and bring peace and stability to the realm. Randell saw right through the snake.

For the time being, Drogos needed every man present in this tavern, but what would happen once Varkuvia was taken? During the preparations, Drogos had symbolized the east as a pack of wolves while the lands of the Five Kings were a herd of sheep ripe for the slaughter. He had said that the Order of Acrium had been the shepherd, and without them, the wolves would fall upon the helpless sheep, rending their flesh. But what would happen once all the sheep were gone? The wolves would turn on each other for survival, devouring one another. And Randell knew who would be the vulture sitting in the background, waiting until the wolves had killed one another, feasting on the remains. Drogos.

The sly lord was playing his own game, and for the time being, Randell had no choice but to go along with it. Without Drogos's many agents throughout Varkuvia, the invasion would certainly fail. *One day there will be a reckoning*, thought Randell, *and I will be damned if I am on the wrong side of the dagger plunging toward my back. Better me plunging the blade into Drogos's black heart.* Randell's mind was dragged back to the present when he felt Drogos's soulless eyes drilling into him. The jet black eyes nearly merged perfectly with the pupils. The piercing gaze seemed to look right into the depths of his soul. Randell shivered despite himself. Could the man read minds?

Still looking Randell in the eye, Drogos spoke. "I fear that the hour is growing late, and if we are all agreed upon what needs to be done, then I do believe I hear my bed beckoning me." He rose, signaling the end of the meeting. "Until the spring, my lords."

The other eastern lords followed Drogos's lead, rising and saying their farewells. Drogos and Dorian retired to the upstairs of the tavern while Nikolaos and Randell drew the hoods of their cloaks tightly around their faces, moving toward the entrance. Each man had gone through careful precautions to make sure nobody knew they were in Sura. All it would take was one Varkuvian agent catching a glimpse of all of the eastern lords gathered together for their plans to come to naught. Nikolaos lifted the locking bar off the door and opened it.

Randell braced himself against the bitter wind that was sure to follow. He was relieved when a refreshing breeze brushed against his skin. Winter was finally coming to a close; spring just on the horizon. Stepping outside, Randell saw the sun of predawn had painted the sky a pink hue. For a moment, the lord of Cabalo's weariness was forgotten in the majesty of the approaching sunrise.

A light snow had fallen during the night, coating the cobblestoned streets of Sura. Randell could already see that the snow was beginning to melt with the coming of the dawn. Glancing toward the sky, he saw the last of the previous night's snow clouds moving toward the west. Randell smiled to himself at the irony of the moment. Dawn was rising on the eastern city-states, a storm sweeping toward the Five Kings. Spring was fast approaching, and Randell relished the thought that King Stefanos would see his last winter. The stout lord drew in a deep breath, filling his lungs with the sweet-tasting morning air. He nodded his farewells to Nikolaos.

Sloshing through the melting snow, Randell began the walk back to the stables where his prized stallion had been kept for the night. Exhaustion began to creep into his soul; the night's planning finally taking its toll. Randell was approaching his late forties and had not stayed up to see the sunrise since the days of his youth. Knowing his tired body needed to rest, he contemplated catching a quick nap at an inn before returning to Cabalo. Almost immediately, he dismissed the idea. He couldn't take the risk of someone recognizing him.

Randell's most loyal advisor, Kleitos, was camped in a stand of woods not two miles from Sura. Randell would merely have to wait before he could rest. However, the thought of sleeping on a hard-packed ground filled him with no joy. The old spear wound in his left shoulder was already beginning to bother him. A souvenir he received from a northern tribesman in the arrogant days of his youth when he believed himself invulnerable to harm. The wound always bothered him when the weather turned wet or cold. Randell knew that once he was back in the sanctuary of Cabalo, he would need to have his shoulder tended to, and most likely rest for the remainder of the day.

Randell and Kleitos had informed their wives, along with the remainder of Randell's advisors, that they were going hunting. The rouse had been believed, Randell's subjects seeing how stressed his duties were making him. The lord of Cabalo knew it was far more than his duties that caused his stress. A constant pit remained in his stomach, and he would never voice aloud the cause of it, not even to Kleitos, who was not just his advisor, but his most trusted friend as well. If truth be told, Randell did not like this venture into Varkuvia.

His reasons for joining the other eastern lords were purely selfish. If he could kill King Stefanos and reclaim his birthright without the other kings getting involved, he would do so. However, to reach Stefanos, Randell would have to cross the Stone Realm, ruled by King Markos. Markos, a loyal friend to Stefanos since they were children, would never allow this. Randell sighed aloud to himself.

King Markos was the only king whom Randell had met before. The Stone Realm was the closest to the eastern lands, and King Markos would need to be conquered first for an invasion to have any hope of success. Six years earlier when the planning had begun in earnest, Randell decided to travel to Markos's three-walled fortress capital of Karalis. Randell was renegotiating trade agreements with the king to allow for more wool and grain to be imported to his city. Instead of allowing his merchants to handle the agreement, Randell had written that he would personally travel to Karalis to deal with the negotiations. It would give Randell a perfect opportunity to assess the defenses himself.

Markos had graciously written back that he was honored Randell would take the time out of his busy schedule for such a trip. Choosing twenty men as an escort, Randell and his wife, Lady Myra, traveled to Karalis. Despite Randell's objections, Myra had been quite persistent she come along with him. It took weeks to finally reach the city, and Randell noted the mountain ranges they traveled between to reach the fortress city. Most of the terrain leading through the Stone Realm was impassable, and an approaching army would have to besiege Karalis to gain access to the rest of Varkuvia. After taking the fortress-city, an army could flood into the plains beyond the city and have a clear path to any other realm in Varkuvia. The only other land route lay far to the north, and even if an army took this path, they would have to take the Haraliam Wall, which stretched from the northern Bale Mountains to the Okhelm Sea. Even if this formidable wall was taken, they would have to worry about an army sallying forth from Karalis to attack its rear flanks.

They passed several villages nestled in the nook of the mountains, for the most part mining and farming communities, and had only passed two forts made of stone on the way to Karalis. Randell noted the walls of the forts weren't overly maintained, and he saw many hand-holds in the stone that a besieging force could climb easily enough. This lack of maintenance only emphasized that King Markos held the eastern lords, along with the northern tribes, in contempt. Randell found his irritation growing.

Approaching the fortress city, he remembered his mission, study-ing the immense fortifications. The walls were close to fifteen feet thick, standing over fifty feet high, with square towers positioned every fifty paces. Randell scanned the walls, looking for any weaknesses or cracks in the foundations, just like the forts they had passed. It appeared the stonemasons had done their jobs well, and he noted sourly that he could find no immediate weaknesses in the wall. Glancing to his left and right, Randell saw that the wall merged perfectly with the Bale Mountains to the north, and the Amarro Mountains to the south. A besieging army would be forced to attack from the front, the moun-tain ranges preventing an encircling maneuver. Passing underneath the gatehouse of wall one, Randell had spotted murder holes above him. These would allow the defenders to pour boiling pitch, heavy stones, or molten lead down upon any foolish enough attempting to breach the gates. It would take a massive army combined with well-made siege equipment to take these walls.

Emerging from under the gatehouse, Randell was horrified to see no buildings lay between walls one and two. Only open ground with a steep gradient met Randell's eyes for over two hundred yards. An attacking force would not only take fearful losses taking wall one, but they would also have to endure another gauntlet of arrows to besiege the second wall. As a student of war, Randell knew this would dishearten any besieging army, lowering their morale and tenacity. And just like the first wall, the second merged with the mountain ranges, allowing for only a frontal assault. Randell was beginning to understand why the fortress was said to be impregnable.

Passing through the second gatehouse, he had finally found a modicum of relief. Here the buildings of the city had spread, eliminating the killing ground between walls two and three. These buildings that ensured economic growth for Karalis would provide cover all the way to wall three for an attacking army. And unlike the first two walls, the third wall did not merge with the mountains, but instead encircled the mighty Keep of Karalis like a protective ring of stone. A besieging army would finally be able to encircle this wall, burning the buildings of the city in the process. Feeling slightly better, Randell continued on his way to the keep where King Markos resided. He was unsure of the reception he would receive from the king, for every person of power knew of Randell's past and of the vengeful oaths he had proclaimed. He was surprised to find King Markos, along with his wife, the beautiful Queen Lorain, awaiting him in the courtyard in front of the keep. He was even more surprised when Markos openly embraced him in front of everyone, thumping him on the back as if he were greeting an old comrade.

A lavish banquet consisting of roasted boar, venison, duck, and fine wines was held in Lord Randell's honor. The celebrations went long into the night, the wine flowing freely. Despite his best efforts, Randell found himself warming to the black-haired king with eyes the color of a winter storm cloud. He was a man who put the well-being of his people before his own personal gain, an uncommon trait in this day and age. The king constantly spoke of his two sons throughout the banquet, notably mentioning his soaring pride when both of them had been initiated into the illustrious ranks of the Order of Acrium. Having a son of his own, Randell could relate with Markos's happiness at his son's accomplishments.

Randell also noted with pleasure that Myra, usually shy at events such as these, seemed to be making best of friends with Queen Lorain. As the night wore on, and the more wine Randell consumed, he found his joy being replaced with a sense of melancholy. If Randell hadn't had his birthright stolen from him, it would've been he, and not King Stefanos, who would've been lifelong friends with King Markos. After this bitter thought, Randell had excused himself from the raucous celebrations, retiring to his bed. Sleep was hard to come by that night; Randell's thoughts were teeming.

The following morning Lord Randell shook hands with King Markos over a successful trade agreement. The king was even gracious enough to present a casket of wine from his personal collection, a clear gift to promote further dealings. He then requested that Randell come out hunting with him that day. Randell respectfully declined, saying he had to return to his own city-state on urgent business. Markos's disappointment had been genuine, and Randell almost reconsidered. Almost.

As Randell said his farewells to Markos, the king insisted he return soon. This offer was bolstered by Queen Lorain's and his Lady Myra's gleeful agreements to return as soon as possible. Despite Myra's constant insisting, Randell never returned to Karalis. Every time Markos sent a letter requesting Randell to go hunting or to be his guest at a banquet, Randell always made up an excuse to not attend and would politely decline. One day he would be forced to watch Markos humbled, and he decided close ties with the king would not be advisable. Still, Randell hoped he wasn't present when Karalis was overrun.

Forcing his mind back to the present, Randell tried unsuccessfully to push Markos's impending demise from his mind. It appeared the day to humble the king was now at hand. Weaving and ducking his way through the back alleyways of Sura, Randell had a sudden urge to no longer be in the choking confines of the port city. He knew that he should stick to the back ways of Sura and keep his face hidden, but to his left was the Market Square, and a shorter route to the stables he was heading to. Exhaustion and bitter memories clouded Randell's judgment.

Cutting to his left, Randell moved across the Market Square. Even with the sun barely cresting the eastern horizon, merchants were already starting to set up shop, getting ready to ply their wares for another day. A group of whores at the edge of the Market Square stood as Randell went to walk by them. Their flimsy dresses hid little, their practiced smiles full of dark promises. Randell ignored the whispered promises of pleasure and caressing hands running down his body as he passed them by. Once it was obvious their potential client wasn't interested, the whores went back to chatting amongst themselves.

As Randell fought down his uncomfortable ardor, he contemplated allowing whores to openly operate in his own city-state of Cabalo. The revenue prostitution could bring in would be prodigious. Chuckling to himself, he dismissed the idea immediately. Whores might warm the beds of many a men, but Myra would make sure his remained cold. Unlike his other eastern lords, Randell had taken only one wife. He loved Myra unconditionally and took her wise words of council to heart. When his wife flashed her smile, he forgave her anything.

Momentarily distracted, Randell didn't notice the slender young man that walked into his path. Bumping into the man, Randell's hood fell out of place, exposing his thick fiery red beard.

"My apologies," muttered Randell, pulling his hood back into place. Cursing himself a fool, he hastily walked away. A momentary lapse of judgment could've just ruined everything. Thankfully, the moment had only been fleeting.

Arriving at the stables, he asked the stable hand, a scrappy boy of nine or ten, to fetch his horse. Bringing his mount out, Randell admired his prized possession. Just under sixteen hands, the black stallion was sleek, powerful, and had incredible stamina. Seeing how well tended his mount had been kept, Randell slipped the stable hand an extra full silver piece. Seeing the sum, the boy's eyes widened in disbelief, and he sprinted away, most likely to show someone his prize.

Randell chuckled as he mounted his horse. Steering the stallion toward the north, he cantered the horse to where Kleitos awaited him. The coming months would test Randell like never before, and he hoped he had the nerve to do what needed to be done. The world was about to change, whether it was for better or for worse, Randell could not say. Lord Nikolaos was in the most part a good man, and Randell hoped he also fell under that category. Lord Dorian was a cowardly man and left to his own devices was completely harmless. But was giving a man the likes of Drogos even more power a good idea? Pushing such somber thoughts from his mind, he decided to enjoy the horse ride for the time being.

In the shadows of the stables, the young man whom Randell had bumped into emerged into the gathering sunlight. His eyes squinted as he observed the eastern lord's graceful riding style, noting the lavish horse the man rode. A horse meant for a king. He watched Randell until he rode from sight. The slender man subconsciously rubbed at the pale scar upon his cheek then slipped into a side alleyway.

# CHAPTER ONE

rystan was bone weary as his gray mare plodded through the Harrowing Woods, situated at the northern border of King Stefanos's realm. It had been over six months since the Order of Acrium had been disbanded, and the almost twenty-five-year-old was unused to being in a saddle for such an extended period of time. Stretching his lower back, Trystan gazed up through the bare branches of the gnarled oak trees surrounding him. Dusk was fast approaching, and he began scouting around for a good campsite for the night.

Spotting a small hollow to his right, Trystan guided his tired mount toward where he would rest. Emerging into the clearing, he saw a large boulder that formed an overhanging shelf. *A perfect spot to escape the chilling wind once the weather begins to plummet*, he observed. Dismounting, Trystan secured the reins of his horse on a low-hanging branch. After feeding and brushing his mount, he threw a woolen blanket over the mare's back. With the mare properly tended to, he began preparing a fire for himself.

Spreading a pile of shredded leaves beneath a stack of small twigs, he sparked file and flint together to get the blaze started. His fingertips were starting to grow numb from the dropping cold, making his first attempt clumsy. Taking a deep breath, he calmed himself and tried once more. This time the flint sparked and the beginnings of a fire glowed. After tossing on more twigs to get the fire going, the young man gathered his feet and stood. Then he moved off into the shadowy woods to find suitable firewood. Darkness had fully descended by the time he returned, an ample bundle of wood cradled in his arms, which would see him warmly through the night.

As he approached his meager campsite, he was happy to note that the boulder face hid most of the glow from his fire. The Harrowing Woods had become increasingly known for marauding outlaws over the last few months, and the last thing Trystan needed was someone creeping into his camp and slitting his throat while he slept. Sitting cross-legged in front of the fire, he drew an oatcake from his pack and began to eat. It was stale and far from his liking. To take his mind off his disappointing meal, Trystan flew back in his mind's eye to the months before the disbandment of the Order of Acrium.

For the Five Kings to sign the decree that sent the finest warriors in all of Varkuvia back home was a stupidity beyond Trystan's comprehension. Every report the Order had received over the last few years pointed toward a joint eastern invasion. Lord Randell and Lord Nikolaos of the east had steadily increased the power of their military over the last year. They maintained this was to counterbalance an increased threat from the tribesmen of the Northern Woods. This was so false that Trystan had almost laughed aloud when he heard the news. Lord Nikolaos's city-state of Seren lay far to the south, out of harm's way from the tribesmen, and everyone knew of the oaths Lord Randell had sworn to reclaim the throne from King Stefanos.

Trystan had been in utter disbelief when he discovered the Five Kings weren't going to take any action against the east. Instead, they had reached an agreement with the eastern lords, requesting that they maneuver their troops far from Varkuvian borders. Lord Randell and Lord Nikolaos had graciously accepted, saying they had no intentions of bringing their soldiers onto Varkuvian soil. Trystan shook his head as he took another bite of his oatcake. The armies of the east had always been more than adequate in dealing with even the boldest of chieftains in the north. If he, a lowly member of the Order, could see that, how couldn't the Five Kings who were meant to protect the welfare and well-being of their people?

Even with an increased eastern presence, the people of Varkuvia still slept soundly at night for they had the finest military force in history to spearhead their armies if an invasion were to occur. Then disaster struck. Just as the leaves were beginning to fall from the trees, a herald had arrived at the Fortress of the Van, the home of the Order. All training had stopped as every member of the Order was summoned to the main courtyard. Men milled around confused; no one knowing what was going on. Then the herald had emerged from the main hall, sweat shining from his balding head. He had appeared nervous as he walked onto a platform that overlooked the gathered warriors. Silence fell as he unrolled a scroll of parchment.

"I have a royal decree signed by each of the Five Kings of Varkuvia." His shaky voice carried out over the silent courtyard. "By unanimous decision, the rulers of these realms have decided that the Order of Acrium is both too costly to maintain and is no longer necessary in bringing peace to these lands. By command of the Five Kings, you are all hereby disbanded and ordered to return to your homes immediately." A huge uproar met these words. "I have here the five signatures and royal seals from each of the Five Kings," finished the herald, screaming over the noise. He faced the decree toward the outraged warriors, showing them all.

After finishing what he came there to do, the herald, sweating profusely, got on his horse and galloped from the fortress. How nobody in the crowd had killed the man, or at least attempted to stop him, Trystan still did not know. Perhaps everyone was just as shocked as he was at the news. Everybody was still talking in angry voices when First Master Roderic, the head of the Order, stepped onto the platform to address his students and fellow members.

Roderic had been a noted warrior in his youth; the man's very name striking fear into the hearts of his enemy. Now, close to seventy, he was undisputedly the most respected member of the Order, despite advanced arthritis making his sword arm all but useless. Roderic's heroics and deeds while younger had assured him a life of ideal luxury in any major city of his choosing. Instead, he had opted to stay a part of the Order to teach and train future generations. Raising his one good arm, Roderic called for silence. It took several minutes, but finally the courtyard remained quiet once more.

"My dear brothers in arms, this must be a mistake our gracious kings have made," Roderic said, his voice still ringing with accustomed authority despite his physical frailty. "On the morrow, I will personally lead an envoy to the gathered kings at Karalis and plead with them to listen to reason. I have fought for this Order for most of my life. In my youth, I even fought beside some of you. And I will continue to fight for this Order until my final breath leaves my body. Tomorrow I leave at first light to fight for the right of this Order to be preserved. For the time being, go about your training and your duties. In a week's time, when I return, we will put this foolish business behind us."

Finished with his speech, Roderic stepped down from the platform, signaling for the four other masters and leaders of the Order to follow him. The most respected living members of the Order filed in behind the shuffling figure of Roderic. The following morning, Roderic stayed true to his word and emerged from the great hall to mount his white stallion. Trystan saw him don a white cloak lined with white wolves' fur with five interlocking silver circles expertly stitched in a circular motion at the center, the symbol of the Order of Acrium. Only the first master of the Order was allowed to wear the white fur-lined cloak while the rest of the members, both teachers and students alike, wore black cloaks. Roderic, along with a majority of the leaders of the Order, departed for Karalis. Only Layne, the Master of Sword, remained behind to maintain the Order.

Each day that passed after Roderic's departure saw the inner fears of each member increase. Every man thought about what they would do if they truly were to be disbanded. For the members of noble birth, it would mean dishonor to their families. None of them wanted to be remembered in the history books as being part of the Order when it was disbanded due to its uselessness. For the members of peasant stock, it would mean a life of hard work and labor once again. Many amongst them knew no other occupation than being a soldier. What would they do if the Order was disbanded? Would any of the Five Kings allow them into the ranks of their armies after being dishonored in such a way? What was certain was that each man there simply wanted closure. Patience was not a virtue shared by any of them in this matter. Ten days after Roderic's departure, the warriors would get the closure they had fervently waited for.

A single horn note blasted through the morning air, signaling the arrival of riders. Trystan remembered the dreary day. A light rain had been falling, soaking the members as they began to assemble in the main courtyard once more. He recalled the shock he had felt as he emerged into the courtyard for over a thousand armed men rung the perimeter. Trystan saw the banners of the Five Kings set upon poles around the courtyard, flapping in the storm's wind. There was the black-and-green checkered banner with a rearing griffin upon it, signifying King Eryk's house, ruler of the Wood Realm. The red-and-gold striped banner with a jeweled crown upon it to represent King Alaric's House, ruler of the Iron Realm. A hand clutching the burning sun with a black background for King Lucan's house, ruler of the Gold Realm. Then there was the rearing black stallion with a golden background for King Stefanos's house, ruler of the Horse Realm. Trystan noted he did not see the gray keep with blue background that would herald King Markos's house, ruler of the Stone Realm.

Of Roderic and the other leaders, there was no sign. Instead, standing on the platform was a middle-aged man with iron-gray hair, armed soldiers lined up menacingly behind him. Despite the light rain, his hair looked freshly groomed, his attire appearing extravagant. When all of the Order was assembled, the new herald drew another scroll. He did not bother to unroll it but instead pointed it at the gathered men as if it were a sword.

"Gracious warriors of the Order of Acrium, the esteemed rulers of Varkuvia have asked you to disperse back to your homes. Already this message has been delivered, yet all of you remain." The herald scanned the faces in the crowd. "I have been instructed to inform you that this slight will be forgotten. All of you will return home as heroes with no dishonor to your families. Furthermore, you will each be paid for six months' work to start you in your new lives for the services you have performed in these lands." The man paused to let the words sink in. "However, if you refuse to leave peacefully, the rulers of these lands will have no choice but to brand each and every one of you as traitors of Varkuvia. Any of you of noble birth will have your lands and titles stripped from you. Those of you who are commoners will have your families named traitors along with you. There will be nowhere safe for you in all of Varkuvia. The choice is yours. You have until tomorrow morning to make your decision." Finishing his speech, the herald turned to leave the platform.

"And where pray tell is First Master Roderic, along with our other noble leaders?" A voice yelled from the crowd. Trystan saw that it was Layne, the Master of Sword, his dark hair tied at the nape of his neck in a ponytail. "What have you done with our leaders?"

Many in the crowd shouted their agreement as the herald turned around to address the gathered warriors once more. He could tell the situation was close to becoming ugly, and this time he forced a practiced smile. "Master Roderic has listened to the wise counsel of his kings. He has been granted lands and wealth as befits a man of his reputation and stature. All of you should follow his lead."

Not one person in the crowd believed Roderic would leave without so much as a word, but the repercussions of refusing the herald's offer were too strong to ignore. The Fortress of the Van was situated directly on the border of three of the kings. To the east lays King Markos; to the south, King Stefanos; and to the north, King Eryk. If they refused, it would mean open rebellion, and then the Five Kings would move their combined forces against them. The Order of Acrium was second to none on the field of battle, but these three kings alone could muster close to thirty thousand men. There was no way three thousand men, no matter how skilled they were in combat, could overcome such odds set against them. Even if by some miracle they were able to defeat these forces, King Lucan and King Alaric further to the west could bring to field a force of similar size. King Lucan alone could summon up to twenty-five thousand trained soldiers.

As with the first herald, no one voiced their opinions out loud, and the unspoken tension was left untempered. Thus ended the era of the Order of Acrium without so much as a fight. The following morning, every warrior began the procession back to their respected homes.

Now, six months later, Trystan sat alone in a dark forest, eating a stale oatcake. After gobbling down the last remnants of his meager meal, the young man wiped the crumbs off the front of his leather jerkin lined with fleece. Throwing a large branch onto the fire, he spread himself out before the blaze. Watching the flames dance, his mind wandered into the past once again.

It was one thing to be ordered to go home, but it was quite another to follow that order. Trystan had no actual home and no living relatives he knew of. His childhood had been spent in the massive city of King Lucan's capital of Calydon. His mother passed away just before his twelfth birthday, and his last memory of her had been of a thread-like woman who coughed up blood. He could not remember a single time when she laughed or smiled. Trystan was overwhelmed with the responsibility of taking care of her and watched her pass away long before her time. Of his father, he had no recollection. He had left his mother before Trystan had even been born and had not been a part of his life. With no relatives to care for him as a child, Trystan had turned to a life of thievery to survive. The boy he once was, was forced into manhood long before nature intended him to.

Being fleet of foot and swift of hand, Trystan soon discovered that not only could he survive as a thief but also that he excelled at it. After successfully relieving someone of their possessions, he would simply slip away into the many warrens of Calydon's backstreets. His sure-footedness allowed him to leap across the closely spaced rooftops, easily avoiding the city watch. He could still recall the day when everything had gone terribly wrong. Winter was fast approaching and times were getting tough for the young thief, and so he made a daring move.

Under the cover of darkness, he climbed the walls of the rich merchant Caliphos's estate, sneaking into the overly elaborate residence.

There were certain people in the city of Calydon that thieves knew not to steal from, a high end of society known as the Untouchables. These were the type of people that were well connected, and death would be instantaneous to anyone caught stealing from them. Caliphos was the worst kind of Untouchable. Not only was he wealthy beyond the wildest fantasies of mere mortals, he also had close ties to King Lucan himself, and the full wrath of the city watch would be turned loose on anyone foolish enough to wrong the merchant. But Trystan had been desperate, and though it was a huge gamble, the fine goods stolen from the estate would ensure his survival through the bitter months of winter.

He used all of his exceptional skill that night, avoiding the guards and watchdogs that patrolled the estate, determined not to get caught. It all went so perfectly, his pack filled with valuable possessions that would see him through winter and beyond. As dawn fast approached, Trystan made his way through the estate, back to the wall and back to safety, but luck had not been with him. As he crossed before the bedchambers of Caliphos, the door suddenly swung outward. The merchant, still yawning, walked into the corridor beyond, his half open eyes falling upon the young man in ratty clothing standing before him. Then his gaze flicked to the bulging pack thrown over Trystan's shoulder. A golden goblet studded with jewels fell through a rip in the bag, clattering against the marble floor.

Caliphos's eyes widened. "Guards!" the merchant bellowed. Trystan heard Caliphos yelling long after he turned to run as fast as he could, his arms and legs pumping.

As he approached the wall, he heard the pounding of feet behind him and shouts from the merchant's guards. Scaling the wall, the hole in his pack caught on a jutting vine, ripping it cleanly in half. Everything he worked so hard to steal during the night tumbled to the ground. Trystan stared longingly at all of the expensive trinkets and silverware that would've ensured his survival. For the merest moment, he contemplated jumping to the ground and grabbing what he could. Looking back toward the estate, he saw a score of guards rapidly approaching him, their drawn swords flashing in the gathering dawn sun. Cursing inwardly, Trystan topped the wall, and jumped to the ground beyond, his heart beating wildly. He heard shouts of pursuit from all around him. The chase was on.

He bolted straight ahead into a side alley, confident he would lose his followers now that he was back in his domain. But luck evaded him once again. Emerging out of an alleyway, he ran directly into a patrolling group of the city watch. They stared incongruously at the young man, noting his thread-worn attire, their curiosity aroused. Then they heard the angry shouts from the pursuing guards. One of them made a grab at Trystan, but he ducked away, slipping into another alleyway. To get caught now would mean an immediate trip to the executioner's block. He heard a group moving in the alleyway adjacent to him. His pursuers were tightening the circle around him, cutting off all avenues of escape. Growing desperate, Trystan opened a side door to a bakery, rushing inside. If anyone was inside, and saw him, he would be doomed, for he knew anyone would willingly comply with the city watch, or guards bearing the insignia of Caliphos.

The bakery appeared vacant, and he had darted behind a stack of barrels filled with flour. Sweat flowed freely down his face, his breathing coming in quick gasps. He relaxed, believing he was finally safe. Swiveling his head to the left, he saw a girl, no more than thirteen, staring at him with wide eyes. She wore an apron speckled with flour, her face similarly covered. But Trystan was drawn to those wide eyes. Never before had he seen eyes so beautiful, the sunlight beaming through the windows reflecting off them. One moment they were the lightest of browns, the next hazel with golden flecks. Trystan became so mesmerized by those eyes that for one blissful moment he forgot the peril he was in. Reality came rushing back at him as the front door of the bakery crashed inward. The startled young girl jumped as a pair of guards barged in.

Trystan pressed himself hard against the barrels, wishing he were invisible. "You there, girl," he heard one of the guards growl in a grating voice. "Have you seen a boy wearing tattered clothing around here?"

The young man's heart was in his throat. It was over. She would rat him out in an instant. And who could blame her? She owed him nothing. He closed his eyes, a sense of resignation washing over him. The only thing he hoped for now was a swift death when the time came.

"No, sirs, I'm afraid I haven't," the girl replied sweetly. Trystan's eyes snapped open. "As you can see, I have been hard at work, and the only thing I have seen all morning is the bread rising over there. You are welcome to help yourselves to some if you would like."

A few tense moments passed. "Are you sure, girl? This boy is quite dangerous and wanted by the city watch as a thief and a scoundrel."

"I assure you that I have not seen the boy you are searching for. I wish there was more I could do to help you."

The guards began talking in low tones. Trystan, hidden behind the barrels, could not hear the exchange. "All right," one of them finally said. "If you see anyone out of the ordinary, you let us know, agreed?"

The girl said her good-byes, wishing the guards good luck. They shut the door behind them. For several minutes Trystan could not move, still unable to believe what just happened. Eventually he stood on shaky legs, facing toward the girl who just saved his life. Once again, he was drawn to those eyes. She was already quite attractive yet only just reaching puberty.

"Why?" Trystan simply asked.

She shrugged, causing her curly auburn hair to bounce ever so slightly. "You just looked so scared. I find it hard to believe that someone looking as frightened as you could be as dangerous as they said."

Trystan was at an utter loss for words. This was the first moment in all his years that he could recall anyone showing compassion toward him. He had no idea how to react. Outside, he heard the sounds of his pursuers fading away. He had to get away from here before they came back. Without a word, he moved to the doorway. Grabbing the handle, he opened the door halfway and then paused.

"What is your name?" he asked.

"Arianna," she replied. "And who might you be?"

"I am Trystan." He hesitated. "Thank you, Arianna."

And then he was in the streets beyond. With the immediate danger behind him, he roamed through the city, his mind racing, planning his next move. He knew he could not stay in Calydon, not now. He had stolen from the wrong man, someone far superior to him in every way. A reward would most assuredly be given to anyone with information regarding the young thief. It would only be a matter of time before he was brought to justice. He would have to leave the city. But where would he go? And how would he survive? Stumbling into the city square, he found his salvation.

Addressing a gathered crowd was a handsome man wearing splendid armor, his black cape billowing lightly in the wind. He spoke movingly of recruiting noble young men to join the Order of Acrium, to protect the lands from the evils of the world. His voice had roared over the attentive crowd as they hung onto his every word. As he finished his speech, men of all ages eagerly rushed forward to sign up, believing they would forge their own legends. All Trystan heard was a means to escape the city with his head still attached.

The minimum age for signing on had been sixteen, but Trystan, looking older than his fifteen years, had not been questioned. As Trystan and the other recruits topped the final rise that would leave Calydon behind them, he glanced back at the massive city. He found himself wishing he had sought out Arianna one last time just to say good-bye. *She has most likely forgotten about you already*, he thought. And then he turned around, leaving the city of his childhood behind him.

In the months that followed for the first time in the young man's life, he discovered joy. Trystan's incredible hand-eye coordination not only allowed him to make the initiation into joining the Order but soon established him as a formidable swordsman as well. The Master of Sword, Layne, soon took an interest in the wolf-lean, olive-skinned youth with eyes the color of dark emeralds. Layne saw a younger version of himself in Trystan, passing down decades of knowledge and codes of honor to the young man. The Master of Sword was the closest thing to a father figure Trystan ever had in his young life.

It was also in the Order that Trystan forged his first true friendship. In the suffocating streets of Calydon, a friendship might have been his downfall, and survival had always taken precedence over such petty things as friends. It was this precise reason that Trystan still could not explain how easily he and the giant Jaxon became friends. Jaxon was just a shade under six and a half feet tall, barrel-chested, with an enormous breadth of shoulder, and a thick dark beard framing his closely shaved head. The best way to describe him would be to call him a bear of a man though he doubted if even a grizzly bear had the nerve to go against him. The big man was often seen in the middle of a good jest, his booming laughter sounding out.

Trystan's childhood caused him to be reluctant around the company of people. With Jaxon's easy personality, he learned to open up over the years, the bitterness of his youth becoming a distant memory. Jaxon was more than a friend, he was a brother. He was the only reason Trystan was camped in the Harrowing Woods at all. Trystan tried unsuccessfully to become a farmer in King Stefanos's realm after the disbandment. This mundane lifestyle did not suit the once-elusive thief, and he shortly thereafter wrote to Jaxon, informing him he was coming to visit. Trystan wrote the words large for Jaxon to read. The Order deemed it necessary for every member to know how to read and write, and Jaxon, despite his immense physical prowess, found it extremely difficult to learn the symbols. Jaxon used the money he saved from the Order to start his own small farm just north of the Harrowing Woods in the fertile lands of King Eryk's realm. Too eager to wait for a reply, Trystan left a few days later, heading north toward his friend's farm.

He found his mind wandering back to First Master Roderic. Months after the disbandment, it surfaced that the head of the Order was arrested, soon after speaking with the Five Kings, along with the other masters. They were thrown in the dungeons for over a month before being sentenced to exile, never again to return to Varkuvia. After discovering the fates of the exiled masters, a few hundred warriors of the Order reformed, attempting to incite a rebellion. News of their treacherous plans reached the king's ears long before any sufficient damage could be dealt, and the rebellion was crushed in its infancy. The rebels of the Order were crucified, a clear warning to any others that might harbor the same feelings and ideas.

Trystan forced his mind back to the present, pushing the depressing thoughts of his past behind him. Tomorrow he would reach Jaxon's farm, the thought comforting him. Wrapping a blanket around himself, he once more watched the flames of the fire dance, leap, and twirl. The warmth of the fire overcame him, weariness falling upon him like a spell, and he felt his eyes growing heavy. He fell asleep to the crackling of wood and slept without dreaming.

The breaking of wood roused Trystan from his sleep, his eyes snapping open. Instantly alert, he rolled to his feet. Dawn lit the sky, the fire behind him dying sometime in the night. A distant bird chirped, the sound echoing through the silent woods. Trystan's attentive gaze swept the small hallow, searching for any signs of danger. But there was no danger to be found. *Perhaps it was just a bad dream I experienced,* he thought. He was starting to feel foolish when four men emerged from the bushes ringing the hollow. Trystan's eyes narrowed, gauging the men.

It was apparent the men had fallen on hard times. Their clothes were threadbare, dirt was deeply ingrained into their features, and there wasn't an ounce of fat on any of them. Trystan's eyes fell upon his sheathed sword, some ten feet away from where he was standing. He cursed himself a fool, for he always slept with the blade close at the hand. The damn fire had distracted him the night before. The robbers spread out in a half circle, cutting off Trystan's escape routes.

Trystan's gaze fell upon each of the robbers, noting the weapons they carried. A sandy-haired man with a round face carried a short bow, an arrow notched to its string, while two of the others carried simple daggers to Trystan's left and right. Standing directly in front of Trystan was a man with a sword pitted with rust. The other robbers kept glancing at the one with the sword, an ugly fellow with a pockmarked face. It seemed like he was the leader, and Trystan turned his full attention on him.

Pockmark face drew a dirty sleeve across his runny nose before saying, "Me and my companions here were out hunting when we saw the smoke from your campfire. We hoped to share a meal with a nice fellow. Are you a nice fellow, boy?" the man asked, flashing a smile of broken teeth.

Trystan heard the other robbers snicker at the comment and knew the leader was toying with him. He tried to control his building anger. The robbers saw before them a young man unarmed and alone, but they could have no idea of his training or background. When Trystan spoke, his voice was colder than winter.

"I know what you and your 'companions' planned to find here, and I will only warn you once. Leave now from this hollow, and I will allow each of you to leave with your lives. Live or die, the choice is yours."

The smile left Pockmark's face. "You arrogant little shit. There are four of us, and you're unarmed. I'm going to carve open that big mouth of yours. Kill him, lads, and let's be done with this prick."

As Pockmark spoke, Trystan relaxed his body, his mind totally engrossed in his surroundings. Just to Pockmark's right, he saw the sandy-haired archer draw back his arrow. Trystan dove to the left just as the arrow was released, the projectile bouncing harmlessly off the rock face behind him. Coming to his feet in a tumbler's roll, he was just in time to block a dagger thrust with his forearm. Trystan brought his open palm up into the man's nose. The bone crushed upward into the thin membrane of the brain.

The man fell without a sound, the dagger falling from nerveless fingers. Scooping up the blade, Trystan turned to face a fresh attacker. He sidestepped a dagger thrust, keeping his body angled so Sandy Hair couldn't release another arrow at him. Slapping aside a clumsy lunge, Trystan stepped in close, driving the point of his dagger up through the man's jaw, the iron piercing his brain. Standing nose to nose with the thief, Trystan saw the fear and desperation in his opponent's frantic eyes. Withdrawing the dagger, blood pumped from the mortal wound, drenching his hands.

Trystan used the corpse as a shield as Sandy Hair hastily released another arrow. The arrow buried itself deep in the dead robber's back, and the archer hurriedly drew another arrow. Still using the corpse as a shield, Trystan drew his arm back and threw his dagger at the archer. He was aiming for the archer's chest, but the balance of the dagger was off. Instead, it hit the man full in the throat.

Dropping his bow, Sandy Hair scrabbled frantically at the hilt jutting from his throat. He fell to his knees before falling face-first onto the ground. Dropping the body of the dead knifeman, Trystan turned casually toward Pockmark. The man licked his lips nervously, fear apparent in his eyes, sweat beading on his forehead. Gripping his rusted sword double-handed, he advanced upon Trystan. Without a moment's hesitation, Trystan moved to meet him.

Pockmark tried a wild slash. Sidestepping to the left, Trystan punched the robber full in the face with a left cross. He heard the snapping of bone and instantly knew he had broken the man's nose. Blinded by pain, Pockmark dropped his sword, his hands instinctively going to his ruined nose, his eyes streaming with tears. In one fluid motion, Trystan picked up the fallen sword, driving it into the ugly man's gut. Pockmark let out a scream that was barely human as Trystan leaned in close.

"I warned you, you miserable whoreson," he hissed into the dying man's ear.

Twisting the blade savagely, Trystan pulled the rusty sword clear. Pockmark let out one final gasp of air then fell to the ground, joining his fellow would-be robbers. Trystan flung the blade from him, drawing in a deep refreshing breath to calm himself. Glancing down at his blood-covered hands, he saw he was trembling. With his blood pumping furiously during combat, danger had eluded him. Now the aftershock was settling in. It was always the same after a fight for Trystan. He felt his blood run cold while his legs wobbled beneath him.

To push his mind from the matter, the young man began busying himself. Gathering his belongings, he banked the fire, crushing any remaining embers. Moving to his horse, he saw the animal's ears were flat to its skull. The smell of blood had terrified the horse. Moving in close, Trystan whispered soothing words to his mount, gently stroking its flanks. Calmed by its master's words, the mare began to relax. Still calming the horse, Trystan saddled her.

Finally, he moved to pick up his sword, hesitated for a moment, and then drew the blade. The gathering sunlight gleamed off the metal, making it shimmer different colors of gold and green. Forged from the rarest metal in the world just off the coast of King Alaric's realm, the sword would never rust and would cut cleanly through all but the strongest steel armor as if it were simple cloth. Master of Sword, Layne, presented it to the young man on his final day in the Order, and he was at a loss for words. The balance of the sword was perfect, the hilt intertwined with woven silver, a round black pearl set into the pommel. The rare sword was worth twice a man's weight in gold, but not once had

Trystan considered selling it. The gift was a prize beyond comprehension, normally reserved for royalty. Sheathing the sword once more, Trystan moved to his horse.

Vaulting into the saddle, Trystan noticed for the first time an appalling stench had crept into the hollow. It clung to his nostrils and made his stomach heave. *This is the heroic deeds the bards sing of,* he thought. *One man set against four outlaws and prevailing victorious.* It was funny how the singers never mentioned the trembling hands, sleepless nights, or the dead defecating themselves. Trystan wondered if any bard had ever actually been in a battle or even a fight for that matter. Glancing toward the edge of the hollow, he spotted a red fox eyeing the corpses greedily.

These men had been alive just minutes ago, each with their own personal desires and ambitions. Some of them might have had family, a brother, a wife, maybe even children though Trystan could not imagine a woman who would marry a man as ugly as Pockmark. Now they lay unburied, merely food for the likes of foxes and carrion birds. A gentle breeze blew, brushing across Trystan's stomach. Looking down, he saw a tear in his leather jerkin where Pockmark had slashed at him. Had his opponent been more skilled or Trystan's timing a fraction off, the sword would have disemboweled him. And then it would've been he that would be carrion, not these robbers.

Trystan knew he allowed anger to cloud his judgment. Master Layne chided him through the recesses of his memory, *"Anger in battle is death's brother. To lose control of your emotions is to embrace death itself."* Trystan would not make the same mistake again. Cantering his mare toward Jaxon's farm, he left the small hollow full of death behind him. Not once did he glance back, and the fox darted in to feed.

Just before midday, five dark-garbed riders thundered into the hollow. They pulled hard on their reins when they saw the dead bodies. Their clothing was constructed from the finest materials as were the swords of black steel they wore at their sides. Their leader, Orpheus, a battle hardened man with cold eyes, gazed upon the corpses.

"Draven," he barked out, "scan the area. Tell us what happened here."

Draven, a tall man with pale blue eyes, dismounted smoothly. The rest of his comrades sat patiently upon their mounts as the tracker scanned the area. Draven's talent to track was legendary, and it was said he could read a man's life in the tracks he left behind. After thoroughly scanning the area, Draven outlined the short battle that took place. He finished with "It appears he not only defeated four armed opponents, but he did so easily. Only a man trained in the art of war for nearly a decade could accomplish such a feat. This is definitely the man we're looking for."

Orpheus was irritated. Had they arrived but a few hours earlier, they could have killed the man, blaming outlaws for his death. His master's orders were explicit in discretion, and Orpheus was one who obeyed without question. Now, the man they were tracking was leaving the Harrowing Woods, and the coldhearted leader would have to rethink his strategy. His party was starting to run low on supplies, and his options were becoming limited.

It still outraged the leader that five men were required to kill this "Trystan." The orders Orpheus received described the man as "deadly" and "to use caution." Orpheus snorted. He had yet to meet a man who could match him with a blade. He had heard the rumors about this Trystan; an orphan child who deserved no right to be called one of the best swordsmen in the Order of Acrium. Orpheus had received a letter from his master days before conveying that the so-called swordsman was traveling to another disbanded member's farm. A new order was contained in the contents of the letter, requesting that Orpheus dispose of the other member, Jaxon, as well. It seemed that discretion was no longer an option. Orpheus would have to kill Trystan and Jaxon along with anyone else unfortunate enough to be at the farm. Then he could torch and loot the farm, putting the killings down to bandits. It was a sloppy plan, but at least Orpheus might get the opportunity to challenge Trystan with a blade.

His decision made, Orpheus gave the order to move out. His party arrived nearly a week earlier at the farm Trystan was said to work at only to find he had left that morning. No one could say where he went, for Trystan was a solitary man who kept to himself. Orpheus was forced to wait another two days for his master to send word of Trystan's whereabouts. Not accustomed to being patient, Orpheus was furious at his prey for prolonging the kill. His frustration was momentarily eased as he pictured with savage joy his dark blade plunging into Trystan's heart. The orphan would not be the first warrior of the Order Orpheus had killed. Nor would he be the last.

Orpheus's irritation at his mission flared once more. He had personally written to his master, requesting a notable warrior of the Order to slay. He hoped to be given the swordsman, Kaleb. Kaleb was the only son of Lord Rickart, a powerful lord in service to the mighty King Lucan. The twenty-six-year-old son had been one of the most skilled swordsmen in the Order, said to rival even the Master of Sword, Layne. A man truly worthy of Orpheus's expertise and talents. Slaying Kaleb would have helped further establish the dark legacy beginning to shroud his name.

*Instead, I am riding toward a little shit farm to butcher some peasant rumored to handle a sword well,* the leader thought maliciously. *The bastard probably doesn't even know which end of the sword to stab someone with.* Orpheus's jaw clenched tightly. He would make sure that Trystan suffered before he killed him. Maybe he would tear Jaxon's heart out right in front of the orphan. So many options went through the leader's mind on how he could prolong the man's agony. Impatience roared through him, and he spurred his horse ahead. The rest of his party followed his lead, and they raced on toward the farm where their destiny awaited them.

# Chapter Two

aleb awoke in the dead of night, stifling the beginnings of a scream in his throat. His breathing came in quick gasps, his nostrils flared, his eyes scanning the dark room. After a few moments, he realized his fears had spawned from a nightmare. Drawing in a deep breath, Kaleb began to relax.

Cold sweat drenched his forehead, his shoulder-length hair clinging to his scalp. He was beginning to feel foolish as he wiped the sweat away with the back of his hand. The last time he experienced such dreams, he was a mere child. His father, Lord Rickart, put an end to those childish fears. He remembered all too well just how his father stopped such foolishness.

At the tender age of seven, the child Kaleb awakened in the dead night from a terrible nightmare. His bedside candle guttered sometime in the night, leaving his room in total darkness. The child sobbed piteously, believing monsters were coming in the night to spirit him away. His caretaker, unable to console the frightened child, reluctantly summoned his parents.

His mother, a kindly woman with gentle eyes, comforted Kaleb with soothing words while his father stood back, arms crossed, his expression as still as a crypt. The following morning, Lord Rickart cancelled his duties for the day, instead opting to spend it with his only son. The seven-year-old was ecstatic. His father never spent time with him, and the child's joy was a sight to warm even the coldest of hearts.

After a short ride, both father and son arrived at a cave just on the outskirts of the castle they dwelled in. Gathering a torch, Lord Rickart took the lead traveling into the cave, gesturing for his son to follow him. Kaleb hesitated. The cave mouth looked dark and sinister. Pushing his fears aside, Kaleb followed the strong figure of his father. If there were any monsters lurking in the dark, his father would surely deal with them.

They traveled for several minutes, walking ever deeper into the catacombs of the cave. Kaleb shadowed his father's footsteps, his eyes glued to Lord Rickart's back, not daring to look at the darkness surrounding them just outside the torch's glare. Suddenly his father stopped, spinning around to look down upon his son. Kaleb's bright blue eyes looked up into his father's stern face.

"I will not have it said that my son is a weakling," his father told him. "You wept like a young maiden last night for the whole castle to hear your shame. You come from a long bloodline of strong men, and the way you acted last night shamed our ancestors. Today you will learn to face your fears." Lord Rickart snuffed out the flame of the torch and walked away from the terrified child.

Kaleb's screams echoed off the cave walls, reverberating back at him. Falling to his knees, he screamed over and over again for his father until his voice went hoarse. All to no avail. Drawing his knees into his chest, he rocked back and forth, sobbing shamelessly. Believing his father had left him there to die, Kaleb wet himself in fear. And so he sat for hours, sobbing, in a pool of his own urine, his fear all-consuming.

After what felt like an eternity, the child finally saw the glow of the torchlight. Lord Rickart approached his son, staring down into the boy's puffy eyes. That was the first time in Kaleb's young life that he realized just how cruel his father's face was. There was no warmth in his eyes, no joy to be found anywhere upon his broad face.

When Lord Rickart spoke, there was an emotional detachment in his voice that Kaleb hadn't noticed before. "From this day forward, you will act like a man. There will be no more of these childish fears." His father looked down in disgust at his son's soiled clothing. "You make me ashamed to call you my son."

In the months that followed, Kaleb had experienced awful nightmares. He was always back in the cave. In many of his dreams, his father had taken on the shape of a monster with sharp teeth and red eyes that would chase him through the never-ending cave. Whenever Kaleb ran in these terror-stricken dreams, his legs would turn to lead, as if he were moving through mud, while his father fast approached him. No matter how much Kaleb willed himself to run faster, the monster form of his father was always quicker. Just before Rickart would descend upon him, Kaleb would awaken from the nightmare, trembling and sobbing. Not ever wanting to go back to that dreaded cave, Kaleb at least learned to hide his fears from his father. Instead, it was his mother who became the child's savior. Were it not for her gentle words and kind smile, the child may never have recovered from that ordeal.

Even that solace was taken from him around his thirteenth name day. Kaleb wakened in the dead of night to overhear an argument between his parents. Even through the walls that separated Kaleb from his parent's bedchambers, he could tell the words were far more heated than usual. He stealthily approached his parent's bedroom door so he could better hear the argument when a woman's scream filled the castle corridor. The sound was abruptly cut off as Kaleb ran the final length of the corridor that led to his parent's bedchambers. The youth opened the door only to find his father standing over his mother's body, blood pooling from a wound in her head. She wasn't moving at all.

So enraged was his father that night, he'd not even noticed Kaleb standing in the doorway. Learning long ago to mask his feelings, the youth silently closed the door and slipped back into his own bed. He did not sleep at all that night, the image of his mother's dead body burned into his memory. The following morning it circulated around the castle that his mother had slipped, fatally cracking her head. Everybody was grief stricken for Lord Rickart at the horrible twist of fate that took his gentle wife from him. Only Kaleb knew the truth. His father murdered his mother in cold blood. He never dared to voice the truth out loud but instead kept the terrible secret to himself, letting it bury itself deep into his heart like a parasite.

For Kaleb's sixteenth name day, he requested enlistment into the Order of Acrium. His father, with a new wife by his side, granted this. Not once had he missed his father or the home of his childhood in the years that followed. Determined never to be like his father, Kaleb plunged into his training with relentless fervor. With a sword, no one in the Order had been his equal, save for perhaps, Layne, the Master of Sword. Only the orphan, Trystan, could hold his own in the training yard against him.

Kaleb's incredible ability with the blade soon convinced him that he had the blood of the all-but-extinct Verillion race running through his veins. The Verillions were destroyed close to eight hundred years ago when the Western people first settled the lands that were now Varkuvia. This ancient race was a peaceful people and stood no chance against the more volatile ancestors of Varkuvia. However, according to legend, this race of old was said to have certain powers the Varkuvian people did not possess. Verillions had incredible reflexes and were ambidextrous while even more of their people were said to be seers who could predict the future. It was also said that a few could perform magic, controlling the elements to their will. The prophet who predicted the coming evil when the Order was first formed was supposedly a descendent of the ancient race. The Western people, fearing the Verillion race would one day use their powers against them, slaughtered them. Those who fled were hunted down and butchered like animals. The Verillion genocide was a time of great fear and bloodshed.

However, the entire Verillion race was not wiped out. Pockets of survivors prevailed and made a new life for themselves after the geno-cide of their people. Tall tales claimed that a warrior descended from

Verillion blood could defeat any opponent in combat. The Legendary Arrturi, a warrior of the Order, had been such a man. No one could stand against the man and hope to live. Arrturi lived over two centuries ago, and no member of the Order was as skilled with a blade since that time. Kaleb, being ambidextrous, believed with his skill he could surpass even Arrturi. He had approached his mentor, Layne, hoping the man could help him develop his talents further. Layne had moments in battle during his youth when the old blood had coursed through his veins. Kaleb etched the conversation into his memory.

Layne's violet eyes gleamed with remembered past glories. "Aye, there have been a few times throughout my life when I knew I had the ancient blood coursing through me. Each time was in battle, when either my closest companions' lives were in mortal danger or my own. It felt as if someone else took over my body. I could read my enemy's moves before they even could. Anyone foolish enough to stand in my path was killed with consummate ease. It did not matter the size or skill of my opponent, for they would fall choking on their own blood. The last time was over a decade ago. Each occurrence was fleeting though, and I never learned to fully control it. If a Verillion descendent could ever learn to fully harness their power, he or she would become the most renowned warrior in known history. Unfortunately, these days only one out of every million is born with Verillion blood, and I fear such a swordsman will not appear in our lifetimes, if ever."

After hearing this, Kaleb pushed himself even further in his training, determined to prove Layne's prediction wrong. When the other warriors rested after a long day of training, Kaleb would remain. Every day, he pushed his weary body to new feats, daring his exhausted bones to betray him. He hoped combat would help unleash his powers, but this thought was brutally crushed. The only battle he had taken part in was against the tribesmen of the Northern Woods, when they invaded the Stone Realm. Kaleb alone killed three and wounded two others during the battle, but he did not experience the feeling that Layne described. The young man swallowed his disappointment, determined that given time he would discover he had the blood of the ancient race in him. Even this dream was shattered.

He still remembered the utter disbelief that seized him when the command to disband was given. Right up to the moment when he walked through the main gateway at the Fortress of the Van, he held to the belief everything would work itself out. His one all-consuming ambition was to become the greatest swordsman in the history of the Order, greater even than the Legendary Arrturi. It was hard not to feel any resentment at being denied his dreams. Any happiness Kaleb experienced in his life was stripped from him. With the lack of any kind of affection from his father, the murder of his mother, and then the disbandment of the Order, it was easy for bitterness to seep into his soul.

Unpleasant thoughts made it impossible for Kaleb to fall back asleep. Throwing his sheepskin blanket from his muscular frame, the young man walked to his window that overlooked the castle courtyard below. Flinging the window open, Kaleb enjoyed the icy wind that blew across the bare chest of his still bed-warmed body. Movement at the edge of his vision made him glance down at the main courtyard. For a fleeting moment, he thought he saw a figure merge into the shadows of his father's personal stables. His mind must've been playing tricks on him, for the hour was late.

Feeling a sudden urge to walk, Kaleb moved to his clothes chest at the foot of his bed. As he dressed in warm clothes, he thought about his friend Kastor who was visiting a local tavern in the town beyond his father's stone walls. Kastor was a former warrior of the Order along with Kaleb, and over the years, their friendship grew. His friend was also a noble, being the eldest son to King Stefanos, and next in line to the throne. His sole reason for being in the far western lands Lord Rickart occupied was to visit Kaleb and escape his duties for a few weeks. Kaleb knew that in all likelihood, Kastor was entertaining a young maiden or two. For once, Kaleb hoped he was wrong as Kastor had an uncanny ability to cheer him up, regardless of the situation.

Donning a pair of fine leather gloves, Kaleb spotted dual scabbards of lacquered wood at the bottom of the chest. These housed the two short swords he once wielded in the Order. Force of habit caused him to hone the blades every night, leaving the edges razor sharp. On a whim, Kaleb buckled the swords. The weight of them always seemed to comfort him.

Throwing on a hooded cloak, Kaleb left his room, descending the stairs that led to his sleeping quarters. There was no activity in the great hall below, and Kaleb was able to walk out into the courtyard beyond without someone questioning where the lord's son was going at such an hour. The night sky overhead was cloudless. The moon shined brightly, the stars sparkling like thousands of distant glittering lanterns. Kaleb drank in the beauty of the night as he walked toward the postern gate that led to the sprawling town beyond.

A sentry whose name Kaleb could not place snapped to startled attention as the young noble approached. "M-m'lord," stammered the slim sentry. "What can I do for you at this hour?"

Kaleb gave an easy smile. He didn't want it reported back to his father that he was going out now. The last thing he wanted was Lord Rickart finding out his only son was out cavorting with whores and getting rowdy in town even if the rumors weren't true. Depending on how the night went, they might be proven true, but still, if Kaleb could avoid confrontation with his father, he would. Gods, what was the sentry's name? It was on the tip of his tongue. Rae! That was it.

"Not a thing, Rae," said Kaleb, his tone friendly. "It can be quite suffocating in a castle on such a nice night like this. One sometimes feels the need to go for a walk." He slipped the sentry a silver piece.

Rae expertly pocketed the coin, giving a gap-toothed smile. "Aye, m'lord, I know the feeling." He removed the bar to the gate as he spoke.

The noble squeezed the sentry on the shoulder as he walked by. "Let's try and keep this little walk between the two of us, eh, Rae?" As a reassuring afterthought, he slipped the man another silver piece.

The sentry gave another gap-toothed smile. "You can have my word on that, m'lord. If you don't mind me saying, I would try and finish your walking before dawn. That's when my shift is over."

"Good man," Kaleb said. Drawing the hood of his cloak tightly around his face, he began walking down the path that led to the town below.

The walk was a short one, for the tavern was located close to the walls of his father's castle. Kaleb insisted Kastor stay in the guest room, next to his own, but Kastor laughed at the suggestion. The Boars Edge Inn where Kastor was staying was renowned for having some of the prettiest maidservants, and Kastor said he was in need of some company after such a long trip. Kaleb shared a few drinks with Kastor and then retired to his own bed. Kastor was disheartened, but Kaleb was in no mood to deal with his father's surly manner.

Kaleb opened the door of the inn, noting that most of the revelers had retired for the night. Only a handful of regulars remained at the tables, nursing their mugs of dark ale. A serving woman wiping down tables seized her activities and approached Kaleb. The woman was young and attractive with honey-colored hair and dazzling blue eyes. Kaleb found himself staring. He was already starting to regret not joining his friend in a night of revelry.

"Can I help you, m'lord?" asked the serving woman, noting Kaleb's extravagant attire.

Kaleb gave a practiced smile, reserved only for beautiful woman. "I was looking for my friend, Kastor. Perhaps you could direct me to which room he's staying in."

The serving woman liked his smile and found herself returning it. "Prince Kastor is upstairs. Second door on the left. I have to warn you though, he went to bed with a woman. Now might not be the best time to meet with him, if you catch my meaning." She winked at Kaleb.

The young noble chuckled. Kastor assured Kaleb he would keep a low profile while outside the safety of Lord Rickart's walls. *I see that lasted long,* thought Kaleb. "Well, it couldn't hurt to at least go check on the young princeling," said Kaleb, noting the curves of the serving woman's body. "If he's…busy as you say, maybe I could return here and enjoy your company instead," he proposed, throwing in his best smile.

The serving woman laughed, the sound enchanting. "You are a rogue, sir." She ran her hand through her long hair. "I wonder how many a fair maiden's heart you've won over with that smile." For a short while, she studied Kaleb, noting his blue eyes, the color of a summer sky, and his well-groomed, short-cropped beard. She bit her bottom lip, toying with the idea of accepting. "My shift's over in a half hour. I'd be inclined to at least give you the opportunity to show me you're more than just a practiced smile. My name is Rachel by the way."

Kaleb flashed Rachel another smile. Taking her hand, he kissed it, looking her in the eye while he did so. "Until then, m'Lady."

He noticed with satisfaction the blush that spread across her face as he moved off to the stairwell. *Sometimes it's a curse being so naturally good-looking*, thought Kaleb. *All the sport goes right out the window.* Already feeling in a better mood, Kaleb approached the room he was told his friend was occupying. Pressing his ear to the door, he strained to hear any noise from within. He couldn't hear anything and contemplated heading back downstairs to further woo his future prize. Then he figured he would at least see if Kastor was awake. He made this trip to see him after all.

Opening the door as silently as he could, Kaleb peered into the darkness toward the bed, looking for any signs of movement. His gaze couldn't pierce the dark shroud that draped the room, and he gingerly took a step inside. His foot struck something solid. Gazing down, he found himself staring into Kastor's open brown eyes. Blood was still flowing from the prince's severed throat, his eyes glazed over in death. The whisper of cloth on wood to his left made him instinctively dive into the room.

A sword blade thundered into the wooden doorframe where Kaleb was standing mere heartbeats before. Rolling to his knees, he smoothly drew his short swords, turned, and was just in time to block a savage downward cut. Kaleb drove forward, forcing his opponent back. The only light in the room was from the hallway beyond, and Kaleb couldn't make out the man's features facing him. Still, he could tell his foe was skilled beyond the hopes of most ordinary swordsmen. His reflexes were astounding, his sword work graceful.

But few men in the known world were as skilled as Kaleb. With the shock of Kastor's death dissipating, he began unleashing all of the skill he possessed. His opponent could tell he was hopelessly outclassed, desperation beginning to show in his every movement. Kaleb blocked a thrust, rolled his wrist, and plunged his blade into his opponent's shoulder. Moving in for the kill, Kaleb heard a floorboard creak behind him.

Reversing the sword in his left hand, holding it like a dagger, he dropped to his knees. A sword whistled by his head. Kaleb plunged the reversed sword backwards directly into his new adversary's stomach. Simultaneously, he plunged his other sword blade forward into his injured opponent's groin. Wrenching both blades clear, Kaleb heard the assassins fall to the ground, writhing in pain.

Still alert, Kaleb looked around the room, making sure there were no more fresh opponents to face. Satisfied he was alone, his gaze was drawn to the bed. The dim light from the hallway shown on the woman Kastor had been entertaining. He could not make out the woman's facial features, but she was naked, and he could tell her throat was slit in the similar fashion as Kastor, for the bedsheets were soaked with blood. Kaleb found anger coursing through his body. With his vision adjusted to the darkness, he could now make out the signs of an evident struggle around the room. Chairs were knocked over, and he spotted several broken pieces of pottery scattered across the floor. Kastor must have awakened at the sound of men entering his room and attempted to fend them off. Half-asleep, naked, and taken by surprise, his friend stood no chance. Kaleb looked at Kastor's dead body once more, anger and grief threatening to overwhelm him.

The discordant ring of metal on metal had awakened many of the inn's customers who were fast asleep in their beds. Curious eyes peered into the room from the hallway beyond, wondering what had just taken place. Kaleb saw Rachel pushing her way past the gathering crowd into the room. Her jaw dropped as her eyes fell upon the bodies. Before she could scream, Kaleb cut her off.

"Rachel, go and fetch the night's watch. I need to have a word with these men before they get here." Rachel's blue eyes were fixed on Kastor's dead body, her features pale with shock. Kaleb lightly snapped to get her attention. She looked into his face, tears brimming her blue eyes. "Go and get the night's watch for me," he repeated softly.

This time Rachel nodded dumbly, turned, and hurried from the room. After she left, Kaleb lit a lantern, sheathed his short swords, and closed the door against any prying eyes. Moving to the man he stabbed in the groin, he saw he already bled to death. With light in the room for the first time, he studied the man's attire and features. The dead assassin's dark garbs appeared expensive, his face was round, and his open eyes doe-like. It looked like a face someone could trust, not someone who would slit a person's throat in their sleep. *It just goes to show you can't judge a person's character on their appearance alone*, reflected Kaleb.

Transferring his attention to the other man, he saw that Kastor's murderer had propped himself up against the far wall and was desperately trying to stanch his wound. Kaleb thought he had stabbed him in the stomach, but his backward thrust had been off and instead he had pierced the assassin's hip. The wound appeared deep, and if it wasn't immediately attended to, the man would join his dead companion. Kaleb had no intention of getting the murderer medical attention. He knelt down in front of the assassin, staring the swarthy man in the face. Kaleb noticed the man's clothing was almost identical to his companion's.

"I am going to ask you some questions," said Kaleb, his anger barely suppressed. "You are going to answer these questions, or I will make sure your final moments are agonizing in the extreme. Do you understand me?"

The swarthy man gazed malevolently at Kaleb. A jagged scar ran from the right side of his face, barely missing his eye, and down through his upper lip, giving him a lopsided smile. The assassin lifted his chin in defiance, ignoring Kaleb totally. The chains holding Kaleb's anger snapped. He openhandedly struck the man full in the face, knocking him sideways. The man's head bounced off the wooden floorboards. As he was spitting blood and bits of broken teeth from his mouth, Kaleb dug his fingers into his hip wound. The assassin let out an anguished scream.

"Do you understand me?" Kaleb screamed into his face.

The assassin nodded through gritted teeth. Kaleb removed his fingers from the wound, and the swarthy man slumped back down, sweat bathing his face. "Now, judging from your expensive clothing and the skill you displayed, I can assume you and your dead companion aren't just simple thieves," began Kaleb. "What I want to know is, who sent you to murder my friend, and why?"

The swarthy man propped himself up against the wall once again, and his dark gaze stared directly into Kaleb's eyes. His breathing was short and shallow. After a few moments when he didn't answer him, Kaleb thought he was ignoring him again. This time he clenched his hand into a fist, ready to drive it into the bastard's face. When the assassin spoke, there was no fear in his voice.

"A fire is sweeping toward Varkuvia," he said, his voice heavily accented from the east. "Prince Kastor was said to be someone who could quench the flames that will soon be spreading through these lands. My brothers and I have been instructed to remove such men for quite some time now." The assassin smiled through blood-soaked broken teeth. "It is also said you are such a man, son of Lord Rickart. I die with happiness in my heart knowing you will soon follow me. Then there will be no one to stop the flames that will consume these lands." The man laughed, the action causing him to cough up even more blood.

The words cut through Kaleb's anger. The assassin knew who he was. The conviction in the dying man's voice was strong, and Kaleb did not think he was lying. He thought to hear the assassin tell him about someone Kastor had wronged or even to a more extreme, someone hoping to claim the throne from his friend. Instead, he was being told not only was this false, but others, himself included, would soon be targeted, if not already. The thought was not a comforting one. Grabbing the front of the swarthy man's expensive tunic, Kaleb shook him violently. The man barely responded to the violence, and it was obvious he was fading fast.

"Listen to me, you bastard! What is coming? Who is going to come after me?"

The assassin suddenly started convulsing, blood bubbling from his mouth. Letting out one last rasp of air, he sagged in Kaleb's grip. Fear overtook Kaleb. His grip was so tight on the dead man's tunic that the whites of his knuckles showed. Flinging the corpse from him, he abruptly stood up, an edge of panic in his movements. He still had no idea who sent the assassins. Something bad was coming to Varkuvia. The assassin also spoke of others being targeted. What others? How had the man known who he was? All questions that would now remain unanswered.

All thoughts of personal danger and panic fled Kaleb as his gaze fell upon the dead body of Kastor once more. Kastor's eyes were still open, and Kaleb moved to the dead prince. Kneeling down, he gently placed a hand on Kastor's broad chest, closing his open eyes with the other hand. Grief overwhelmed Kaleb. Kastor might have been boisterous and slightly arrogant, but he was a friend beyond comparison. Kind and caring, Kastor constantly spoke of building hospitals and universities when he became king. He wanted to make a better life for his people, no thoughts of expanding his kingdom crossing his mind. Now he would never be given that opportunity. Kaleb bowed his head, his jaw clenching and unclenching, attempting to control his swarming emotions.

"You were more than a friend to me, Kastor," he told the departed prince, his voice thick with emotion. "You were my brother, and a better one I could not ever ask for. I could not imagine a more terrible way for you to die. Destiny declared you would be a great king, but fate had plans of its own. I will do everything within my power to avenge you. No matter what it takes, I will. I swear it upon all that is holy." His voice broke at the end.

He heard boots walking up the stairs outside the door. He rose to his feet, composing himself quickly as the captain of the night's watch politely opened the door. The captain was a stoop-shouldered, middle-aged man, who appeared anything but a soldier. Only his piercing eyes gave any evidence he was a man of action. It was those eyes that swept over the carnage in the room, finally coming to rest on the dead woman still naked in the bed. He shook his head and then addressed Kaleb.

"My eyes needed to see it to believe it. Kaleb, I am sorry for the death of Kastor. I know you two were close in your years at the Order." The captain looked at the dead assassins. "I will just presume these men died from the wounds they received while you defended yourself. Is this correct?" Kaleb nodded. "Then all I need is your account of the events that occurred here, and then I will allow you to be on your way."

Kaleb nodded again, devoid of emotion. He retold the captain what happened, leaving out the assassin's final words. He didn't know who he could trust anymore and thought it best to leave the words to himself for the time being. The captain dismissed him, and Kaleb walked out of the room into the hallway beyond, crowded with people. Kaleb ignored the probing questions being thrown at him, shouldering his way through the mass of people. Walking back to his father's castle, Kaleb felt like the walking dead. His mind still refused to process

Kastor was dead. A wolf howled in the distance, echoing the sorrow in his heart. Dawn was fast approaching as he pounded on the postern gate.

Rae opened a slot in the gate, grinning as he saw Kaleb. The grin froze on his face when he saw the depression etched on the young noble's features. Then fear appeared in his eyes when he saw the dried blood on Kaleb's hands and clothing. Opening the gate hurriedly, Rae ushered Kaleb through.

"M'lord, what in the seven hells happened?"

Kaleb rubbed at his eyes with thumb and forefinger. "Nothing that need concern you, Rae. The blood is not my own."

A new kind of fear appeared in Rae's eyes, and Kaleb knew the cause. If any harm or danger had befallen the lord's son, Rae was certain to be punished for allowing him through the gate. "Don't worry, Rae. I won't implicate you when the events of tonight reach my father's ears. You weren't at fault. The blame is mine alone to bear."

The words seemed to comfort Rae, his relief evident. "Much obliged, m'lord. You will make a good ruler someday I think."

In no mood for conversation, Kaleb nodded and moved past the sentry, making his way back to his sleeping quarters. Walking through the great hall, he heard busied activity from the castle servants. Wafting through the dual doors of the kitchen at the far end of the hall came the smell of freshly baked bread. The castle baker was already hard at work, yet the sun had barely risen. The mouthwatering smells were lost on Kaleb. Walking up the stairs, he suddenly stopped. What if more assassins waited for him in his room? The thought sent a fresh wave of panic through him, but he quelled it savagely. *I will not run*, he told himself.

Loosening his swords in their scabbards, Kaleb walked cautiously to his bedroom door. Flinging the door inward, he stepped boldly into the room, every sense alert to danger. There on his bed sat his father, Lord Rickart. The lord's black hair had become speckled with silver over the years, and he had grown a goatee, giving his serious face a sardonic look. He was dressed in a tunic of fine black silk, his leggings in matching fashion. Lord Rickart casually stood and met his son's shocked face.

"I hope you haven't come to slay the man that sired you," his father said, his voice deep and resonant.

Kaleb quickly composed himself, feeling slightly foolish. "I wasn't expecting you," he muttered.

An amused gleam appeared in Rickart's eyes at his son's discomfort. Kaleb's anger flared. He already had been through enough turmoil the previous night without having to deal with his father as well. "What is it you want, Father?" snapped Kaleb, an edge to his voice.

Rickart's eyes narrowed. "Such a disrespectful tone from an insolent boy. Being lord of these lands, it has reached my ears about what occurred last night. I was slightly taken aback to hear Kastor, the son of one of our allies, died while under the protection of my lands. Then, I was genuinely surprised to learn my son had some involvement in the events that took place. I understand Kastor was a friend of yours, and it is unfortunate what happened to him, but already rumors are beginning to circulate. Now, tell me what happened."

Kaleb thought about ignoring his father as he had done a hundred times in the past. Instead, he shrugged and found himself telling him everything that took place. He even found himself telling Rickart the assassin's last words and confessing his fears at the repercussions of those words. Through it all, his father listened intently, not interrupting. When Kaleb finished, Rickart remained silent. After several long moments, Kaleb couldn't take the silence anymore.

"Nothing to say, Father?" He couldn't help but keep the contempt from his voice. "Not going to tell me to quit acting like a young maiden and act like a man for once in my life?"

His father ignored the dripping sarcasm. "It seems we have little option available to us. You must leave. If you stay here, no matter how wary we remain, these men will find a way to get to you. They were bold enough to slay the son of a king in—I say this without boasting—a powerful lord's lands. I don't see them concerning themselves with that same lord's son." Rickart stood, lost in thought.

"I will send you to King Markos. The king's name day is fast approaching, and you can go there to convey my happiness at another year of his reign. As I recall, you were friends with his two sons while you were part of the Order and became close with the younger of the two princes, Vasilis.

"I will send word ahead of you, warning Markos to remain vigilant. If there are more targets as this assassin claimed, the king might be among them. I will also discretely send word to the other kings. If something is coming toward Varkuvia, I would rather be prepared when it comes."

Kaleb was utterly shocked. His father, who had remained cold and distant toward him his entire life, and had even murdered his own mother, was actually concerned about him. For some time he was at a loss for words.

"Why do you care so much about my fate, Father?" he asked softly.

"You are my son," his father replied simply.

Kaleb's irritation grew. "And you've done a great job showing your undying affection toward your family so far in your life. Were you concerned about Mother after you murdered her, standing over her still body?"

As soon as the words left Kaleb's mouth, he immediately regretted them. Still no emotion showed on Rickart's face. Only the anger in his eyes showed he even registered what Kaleb just said. When he spoke, Kaleb thought it sounded like his father was trying to control his emotions. Something he never saw him do before.

"I thought I heard a door click shut that night. You know nothing, boy. Your mother was a whore and consorted with any handsome man that just so happened to look her way. Half of the castle staff, for example. She shamed me, and you should be ashamed to call that woman your mother. I don't regret what I did that night. I only wish I had known sooner. I loved her in my own fashion, and what she did to me cut deeper than any blade ever could. We will speak more about this matter when you return, hopefully when you have marshaled your thoughts and learned to guard your tongue a little better. I will send someone to help you pack your belongings, and I will also personally pick your escort, the best and most loyal men in my service. The sooner you leave, the better."

Kaleb had nothing to say as his father left the room. For the first time in his life, his father had displayed some form of emotion toward him. Instead of embracing the moment, he blurted out a secret he kept for half of his life. The words his father had spoken finally sunk in. He said his mother was unfaithful to him. Picturing his mother through the innocence of a child's eyes, he remembered her kind face and gentle words. Looking back now through an adult's eyes, he recalled the easy way she smiled and laughed with the servants and guards, constantly touching them. As he had grown older, he was blinded to this, only remembering the fact his murderous father had denied him a mother. Just as his father was blinded by love, believing his wife would never do anything to betray him in such a way.

Everything that took place the previous night and the following morning came rushing at Kaleb all at once. His head swimming with overwhelming thoughts, he sat down roughly upon his bed. Events were occurring at a rapid pace, and Kaleb feared they were far from over. His whole life, he tried to be unlike Lord Rickart, pushing himself well beyond the borders of his limits to prove he was an honest and courageous man. He wanted to be someone whom people could look up to as a hero and someone they could rely upon. Yet tonight he lost control of the inner demons he normally kept caged. Looking back at his questioning of the assassin, he realized with a sickening feeling the elation he felt as he tortured the man. Even worse, if the man had lived longer, he would have prolonged his suffering. He unleashed his inner beast, and he wondered how much different he really was from his father.

He put the torturing of the assassin down to the loss of his friend and pushed the thought from his mind. He did not regret the death of the man, for his actions had condemned him. The only thing he regretted were the dark feelings raging through him. Kaleb made a promise to himself that he wouldn't allow the dark side of his soul to resurface again. *I will never be like you, Father*, he thought. With that, he forced his weary body to stand and began packing his belongings.

By midday, Kaleb was ready to leave. With an entourage of twenty mounted soldiers, a wagon possessing his clothing, and supplies for the trip, the group embarked upon their journey. Kaleb knew each of the soldiers by name, all grizzled veterans of many a battle, and utterly loyal to Lord Rickart. Or so he hoped. It would be a long trip to King Markos and the Stone Realm. King Lucan, the liege Lord Rickart served, lived on the Golden Peninsula at the westernmost part of the realms of the Five Kings. The trip to Markos would take some weeks, and Kaleb prayed the trip would be uneventful.

# CHAPTER THREE

Trystan was overjoyed as he rode his mare up the hard-packed dirt road that led to Jaxon's farm. For once, the weather was warm, and after emerging from the Harrowing Woods, he doffed his leather jerkin lined with heavy fleece. Now, he simply wore a soft woolen long sleeve shirt the color of peaches. The sun was bright overhead, birds chirping in the distance. It was a nice day, and Trystan felt at peace for the first time in weeks. Cantering closer to Jaxon's farm, Trystan saw the road he was on led directly to a well-constructed two-story house made of seasoned timber. Behind the house, he saw a large barn of freshly laid red paint. Bypassing the house, he moved toward the barn in the back.

Coming around the corner of the house, Trystan saw bustling activity. To his left, just next to the barn, was a paddock fence that penned in a large herd of cattle. A hill dipped to his right, and he could see barren fields intended for crops. Trystan saw men already tilling the soil, not wasting a moment of the first nice day of the year. It seemed Jaxon's small farm, the one he'd written of, had grown in the months since they talked. Trystan still hadn't spied his large friend and began searching in earnest for him. He finally spotted the giant with a small group of men gathered around a stone wall some distance behind the grazing cattle.

As Trystan cantered his horse toward the gathered men, he noticed the stone wall, which must've marked the border of Jaxon's property, was broken in a spot. Jaxon, along with a handful of his workers, were moving stones in place to repair the damaged wall. The giant took off his shirt in the gathering warmth of the day, and Trystan still could not get over the sheer immensity of the man. Whereas most large muscular men were toned, Jaxon was just sheer raw muscle. He saw his friend bend down and hook his hands beneath a stone so massive it would've taken two grown men just to budge it. With a huge surge of effort, Jaxon lifted the stone to his chest and then heaved it onto the wall where his workers packed it down with mortar.

Trystan stood his mount some distance from the small working party. Not a single one of them noticed his approach so engrossed were they in their work. Leaning forward on the pommel of his saddle, Trystan shouted out to Jaxon, "Hey, you big lummox! Where's a decent man to get a good meal around here?"

The men stopped working, turning toward the disruptive shouting that had interrupted their work. When Jaxon saw who it was, a broad smile crossed his bearded face. "Trys, you rascal!" the giant's voice boomed out. "Get your scrawny arse over here. Let me get a look ya."

Smiling, Trystan trotted his horse forward. Jaxon turned to his workers. "I think that's about it for today, lads. We'll try and finish up the wall tomorrow, no reason to kill ourselves. Go and grab yourselves something to eat if you'd like, you've earned it. After that, if you're done with your duties for the day, return to your homes, and I'll be seeing you in the morning."

As Trystan reined in his horse next to Jaxon, he noticed the easy familiarity in his workers as they said their farewells. They didn't see

Jaxon just as their boss but also as their friend. It was hard not to like Jaxon with his easy personality and booming laughter. Trystan suddenly realized just how much he missed the man. Leaning forward in his saddle, he gripped his friend wrist to wrist in the warrior tradition.

Removing a white linen towel tucked into his pants buckle, Jaxon wiped down the sweat of his upper torso. He then donned his shirt of similar material, the tight-fitting tunic barely covering his breadth of shoulder. "Well, Trys, I received your letter not two days ago, and I appreciate you writing the words large for me too, you bastard. Now, to my recollection, it should take over a week to travel from the farm you worked at to get here." He suspiciously eyed the gentle mare that Trystan was seated upon. "That's a mighty steed you got there to get you here in just two days."

Trystan laughed good-heartedly. "Ah, but I did miss you so, Jaxon. I fear not all of us are built for the farm life like you. If I had stayed there but one more day, I would've lost my mind, so I left as soon as possible." He leaned over, gripping the big man's shoulder, a serious note entering his voice. "I hope I'm not being an inconvenience on you, Jax."

Jaxon waved his hand, swatting away the words as if they were flies. "Don't be foolish, lad. You are always welcome at my hearth, and for as long as you like too. Now let's get back to the house and get some meat on that bony frame of yours. I can see your ribs poking out from under your shirt. How did you survive the journey here with such little fat on you? I feel as though I'm talking to a skeleton rather than a man."

The duo began moving back toward the house, Trystan walking his horse next to his friend. He chuckled at Jaxon's comment. "You caught me, Jax. I starved myself for days, just so I could have my dear old bearded mother Jax take care of me."

Jax snorted derisively. Looking up into Trystan's face, he studied it vigorously. "There must be some truth to what you say. I guess only a mother could love a face like that, huh?"

Their laughter rolled over the cattle grazing inside the paddock fence. Many looked up at the noise, still munching on mouthfuls of grass. "I see you have retained your famous humor." Trystan leaned over, smelling his friend. He reeled back in mock horror, waving a hand in front of his face. "I also see you still don't believe in bathing. By the gods, man, the smell from you could lay waste to the whole herd of cattle over there. Is water not a commodity on your farm?"

Sniffing at his armpit, Jaxon smiled amiably. "Now I know you're lying, little man. My wife, Margaret, would have my hide if I smelled of anything less than roses. The woman is extremely high on personal cleanliness for reasons I still cannot understand."

For a few moments, Trystan was taken back. Jaxon had not written of a wife in the last letter he received. "You don't waste much time do you, Jax? Barely six months out of the Order and already married."

The big man chuckled, the sound like rumbling thunder. "Not just married, Trys. Margaret's a few months pregnant, and I'll soon have little Jaxons running amuck around this farm. The wife and I were childhood sweethearts, and after I returned from the disbandment, I was blessed by the gods to find out she still wasn't betrothed to anyone. She told me she was waiting for me to return before she would marry." He shook his head in disbelief. "I never thought anyone would wait a near decade for me. We were married within the week of my return, and it seems as each day passes, the more my affection for her seems to grow. I'm in love with her. I never thought I'd sound like one of those fools we always made fun of, spouting their nonsense of true love, but I honestly don't know what I would do without her." He sniffed. "Damn, but I sound maudlin now. Old age must finally be catching up to me. Let's go get drunk and have a merry time."

He led Trystan to where his stables were located inside the barn. Trystan dismounted from his mare, leading the horse toward a stall at the far end. Unsaddling his steed, Trystan gathered some straw off the ground and wiped down the horse's flanks. Leaving the horse with enough grain for the night, he followed Jaxon through the back door into the house beyond. The room they entered was large, extending from the back of the house to the front door, which led to the dirt road. A finely embroidered red carpet lay upon the floor between two soft couches and several armchairs. The furniture surrounded a stone fireplace set in the far wall. The floor was laid from fine timber located in the forests of the Wood Realm. Glancing up at the mantle above the fireplace, Trystan saw the ax that Jaxon had wielded in the Order hanging there. The butterfly blades of the giant war ax still appeared as sharp as ever, a fresh sheen of oil laid over them, the long haft of the weapon wrapped in tightly bound, dark leather. The room was well kept, not a speck of dust showing on the floor or furniture.

Jaxon took off his boots, tossing them next to the back door. "My dearest Margaret!" His voice boomed. "Your beloved has returned home, and I've brought a stray dog in from the field. Try not to put him down when you see him."

His wife emerged from around a corner. Trystan guessed she came from the kitchen due to the leather apron she still wore. She was a pretty woman with a nose a shade too big for her face. She was tall for a woman, standing just above six foot. Her chestnut brown hair hung in curls down to the small of her back, her light brown eyes sparkling with joy when she saw her husband. Margaret's smile at the sight of Jaxon lit up the room, the woman instantly changing from mildly attractive to stunning. She ran across the room, directly into her husband's open embrace. The big man picked her up in his arms and spun her joyfully.

Trystan was forgotten as the married couple merrily greeted one another after a long day of work. Setting his wife down, Jaxon kissed her full on the lips and then draped his arm over her shoulder, turning her toward Trystan to introduce him. "This man, my dear, is the famous swordsman of the Order of Acrium, Trystan. The lad traveled a long way, most likely on some gallant quest he's on, saving a princess or some such. This modern-day hero will be staying with us for some time. I expect you to treat him as you would a relative."

Margaret playfully smacked her husband on the chest. "I know who he is, you big fool," she said, her voice pleasant and sweet. "You've talked of little else since you received his letter." Stepping forward, she embraced Trystan, the warmth in the hug genuine. "It's nice to finally meet you, Trystan. I have heard many a great things about you, and I feel as if I know you already." Taking a step back, a more serious look crossed her face, the smile disappearing. "I also heard if it wasn't for you, my husband wouldn't be standing beside me today. I'm truly grateful to you for that."

Trystan felt uncomfortable at the compliment and sudden contact, his upbringing still causing him to be shy around strangers. He hoped his discomfort didn't show on his face, for he didn't wish to make a bad first impression. He spoke hurriedly, hoping to hide his shy demeanor behind a shield of words. "It's a pleasure to meet you, Margaret. I have also heard nothing but good things about you. It seems you have captured the heart of my friend here. He spoke of little else on the walk back to the house."

Now it was Jaxon who looked embarrassed. Margaret laughed at her husband's discomfort. "Ashamed of your friend telling me how you feel about me, are you? Oh, but he is a sensitive one isn't he, Trystan?"

Trystan joined in with her laughter. He could see why the two had fallen in love so easily. They both had that easy personality that could make friends of anyone, and their laughs were infectious. While Jaxon's laugh was booming, filling the room, Margaret's laughter, sounding like music, had the same effect. The two were a perfect match, and Trystan was filled with joy at his friend's happiness.

Jaxon's embarrassment left his face, replaced by a look of love in his eyes. Trystan suddenly felt as if he was imposing on the happily married couple, and he wondered if coming to the farm was such a good idea after all.

With some sixth sense he possessed, Jaxon detected Trystan's unease almost immediately. "All right, lass, I promised good ol' Trys here a meal fit for kings." He turned toward Trystan. "There isn't a cook in all the courts of the Five Realms that can rival her. Well, when she puts the effort in that is," he finished, throwing Trystan a quick wink.

Margaret smacked Jaxon's chest harder this time, a look of mock hurt on her face. "You have quite some nerve, you big horse's ass. I am going to dismiss your ill manners this time, only for Trystan's sake. Now, make yourself useful and go fetch a few flagons of ale from the cellar, and while you're up and about, grab a few logs of wood for the fireplace. It could be a cold night, and a roaring fire may be just the cure."

The big man didn't look happy about fetching anything, preferring to stretch himself out on the couch after a long day of work. With a resigned nod of his head, he went to give his wife another kiss on the lips. She playfully spun away from his embrace, blowing him a kiss as she walked off to the kitchen. Trystan noticed Jaxon's gaze lingering on the swish of his wife's hips as she disappeared around the corner. His friend stood transfixed before shaking his head and coming back to reality.

"I truly believe that woman has bewitched me." Jaxon sighed. "And to be honest, I couldn't care less."

The two men moved off to the cellar entrance at the rear of the house. As they walked, Trystan inquired how Jaxon's farm was faring. Jaxon chuckled in response. "For every piece of silver I have spent on the farm, I have made seven in profit. A few months back, during the bitter months of winter, a lung blight swept through the cattle of the Wood Realm, decimating entire herds and skyrocketing the sales for cattle. Against all odds, the blight skipped over my farm, and within no time at all, I had buyers coming from all corners of the realm to purchase my cattle. A representative for King Eryk himself even arrived at my farm. With the money I earned from selling my herd, I was able to purchase a few horses, even more cattle, and construct the barn. Now I have fifteen able-bodied workers helping out around the farm. Most of them live in a town called Cavall just a few miles up the road, but two of them stay in a small cabin I constructed to the side of my own house. The two men, Jorkii and Yorgos, had nowhere to stay so I took them in and have proven to be loyal and hard workers. I don't want to say it for fear of offending the gods, but it seems as though I'm on the verge of becoming wealthy. Would you have ever imagined I would prove to be such a capable businessman?"

As Jaxon flung open the cellar door just to the left of the back door, and descended the steps, he brought up a fresh new subject. "By the gods, I forgot to mention that rascal Gavin is staying in the same town my workers live in. I was going to offer him a job at the farm, but he has already established himself as a famed hunter." Jaxon laughed. "The men were saying just the other day they swear Gavin could neuter a fly from thirty paces."

Trystan laughed along with his friend as they gathered the ale from the cellar. Gavin was also a member of the Order but, unlike Trystan or Jaxon, was not as skilled with an ax or sword. The man's medium height put him at a disadvantage when facing taller opponents, their longer reach coming into play. Rather, the man was one of the most gifted bowman either of them had ever seen. Gavin's ability to gauge distance and wind resistance, along with eyes that could rival those of an eagle, soon established him as a renowned archer.

During the battle with the tribesmen five years ago, just before the barbarians broke and ran, a group of painted tribesmen surrounded Jaxon. Jaxon's horse was dead underneath him, but he stood his ground, his giant ax cutting left and right, the silver armor of the Order making him stand out like a shining beacon. It was only a matter of time before the weight of numbers would drag Jaxon down, and Trystan single-handedly attempted a suicidal charge on the group encircling the axman. He had not expected anybody to be beside him and was overly surprised to see Gavin fighting alongside him. Trystan still recalled Gavin's strong fingers drawing arrow upon arrow to his cheek, releasing them in one fluid motion into the massed ranks of the tribesmen. Each one of his arrows found its mark, and the group scattered before the ferocity of the warriors, the battle soon becoming a rout. Not a day went by that Jaxon didn't thank the swordsman or the archer for saving his life. Apart from Jaxon, Gavin was one of Trystan's closest friend's while he was part of the Order. He hoped there was time to visit the archer while staying at the farm.

Placing the jugs of ale at the dinner table, exquisite smells struck both Trystan and Jaxon. Their mouths salivated from the intoxicating aroma of cooked duck filling the house. Margaret, sensing the men's hunger in the kitchen beyond, called out, "I hope you men got the firewood as well, or it looks like Jorkii and Yorgos will have a mighty feast upon their hands."

The workers were still toiling away in the fields, and Jaxon scowled at the prospect that the two would enjoy a meal meant for him. As was Jaxon's nature, his momentary irritation soon passed, and he shrugged it off, moving outside to the supply of firewood. The wood was stacked against the back wall, next to the cellar, providing a dual effect. Not only were the split logs used for roaring fires, but the wood stacked against the wall provided much-needed insulation during the frosty cold of winter. As Trystan gathered up an armful of split wood, he noticed a long-handled ax embedded in a tree stump close by, a self-made block for cutting wood. He imagined Jaxon wielding the ax like a veteran logger, carving wood logs with ease.

Both of the men, overburdened with split hunks of wood, made the procession back to the empty fireplace. The thought of a good meal loomed in the near future, and the two swapped jests as dusk fell upon Jaxon's farm, turning the sky bloodred. It was then the thunder of hooves reached their ears. Jaxon was perplexed, for no riders were expected at this hour.

Moving through the living room, Jaxon unceremoniously dumped the wood in front of the fireplace, curious as to who would be here at such a strange hour. Trystan also dropped his pile of wood then followed his friend to a shuttered window, which overlooked the road leading to the house. Peering through the window, the two saw five darkly garbed men seated upon horses that were at least sixteen hands tall, just sitting on their mounts observing the house. Jaxon glanced to the right, and Trystan followed his gaze. Coming around the corner of the house were two other men Trystan took for Jorkii and Yorgos from their dirty work attire. One was short and plump while the other was tall and stick-thin. Both had friendly smiles on their faces as they approached the mounted men.

The two workers greeted the five strangers with a wave then said something to the gathered riders. The window Trystan gazed through muffled the exchange though it appeared as if the workers were inquiring as to how they could help the newcomers. The rider in the middle, a man with a hard face and cold eyes, said something to his companions. The four other dark garbed riders dismounted. What happened next froze Trystan's blood.

Without so much as a word, the riders drew their swords of dark steel and cut down the two workers where they stood. The action happened so fast Trystan doubted they even had time to register the blades delivering the death strokes. The man with the hard face, still mounted, turned his cold gaze once more upon the house. He barked out another command to his companions, and Trystan saw the four men turn their attention to the front door. As when the leader gave the order to cut down Yorgos and Jorkii, they advanced upon the door without a moment's hesitation.

Trystan's shock evaporated. These men had come to his friend's house to butcher and murder. He would be damned if he was going to allow that to happen. Glancing toward Jaxon, he saw that his jaw was clenched, and a vein jutted from his forehead in fury. Turning to Trystan, their eyes met. Understanding flowed between them and Jaxon nodded. Trystan left his sword upstairs in the room Margaret prepared for him. As Trystan moved toward the staircase, he saw Jaxon taking his war ax down from above the fireplace. Vaulting the steps two at a time, Trystan raced to his room, flinging the door open. His sword lay upon the bed. Unsheathing the blade, he flung the scabbard aside and sprinted back to the stairs to join his companion.

As he reached the top of the stairs, he saw Jaxon kick the front door open with ax in hand, his massive size taking up the width of the doorframe. "Thought to come here and kill unsuspecting innocents, did you?" he raged at the dark-garbed warriors who stood rooted to the spot. "Well, here I am, you bastards! Let's see what you cowards are made of!"

He charged into the advancing men, channeling his fury into an unrelenting war cry that promised death to any that opposed him. Trystan, fearing for his friend, sprinted down the stairs. Leaping down the few remaining steps, he rushed to his aid. As he emerged outside, he saw Jaxon battling desperately against three opponents. One of the men lay dead, his brains scattered across the ground. The leader still sat in his saddle, watching the action unfold. Trystan shouted at the top of his lungs, seeking to distract the men assailing Jaxon. One of the attackers broke off and focused his attention on the screaming young man. Dark steel met Trystan's shimmering blade as the two combatants clashed together. The man facing Trystan was talented, his sword blade moving at blistering speed. Trystan blocked, parried, and lunged, praying for an opening and determined to help Jaxon.

As his opponent lunged forward, Trystan sidestepped the blade, kicking out at his exposed knee. He heard the splintering of bone as his boot connected, the kneecap shattering on impact. The man screamed in pain and tried another lunge through gritted teeth. His broken leg made the attempt clumsy, and this time Trystan spun around the plunging blade, bringing the hilt of his sword crashing into the back of the man's head. He fell unconscious to the ground, landing on his face. Trystan turned his attention on Jaxon, ready to go to his aid. His friend was steadily being pushed back toward the open front door by the two opponents facing him.

A tall man with pale blue eyes was trying to circle behind Jaxon, seeking an opening. Trystan rushed to help Jaxon who was already bleeding from a shallow wound to his scalp and shoulder. Jaxon's breathing was starting to come in short gasps, sweat coursing down his face. He was already exhausted from working on the farm all day, and the battle was taking a rapid toll on his beleaguered body. Trystan feared he was going to be too late. The tall man drew his arm back, ready to drive his dark sword into Jaxon's unprotected back when suddenly his back arched, his face convulsing in agony. He scrabbled behind his back as if he were trying to pry something loose. Suddenly all movement seized, the man slumping dead to the ground. As he fell, Trystan saw Margaret standing there, her apron still on. A bloody kitchen knife slipped from her trembling hands. Her face was pale white, her eyes still resting on the man she had just killed.

Jaxon, still facing an opponent, blocked a savage cut that would've dismembered him with the sharp blades of his ax. Brushing aside another sword thrust, Jaxon slashed open a terrible wound in the man's upper thigh. As his opponent fell to his knees in agony, Jaxon brought the war ax over his head. With all of his mighty strength, the giant brought the ax down into his fallen foe's head, splitting it like a melon. Brain and bone shards exploded around the blade.

Trystan didn't even have time to reach his friend before the action was over. Remembering one of the riders sat on his mount, he spun around, scanning for the leader of the group. There he sat, still on his mount, his cold gaze fixed upon Trystan. He sat there the whole time while his men died around him. What kind of leader would do that to his own men?

The muscular built leader dismounted from his horse casually, almost carefree. Drawing his sword, he slashed the dark blade through the air, loosening his shoulders. When he spoke, the tone of his voice was bored. "So it seems I finally get to challenge the famed *Trystan*. I have to say, after watching you in action, I'm not even impressed.

Before we begin, let me introduce myself. My name is Orpheus, and I am going to carve that name into your heart. I am going to kill you, and then I will kill the big farmer. But first, I think I will make him watch as I enjoy his wife. The bitch had no right killing an anointed brother."

Jaxon went to meet the man head on, his face purple with fury, but Trystan held out his hand, stopping him. Jaxon's angry gaze locked to Trystan's, but the swordsman gave a shake of his head. Reluctantly, Jaxon stepped back, his hands clenching the haft of his ax tightly. As Trystan approached Orpheus cautiously, he noted the catlike movements in the leader's fluid motion. *This man will be skilled,* he observed, *but he is also extremely arrogant, his manner far too casual. That will soon change, his doubts eroding at his confidence. That's when I will make my move.*

Orpheus attacked first, dark steel licking out with incredible speed. Trystan barely blocked the blur. And so the duel began. In the beginning stages of the fight, Trystan didn't move on the offensive at all, instead choosing to defend and study his opponent. Orpheus, mistaking Trystan's defensive stance as a sign of weakness, attempted to taunt his opponent as they fought across the dirt road. "What's the matter, orphan child? Too scared to fight back, or is it merely that you're outclassed?"

Trystan didn't respond, his mind totally engrossed in the duel. He allowed anger to cloud his judgment back in the Harrowing Woods. He wouldn't let that happen here, not with just his life on the line, but the lives of his friends as well. Irritation blazed in Orpheus's eyes. His opponents always responded, either with mocking words of their own or fear in their actions. Yet no emotion showed on Trystan's face, his expression as blank as a clear autumn sky. *No matter,* thought Orpheus. *It is time to put an end to this farce.*

He began moving his sword in a movement of bewildering speed, attacking Trystan with everything he had. Trystan backpedaled furiously, desperately defending himself. Twice, Orpheus's blade got past his defenses, opening a shallow wound in his upper chest, and another opening a cut on the side of his neck. The neck wound was a hairbreadth away from slicing open his jugular and ending the fight. As the duel wore on, and Orpheus still couldn't deliver the killing stroke, a termite began to eat its way through his wooden fortress of confidence. *This isn't possible,* his mind screamed. *I am Orpheus, the most talented swordsman in the east. No one can go toe to toe with me with a blade and win.*

In a desperate attempt to regain control of the situation, Orpheus tried goading his opponent one more time as their blades clashed together. "How does it feel knowing you are going to die today, you insignificant worm?"

Trystan met Orpheus's gaze and smiled. That simple action set anger coursing through Orpheus. Nobody treated him with such disdain, especially not a lowly peasant like Trystan. Blinded by rage, Orpheus gripped his sword doublehanded and aimed to chop the bastard's head off. Trystan ducked under the sweep, dropping to his knee. From that moment on, it was as if Orpheus's movements were underwater, and he was helpless as he watched Trystan plunge his blade toward his chest. Searing pain erupted through Orpheus as Trystan's sword cut through his dark tunic and steel mail shirt beneath as if it were wool. The blade pierced one of his lungs, and he felt blood choking his airway. Panic engulfed Orpheus. He would shake this wound off and slay Trystan along with the massive farmer. Orpheus went to raise his blade to do just that when he realized he was on his knees, his weapon on the ground beside him. Looking up groggily, he saw Jaxon striding toward him.

"Looks like you're not going to enjoy my wife while I watch, are you now?" The last image Orpheus had was of Jaxon's giant war ax sweeping toward his unprotected neck.

Trystan walked away as Orpheus's body struck the ground, the dead man's head rolling across the dirt road. Margaret still stood at the front door, her features pale. She held a shaking hand to her mouth, tears spilling down her cheeks. Jaxon, seeing that his wife was petrified, dropped his ax and ran to her, embracing her tightly. He whispered soothing words while rubbing her back. Margaret sobbed into her husband's chest, wrapping her arms around his waist as if her life depended on it.

Ignoring the couple, Trystan let them share their own private moment. Moving to the rider he had knocked unconscious earlier, he saw blood matted to his dark hair where he struck him with the hilt of his sword. Flipping him onto his back with his boot, Trystan saw the man was still out cold. Looking down at his adversary's leg, he saw it was twisted at a terrible angle just below the kneecap. He wouldn't be going anywhere anytime soon. The man's dark sword was still within reach, and Trystan tossed it away.

Moving past the distraught married couple, Trystan moved into the house, looking for something to bind the man's hands. Jaxon, observing his friend's activity, kissed his wife on the crown of her head. "Margaret, I'm going to need you to go back inside for a little. Have no fear, lass, I will join you shortly."

Margaret had stopped crying and wiped the last remaining tears from her face. Her swollen eyes looked up into her husband's face. "I love you, Jax."

Jaxon kissed her tenderly. "And I love you, my beautiful wife. You have my word that no one will harm you as long as I draw breath. Go on in the house now."

This time Margaret nodded and stumbled back through the front door. Moments later, Trystan emerged with a length of hemp rope. Side by side, they moved back to the man who still lay unconscious. Jaxon dragged the dark-haired man to the front wall of his house and sat him in an upright position, his back propped against the wall.

Trystan bound the man's hands behind his back then turned to Jaxon. "Go and fetch a pale of water, my friend. Let's wake this bastard up and find out who he is."

Jaxon returned moments later and poured a full pail of water on their prisoner's head. The man's eyes opened in a flurry, water sputtering from his mouth. A scream of agony ripped from his throat when he tried to stand up, pain erupting from his broken limb. Gritting his teeth against the unaccustomed pain, he stared up at Trystan and Jaxon, fear apparent in his pale gaze. The two warriors knelt down in front of the frightened man, their faces set.

Trystan spoke first. "If you couldn't tell by now, your leg is badly broken. Now, unlike you and your dead companions, I am a man of my word. If your information proves useful, I will tend to your wound though you will be my prisoner. If not"—he shook his head, making a clicking noise with his tongue—"I could make it quite unpleasant for you. Do you understand?"

The man's nervous gaze flicked back and forth between Trystan and the imposing figure of Jaxon, judging their words. His eyes dropped to the ground, and he nodded meekly. Trystan pressed forward. "Even a blind man could tell that you and your companions are no simple ragtag group of bandits. The swords you carry are crafted by a master blacksmith, and I have seen kings wear clothing less lavish than yours. Your dead leader over there, whose head seems to have fallen off, made the unfortunate mistake of saying he knew my name before he met his demise. As far as I know, I have not wronged anyone, man or woman, since my adolescence. Not once since then have I stolen from someone, harmed a woman, or committed a deed that would shame me. Nor have I ever seen my companion here do the same. Which makes me wonder, why would anyone wish death upon us? We are only simple farmers."

Despite the man's anguish, he managed a smile. "Ah yes, simple farmers who managed to defeat five of the Brotherhood." His voice was thick with agony, his face contorted in pain. "My brothers and I knew you before we even saw you, Trystan of the Order of Acrium." He nodded toward Jaxon. "The giant one as well. We received orders from our master himself to get rid of you two and to do it quickly. The Brotherhood lives to obey, for it is not in our nature to question who we are to kill, whether it be man or woman. We have even been ordered to eliminate children before." An evil grin spread across his face as he looked at Jaxon.

Trystan could see that Jaxon was close to killing the man. He obviously had information Margaret was pregnant. Trystan placed a hand on his friend's tense shoulder. Jaxon looked closely at the man that came to bring death to him and his wife, murderous intent in his eyes. With a savage curse, he got up and stormed some feet away. Trystan turned his attention back on the assassin, anger showing in his eyes as well.

"If you provoke either of us like that again, I will slit your throat where you sit. I am this close"—he held up his thumb and index finger, barely an inch apart from each other—"from allowing my companion to rip you in half with his bare hands. Now, who is this master? What Brotherhood are you speaking of?"

There was no longer any terror evident on the interrogated man's face. "Even if I wanted to, I could not give you my master's name, for not even Orpheus knew. We are paid a small fortune to not ask questions. What I can tell you is my Brotherhood was formed to see all of Varkuvia come crashing down. For some months now, we have been eliminating disbanded warriors of the Order of Acrium. Discretion was important in the beginning, only targeting lowly members. The last few weeks have seen us eliminate more high-value targets." A dark gleam appeared in his eyes. "If the Order were to reform today, I'm sad to say it would no longer be able to deal with any major threat. In fact, the two of you might be the only ones left." The man started laughing, the sound malicious.

Trystan snapped, punching the man full in the face. His head rocked off the wall of the house behind him. Blood ran from a gash just below the assassin's left eye, flowing freely down his face. He smiled at Trystan again, a look of utter contempt in his eyes. Trystan lost all restraint. Grabbing the front of the murderer's black tunic, he began unmercifully pummeling the man's unprotected face. Jaxon dragged Trystan some feet away from the bludgeoned man. The assassin, his face a mask of blood and swollen bruises, spit a mouthful of blood after the two, laughing maniacally.

Trystan went to go after him again, but Jaxon's massive strength held him in place. "Dammit, Trys! We have no choice but to keep the bastard alive. Don't you see he's the only living proof we can bring before the Five Kings? We must find out the truth of his words, and if they are true, we must take action. The world needs to know what's happening."

The swordsman was about to respond when the assassin's words cut through his train of thought. "Enjoy your lives while you can, you Varkuvian dogs. Within a fortnight, more men will come for you and finish what my brothers and I started here today. Live the remaining days of your lives in fear."

Turning angrily toward him, Trystan moved to beat him more despite the truth of Jaxon's words. He stopped in his tracks when he saw the assassin had unbound his hands from behind his back and had a balled up leaf of reddish-green color in his hand. Before either Jaxon or Trystan could respond, the man threw the leaf in his mouth and began chewing vigorously, a look of triumph on his face. Trystan and Jaxon moved quickly to their prisoner's side, but it was too late. Within seconds, the man's mouth was frothing, his eyes glazed over in death.

Lifting up the arm of the corpse, Trystan inspected the sleeve. A secret pocket was stitched into the inside of the cloth where he had kept the poisonous plant. A shredded leaf could still be seen on the sleeve, and Trystan recognized it immediately. The plant was called Death Root and only came from the swamplands from the Far East. The plant's name alone spoke of its properties. He taunted Trystan on purpose, just so he could get his hands free without any noticed suspicion. Then, when the warriors were far enough away, he slipped the plant into his hand. He would rather kill himself than be taken alive. *What nature of men are we dealing with?* Trystan wondered.

Trystan's mind was reeling. Before committing suicide, the man confessed this Brotherhood of assassins was targeting former members of the Order. He found himself wondering how many of the recently dispersed Order of Acrium remained. Were Jaxon and himself truly the only ones left? Regardless, they couldn't stay at the farm. This Brotherhood already knew of the place, and once they discovered the assassins they sent failed, it would only be a matter of time before they dispatched more. Looking at his friend, he saw Jaxon realized this as well, a look of sadness etched into his face.

Without a word, Jaxon disappeared into the house, emerging moments later with two shovels. Handing one to Trystan he moved off some distance to the side and began digging. Trystan joined him, and after some time, they had two shallow graves dug for Jaxon's recently murdered farm hands. Closing the eyes of his workers, Jaxon carried the bodies and placed them gently in the graves. After a few nice words for the recently departed, they quickly buried them, patting the dirt down with their shovels. Trystan had not known them, but Jaxon clearly trusted them enough to allow them to live on his land, and his first thoughts after the action was over were to see them buried. Out of respect for his friend, he wished the men a safe passage in the journey afterlife.

Gathering the five bodies of the assassins, Trystan and Jaxon searched them for any remaining insight into the Brotherhood they were said to be a part of and who their master might be. Coming to the body of the tall man Margaret stabbed, Trystan found a ring hidden in his pants pocket. The metal of the ring was dark and finely crafted with the initials SV inscribed on the inside, and the inset into the ring was a golden sun. Curious, Trystan searched the bodies once more, this time more thoroughly. Each assassin had a hidden pocket somewhere on their person, and in each of these, he found a ring that matched the first one. Trystan realized the sun was an obvious symbol of the assassins and hoped it would shed some light onto the name the Brotherhood carried.

Pocketing the rings, Trystan and Jaxon carried the bodies one by one into the backyard and away from any onlooker's eyes. There they stacked the bodies and set them ablaze, destroying any evidence of them ever being there. Then they moved to the Brotherhood's horses that, without their riders to guide them, began grazing on the grass on the side of the road. They unsaddled the beasts and slapped them on the rear, sending them running off into the wilderness. Blood patches still covered the ground, but storm clouds could be seen in the fading light, moving in from the north. With luck, the storm would wash the blood away.

Just as darkness descended, the two companions went inside, satisfied for the time being they were safe. Margaret sat upon one of the couches in the living room, staring emotionlessly into a roaring fire, which she prepared in the fireplace. The meal that smelled so enticing little over an hour before was forgotten in her trauma. Jaxon slumped down next to his wife, drawing her to him, while Trystan moved to a deep armchair, watching the flames. The trio sat in silence for some time, darkness fully falling outside the house.

Rain began petering off the roof of the house as Trystan leaned forward on the edge of his seat. "Since nobody else wants to say it, I suppose I will. It is only a matter of time before the master of this Brotherhood realizes the men he sent failed him. I believe it's safe to say he will dispatch more assassins once their failure reaches his ears. Now, I can't force you to leave here, Jaxon and Margaret. It is your lives, and your farm, but if you stay here, you will be vulnerable. For the time being, we have bought ourselves a small window, and we should use it to our advantage. In the morning, I am going to travel to Cavall where your workers live and purchase supplies. From there, I will see if Gavin still lives, and if he does, I will ask him to accompany me eastward to Karalis where King Markos resides. Markos is the only king whose banner was not present when the Order was disbanded. His realm is the closest to danger, and it is my belief that he alone defended the importance of the Order to the other kings. I will go before him and tell him of what happened here today. I won't ask you to come with me, Jaxon, for you have a family to think about, and this trip will most assuredly be dangerous. This Brotherhood has a far grander scheme in mind other than assassinating disbanded warriors of the Order. Until this day, their work was done only in the shadows, and if they discover I plan to warn one of the Five Kings of impending peril, they will seek to eliminate me with even more gusto. But I urge you, for the time being, to leave your farm. Tell no one of where you are going and lay low until this is all over."

Jaxon sat for a long time, lounged on the couch, his normal jovial face cast in seriousness. The shadows from the flames played off of his bearded face, the lines on his forehead appearing chiseled from granite. In the light, he appeared far older than his twenty-eight years. Margaret still lay curled up on the couch, cuddled close to her husband.

"I hear your words, Trys," Jaxon said at last, an edge of sorrow in his voice. "But as long as the master of this Brother remains alive, all of our lives will remain in peril." He looked down at his wife, his emotions barely masked. "It pains me to say this, Margaret, but tomorrow we will travel to Cavall. After purchasing supplies, Trystan and I will escort you to your mother's home. Then I will ride with him to Karalis and plead our case before the king. Without you." Margaret sat up, anger flashing in her eyes. She went to object, but Jaxon cut her off. "Don't make this any harder than it has to be, Margaret. One of those men who tried to kill us made it clear that disbanded warriors of the Order are being targeted. As long as you stay by my side, your life will be in constant danger." His voice choked up. "The thought of you not being with me every day is an unbearable one, but I am trying to do what's best for you. And for our baby." He gently placed his hand on his wife's stomach.

Margaret looked ready to burst into tears. "I don't want you to leave me," she said, her voice shaking.

Both husband and wife held each other closely, Jaxon stroking her chestnut hair. Seeing the couple needed some time alone, Trystan politely stood up and walked upstairs, leaving them to their privacy. As Trystan walked to his room, he heard muffled talking from the spouses below. Clicking the door shut behind him, he moved to a window set into the wall overlooking the front yard of the house. For some time, he stood there watching the rain outside that turned torrential. As lightning lit up the sky, Trystan's eyes were drawn to the two graves they dug earlier.

As he watched Mother Nature at her best, Trystan lost track of time within the relative safety of the house. Hearing the creaking of the stairs, he knew Jaxon and Margaret finally made their way upstairs. They did not say good night to their guest, instead going directly to their bedroom at the end of the hallway. Trystan heard the door shut behind them. Getting undressed, he got into bed himself. Sleep was hard to come by, but when it did, it was sudden. For the second night in a row, he slept without dreams.

The following morning Jaxon's workforce began arriving for a day of labor. Jaxon met them in traveling clothes and laid out his future plans as cautiously as possible. He addressed the head farm hand Kody.

"I am going to be gone for some time, Kody. While I am away, I am leaving you in charge of the farm. You will receive 30 percent of all profits that are made, and I will make sure each of you here is paid in full for the time I am gone." Jaxon took out a heavy pouch full of coin. "Here is a month's wages to start off with. When I return, if I believe each of you has done their job to the fullest, I will greatly reward each of you. For today, all of you are dismissed to return home. Enjoy your day of relaxation."

Kody stepped forward. A large hooked nose jutted from his narrow face. "You can rely on us, Jaxon. There isn't a single one of us that can say you have treated us unfairly. You have my word we won't let you down."

After his workers departed, Jaxon led Trystan down to the cellar where they had gotten the ale from the previous night. Jax said he had a surprise to show him, and Trystan was more than curious to see what it could possibly be. Striding to the corner of the cellar, Jaxon pushed a stone block set into the wall. The block turned out to be a handle, and the wall swung inward, revealing a hidden room beyond. Trystan followed Jaxon into the room. In the middle of this new room, on stands, stood two full suits of shining armor only warriors in the Order of Acrium wore.

Jaxon moved to a chest set against the wall as Trystan moved forward, awestruck that his friend kept the suits after the disbandment. The breastplates, with long-sleeved mailed shirts underneath that extended to just above the knees, greaves, gauntlets, and winged helmets with visors that just covered the eyes, shone brightly as if they were brand new. Each piece of armor was crafted from an expensive metal mainly found in the Iron Realm, King Alaric's domain, and was reserved only for the Order. The metal was strong and would stop a sword thrust yet was light, allowing for flexibility of movement. On the front of every shining breastplate was the symbol of the Order, the five interlocking circles in a circular motion, symbolizing the unity of Varkuvia.

Each breastplate was designed specifically for the wearer to allow for better comfort. Trystan approached the armor on the right, tracing his fingers down the interlocking circles on the breastplate. This was the armor he had worn in the Order. Jaxon came up behind him, holding two rolled-up black cloaks in his big hands. Handing one to Trystan, he unfurled the cloak remaining in his hands. The interlocking silver circles on the cloak matched those on the breastplates.

Looking thoughtfully at the armor, Jaxon spoke to Trystan. "I hoped to give you the armor as a gift of remembered days, maybe even wear it if you wanted to. But it seems that's not going to happen now. We would attract the Brotherhood like dishonest men to a whorehouse."

Trystan stood lost in thought and then looked up into his friend's eyes. "Maybe not, Jax. It seems no matter what we do, these men will come after us. I say after we see Margaret safely to her mother's house, we don the armor once more. Let every town, village, and city we pass through know the Order of Acrium has returned. Let us bring hope back to these troubled lands. And with luck, any members of the Order that have survived the Brotherhood's attacks will flock to us. I think it's time we let this Brotherhood know we aren't scared of them and fight them head on, silver against black."

Jaxon chuckled, shaking his head. "I always knew you were a crazy bastard, Trys, but this is insane." He pointed to the armor. "To wear that armor might royally piss off the Five Kings that rule these lands who, if you haven't forgotten, signed a decree that disbanded us in the first place." He looked into Trystan's eyes, seeing the resolution there. "You're serious about this, aren't you?"

"I am."

Jaxon stood for a moment looking at his friend, rubbing his hand through his thick beard. "The gods might call me a crazy bastard for saying this, but I'm with you. If we're going to die, we might as well go out in a grand style." He held out his hand. "Brothers 'til the very end."

Trystan smiled, clasping Jaxon's outstretched hand. "Brothers 'til the very end," he agreed.

# CHAPTER FOUR

The trio set out just before midday. Jaxon drove a wagon containing his wife's belongings and the armor of Acrium. Two horses rode tethered to the back of the wagon. Once they saw Margaret safely to her mother's house, they would abandon the cumbersome wagon that would slow them down. One of the horses was intended for Jaxon to ride, the other was a packhorse, and would carry the armor and supplies for the trip. Margaret sat with her husband at the front of the wagon while Trystan rode his mare alongside the ox-drawn wagon.

The ride to Cavall was taken in relative silence, each of them with their own thoughts. Margaret feared her husband would never return but dared not voice her fears aloud. Jaxon hoped he would be given the opportunity to raise the child his wife carried. And finally, Trystan's mind was consumed with a single driving focus that would see the Brotherhood toppled. Then they could return to their lives in peace.

Thankfully, the trip was short, and after topping a rise, the town of Cavall lay sprawled out before them. The town consisted of some one hundred homes, for the most part well-constructed from stone or timber with a few showing chimneys made of red brick. It was obvious Cavall was expanding, slowly moving from a small community to a bustling town. The homes on the outskirts of town were made from freshly cut timber, and just by gazing upon them, Trystan could almost smell the newly fallen sawdust. A blacksmith's shop could be seen just at the edge of town, thick black smoke rising from its bellows, the smith hard at work. Several travelers were seen making their procession toward the center of town where an inn dominated the center of Cavall. The group set off toward the inn to purchase further supplies.

Approaching the center of town, the traffic pressed all around them as the townspeople went about their daily business. Trystan turned in his saddle. "Jax, where is Gavin staying in Cavall?" he yelled over the commotion.

"In a cabin just on the outskirts of town, bordering a forest of pine to the east," shouted Jaxon. "You can't miss it."

"If it's all the same to you, I think I will go and visit our old friend," said Trystan. He eyed the people all around him warily, feeling the suppressed tension in the air. "I cannot stand this press of people. You and Margaret purchase the supplies. I will return shortly."

Trystan angled his horse around the wagon, navigating his way through the crowded center of Cavall. After leaving the town behind him, he emerged onto an open plain that ran directly to the pine forest Jaxon described. He snapped the reins of his mount, the mare obeying instantly. Galloping across the open ground, he realized just how foolish he was. The plain looked flat, but Trystan knew it was deceptive. The seemingly flat ground was full of hidden dips, and all it would take was the horse's hoof catching on a hidden root or stepping in a rabbit hole for the animal to break its leg. He suddenly realized he didn't care. Enjoying the wind in his face, he let the horse pound across the plain.

After letting the horse run for some distance, he drew rein, slowing the gray mare. The mare slowed to a walk, its breathing ragged.

Leaning forward in his saddle, Trystan patted the horse's neck. Looking up, he spotted a wooden cabin with a sloping roof of slate, with a chimney protruding from it, just on the border of the forest he was traveling toward. Approaching the cabin, he heard the chopping of wood echoing across the silent plain. There stood Gavin, bare-chested and cutting blocks of wood with a fluidity of motion. Trystan's relief at seeing the archer alive was instant.

Hearing a horse approaching, the stocky man halted his work. Gavin had a thick dark beard with matching close-cropped hair and dark brown eyes. His swarthy features were evidence he was raised in the warmer climate of the south. The medium-sized disbanded archer of the Order had powerfully built, hairy arms, perfect for pulling a longbow effectively. Trystan rarely saw the man smile, but when he did, the merest of grins would touch his lips, a twinkle appearing in those dark eyes. That slight grin crossed his face when he saw it was Trystan riding toward his cabin.

"Do my eyes deceive me?" asked Gavin, his voice deep. "Could this be the famed hero Trystan standing before me? The man who with a single swipe of his blade defeated the savage tribesmen when they invaded the peaceful lands of the Five Kings? The one that bards sing of at inns across the world?"

Trystan dismounted smoothly, approaching the archer with a smile on his face. The two gripped hands in the warrior fashion then embraced each other as brothers would. "Ah, but it is good to see you, Gavin. I missed you, my friend."

"Let's not get maudlin now," Gavin said, throwing on a shirt of blue wool. "Step in to my humble abode. Let me get you something to drink."

Entering his friend's cabin, Trystan saw a table made of pine with four chairs surrounding it. Gavin told him to take a seat, and as he did so, he looked around Gavin's home. The archer's cabin was spartanly furnished. A few shelves were set into the wall, on which plates and silverware were set. A few dented pots and pans hung from hooks of brass on the walls. Other than the chairs surrounding the table, the only other furniture was a small worn-out armchair set before a scorched fireplace. In a side room was a narrow bed covered in furs.

Trystan couldn't help but notice that the bed was meant for one, and it seemed as though Gavin lived alone. This surprised him, for Gavin had spoken often of settling down after the disbandment. Glancing through a window at the back of the cabin, he could see a well-constructed shed where Gavin most likely hung his meat after a successful day of hunting.

Bringing two cups of watered-down wine, Gavin sat down beside his guest. Sipping on the wine, the hunter leaned back in his chair. "This is quite an unexpected surprise, Trys. What brings you to my neck of the woods?"

Trystan gripped his cup of wine two-handed, hunched over the table, his expression solemn. Gavin noticed the change in the atmosphere immediately. As a hunter, his patience was infinite, so he sat silently by while Trystan sat lost in reflection. After taking a large swig of wine, Trystan told Gavin everything that had taken place at Jaxon's farm. He told him of the assassination attempt, the assassin's words before committing suicide, and of the aid they would seek from King Markos. Finally, he told Gavin how he planned on donning the armor of Acrium once more. Through it all Gavin listened intently, his expression betraying nothing of his reaction to the news.

Taking another sip of his wine, Gavin tapped his fingers on the tabletop. His expression was set when he spoke. "Yesterday morning, two men wearing the same dark clothing you described came by my cabin. They told me they were traveling merchants and, hearing my skills as a hunter, wanted to purchase meat from me. I know the look of a warrior when I see one though, and these two looked deadly. I lied to them and told them I just had an order filled and had nothing to spare. Their manner was easy enough, but some inner itch made me feel as if they meant me harm. After they left, I went inside and strung my bow. They didn't return, but the sense of unease remained. Now I know why."

Trystan nodded. Gavin always seemed to have an unspoken sense of when danger was close. He wondered if his friend had some of the ancient Verillion blood in him or if it was just his inner warrior. "If that's the case, Gavin, you need to leave here. Eventually those men are going to make an attempt on your life. Even if you defeat them, they will simply send more. The assassin at Jaxon's farm told me as much just before he killed himself. His master, whoever he may be, believes the Order is the key to something. Join Jaxon and I. Separated, they will pick us off one by one, but together we can find out who this master is and make him pay for the warriors of the Order that lost their lives."

Gavin stood up, wine in hand. He moved to the window, which overlooked the pine forest in the back of his cabin, appearing lost in thought. Trystan turned in his seat, looking toward the stout archer.

"You know I came here to settle down and start a family." The statement was rhetorical, and Trystan didn't answer, sensing Gavin had more to say. "Within a month of returning home, I thought I had found the one. I felt it deep in my soul the first time I laid eyes on her. I never felt more certain about anything in my entire life. Sophia was her name. She had a smile unlike anything I had ever seen, and when she sang, her voice could rival the finest singers at any court. For three months, we were inseparable, and once spring came, I was going to ask for her hand in marriage. She told me she loved me, and I was the only one for her. It was the happiest I could ever remember being." He sighed. "It turned out I was more like one of fifty. Whenever I wasn't with her, she was entertaining another man. Everybody seemed to know, except for me. The day I found out, I felt as if someone had stabbed me in the heart. That same day I moved out of town and, with the money I earned from the Order, built this cabin. Not once did she come to me and apologize for what she did to me. Not once did she try and win me back. And here I have lived for over two months, only dealing with people when I need to. Cavall holds nothing for me anymore." He turned away from the window and looked directly at Trystan. "You and Jaxon are the only two who have truly been there for me when I needed you. I will travel with you, and do so gladly."

Trystan gave a nod of his head. "We will be honored to have you, Gavin. I hoped to stay ahead of the assassins tracking us, but the men who visited you yesterday will assuredly have reported my presence in town by now. The sooner we leave, the better. We will have to travel with speed to reach King Markos."

"I agree. Let me pack a few things, and we will be going."

After throwing everything he needed in a canvas sack, Gavin moved outside to where his horse was hobbled inside a small stall on the side of the cabin. Gavin saddled his mount, an old gentle brown-and-white piebald. The whole time Trystan stood outside, scanning the horizon for any signs of travelers and, more importantly, for any signs of trouble. After he strapped on everything he needed for the trip, Gavin moved back inside. Trystan followed him. Moving to a chest nestled in a corner of the cabin, Gavin withdrew a dull gray key from his pants pocket. Unlocking the chest, he hurled open the lid. Nestled perfectly inside was the armor of Acrium. A beam of sunlight from the window made the polished silver shine brightly.

Gavin gave one of his slight grins, his eyes sparkling. "We might as well match on this adventure."

Trystan smiled and then proceeded to help Gavin put the armor on the back of the piebald. "We will have to purchase you a new mount once we get back to Cavall. I don't see this piebald surviving a trip carrying your weight along with a suit of armor."

Moving back inside, Gavin quickly picked up his longbow made of yew, looped a quiver of arrows that he personally crafted over his shoulder and strapped a long hunting knife to his belt. Going back outside, both men mounted their horses. Trystan kicked his horse into a gallop and moved off toward Cavall. Gavin gave one quick glance at his home and thundered after Trystan.

Arriving back in town, they found Jaxon sitting in the back of his wagon with Margaret, the supplies already purchased. Greeting Gavin with a wide smile and a thump on his back, Jaxon introduced him to his wife. After a few pleasantries, Gavin informed the group he had to stop by the blacksmith before they left to acquire more arrows. He then requested Trystan sell his horse for him and buy another mount for him to save time. After handing Trystan more coin to purchase a better mount, Gavin moved off on foot to Cavall's blacksmith. Trystan left his mare with Jaxon and set off on the piebald to the stables.

The stable owner named Garret, a tall man with thinning hair, inspected the piebald thoroughly, nodding his approval. "Aye, I know a farmer that could use your horse to pull a plow for him. I will offer you seven silver pieces."

Trystan thought the price over. The piebald was old, and he wouldn't get a better offer. "I accept. Now I need another mount. Preferably one that is fast but with good stamina."

Garret ran a hand through his thinning hair. "I have a horse fitting that description. A nice gray-and-white stallion of some fifteen hands. Won't run in a hairy situation either if you catch my drift. Got a bit of a mean spirit in it though. Beast trampled its previous owner to death."

"Let me see the stallion, and I will make the judgment for myself.'

Garret led Trystan to the stall the stallion occupied. The stallion eyed Trystan warily as he approached him. Looking over the horse, Trystan saw scar marks around the mouth and whip marks on its flanks. *No wonder he trampled his last owner*, thought Trystan. *Treat any creature, whether they are animal or human, with such cruelty, and eventually there would be retaliation.*

He thought it over. "How much are you asking for?"

"Twenty silver. Thirteen if you include what I am paying you for the piebald."

"Eight after you take out what you owe me. With a saddle thrown in"

Garret adopted a look of outrage. "With a saddle thrown in? What does this look like to you, a charity?"

Ignoring the man's sarcasm, Trystan pressed forward. "I am offering you a fair price. Nobody wants a horse that killed its last owner. If you end up having to sell the mount for glue, you will get what? A half silver, if that. I am offering you eight. It is better than getting barely anything."

Walking away a few paces, Garret ran his hand through his hair once more. "All right, nine silver pieces. And I will throw the saddle in with it though it will be one of my choosing. That is my final offer."

"You have a deal," agreed Trystan, extending his hand.

The two shook hands, and Trystan counted out the silver pieces. "I will throw in another two silver pieces if you could saddle the horse now. I am kind of in a hurry."

"I will have my stable hand do it at once," promised Garret.

True to his word, the horse was soon saddled. The stallion stood statue still as Trystan approached, his eyes watching him the entire time. Whispering soothing words, Trystan mounted the horse and guided him back to where the rest of the group awaited him. He returned to see Gavin sitting in the back of the wagon, a fresh quiver of arrows at his side. Withdrawing an arrow from the quiver, Trystan saw the tip of it was a bodkin point, meant to pierce armor. Jaxon and Margaret sat alongside him. Gavin placed the arrow back in the quiver and stood as he approached, inspecting the horse over. He looked skeptical when he saw the horse staring him in the eye.

"I don't know about this one, Trys. He looks like a cantankerous animal. Even now, just standing here, he looks like he wants to bite my hand off."

Jaxon gave a rumbling chuckle. Standing up, he approached the stallion. "Nonsense, Gavin. It's just a horse."

Reaching out his hand, Jaxon went to pet the horse's head. Snorting, the stallion snapped at his hand, his teeth inches away from ripping Jaxon's fingers off. Snatching his hand back quickly, Jaxon took a hasty step backwards, stumbling over his own feet. The others laughed wholeheartedly as he landed in a puddle of murky water.

"Aye, that might be a foul-tempered bastard," said Jaxon, staring balefully up at the horse.

Still chuckling, Gavin turned to Trystan. "You did quite the stand-up job buying my horse, Trys. Why don't we just switch mounts, eh? That way you can worry about when that thing is going to bite your balls off, and not me."

Jaxon stood up, brushing his hands across his soaked leggings. "If that bastard does that again, I am going to sell him for glue."

The stallion gave a derisive snort and shook its head. Trystan chuckled. "I think our new friend here thinks it will be you turned into glue if you try it."

Even Jaxon chuckled at the thought of a horse turning him into glue. "Enough of this dillydallying," said the big man, wiping his hand across his wet leggings once more. "We have a mission to embark upon."

"On the ride back from my cabin, I was thinking about the route we should take to reach King Markos," Gavin said. "The fastest route would be to take the Green Ridge Road that leads straight to Karalis where King Markos resides. However, the Brotherhood will most likely be aware of this information as well and will undoubtedly have men stationed on the road ready to waylay us. I say we travel on the road for some time and then cut off it and enter the Black Forest. The forest stretches to within sight of Karalis. We will be exposed on the last stretch of the trip, but I would rather be exposed for a short period of time than waylaid on the road. If you can think of any other options, I am all ears."

Jaxon sniffed. "I have never traveled the route we are taking before. I can offer no better counsel."

"I believe a former warrior of the Order lives in a village just at the edge of the Black Forest," Trystan offered. "Fursta, I believe the village is called. We should stop there and see if he still lives. If he does, we will ask him to join us. The more men of the Order we bring to Karalis, the better to argue our case."

Gavin nodded. "Aye, I know the man you're thinking of. Kole is utterly deadly with spear and dagger. I believe he took over ownership of an inn after the disbandment. Recruiting him would greatly aid our cause."

Jaxon clapped his hands together. "Now that were all settled, let's be going, lads."

The group headed off north where Margaret's mother lived in a small village called Modina. As dusk was falling, they came upon the mother's house, a modest cottage made of stone with a thatched roof. Their reception was a warm one, and it was obvious to all that Margaret's mother greatly liked Jaxon. During the trip to Modina, Trystan discovered Margaret's father was taken by the plague that swept through the lands years ago when she was only a child. It was obvious he was a good man in the way the mother affectionately spoke of him, so Trystan made it a point to try and not bring up the subject. That evening they were cooked a fine meal and all of their cares and worries were lost for a single evening.

The following morning, Jaxon warmly embraced his wife in front of the small cottage. The group left the wagon at the cottage and transferred their supplies to the packhorse. Then each man put on their own suits of armor. Trystan readjusted the sword on his belt. The armor felt like a second set of skin, fitting perfectly to his form. Jaxon stepped up to his horse, putting his war ax in a giant sheath on the side of the mount so he could easily withdraw it in case of danger.

By donning the armor of Acrium once again, each of them looked like what they were born to be. Moments before, these men had been a gentle farmer, a wanderer, and a vigilant hunter. Now in their place stood warriors born, men trained in the art of war every single day for a decade. This is what they were destined to be, and each of them felt it. Trystan drew in a deep breath and mounted his horse while Jaxon said his final farewells to Margaret.

With one last wave to his wife, the trio galloped off toward the Green Ridge Road. The road was well constructed of paved stone and connected to every major city in Varkuvia. This made it possible for a messenger or marching army to reach its destination as quickly as possible. After all, traveling on a paved road was much faster than moving across a muddy dirt road. The builders tried to extend the road to the eastern city-states but surprisingly were attacked by tribesmen every time they attempted it, and over time, they eventually gave up. The group traveled on the road until they merged into the borders of the forbidding Black Forest. Then they cut right into the forest, making for the town of Fursta, which was only a few miles from their current location.

Gavin hung back when they left the road, covering their tracks as best he could. Tracing his horse back, he made a false trail going left into the woods for anyone who might be following them. Satisfied the trail was convincing enough, he set off after his companions, covering his own trail as he went. The false trail wouldn't cause their pursuers to give up, but it might throw them off the trio for some time, and that time might be all they needed to make it to Karalis.

After a short ride, they emerged from the wood line of the Black Forest into the town of Fursta. The town was a timber-producing community, and Trystan could see groups of workers at the edge of the forest cutting down trees to be brought back into town. One group of loggers cut down trees while another stripped the trunks of branches. Finally, the stripped tree was loaded onto wagons and hauled back to town. There was also a silver mine some miles to the south, and Trystan saw many men covered in the sweat and grime from working in a mine shaft all day, their pickaxs and tools either held in their hands or laid on the ground beside them.

The fading sunlight blazed off Trystan's armor as he cantered his stallion through town. All work seized as they rode past. Everybody recognized the symbol of the Order. Just as everyone knew the Order of Acrium had been disbanded over six months ago. Many people began muttering about what was going on, as if they needed to confirm what their disbelieving eyes were seeing. Had the Order reformed? Was a rebellion against the Five Kings stirring? By the time the group reached the inn Kole operated, a crowd had gathered.

Trystan ignored the throng of people as he dismounted. Many of the looks from the people in the crowd hinted at a dark forewarning, and Jaxon's unease grew like an itch at his backside. He went to withdraw his battle-ax from its sheath, but Trystan gripped his arm, stopping him.

"It wouldn't exactly be a good first impression if we looked as though we meant harm to these people," he cautioned. "By all means, take the ax off the horse but keep it sheathed."

Jaxon didn't look happy about it, but he listened regardless, strapping the massive ax to his back. Gavin dismounted, his manner carefree and completely oblivious to the mass of people that gathered. "I will bring our mounts to the local stable. The light is fading fast, and I say we rent a room and catch a good night's rest here. Hopefully by the morning we will have Kole accompanying us."

"Sounds good to me," said Trystan, his voice strained.

Trystan and Jaxon walked into the inn while Gavin led the horses to the local stables. The crowd seemed incredibly tense, more hostile than friendly, and it seemed all it would take was one spark for violence to ensue. Trystan couldn't understand it. Had the Order of Acrium not defended the people of Varkuvia for over three centuries? Why would they react with such hostility at seeing the symbol of the Order once again? It baffled the young man, and he suddenly found himself doubting if he was right about donning the armor once more.

Opening the door to the inn, Trystan's ears were swamped with a cacophony of noise. The inn was packed with people, and he noticed many of the patrons looked like mine workers, the dull eyes of men worked to the bone set into their soot-covered faces. All noise in the inn died at once as every eye turned on Trystan and Jaxon. The silence was deafening and lasted several heartbeats with the two just standing there. Jaxon mumbled a curse and walked to the bar where Kole was staring openly at them, an apron wrapped around his stocky frame. The tension passed and conversation picked up once again though Trystan couldn't help but notice that every eye was still upon them, and he could easily guess what everybody was talking about.

Kole was cleaning out a pewter mug with a linen cloth as they approached the bar. The man had added a little bit of weight since the disbandment, but he still looked every inch the warrior. His eyes were dark, his hair a light brown, and his square chin clean-shaven. A pale scar ran from just below his left eye down to his strong chin. His muscular arms showed quite a few scars as well. Kole was always a man to meet his opponents head-on, not giving an inch of ground. A smile was on his face as Trystan leaned on the bar, but he saw the suppressed tension on his old comrade's face.

"I'm hoping you boys wore that armor so I wouldn't have a problem recognizing you," Kole said halfheartedly.

Conversation died down once more as Gavin entered the inn. Ignoring the stares, he made his way straight over to the bar. The anger in Kole's eyes was now evident. "Look, Kole," said Trystan, trying to calm the situation. "We have to talk to you. It's important."

The innkeeper turned his angry gaze upon Trystan. "Listen, Trystan, I mean no disrespect toward you and have nothing against any of you for that matter, but if you are going to ask me to rejoin the Order, then the answer is flat out no. I see where this road is heading, and I will not be a part of any rebellion. Now, payday is tomorrow for the miners and loggers, and as you can see, it is quite busy. I wish I could offer you boys a room, but we're all booked. The best I can offer you is the loft in the barn we got just to the side of the inn. Feel free to

ask any of the serving women for food or drink. We will speak later."
The innkeeper moved off before they could say a word.

"Not much of a warm welcome, was it?" muttered Jaxon.

"Let's just order some food and wait to talk to him once it dies
down," Trystan said. "Maybe he will change his mind when he listens
to what we have to say." He moved off to a newly vacated bench table.
The trios' backs were to the wall, giving them a clear view of the rest
of the patrons in the inn. Many of the customers kept giving them
fleeting glances, their eyes filled more with resentment than curiosity.

Trystan ordered a steak topped with steamed vegetables and a nice
mug of dark ale to wash it all down. The meat was harshly seasoned
and tough to chew, but after a hard day of traveling, it tasted divine. As
he was eating, he noticed a group of men a few tables down that kept
glancing their way. A wide shouldered man with a drooping moustache
kept giving Jaxon scornful looks. As Trystan was finishing the last of
his meal, the burly man got up and started walking toward their table,
his movements arrogant. He kept glancing back at his friends, drawing
strength from their snickering smiles.

As the man approached, Trystan noted his arms were heavily muscled, and his nose appeared as though it had been broken in several
places. He had the looks of a fistfighter about him. Moving directly
to their table, he leaned forward on his hands, staring Jaxon right in
the face. Jaxon ignored the man and picked up his mug of ale, taking
a large swig. The newcomer's lips thinned in aggravation, causing his
moustache to droop even further.

"So you're warriors of the Order of Acrium, are you? Don't look
too impressive to me. I've been watching you three since you walked
in, and I bet I could take each one of you." He turned to Jaxon. "You,
big man, look fat and slow. I bet I could crush—"

Jaxon held up his hand. "Let me stop you right there. You have
had your fun and have obviously impressed your friends. Now why
don't you just go back to your table and let me and my companions
enjoy the rest of our meals. We're not here to cause any problems."

The newcomer's face flushed with anger. "Who the hell do you
think you are ordering me around?" he roared. "Now you've got your-

self a problem. Get on your feet, you bastard. We'll see just how tough you really are."

Picking up his mug of ale, Jaxon went to ignore the man when a large hand smashed the cup out of his hand, shattering it across the wooden floor. A deadly silence blanketed the inn as every patron turned in their seats to look and see what was going on. The situation was perilously close to boiling over. A gleam appeared in the man's eyes as he leaned even closer to Jaxon. When he spoke, his breath reeked of cheap ale. "Not so cocky now are you, fat man? Maybe you're too scared to fight me. I bet that's what it is. I always knew the Order was a bunch of cowardly pieces of—"

The man never saw the right cross coming that smashed his teeth to shards. Jaxon was on his feet before anyone in the inn even noticed. The man, his lips in ruins, screamed in rage and rushed at Jaxon. Ducking under a left hook, Jaxon smashed his fist into the man's midsection. Letting out a *whoosh* of air, the drunkard doubled over, right into Jaxon's rising knee. He hit the floor like a sack of potatoes. His friends stood up hurriedly, scattering chairs across the floor. Pride demanded that they avenge their friend's thrashing, and they went to bull-rush Jaxon. Gavin, still seated, took out his large hunting knife and slammed it point first into the wood table where it stood quivering. His eyes bore into the men, and one by one, they looked away shamefully.

Jaxon's eyes were angry as he scanned the stunned patrons who watched the whole scene unfold. "It is one thing to insult me, but I will never sit idly by while anyone insults any warrior of the Order. We put our own lives at stake so that all of you could sleep soundly in your beds, and this is the thanks we receive?" He pointed forcefully at the unconscious man. Then, he looked up at the man's friends who stood sheepishly by. "Take this scum out of my sight, and when he wakes up, you tell him I said personally that if I ever see him again, I will kill him where he stands."

No one stood in Jaxon's path as he thundered past the men and out of the inn. A short man with fiery red hair came forward to where Trystan and Gavin still sat, his eyes downcast. "I apologize for Toby's behavior. Sometimes the alcohol gets the best of him. It shames me that I goaded him on as well. We will be getting him out of here now if that's all right with you."

The redhead ushered the others forward, and they carried the unconscious Toby out of the inn. Gavin took one final sip of his red wine, wiped his hand across his mouth, and then counted out money for the meal. Tossing the coins on the table, he withdrew his embedded knife, sheathed it, and followed Jaxon out of the inn. Trystan was the last to get up, and as he stood, his eyes met Kole's who stood behind the bar, his powerful arms crossed, and his expression unreadable. Trystan's face hardened, and he quickly walked out of the inn, ignoring the eyes that followed his every move.

Night descended as Trystan emerged outside. He saw Jaxon and Gavin seated upon the hard ground some way to his left. Jaxon was hunched forward, wringing his hands together, and it was obvious his anger hadn't evaporated. Trystan walked over to his friend, the moon overhead making him look like an ethereal figure in his suit of armor. Standing over Jaxon, he clasped a hand to the big man's shoulder. "Come on, let's just go and get some sleep. It's fairly obvious that Kole has no desire to join us and that we're not wanted in this town. We will get a good night's sleep and leave in the morning."

Jaxon turned his still angry eyes up at Trystan. "I didn't leave my pregnant wife for this shit, Trys. Is this what it's going to be like at every town we pass through? Open hostility and scorn? We knew Kole for almost ten damn years, and you saw the look in his eyes when he saw us wearing the armor. We were nothing to him." He swore loudly. "I saved that bastard's life during the tribesmen battle, same as you both saved mine."

"Nobody said it was going to be easy, Jax," Gavin said, twirling a blade of grass in his fingers. "Not every town we come to is going to like the fact that the Order has resurfaced. This winter was a harsh one and a lot of people suffered for it. Somehow, the disbandment of the Order got blamed for it all. The common people didn't blame the Five Kings for it, but instead, put the fault on the shoulders of the actual warriors as if we had a say in the disbandment. They think we are the sole purpose the weather was bad or the reason why they had a bad harvest or their cattle came down with the lung blight." He shrugged. "People are idiots."

Jaxon brushed Trystan's hand off his shoulder and stood up. He took a deep breath and moved off to where the barn was located at the side of the inn. Trystan let his friend go, knowing he wanted to be alone. Jaxon was a good man, but sometimes anger got the best of him. In a few hours, his anger would subside, and he would completely forget the situation with the timber worker in the inn. Jaxon was incapable of holding a grudge. Offering a hand to Gavin, he helped him up.

The duo walked off to join Jaxon at the barn. Any townsperson they passed cast them a withering glance. Trystan had not imagined it like this. In his mind, he imagined that the common people of Varkuvia would rejoice at seeing the armor of Acrium once again. He thought the symbol would bring hope back into people's lives, yet within a day of wearing the armor, an entire town looked like they wanted to slit their throats while they slept. Trystan sighed and moved off to the barn. It seemed he had just learned a life lesson, yet the meaning was lost on him.

Climbing a short ladder inside the barn, he emerged onto a straw-hewn floor. Jaxon sat once more in front of an open window, set close to floor level, which overlooked the town of Fursta. He was still dressed in full armor, his double-bladed ax unsheathed and at his side. His eyes looked sorrowful, and Trystan moved off to a corner of the loft where he began unbuckling his breastplate. As he was unhooking the metal, the sound of approaching horses filled the loft of the barn.

Jaxon sauntered to his feet, looking intently out the window. "You lads might want to come and see this."

Gavin and Trystan joined him at the window, following his gaze. A large group of rough-looking men surrounded the front of Kole's inn; a dozen or so mounted. Many of them carried single-handed axes, long daggers, and Trystan spotted several swords among them. Only a few carried short-curved bows, but many amongst them carried torches. Their clothes were made of homespun green wool though Trystan only spotted a handful of armor of any kind. They weren't the Brotherhood, but they definitely weren't there for a warm meal. A group broke off, all with torches, and began setting the homes of Fursta ablaze.

Over a dozen of the men entered the crowded inn. Moments later, the sounds of shouts and screams pierced the air. Jaxon gathered his ax and went to climb down the ladder. Gavin leaned forward on the window frame, peering intently at the inn, then spun around and gripped Jax's arm tightly, stopping him midstride. Jaxon turned to protest.

Gavin cut him off, pointing toward the inn. "Wait, you lummox! Look at the front of the inn."

Following the pointing finger, Jaxon saw two of the bandits carrying a man from the inn. They forced him to his knees, and it was obvious in the moonlight that blood bathed the side of his face. The downed man turned his dark gaze toward the barn. It was Kole. A portly man dismounted from his horse and approached Kole, turning his head savagely. The fat man hissed a question into the innkeeper's face. Kole responded by spitting his interrogator full in the face. A backhand sent Kole to the ground, and the fat man wiped the spit from his face. He gestured for a broad-shouldered man with a long handled single-bladed ax to dismount.

"What do we do?" Trystan asked, still looking at the downed innkeeper. Jaxon and Gavin looked at him and then turned their attention back on Kole. The portly man was questioning Kole once more down below while the axman stood ominously by.

Emotions had vied for control as Kole watched Trystan exit his inn. More than anything, he wanted to tell his former comrades he would don the armor of Acrium once again. He wanted to tell them he would ride with them into the depths of the underworld once more. But the Order no longer had a purpose in these lands. The Five Kings, with their infinite arrogance, would never admit they were wrong in disbanding them, and any attempt to reform the Order would be seen as a slight against them. And kings did not suffer slights.

Kole was blessed upon returning home from the disbandment. The previous owner of the inn had been family friends with his recently departed father. He told Kole he would sell him the inn for a fraction of the normal cost, for he wanted to move to the city and try his luck out there. Kole had graciously accepted, and in the months that followed, the business flourished. He refurbished the rooms upstairs, the common room, and the kitchens in the back. Then he imported some of the finest wines from the vineyards of King Stefanos's realm in the South. The cost was high, but the profit well worth it.

Now, bordering on wealthy, Trystan and the others emerged into his inn. His first reaction when he saw them was to welcome them as brothers in arms. Realizing they wore the armor of Acrium made him keep his demeanor neutral. He wasn't about to risk his business and his own life for pursuits of battle and glory once again. Then, Toby had insulted Jaxon in front of everyone. Kole had been sorely tempted to pummel the obnoxious timber worker himself when he insulted the Order but instead remained silent as his former comrades stormed out of the inn.

Once things died down for the night, he would go and talk to them. He was beginning to feel bad for treating them so poorly, for they had done nothing to warrant such treatment. He would bring a nice twenty-year-old bottle of brandy he was saving for a special occasion, hoping cracking the bottle open might ease the tension between them.

For the time being, he had no choice but to stay at the inn. Underneath the floorboards of where he was standing was a chest containing the payroll for the miners and timber workers. It was a large sum, and he didn't trust anyone at the inn enough to leave that sort of money lying around. The key to the chest was on a length of twine tied around his neck and only he would have access to the chest. Tomorrow morning, an escort of troops would arrive and the payroll could be distributed to the workers, but until then, he would have to just keep a wary eye open.

A scuffle broke out at the rear of the inn. Kole's hand gripped around the iron-studded cudgel he kept under the bar. If the situation turned sour, he would have no choice but to send everyone home for the night. One fight was bad enough in his establishment, and he would not allow another to occur. Just as he was about to move from behind the bar to keep the situation from escalating, the front door to the inn was thrown open. Kole's head whipped around as a group of men entered. They had weapons on their person, and they were drawn.

The door had struck a thin timber worker, spilling his ale all over his shirt. He whirled around, angrily protesting. His protests were short lived when a hatchet buried itself into his forehead. Everybody in the inn stood stunned as the timber worker's dead body slumped to the floor. Then the spell broke, and everyone began screaming, cowering in fear. The armed men advanced into the inn, striking out at anyone in their path. Blood began to flow onto the floor from the dead and wounded. Kole drew a curved dagger from a hidden sheath in his boot and leapt over the bar. The man wielding the hatchet moved to meet him, pushing scared customers out of the way, his bloody weapon aiming for the innkeeper's head. Kole's powerful hand gripped the man's wrist, twisting it savagely. Screaming in pain, the man dropped the hatchet as Kole's dagger rammed into his throat.

Scooping up the hatchet, he reversed his dagger and stood in a warrior's crouch as the other bandits advanced warily. Nobody moved and the situation became increasingly tense. *When left with little choice, sometimes the best strategy is to attack*, thought Kole. Screaming a battle cry, he charged into them. The bandits stood transfixed as he tore into them. Three of them fell to the frenzied attack before any were able to respond. Kole, the hatchet lost in an opponent's chest, was slashing left and right with his dagger furiously. He sliced the cheek of an opponent open, spraying blood everywhere, before a sword hilt crashed into his temple, knocking him to the ground. He tried to rise, knife in hand, but fists rained down upon him, ending his defiance.

He lost consciousness. When he regained his senses, he was being dragged outside. Another group of bandits was standing stationary outside the front of the inn, five of them mounted. Kole could see clusters of fire spreading through the town behind them. He tried to get his feet underneath him, but a kick from one of the men holding him sent him to his knees. His knee landed heavily on a rock, and he winced as fresh pain shot up his leg. His head was throbbing abominably where the sword hilt had struck him, and he could feel blood flowing freely down the side of his face.

Casting a glance toward the barn where Trystan and the others were staying for the night, he hoped against hope that the warriors had the common sense to stay hidden. There was no way the three of them could defeat the amount of men set against him, no matter how skilled they were. His head was savagely turned back around by a meaty hand. He found himself staring into the beady eyes of a heavyset man with blotchy skin.

"I need you to pay close attention, innkeeper," the fat man hissed, spraying spittle across Kole's face. "We know the payroll money for the workers is here. Now tell us where it is, and we won't hurt anyone else. We will let you live and leave this town."

Kole looked closely at the man. It was a talent he had to know when someone was lying. And he was being lied to right now. He made as though he was about to speak, and the portly leader leaned forward intently. Kole spit right in his face. A look of outrage caused the man's many chins to tremble. He backhanded Kole to the ground. Stars were spinning in front of his eyes when he saw a broad-shouldered man dismounting from his horse, a long-handled ax cradled in his hands.

The men who originally dragged Kole outside pulled him to his knees once more. The axman stood by as the overweight man looked down upon Kole. "I will only ask one more time. Where is the money?"

"Go to hell," Kole responded defiantly.

The leader gestured to the axman, and he moved to stand before Kole, towering over him. Kole's vision was swimming in and out, but even still, he looked up to see the ax blade being raised above the man's bald head. The fires from the town had spread, and the screams of the innocent mixed with Kole's fear. He was about to die. Kole met his executioner's eyes, determined he would meet his end with courage. A look of shock crossed the executioner's face, his ax dropping from his hands. His hand went to his forehead where the shaft of an arrow had emerged. His fingers brushed the wood of the shaft and then he fell backward without a sound. Everyone stood mesmerized, their eyes locked on the dead executioner.

A war cry broke the silence as Jaxon charged from the darkness, Trystan right on his heels. The flames from the burning houses played off their silver armor, giving them the appearance of demons summoned from the pit. A mounted bandit reacted first, charging his horse right at Jaxon. Raising his arms, Jaxon began yelling at the top of his lungs, waving his hands back and forth. The horse, startled by the noise, reared, dumping its rider to the ground. Before the man could raise his weapon, Jaxon's ax cleaved through his neck, half severing it.

One of the archers notched an arrow, aiming it right at Jaxon's chest. An arrow flew from the darkness, lodging into the archer's temple. Gavin emerged from the shadows, another arrow being drawn to his cheek. Releasing the arrow, it took an outlaw in the chest as he was dismounting his horse. A bandit rushed Gavin with his ax raised. Drawing another arrow, he sidestepped a downward cut and stabbed the axman in the eye, withdrawing the arrow smoothly. As the body fell to the ground, he drew the arrow and released it in one fluid motion. This one took a bandit in the throat as he was lunging toward Trystan's exposed back.

Trystan blocked a lunge, opening his opponent's throat with a riposte. The man fell to his knees, choking on his own blood. Trystan didn't even see him fall as he turned around to face a fresh foe. A tall bandit rushed at him with his shield raised high. Trystan gripped his shining sword of green and gold with two hands and brought it down with all of his force, splitting the shield cleanly, the force of the blow carrying on to slice open the shield bearer's face. Hearing the sounds of battle, bandits rushed from all over the burning town, screaming their hatred as they charged the warriors of the Order. A sudden calm descended on Trystan, and he felt himself becoming strangely detached from his body. Instead of panicking at this new sensation, he embraced the moment and charged into the bandits.

Four men rushed at him. The first swung his ax blade in a high arc, but to Trystan, the man appeared to be moving in slow motion. With contemptuous ease, he blocked the swing, cutting the haft of the ax cleanly in half and in the same motion slashed his sword across the man's chest. Two others rushed him, and as they raised their weapons, Trystan gave two quick slashing cuts left and right, killing them where they stood. The last ran at Trystan, the torch in his hand lancing toward his face. Trystan swayed back, his sword moving of its own accord to cut the bandit's hand from his body. His screams were short-lived as Trystan's blade plunged through his open mouth. He was moving to meet new foes before the body even hit the ground. His movements were blinding quick and in his wake lay a pile of corpses.

The horses, terrified by the sounds of battle and the smell of smoke in their nostrils, began moving around skittishly. Their riders were having a hard time controlling them, and many bolted off toward the woods in panic, impeding the bandits running toward the ensuing battle from all over the town. The portly leader, Jarvis, cast a nervous look around. No soldiers were supposed to be in this area until tomorrow, yet these three warriors alone were cutting through his men like a scythe through wheat. Jarvis had never seen anyone like the silver swordsman possess such skill in his entire life. His eyes couldn't even follow the speed of his movements. Anyone that went against him died instantly. The swordsman had to be a demon, for no human being could possibly move that fast.

Just as Jarvis was on the border of sheer panic, the rest of the bandits in the inn, hearing the sounds of battle, rushed outside. The combined weight of his forces pushed the warriors back. Jarvis relaxed, his heavy jowls sagging in relief. Many of his men were down, but the silver warriors were now being surrounded. Weight of numbers would win the day. Just as he was preparing himself to join his men, a cold voice cut through his thoughts of victory.

"Here's your money for you, you bastard."

Jarvis spun around just in time to see the heavy head of an ax blade swinging toward his face. Kole wrenched the long-handled ax from Jarvis's face. Stepping over the body, he charged into the bandits that were moving in to surround the warriors of the Order. The confiscated ax took a bandit in the back, smashing his spine to shards. His screams were cut off as Kole pried the ax loose. Raising the ax, he was just in time to deflect a slashing sword. Releasing the haft, he thundered an uppercut into the man's chin, lifting him off his feet. Another bandit ran at him, his opponent's ax moving in a murderous arc. Kole sidestepped, bringing his own two-handed ax down, severing the man's leg. The man fell to the ground, screaming in anguish, blood pumping from the ruined leg. Kole stomped on his downed foe's skull with his steel-toed boot, extinguishing his life. During a brief respite, Kole gazed around, gauging the battle. More than half of the bandits were down; but Trystan, Jaxon, and Gavin were fighting in a tight-knit circle, completely surrounded. Several dents covered the armor of their upper bodies. Gavin, his longbow discarded, was desperately fending off an attacker with his long hunting knife. If one of them fell, then the bandits would completely overwhelm the others. Then the battle would be over in mere heartbeats. Kole himself was exhausted, the wound at his temple making him feel nauseous. He took a deep breath, steadied himself, and prepared to go to his comrades' aid once more. Men rushed past him, armed with daggers and other weapons from the fallen bandits. Kole could not believe his eyes. It was the loggers and miners who had been cowering at the inn.

With all of their attention focused on the silver warriors, the workers tore into the remnants of the bandits. Sensing the tide of the battle was turning against them, the bandits began running for their lives. The few who remained threw down their weapons, begging for mercy. There was none to be had, and they were swiftly cut down. Little more than a handful of bandits raced off toward the forbidding Black Forest. Many of the townspeople, realizing the action was over, rushed off to battle the flames that were spreading throughout the town. A small crowd gathered around the silver warriors, their armor dented and bathed in blood. Jaxon, whose helmet had been knocked off during the battle, was supporting Gavin, who was limping heavily. Trystan sheathed his sword on the second attempt, his chest heaving.

Kole pushed his way through the gathered crowd and went to Trystan's side. Despite the pain from his injuries, he forced a smile. "You crazy bastards. What were you thinking rushing that many armed opponents?" He thumped Trystan on the shoulder.

Trystan smiled wanly. His knees suddenly buckled, and he sat down heavily upon the ground, a look of bewilderment on his face. The townspeople immediately rushed forward, helping him to his feet. More went to help Gavin and took the weight off Jaxon. One of them was Toby, the man Jaxon had fought earlier.

"Someone go and see if they can find Gerry, the town healer," yelled Kole. "These men need tending to." Even as he spoke, Kole staggered and several men went to his side, helping him inside the inn. The town healer arrived within minutes and rushed to Kole's side to treat him. The innkeeper waved him off. "See to the Order of Acrium first."

Gerry, a short balding man, gave a wary glance at the other wounded men and then moved to Jaxon. The big man was holding his right side, and Gerry asked him to raise his arm. Jaxon winced as he did so. "We need to get this armor off him. I fear he might have broken a rib."

Trystan sat back in the chair he occupied, utterly exhausted. His armor saved his life numerous times during the battle, and only a few minor cuts and bruises covered his upper body. The blood flow had already cleansed these wounds and were starting to heal, but a gash on his right forearm was bleeding profusely. Cursing, he asked a young man standing idly beside him if he knew how to stitch a wound. His face turned ghostly pale, and he moved off to find someone who could better assist Trystan. An elderly woman returned carrying needle and thread and began stitching the wound.

Gritting his teeth against the pain, Trystan leaned back, observing the faces in the crowded inn. Gone were the hostile stares and contempt these people had shown them hours before. Many of them looked truly concerned as the warriors wounds were being tended to. Trystan wondered why everybody wasn't helping to extinguish the flames and asked the old woman.

"Many of those here don't live in town," she informed him, still stitching the wound at his arm. "They are only here to get paid."

Jaxon, his armor and shirt removed, was once again lifting his arm, noticeably wincing against the pain. The healer probed the ugly bruise that spread across Jaxon's side. "You got quite lucky, young man," Gerry told Jaxon. "Nothing is broken, but I would recommend taking it easy for the next few days. Don't do anything that will overly exert yourself. I will give you some minor opiates to help relieve the pain."

Muttering his thanks, Jaxon drew his shirt back on once more. Other than his bruised side, the only other injury he withstood was to the bridge of his nose where blood seeped down his lips and into his thick beard. Gerry cleansed his nose and then moved to Gavin's side. The archer's right ankle was sprained and a deep gash on his shoulder was revealed after he removed his armor along with several ugly bruises.

The doctor wrapped his ankle, stitched the wound, and then made his way over to Trystan. He told him to remove his armor. After Trystan did so, he inspected his body, and after making sure he had no other wounds, finally tended to Kole.

Reflecting back on the battle, Trystan contemplated the feeling that came over him. It was almost as if someone else was controlling his body, yet he was fully aware of every move he made. His opponent's attack against him seemed choreographed, and he responded to them before they ever had the chance to. Three times, it felt as though he had eyes in the back of his head and blocked thrusts behind him that would've killed him. Almost as soon as the battle was over, the feeling passed and exhaustion weighed Trystan down. It felt as though he expended a week's worth of energy in that brief span. Never before had he experienced such a feeling, and he wished Master Layne was there to discuss it with him.

Even still, they had been lucky. There was no way any of them should be alive. He knew the bandits didn't exactly possess the greatest of skill; for the most part, they were cowardly men who would rather steal from others than work an honest day for their food. Trystan knew the feeling that came over him contributed greatly to their survival. Without even thinking, he saved both Jaxon and Gavin from thrusts that would have killed them. During the heat of battle, Trystan hadn't even considered the faces of the bandits. Looking back now, he saw the fear in all of their eyes. They were terrified. Not just terrified, but terrified of him specifically. Trystan shivered. *What happened to me?* he wondered.

The flames from the houses burned brightly through the inn windows, and Trystan gazed through the glass, watching the townspeople desperately trying to save their homes. Leaning his head against the wall behind him, Trystan closed his eyes. If it hadn't been for Jaxon, Gavin, and himself, the whole town would have been slaughtered. The thought comforted him, and he was asleep within minutes.

When he awoke, dawn was tinting the sky outside. Moving his head, he groaned. Sleeping with his head at such an angle all night had caused his neck to cramp badly. Running his hand over his neck, he probed the muscles, easing the pain. Sitting up, a blanket fell from his lap, and he realized someone had covered him during the night. Again, he groaned. His entire body was aching and sore.

Gazing around the inn, he was shocked to see it was overly crowded with people. Men, women, and children covered the floors. Some were asleep, but most still lie awake. Many of their faces and clothes were covered in ash and soot, and Trystan realized these must be the families who lost their homes to the flames the previous night. Tear streaks were evident on the people's faces that were awake. Who could blame them? They had just lost everything in one terrible night.

Standing up, Trystan was relieved to see his armor stacked neatly next to where he was sleeping. Not only was nothing stolen, but someone had taken the time to cleanse it of blood for him. His relief lasted mere moments when he looked up through the inn window once again. Dark smoke still rose from the smoldering ruins that were families' homes. Looking down, he saw a little girl, no more than seven, curled up next to where he was sleeping, a straw doll clutched in her tiny hands. Her parents were nowhere to be seen, and Trystan was saddened by the thought that they most likely were killed during the raid. The bandits were beaten back but at a terrible cost. Taking the blanket that covered him throughout the night, he placed it on the girl's sleeping frame. Winding his way through the mass of people strewn across the floor, he made his way to the entrance. Emerging outside, he took in the full scale of last night's raid.

Some thirty homes were in ruins along with a mill at the edge of town. The houses made of timber stood no chance against the flames that consumed them. An easterly breeze the previous night had fanned the flames further, rapidly spreading them to the other buildings. Bodies scattered the ground, and Trystan was horrified to see not just men and women among them but children as well. *These bandits were monsters,* he thought, disgusted. Men were carrying the bodies of their loved ones to the edge of town, laying them gently in a row. The dead bandits were piled into one mass heap to be burned. He saw Kole some way to the right, leaning heavily on a crutch. He was organizing a group of people trying to save a house that still smoldered. This home at least, looked like it had been saved, only the outside of the house showing signs of the inferno from the previous night.

Trystan waved as he approached the innkeeper. Kole was covered from head to toe in soot; and it was obvious, despite his injuries, he was in town helping with the fire. His eyes were set as Trystan gripped his hand.

"What manner of man would do this, Trys? I can understand wanting to steal the money. But this was just wanton slaughter." He pointed to a woman and small child embraced in death some way down the road. "That was Jocelyn and her six-year-old daughter, Kelly. I never met a nicer woman or a sweeter child. Both were so full of life, and in one horrifying night, their lives were snuffed out. How can such a terrible fate happen to such as these? It just isn't fair."

"Life in general is rarely fair." Trystan's voice was solemn. "Unfortunately, men like those that attacked this town are much more common in today's world than kind-hearted souls like Jocelyn and Kelly. The best you can do is keep their memories alive, that way they will never truly die. Cherish every breath you take, Kole, because you never know when it will be your last."

Kole nodded and looked intently into Trystan's face. "You have changed since the Order was disbanded. I can't put a finger on what it is exactly, but you have." He ran a hand through his light hair, causing ash clung to his scalp to rise up in a shower. "Or maybe it's me that has changed. Everyone here spurned you three when you first rode into town, thinking you were bringing nothing but trouble. Yet you put your own lives at stake to save this town, and the lives of people none of you even knew. No one here will forget that, Trys."

Trystan shrugged. "They will or they won't. It is immaterial." He gripped Kole's shoulder. "I really do need to talk to you about something, Kole, and it's important."

The innkeeper listened as Trystan once again retold the assassination attempts against the Order of Acrium. At the end, he looked away and then cursed loudly. "Do you remember a member of the Order named Ralph?"

Trystan smiled with remembrance. Ralph had been declared the unofficial jester of the Order, for he was always at the center of a prank or joke. Such was his nature, that all forgave him when they were a victim of one of his many pranks. The man was incapable of maturity, yet it was no surprise he made the Order. Ralph was utterly deadly with sword, lance, and bow. Everything was a jest until action was at hand. Then he stowed the jokes away until it was over.

"Who could forget a man like Ralph?"

"Around a month ago, I wrote to him, requesting he take a trip to my inn and catch up on old times. I received a letter back from his sister conveying that Ralph had been killed in a freak accident. Apparently, he fell from a balcony one night after consuming too much alcohol. I grieved for him, but looking back now, none of it adds up. Ralph was always afraid of heights, even just mounting his horse terrified him, and I never saw him consume alcohol. Even if he was drunk, what would he be doing out on a balcony?"

Trystan knew the answer and so did Kole now. "He was a victim of the Brotherhood, Kole. I don't know how many of us remain, but someone is going to great lengths to see our lives extinguished. I will rest for one more day, but after that I ride to Karalis and King Markos."

The innkeeper sighed. "It seems either way I lose. If I stay here, this Brotherhood will come for me, and next time I won't have you on hand to save me. But if I go with you, then King Markos will most likely execute us on the spot. Neither are appealing options. Please take no offense to this, Trys, but let me be alone for a bit. I need to think about my future, which is looking shorter by the second."

Grasping Kole on the shoulder once more, Trystan moved off to find Jaxon and Gavin. He found them in the loft of the barn where the flames had not touched. The remainder of the day was spent there with someone bringing them a small meal consisting of hard bread, sharp cheese, and watered-down wine. Gavin was still moving around with a limp, and Jaxon's side was still badly bruised. However, both agreed they had to leave in the morning; they would just have to deal with the discomfort for the time being. Trystan's forearm was also itching, which even though it was a sign his wound was healing, was still aggravating. He was always a fast healer, even when younger, and he knew within a day the stitches could come out.

He was getting increasingly irritated as he settled down to sleep that night. Kole still hadn't visited. He could have at least given them the courtesy of letting them know they wouldn't be traveling together. Instead, Kole chose to ignore the men who had not only saved his life the night before, but the remainder of the town as well. Trystan went to sleep in a foul mood that night. When he awoke, the feeling had not passed. Instead, he packed up his belongings alongside Jaxon and Gavin, and they mounted their horses to leave town.

Just as they were about to make off for the Black Forest, the plodding of horses came from around the stables. The three men turned in their saddles to see Kole, fully dressed in the armor of Acrium. With him were several men that Trystan had seen battling the fires in town. Kole drew rein, directly in front of Trystan.

"My apologies for being late, my boys," said the stocky innkeeper. "I was talking long into the night with the town councilmen who survived the raid. As you can see, they have decided to come along with us. I think we will be better received with a delegation of men preaching about your heroism."

Trystan's eyes raked the councilmen. Each looked like good, strong men. "I was never one for lying, so I will certainly not start now. Not only do we not know the kind of reception we will receive in Karalis, but also, there are men pursuing us. Their goal is to kill anyone who was a warrior of the Order. I don't doubt for a second they will worry themselves about killing anyone who accompanies us. I truly appreciate all of you for coming forth, but I will not think less of any who wish to change their mind and go back home."

The councilmen shifted nervously in their saddles, glancing at one another. Finally, an elderly man with a hooked nose spoke up for the group. "If you don't mind me saying, we are all agreed you did right by us. We are simple folk, but we are not stupid. This whole town would have been wiped out were it not for you boys. I myself have a wife, four children, and two grandchildren to be grateful for, and a debt must be repaid. We will travel with you to Karalis, and hopefully, the king will listen to what we have to say. Afterwards, we will return to Fursta to rebuild. We aren't going with you to start a war."

Trystan nodded. "Trust me, we are not traveling to a fortress city like Karalis to begin a war. That is the last thing on our minds, right now. I am grateful to all of you for accompanying us."

Jaxon cleared his throat. "As moving as all of these speeches are, we are killing daylight. Let's go and talk to a king."

And with that, the warriors and townspeople skirted the road and merged into the Black Forest. Minutes after they left, a pigeon flew from the edge of town, a message strapped to its leg. The bird flew off to the east, wings flapping furiously. No one had bothered to mention, but today was the first day of spring.

# CHAPTER FIVE

The first few weeks of spring were turning out to be a nightmare for King Markos. Reports flooded in daily that worried the benevolent monarch down to his soul. The first week of spring saw messengers arriving with news that King Ragnar, the brutal leader of the Argarians of the Storm Islands, was massing his entire fleet at his capital of Taranis. This alone was not overly concerning, for the longboats were still beached at the Storm Islands and not yet prowling the Okhelm Sea. The Argarians did not have the manpower to contend with the might of the Five Kings, or so King Markos thought.

The second week of spring saw his hopes dashed. King Ragnar launched the might of his fleet from Taranis. Over two hundred long-boats carrying ten thousand battle-hardened Argarians landed on the shores of King Eryk's domain just as the last of the winter snows were melting away. King Markos was alarmed by the numbers. This was not just a raid but an invasion force. If the Argarian king was able to gain a foothold on Varkuvian soil, then he would be able to ship in more supplies along with more men. The Argarians were vicious fighters, and the Five Kings would be hard-pressed to drive them from their realms.

King Eryk's fighting force relied mainly on the deadliness of their longbow men. At the beginning of his reign, he signed a doctrine, which decreed every man between the ages of sixteen to sixty was to practice daily in the use of the longbow. A longbow, unlike a crossbow, required exceptional skill to use and, in the hands of someone who knew what they were doing, could truly be deadly. At first, King Eryk was mocked for the decree, for the bow was considered a coward's weapon, meant for peasants. When his archers decimated the last raiding force by themselves, the mockery ceased.

The longbow was effective over great distances, but once the battle was joined, the archers in their light-studded armor would be slaughtered. King Eryk's archers would cause untold devastation to the invaders as they raced toward his forces, but he was not known for his infantry. His army would be swept aside by the ferocity of the Argarians. Messages requesting aid arrived daily. Markos knew the same messages were being sent to the other kings as well. Markos and his lifelong friend King Stefanos shared lands that bordered King Eryk's, and they would be expected to respond first.

Stefanos's fighting force was renowned for its cavalry, and he already sent word ahead to Markos relaying that his forces were mobilizing and would be on the march within a week's time. Markos's standing army numbered seven thousand infantry, a thousand cavalry, and five hundred archers. The rest of his force consisted of conscripted militia who gathered only once a month for training. He immediately dispatched five thousand infantry to King Eryk's aid. The situation seemed contained until the third week of spring arrived. It had been on King Markos's forty-third name day that fresh events had unfolded.

A bloody messenger ran headlong into the great hall of Karalis's keep as the king was overlooking a map of the Argarian positions with his senior advisors beside him. He stumbled before Markos, offered a quick bow, and handed him a scroll of parchment. Markos unfurled the parchment as the messenger stood anxiously by. The king read the message twice, crumpled the paper, and then picked up a cup full of wine before spiking it into the nearest wall. The tribesmen of the Northern Woods were engulfing the Stone Realm. Already several towns had been ransacked, and the two forts at the borders of his realm were completely overrun. Now they would have an all but clear path straight through to Karalis. The only good news was the Haraliam Wall, which stretched from the Bale Mountains to the Okhelm Sea in the passageway to the north still held. If this wall were to fall, then he would be finished. The reports came pouring in by the hour after the first messenger arrived, describing the atrocities that were being inflicted upon his countryside. The Stone Realm was being bathed in blood.

He refused to believe the number of tribesmen reported to be in his lands. Even the commoners knew the tribes of the Northern Woods were constantly at war with one another, and they were never considered a full threat as long as they remained divided. Now Markos was hearing of a cold, calculated chieftain named Timon who was uniting the tribes and had close to thirty thousand bloodthirsty savages under his command, ready to willingly die for him. And more were arriving each day. Timon's tribe, the Khali, was imposing their name upon all tribes that joined their cause. Never before had a name of unity been given to the tribes, each instead acting independently, and it seemed they were close to becoming a nation united.

The Stone Realm was in danger of being conquered within a week of the first message. He immediately sent a message to General Hugo, the commander of the army he sent to reinforce King Eryk. In the message, he made it clear that three thousand of his men break off at once. Two thousand were ordered back to Karalis for defense of the city, and the other thousand were sent to the Haraliam Wall to hold off until reinforcements could be gathered. Despite the troubles in his own realm, he couldn't pull the entire army from helping King Eryk. If the Wood Realm was conquered by the Argarians, then Markos would truly be doomed, dealing with enemies on two fronts.

He then sent message to Stefanos, telling him to defeat the Argarians before dealing with the tribesmen. Then the combined forces of Varkuvia could push the tribesmen from his realm. He also sent word to King Lucan and King Alaric, seeking aid. King Alaric promised two thousand heavy infantry to his cause. Alaric was never known as a military tactician, but the finest armor was forged in his realm, and his armies were the best equipped in Varkuvia. King Lucan flat out ignored the conflict that was sweeping through the Five Realms. Markos was furious, for Lucan alone could tip the balance of the war with the amount of men he could bring into the field.

The stresses of the dual invasions were beginning to take their toll on Markos. His sleep at night was tormented, and he barely ate. His eyes were hollow rimmed and sunken. The stress became almost overwhelming when he sent out his cavalry under his general, Corbin, to harass the enemy. The Memure River cut in between the mountain ranges that led to Karalis before flowing South to the Gulf of Ramal. There was only one stone bridge that crossed the river, and with his lands under attack, it was now a strategic location. If the tribesmen were to take control of the bridge and dig in defensively, then the cost of retaking the bridge would be appalling.

He was explicit when he told General Corbin not to engage in any pitched battles. The cavalry was intended for hit-and-run encounters only and to let the tribesmen know they couldn't invade the Stone Realm without a fight but more importantly to prevent them from taking the Memure Bridge. Corbin had been a fool, holding the tribesmen in contempt, and was lured into a trap. Most of his force was slaughtered in the process, along with the general himself. Timon had the heads of the cavalrymen set on pikes on the roads leading to Karalis. Then the grand chieftain advanced further, capturing the Memure Bridge. Now the tribesmen were within a three-day march of the city. Without his full force gathered, Markos would be hard pressed to hold the city. The two hundred or so cavalrymen who returned to Karalis had the look of fear and desperation in their eyes. After that incident, many of the citizens who inhabited Karalis fled to the west in terror.

To add to the growing pit in his stomach, Markos had a personal problem of his own. Prince Leon, his eldest son and next in line to the throne, went out hunting with a group of nobles when the Khali invaded. He hadn't received any word on his son's whereabouts since the invasion, and he feared the worst. Being a family man, he wanted nothing more than to cut a bloody path through the tribesmen and find out where his son was, but common sense held him back. A majority of his forces were made up of conscripted militiamen who were mainly farmers. If he didn't wait until the combined forces of his armies were gathered, he would risk not just his son's life, but the lives of his subjects as well.

The reports weren't focused solely around the dual invasions. A letter from Lord Rickart, a cold man who Markos barely spoke to, wrote to him detailing the events that took place in his own lands. The king had been distraught and shocked when he read about the assassination of Prince Kastor. He liked the young prince and believed he would make a good ruler one day. He knew King Stefanos would be hit hard by the loss, for he constantly doted on the young man. When he read of Kaleb making the trip to Karalis to keep him protected, Markos wanted to laugh aloud. Rickart had sent his only son into a land under a full-scale invasion. Anywhere was safer than here. Then, when he read about the assassin's final words, he was troubled. That evening his food and drink had been tasted for poison, and he had the guard doubled on his door while he slept. His people needed him now more than ever. He would have to be cautious until he could get things under control.

Perhaps the most shocking of reports, almost as shocking as the dual invasions, was the letter he received from Fursta. The raid on the town by bandits wasn't anything overly concerning, especially since it was repelled with the bandits all but wiped out in the process. What was troubling was the townspeople praising a group of warriors they claimed wore the armor of Acrium. Markos didn't know how to respond to the news. When the Order had been disbanded, he wanted to lash out at the other kings for their utter stupidity. His arguments went long into the night, but it was Stefanos who finally convinced him to sign the decree. Even still, he refused to have his banner present when the Order was dispersed. It still sat like acid upon his soul that he signed the doctrine along with the other rulers. Now it seemed the Order had reemerged. More than this, they saved a town under his protection from certain destruction. What did this mean? Were they attempting to rally his own people against him?

Then he read that the warriors were traveling to Karalis, along with a delegation of councilmen from Fursta. Had this happened a month ago, he would have no choice but to imprison these warriors and execute them for disobeying a direct order from the combined decision of the Five Kings. As events stood, if he arrested them, he might have an open rebellion on his hands. With the invasion of his realm, along with King Eryk's, he could not expend more men to deal with further arising problems. He was having a hard enough time coping with everything as it was.

The warriors arrived the previous day, and the city was abuzz that the Order of Acrium came to deliver them from the evil that beset their lands. The following morning, Markos was sitting upon his throne in the great hall when the messenger arrived, his face flushed with excitement. The councilmen from Fursta and the Order respectfully requested an audience with him. Markos dismissed the messenger and turned in his throne to face his son, Prince Vasilis, who was also a warrior of the Order.

"How do you think we should proceed?" asked Markos.

Vasilis thought well before he answered his father. Markos studied his son while he contemplated his answer. He had his mother's cornflower-blue eyes and golden-blond hair, but his father's strong chin and powerful figure. Even though he was in his early twenties, he still could not manage to grow a full beard and opted to keep his face clean-shaven instead. Despite the lack of facial hair, his aquiline features made him strikingly handsome, and many a woman turned her head as he passed. He was promised to Princess Isabelle, the daughter of King Stefanos. The wedding was to have taken place in the summer of this year when Isabelle was considered a woman at sixteen. Markos hoped they were all still alive come summer.

"Well, Father, it is rumored that the swordsman, Trystan, leads the group that seeks an audience with you. I was not personally close with him, but I still have respect for him. In all our years together in the Order, I never heard an ill word spoken about him. He might be slightly solitary, but I don't see a man like Trystan making a trip to Karalis for no reason. To be honest, I don't think he has it in him to spark a rebellion. Trystan has always lacked a certain charisma that is common in most men of power. Regardless of his character he, and those who follow him, did save Fursta. I say you at least hear what he has to say, but greet him coolly. After all, you were a part of the disbandment, and you have to let them see you are not overly pleased with seeing the armor of Acrium once more."

Markos nodded. "Your council is wise, my son. I think your mother and I did a fine job with raising you. What of you and Kaleb? Will you rejoin the Order of Acrium if it is to reform?"

"My loyalty is to you, Father, and to you alone. I would never betray you. If it is your wish that I join them once again, then that is what I will do. Yet if you order me to kill them, then I will do so without hesitation though I will do it with a heavy heart."

"Let us see how events play themselves out first. We aren't exactly in a position to make any rash decisions."

"Shall I have them summoned to the great hall Father?"

"No, I will go and speak to them myself. These men might be considered traitors of the realm for the time being, but they did save Fursta. It is because of them my people still live, and my taxes can still be collected. Have them brought to my personal study. Remain courteous, but make it clear they are not to wear their armor. After you greet them, make sure the guards search them thoroughly for weapons. These are hard times, Vasilis. We must remain vigilant."

Pride flashed in Vasilis's eyes at his father's decision. Almost immediately, it was replaced by a forlorn look. "I wish Leon was here. He always remains calm in situations such as this. Has there been any word of him since the invasion?"

The king sighed. "I am afraid not. There is not a moment that passes throughout the day that I do not think of him. I would endure the horrors of the underworld to save any of my family members even at the cost of my own life. If it was my choice, I would gather the forces we gathered here and sally forth to smite the enemy tooth and nail." Markos's gray eyes looked downcast. "But I have a kingdom to think of. Thousands upon thousands of lives are under my protection. If I make such a rash decision, then my people could be slaughtered, and my lands conquered. I have no choice but to wait and hope that my son still lives. It is not something that sits well with me." He drew in a deep breath. "Let us not speak anymore of this matter. Go and summon your former comrades. I am interested to see what they have to say for themselves."

Trystan found his thoughts troubling as he sat in King Markos's personal study. They finally reached their destination, but now any number of things could go wrong. King Markos could simply order them to be arrested, and then this trip would have all been for nothing. *That is highly unlikely,* he told himself. If that was the king's desire, then he would have done so as soon as they were within sight of Karalis. It didn't seem likely that Markos would summon them to his own study just to have them arrested. Even still, it was a thought he could not push from his mind, and Trystan felt more than vulnerable without his armor or weapons.

Glancing to his left, he saw Kaleb and Prince Vasilis talking in low tones in the corner, while Kole, Gavin, and Jaxon gathered around the king's dark oak desk, chatting amongst themselves. There might have been no distinction of birth in making the Order, but after a member was inducted into the Order of Acrium, it was no wonder the nobles would quickly form their own circles, looking down upon the peasants as if they were nothing. It was a great concept for the peasants to be seen as equals with the nobles but impractical to enforce. Trystan didn't hate them for it though he knew many amongst the Order that did. It wasn't the nobles' fault, for it was how they were raised. Even the esteemed Order of Acrium couldn't get rid of generations of breeding, which enforced the idea they were superior to those who tilled their lands and made their estates wealthier. Trystan had even noticed it with Prince Vasilis. Of course, the young prince greeted them pleasantly enough, but he noticed an underlying superiority Trystan doubted he was even conscious of.

Glancing once more toward Kaleb, he was still surprised he was even here. He and Kaleb were two of the most noted swordsmen in the Order, and Trystan knew the noble's loathing of him went far deeper than their upbringing. Kaleb saw him as a threat and couldn't possibly fathom the notion that a lowborn orphan could be considered his equal, if not in standing, at least with a blade. He also knew the fact Master Layne had taken quite a liking to the young thief Trystan once was didn't help the situation. Several times while they were living together at the Fortress of the Van, Trystan tried to breach the unspoken gap between them. They should be brothers-in-arms not barely concealed rivals. Yet Kaleb would never see it that way. To him, Trystan would always be his competition, and nothing he could say or do would change his mind. It bothered Trystan, for even though Kaleb was slightly narcissistic, he kept the darker side of his soul chained in bonds stronger than steel. Trystan saw the makings of a great man in him if only Kaleb would see beyond his own desires.

Pushing thoughts of his rival amongst the Order from his mind, Trystan focused on the trip to Karalis, which had taken some weeks. If they'd stuck to the Green Ridge Road, they would have arrived in the fortress city over a week ago. Instead, they traversed the entire length of the Black Forest, remaining within the sanctuary of the trees to disguise their approach to the city as best as they could. It was painstakingly slow. During the day, Gavin would scout ahead or go back and hide their tracks as much as possible. At night, they would each take turns sitting watch, placing perfectly concealed traps to warn them of any intruder's approach. Trystan expected a race against time with the Brotherhood to reach Karalis and took every precaution necessary to ensure they arrived safely to the city. Yet the trip was made without incident. The young warrior was still unsure if this was a sign of weakness or if the Brotherhood was gathering its forces after the setbacks he caused them. As much as he wanted to believe they were no longer an issue, Trystan was wise enough to know otherwise. He could almost sense their presence, waiting in the shadows for their moment to strike. It left him uneasy.

The news of the dual invasions hadn't reached their ears until they entered the outskirts of the city. Karalis was abuzz with the news of war. Many of the citizens they spoke to boasted loudly of how the Khali, a name the tribesmen were styling themselves as, would fall beneath the shining blades of the brave Varkuvian soldiers. Trystan sensed the fear underlying the words. The citizens needed to believe the tribesmen could be dealt with easily. Most of them lived in the city their entire lives in relative peace with the thought of war being an alien concept to them. The fear in Karalis almost seemed to seethe from the buildings themselves like lantern oil. All it would take was one spark to ignite the city in flames.

Trystan knew the arrival of warriors wearing the armor of Acrium could be such a spark. Their arrival was the exact opposite of the reception they received in Fursta. Here the people looked at them with gleaming hope in their eyes. To them, the undefeated Order of Acrium had reemerged to save them from the evil tribesmen that were ripping their country apart. More than this, the Five Kings were proven utterly wrong. Not even a year had passed since the disbandment, yet their lands were in danger of being conquered by foreign invasion. The situation was looking perilous indeed, and Trystan knew it was one of the main reasons King Markos ever agreed to listen to their council.

His mind was jerked back to the present when a guard opened the door to the study. He was dressed as one of the Stone Guards, King Markos's royal guard. A knee-length cape of royal blue fringed with gold was clasped at the shoulders of the steel breastplate he wore. Hard eyes could be seen through the T-shape opening of the one-piece helmet he wore. The gauntlet he wore gripped tightly around the shaft of the ash-colored spear in his hand. Hitting the butt of the spear against the dark granite floor, he commanded instant silence.

"All kneel before King Markos the Benevolent, Protector of the Stone Realm, and one of the esteemed Five Kings of Varkuvia."

Only Prince Vasilis and Kole fell under King Markos's jurisdiction, so no one else in the room was obligated to kneel. Even still, Trystan, along with the others, knelt out of respect as the king entered the room, flanked by four more of his Stone Guards. The Stone Guards spread around the room, their hands resting on the hilts of the swords sheathed at their sides, ready to react at the first sign of danger. King Markos looked down upon the men kneeling at his feet. Within a matter of moments, he established his superiority over the gathered men in his study. Trystan glanced up. The king looked awful. His pale skin was drawn tight, and his gray eyes were sunk into his skull from sleep deprivation. Even his salt-and-pepper hair seemed to lack luster. Even still, everything about the king emphasized power in the way he held himself and the strength in his gaze despite the lack of sleep. There was no doubt they were in the presence of a king.

"You all may rise," he said, turning his attention away from Vasilis and Kaleb. "Then I want some immediate answers as to why the symbol of the Order of Acrium is in my city. After I have listened to what you have to say, I will pass judgment on whether I should imprison the four of you or not."

The four warriors stood and didn't say a word. Jaxon's, Kole's, and Gavin's body language all turned toward Trystan. Trystan's heart sunk. Ever since the raid at Fursta, he was elected the unspoken leader. Even Jaxon, his closest friend, looked to him for instruction. It was not exactly a role he desired. Whether he wanted it or not, the others expected him to speak for the group. The king noticed it as well and looked him directly in the eye. Storm gray eyes met eyes the color of a deep emerald sea. Almost immediately, Trystan regretted the comparison, for the two never met without tumultuous results.

"First, I want to convey my gratitude that you took the time out of your busy schedule for us, Your Majesty. I understand you have other pressing matters, so I will try to be as brief as possible."

And so it was, Trystan once again retold the events that took place at Jaxon's farm, the discovery of the Brotherhood, the donning of the armor, and the repulsing of the bandit attack at Fursta. Through it all, Trystan felt his heart thudding loudly in his chest. All of the events from the past few weeks led up to this moment, and if he didn't say the right words, then he and his companions would be thrown in shackles and escorted to the dungeons. Thankfully, his voice did not show his inner fears; and before he knew it, he finished retelling the events. King Markos didn't say anything, his powerful eyes staring into Trystan's. Trystan's gaze did not falter.

After several excruciatingly silent moments, Markos gestured to Kaleb with his hand. "If it wasn't for young Kaleb over there, or the fact I have already spoken to the leaders of Fursta, I would have a hard time believing everything you just told me. An attempt was made on Kaleb's life not too long ago, and he was not only lucky enough to escape with his life but also slayed the assassins in the process. Prince Kastor was not as fortunate. He was murdered in his sleep. Since Kaleb's arrival, I have been gathering as much information as possible on other disbanded members of the Order. Many of those I inquired about were dead, and almost every death was 'accidental' or they 'committed suicide.' Now, it's either that many of your disbanded brethren had extreme suicidal tendencies or this Brotherhood you spoke of truly exists. Even more so, I believe I know the leader and the name of them as well. My question to you now is, what do you plan to do it about it?"

Trystan took a deep breath. He hoped the assassin was exaggerating the number of deaths. This hope, like so many hopes in recent days, had just been brutally dashed. He marshaled his thoughts quickly. "I planned to prevail upon you to aid us to the best of your ability, Your Majesty. However, with the invasion of your lands, it would be near impossible. Then, I hoped to at least warn you of the assassination attempts and to proceed with caution, but it seems Kaleb has already done so. I could tell you my comrades and I will hunt down the leader of this Brotherhood and help you sleep easier at night. However, we are yet to ascertain who is pulling the strings. I can't say this without sounding arrogant, but we are the finest warriors in all of Varkuvia. We were trained by the best, and thus became the best. In short, we cannot help you unless you help us, Your Majesty."

Markos looked at Trystan, seeing him in a new light. This was a young man to be noted. "The Brotherhood is known as the Sons of Vikundo. They operate in the city-state of Yursa to the east, under the protection of Lord Drogos. I cannot prove that Lord Drogos is the one giving the orders, but I have strong suspicion to believe that he is. Now that I have shared this valuable piece of information with you, what are your plans? Will the four of you march east and defeat a horde of tribesmen to reach Drogos?"

"With respect, Your Majesty, we would like to offer you our services. Each of us was not only instructed on how to fight, but we were also taught the subtleties of strategy. We need not boast of our fighting skills, for they were already displayed at Fursta. We will swear whatever oaths of fealty you require of us and fight unto death for you in defense of Karalis. The only thing we ask in return is you allow us to wear the armor of Acrium once again and allow for any surviving warriors to join our ranks without repercussion. When the Khali have been repulsed from the Stone Realm, we will speak again about these Sons of Vikundo."

The king's laughter filled the study. "You men aren't exactly in a position to negotiate. I will admit, my forces would be bolstered by your exceptional skills in battle. Then again, if I allowed you to fight for me, that might cause some resentment amongst my neighboring kings and allies. If they were angered enough by my decision, then they might not send their armies to help protect my lands. I did not study strategy as you boys did, but I do believe the tens of thousands they would be bringing to my aid would help far more than you four ever could."

Trystan's irritation flared. "Well, Your Majesty, you keep asking what we plan to do. I have told you, yet you still stand here and ridicule my companions and me. We did not travel all this way to be made a mockery of nor did we put our own lives in danger to save your people just so you could spit in our faces. It was my hope you would see us as your allies. Since this meeting is rapidly going nowhere, why don't you tell *us* what *you* want?"

The Stone Guard closest to the king cast a malevolent glance at Trystan. "You are addressing one of the Five Kings of Varkuvia. Be sure to show some respect the next time you speak to him, or I will teach you a lesson in manners, you insolent peasant."

Still looking at Markos, Trystan said, "I was speaking to the king. If I want to hear a dog bark, then I will go to the kennels."

The guard's lips thinned inside his helmet. His hand wrapped around the hilt of his sword, and he made to draw it. King Markos turned to the guard, his voice ringing out. "Keep your sword sheathed!" He turned his angry gaze back upon Trystan. "Provoke any of my guards in such a manner again, and I will see you thrown in the dungeons."

Jaxon drew himself up to his full height behind Trystan, crossing his powerful arms. Kole and Gavin followed his lead. Markos cast a quick look around the room. The situation was close to becoming dangerous. Ignoring the building tension, he spoke to Trystan once again. "There is something you could do that might allow me to consider your proposal."

"We are listening," responded Trystan, skeptically.

"I received a message just before I entered the study regarding my eldest son's whereabouts," said Markos. Vasilis's head perked up at the news, and he went to say something, but his father raised his hand, silencing him. "The barbarians have seized the Bale Fort, which is a half-day's march from the Memure Bridge. A farmer who escaped the initial invasion, and made it with the other refugees to Karalis, spoke of prisoners being brought inside of the fort. One such prisoner met the exact description of my son, Prince Leon. I do not presently have the manpower to launch an attack on the Memure Bridge, and I cannot allocate any more of my soldiers to organize a rescue mission nor can I think of a single soldier under my command that possess the skills you men do. I have found in the twenty years of my reign it is foolish to trust any one person. Yet now I am forced to trust four men I know nothing of. If you can go behind enemy lines, rescue my son, and bring him back safely, then you will fall under my protection. Then we will speak of your terms."

Nobody in the room spoke. Finally, Gavin stepped forward. "Your Majesty, I know the terrain of these lands extensively, and there is only one route to the eastern part of the Stone Realm. And it's the Memure Bridge. The enemy has taken the bridge and dug in defensively. Normally, I would suggest attempting to swim the Memure River for at certain bends it only spans *thirty paces*. But with spring causing the snow to melt down from the Bale Mountains, the river will be gorged and overflowing with the current much stronger than usual. And there's no way we could reclaim the bridge by ourselves. How then do you suggest we rescue Prince Leon?"

"I haven't been able to give much thought to the matter, seeing as how I was just privileged to the information myself," began Markos. "If memory serves me correctly, there is a bend in the river with an abandoned mill on the eastern bank. The current at this bend is not nearly as strong as other parts of the river and is relatively short across. You shouldn't have a problem making the crossing at this point. For the time being, the tribesmen are not advancing farther into my realm. It is my belief they are stripping the forests clean to construct equipment so they can lay siege to Karalis, and your trip to the river should be fairly without incident. The trip back however will prove to be far more difficult. It is also a fear of mine that I have a traitor within the city. The tribesmen know far too much about my lands for it to be otherwise. You could come to this bend I spoke of only to discover the enemy has fortified the bank. The options are not appealing, but this is the only way I will allow the Order of Acrium to remain under my jurisdiction without consequences. The choice is yours."

"We will do it," replied Trystan instantly. "Provide us with supplies, and we will leave as soon as possible. We will bring Prince Leon back to you or die in the attempt."

"I will have rooms arranged for you immediately. However, the armor of Acrium will remain behind. That gaudy armor will draw too much unwanted attention for my liking. Tell the servants who show you to your rooms anything you might require for the trip, and it will be brought to you. Your weapons will be returned once you are safely outside of the city limits. Good luck to you, men. Bring the heir to my throne back to me safely, and you have my word, each of you will be greatly rewarded. You are dismissed." Markos signaled to Kaleb and his son. "You two remain behind. Guards, escort these men to their rooms and leave us."

The Stone Guards bowed to their king and then flanked the warriors as they left the study, their blue and gold capes flicking back and forth as they exited. Markos turned his attention on the two young men as the door clicked shut. "Neither of you is to join them."

Both of them appeared outraged, and Markos saw Vasilis's face turn red under his tanned features. "But, Father, they are going to rescue my brother. I am no coward. You must let me go with them. Besides, how can we be sure that once they leave the city they will not simply try and make it on their own? You must let me go," he repeated.

"I cannot go on the word of a single farmer that Leon is being held captive at the Bale Fort. For all I know it could be a trap set up by the enemy to lure me out of Karalis. This grand chieftain, Timon, has already proved to be more than the average leader of these savages. He could be waiting for me to make such a daring move. They might even expect me to send a group of men to save him. I will not send my only other son into a situation that reeks of a trap. No, instead I will send these heroic warriors to do it. If it is a trap, as I suspect, then they will be killed, and I will no longer have to worry about them. If Leon is not in the Bale Fort, and by some miracle, they return, then I will have them executed for treason. But if he is truly being held prisoner at the fort, and they do rescue him, then I will grant them everything I promised. They will return as heroes and be welcomed by the people of this city. Some of the other kings might be angered by the fact they will be under my protection, but then the rest will see they rescued the heir to my throne. Whichever way this turns out, it will be a win-win situation for me. I could either eliminate the potential problem the Order might bring, or I will get my son back. However, my decision is final. Kaleb, you will also remain behind. Your father sent you here to keep you safe, and even though my realm is beset by invasion, I will honor this charge to the best of my ability."

Kaleb looked angry. Without a word, he stormed out of the study. Vasilis looked his father in the eye, as if seeing him for the first time, and then followed Kaleb's lead. Markos sighed. One day his son would learn that not even a prince always got his way. Hell's teeth, most of the time a king did not get the things he desired. Every problem in his kingdom rested solely on Markos's shoulders, and he learned long ago, leadership was a lonely place. In the end, every decision he made, whether it was good or bad, would be on his conscience. It was a burden he had grown to live with over the years. If Leon was dead, as Markos feared, then Vasilis would become heir to the Stone Realm. He was a good son, and in times of peace, the country would flourish under his rule. The coming months might see Markos slain, and it was something he simply had to accept. He loved Vasilis to death, but he had too much of his mother in him. The coming war required a kind of steel that Markos feared his younger son simply did not possess. *Only the future will tell*, thought the king.

Trystan was still troubled as he was escorted to his new quarters. Each of his companions was assigned separate rooms, and now he was alone as he walked down one of the many corridors of the Keep of Karalis. The Stone Guard walking beside him did not say a word, and Trystan found his thoughts wandering. The meeting was worrying him. The king had agreed to terms far too quickly for his liking, and Trystan feared this quest to save Prince Leon would be wrought with peril, and not just from the tribesmen. For all he knew, King Markos might have men stationed on the path to the Memure River, waiting to waylay them. The blame could easily be put down to the tribesmen. Then the people of his city would still be placated, knowing the warriors died valiantly while attempting to rescue their dear Prince Leon.

Yet what choice did he have but to agree? They could try to make a run for it once the city was safely behind them. But where would they go? Ahead of them would be a horde of bloodthirsty savages who were terrorizing the surrounding countryside. They would never make it safely out of the Stone Realm. Even if they did, where would they go? One of the eastern city-states? The assassins that tried to kill them were based in the city-state of Yursa. How long would it be before more assassins found them and slit their throats or waylaid them in some dark alleyway? Trystan realized with a sick heart that they had no choice but to go along with Markos's will and hope he stayed true to his word. It was not a situation he was comfortable with being forced to react. *I have brought us to this*, thought Trystan. *I will see it through until the end.*

He was thinking of possible things that could go wrong when a serving woman came around the corner, bearing a tray of food. Trystan collided with her. The tray clattered to the floor, scattering food and wine across the corridor. She cast him a look of death and then bent over, pulling clear a rag to clean up the mess. Cursing himself a fool, Trystan knelt down and joined her on the ground.

"My apologies," he mumbled. "My mind was far away. I never intended for that to happen."

She looked up, and Trystan's breath caught in his throat. She was without a doubt the most beautiful woman he ever laid eyes upon. Her auburn hair was drawn tightly back, causing strands of curly locks to hang down at her temples. He found himself studying her face with her small nose, lush lips, and rosy color in her high cheekbones. It wasn't the exquisite beauty of her face that drew his attention though but her eyes. Depending on how the light hit them, they shimmered from hazel flecked with gold to light brown. They were eyes that reminded him of a time from his youth, a time when he fled before the city watch. Eyes that saved him from certain execution.

"Arianna?" he barely whispered.

She jumped at the name. "What did you say?" she asked while still cleaning the scattered food. Her eyes narrowed as she studied the man who bumped into her. "Do I know you?"

Trystan's heart sunk as he realized she did not recognize him. It had been nearly ten years since he last saw the girl who saved his life. Ten years since he had seen the only person who showed him any compassion in the rough days of his youth. And she did not even recognize him. *What did you expect?* he asked himself. *That she would remember some gutter rat from Calydon she barely spoke to?* There was one thing that was certain. She was no longer an adolescent girl but a woman grown. Despite himself, his eyes were drawn to the curve of her smooth neck, drawing ever lower.

"Is it customary where you're from to stare at a woman's breasts?" asked Arianna, an edge to her voice. Trystan's head shot up, his face flushed. "Now that you're more focused, I will ask you again. What did you say?"

Trystan cleared his throat, blushing furiously. "My apologies again. I thought you were someone I once knew." He hesitated. "I am Trystan." He offered her his hand.

Her brow scrunched as if the name almost jarred something from her memory. Then she lightly gripped his outstretched hand. "I suppose I can excuse your boorish behavior just this once. I am Arianna." She flashed him a smile.

The smile was angelic, and Trystan reeled back as though he'd been struck between the eyes by a hammer. His eyes drifted beyond her neck, roaming the curves of her body beneath the green wool dress she wore.

Her hand tore from his grip. "You are staring again," she chided him.

He took a deep breath, composing himself. *What is the matter with you?* he asked himself. Much of the wasted food was cleaned up now and placed in an unceremonious heap on the tray. The two stood. Arianna brushed the dirt off her dress while Trystan desperately thought of something he could say.

"I truly am sorry," he said, trying once more. "It seems I have made a complete fool of myself."

"That is a safe assessment," replied Arianna. She looked up into Trystan's face, and the dawning of recognition finally flashed in her eyes. "You are the boy I helped back at my father's bakery in Calydon! I always wondered what became of you. You have the same exact frightened expression on your face as you did back then. Am I truly as terrifying as those guards that were chasing you?"

Trystan forced a smile, relieved she finally remembered him. "Close enough. I've never been comfortable in the company of women. My tongue swells to twice its size, and I seem to acquire two left feet."

"A common affliction with most men around women," she said sweetly. "You also forgot to mention, your eyes grow to the size of frying pans, as if you were gazing upon some object that fell from the heavens."

"A fact I would be unaware of since I cannot see my own eyes," responded Trystan, chuckling. "I doubt the gods themselves could deliver a more divine object than you though."

A blush crept into Arianna's cheeks. "That was well said for a man who claims to be uncomfortable around women." She smoothed out the creases of her dress. "Well, as much as I would love to stay and chat, I have my duties to attend to. If we happen to meet again, perhaps you could refrain from running into me." She threw in a smile to take away the sting from the words.

The smile left him dumbfounded once again, and he raised his hand in farewell even though she was standing only a foot away. As she walked away, he hit himself on the forehead with the palm of his hand. Why in the seven hells did he just wave at her instead of saying something? Glancing to his left, he could see the Stone Guard who was escorting him was smirking underneath his helmet. Shaking his head, Trystan regained his senses and proceeded to follow the guard to his new room.

Clicking the door shut behind him, Trystan kicked off his boots and stretched himself out on the bed set in the corner of the room. For the first time in weeks, he allowed himself to relax. Whatever tomorrow may bring, today he was safe. If safe could be defined as sitting borderline hostage in a keep in one the world's greatest fortresses, then yes, for the time being he was safe. There was no doubting the fact, the situation he got himself into was perilous indeed, but not all hope was lost. He would weather this storm and see his brothers-in-arms safely through it. His thoughts turned to Jaxon. His friend left his wife and future child to accompany him. *If I were a true friend, then I would never have allowed him to come*, he thought. *I will see you safely through this, Jaxon.*

Without conscious thought, Arianna's smiling face sprang into his mind. All thoughts of Jaxon and future perils were swept aside. The woman had an effect on him like no other woman ever had before. It wasn't just the fact that she was stunning. No, it was much more than that. Just thinking about the way she tilted her head when she smiled set his heart racing. He found himself remembering much more than the beauty of her face. Her breasts pressed against the fabric of the dress she wore, and Trystan found his thoughts plunging toward the carnal. *What is the matter with you?* Tomorrow he would be traveling into enemy territory and in all likelihood his death, yet he sat in bed daydreaming of a beautiful woman like an adolescent boy.

"You are a fool," he told himself aloud.

A soft knocking came at the door. Trystan sat up, groaning. His body was still sore from the weeks of traveling and sleeping on a hard packed floor. With an effort of will, he pushed himself off the bed and opened the door. Arianna's eyes met his own. Was he still daydreaming? Glancing down, he saw she was bearing a new tray of food. Trystan felt like even more of a jackass. He had knocked his own tray of food out of her hands. *You truly are a fool,* he thought.

Stepping aside, he allowed her to enter, the guard shutting the door behind her. He could think of no words to say as she set the tray of food down on a small table of pine set next to a window overlooking the city below. "So we meet again," he finally managed to say. *What a dumb thing to say. Of course, we are meeting again.*

Arianna glanced his way, amusement in her eyes. "And it appears you refrained from running into me, just as I requested. I heard from the other servants you are a part of the group that arrived wearing the armor of Acrium. I had no idea you went on to join the Order of

Acrium after leaving Calydon. A common street thief turned into a hero. Who would've thought it possible? Are the rumors true for once?"

Trystan felt himself relax if only marginally. She had taken the time to inquire about him. "The rumors are true. My companions and I came here with the hopes of seeking King Markos's aid."

Her laughter rolled out as she poured a cup of wine. The sound was like water to Trystan's parched soul. "You obviously have not had much experience in dealing with kings. All of them are the same. Arrogant in the belief every decision they make is the right one, as if they are not capable of mistakes. In fact, throughout most of my life, I have discovered most men are the same way. As if it is such a tragedy to admit when one makes a mistake. We are human after all."

*Brains and beauty*, observed Trystan. How weird, the two generally did not go hand in hand. It was as if the gods deemed that a man or woman only be blessed with one or the other. Or, to the least fortunate, neither.

"I thought King Markos would be different than the others. It seems I learned the lesson too late," said Trystan, keeping his voice low. He did not want the guard stationed outside his door to hear the conversation and report it back to Markos. "Tomorrow I depart on a suicide mission. I fear I have traveled quite some distance only to face ruin."

He suddenly realized Arianna was a servant of King Markos. For all he knew she could have been sent here with the purpose of dissecting information from him. His heart told him she wouldn't do this, but his head advised caution. Arianna finished placing the food and wine on the table and turned toward him. For the first time he realized they were completely alone in the room, and the space between them seemed substantially smaller than he remembered. His heart pounded inside his chest. The sound was so incredibly loud that he was sure she had to hear it. *Get a hold of yourself*, he thought.

"I also heard you and your companions were the ones who saved Fursta. It is said because of your actions men, women, and children were saved. Servants around the keep speak of you with awe in hushed whispers. Already legends are beginning to unfold that it was you alone that vanquished the bandits. *Trystan of the Blade* I heard one woman call you."

Trystan found himself blushing once more. "I certainly did not do it by myself. We were hopelessly outnumbered and in danger of being overwhelmed when the townspeople joined the fight. If it was up to me, I would rather have the innocent lives claimed during the raid still among the living. Overblown legends mean nothing to me. The bandits not only murdered men in their homes but women and children as well. It is an image that will haunt me for the rest of my days."

Arianna's face softened. She moved closer to Trystan, standing within arm's reach of him. The room suddenly became unbearably warm, and Trystan could feel sweat trickling down his spine. His eyes remained firmly glued to the floor, his discomfort immense.

"What you did for those people was valiant, and even though I cannot relate to the atrocities you saw, many more lives would have been lost if you did not act as you did. Mourn the dead if you must, but do not belittle your deeds. What you did was heroic, and you should be proud of yourself."

Tearing his gaze from the floor, Trystan gazed into Arianna's eyes of shifting color. All nervousness left him. Something he never felt before stirred deep inside of him. Her lips looked moist and inviting. He felt himself being drawn to them. She did not back away, and their lips met. The kiss lingered for several moments, and Trystan felt himself becoming light-headed. He kissed women before in his life but never had he experienced the dizziness that was now swamping his senses. After what felt like a lifetime, or perhaps the beginning of a new one, he pulled back and saw that Arianna's face was flushed, her pupils dilated. Arousal coursed through him, and he went to kiss her again. An intrusive knocking came at the door just as his lips were mere inches from hers. His eyes met hers, and he found himself being lost in the pools of shifting hazel flecked with gold and the lightest of browns that would rival those of a doe. The knocking came again, louder this time, and he tore his gaze from hers and opened the door.

Kaleb stood in the corridor beyond. His clothing was immaculately tailored. He wore a tunic of blue satin with intricate designs in silver thread weaved along the sleeves, a pair of knee-length boots freshly oiled, and gray leggings of the finest fabric. His shoulder-length hair looked newly groomed and was held in place by a silver circlet. Even his close-cropped beard looked as though it was just trimmed. He looked every inch the noble that he was.

"May I have a word with you, Trystan?" inquired the noble.

Trystan went to reply when Arianna brushed past him. She threw a look back as she moved into the hallway. "I have other duties to attend to. It was a pleasure to see you again, Trystan. I pray that it will not be the last time." Her gaze lingered a moment longer then she curtsied and moved off down the corridor.

Trystan was both embarrassed and angry as she walked away. That was the second time now he had not even said farewell to her. Now she probably thought all he wanted was to bed her. *Was that what I wanted?* he asked himself. *No, it was much more than that. But what was it?* His emotions were confusing in the extreme as he turned his attention back on Kaleb. The noble was grinning from cheek to cheek.

"Maybe now wasn't the best of times, eh?" he asked, an impish gleam in his eye.

Trystan tried unsuccessfully not to blush. The effort always made him aware of the warmth that spread through his face. "Please enter and take a seat." Kaleb entered and Trystan shut the door behind him. "What can I do for you, Kaleb?"

Kaleb looked around the room Trystan occupied. He tried to keep the contempt from his eyes at the lack of luxury. It was an extreme failure. His face was an open book, and Trystan could read the pages as he inspected every inch of the room. This was a room meant for a commoner, not for someone of class like Kaleb. Finally, the noble took a seat at the table where Trystan's dinner still remained untouched. Picking up the goblet of wine, he sniffed at it, his nose scrunching at the smell. Putting the wine back down, he placed his hands in his lap. He appeared ill at ease to Trystan though he did not know why. The silence stretched for several moments, and Trystan thought he could cut the unspoken tension with a knife. Finally, Kaleb spoke.

"King Markos has forbidden me to accompany you and the others to rescue Prince Leon. The same goes for Vasilis. He fears the tribesmen might expect such a move and does not want to put us in harm's way. My father, with his boundless generosity, sent me to the Stone Realm to keep me safe from assassination. It seems you also came here for that exact reason. I know we have had our differences when we were a part of the Order, but now we stand on common ground. My reasons are my own, but I also wish to see the leader of these Sons of Vikundo draw his last breath in this world. Let me join your cause. Together we can topple this brotherhood of murderers and cowards. What do you say?"

Trystan picked up the cup of wine and drank deeply. Some of it dribbled down his chin, and he dried it off with the cuff of his sleeve. "I had my suspicions that King Markos might be sending us into a trap, yet what choice did I have but to accept? We have no allies in Karalis, and no other king would have even received us. My initial goal was to find the leader, this Lord Drogos, and end his life. Then the lives of our departed brothers in arms would be avenged, and we could return to the lives we left behind. But things have drastically changed. I fear this brotherhood is merely a pawn in a much bigger game. I have been giving a lot of thought into the dual invasions of Varkuvia since my arrival. The Argarians' invasion of King Eryk's realm at least makes sense, for they have a long history of animosity toward one another. It is the Khali's invasion of the Stone Realm that makes no sense to me. In decades past, they would pillage, loot, and rape their way across the lands, and then they would melt back into the sanctuary of the Northern Woods. Not so now. Even if they were to conquer Karalis, the people of the Stone Realm would never settle for having barbarian masters. They would rise up in their thousands, and the realm would be ripped apart by civil war until either the tribesmen were driven back or they themselves were killed in the effort. It is my belief someone else is pulling the strings here. I do not know who yet, but it is my intention to find out. For me to do this I must stay alive, which with my current situation isn't looking promising. However, I agree, we should join together. Even though we did not always see eye to eye in the Order, I have always respected you. I would be honored to call you my comrade once more."

Kaleb nodded, and Trystan thought for just a heartbeat he looked upon him as an equal. The moment was fleeting, as if Kaleb's noble blood seemed to detect the implied equality, and quickly masked the betrayal his face showed. "I have been thinking about the mission that Markos has assigned you. Even if by some miracle this is not a trap designed by the enemy, it will be nearly impossible. The hills themselves are crawling with tribesmen, and they will undoubtedly have sentries guarding Prince Leon at all hours of the day. Even if you somehow manage to spirit the prince out of the fort, how long will it be before the alarm is raised? Then you will have a horde of tribesmen at your backs all the way to Karalis. Also, I intend no offense toward Jaxon, for I know you two are close friends, but he is not exactly the stealthiest of men. He and Kole are the kind of warrior that when they see the enemy, they charge into their ranks, hoping their skills will see them through the day. In certain situations, such an act is promptly called for. This mission, however, will call for a little bit more subtlety than that. In short, I do not see the four of you being able to pull this off."

"What do you suggest?"

"Five might even the odds."

# CHAPTER SIX

Trystan awoke when a beam of sunlight broke through an opening in the branches overhead. The grass beneath his back felt like feathers, and he wanted nothing more than to pull his cloak over his eyes and go back to sleep. After negotiating with himself on whether he should go back to sleep or not, he rolled onto his stomach and pushed his arms underneath him, groaning at the tightness in his lower back. Gathering his legs, he stood, stretching his back as he did so. Stifling a yawn, he felt pressure in his bladder. The stand of trees he slept beneath the previous night was still dark except for random strands of light that fell in between the branches, and he looked around for a good place to relieve himself. Deciding it didn't matter, he moved to the edge of their camp, accidentally hitting Jaxon's leg as he did so. The slumbering bear grunted and then immediately fell back asleep, the rhythmic sound of snoring coming moments later.

Relieving himself against the base of a giant pine tree, Trystan yawned openly. They were four days into their trip with the Memure River just in sight outside the stand of trees. They stayed away from the road as much as possible, restricting themselves to the woods in the shadows of the majestic Bale Mountains. Only once did they have to endure an open stretch of land, and despite the fact they could be seen more easily, they kept their movements relatively slow. The ground was dry, and if their mounts were to kick up dust, then the Khali could be alerted to their presence. Thankfully, they were not spotted and merged into a jumble of large boulders.

They passed several farms and towns, every one of them abandoned. Passing through one such town was like walking through a place inhabited by spirits. The silence was all-consuming, the only sound coming from the wind whistling between the buildings. The occasional shutter would slam against a window, or a door left open would creak on its hinges. Each one of them breathed a sigh of relief after they departed the town. It was an eerie sight to see so many houses and places of business once full of bustling activity brought to a standstill by the stupidity of war.

What bothered Trystan the most was how uneventful their passage to the Memure River had been. Such a thing should have made him happy, but instead, it left him with a sense of unease. Three times, they spotted Khali outriders, but always they were in the distance, the sunlight glinting off the tips of their spears, their war ponies pounding across the land. They were scouting parties and not ravaging the countryside at all. This was not usually the way the tribesmen conducted a war. In generations past, they would see the enemy, charge them, and hope sheer brutality and weight of numbers would overwhelm their foes. Then, after they raped and pillaged, they would return to their villages in the Northern Woods. Yet with this war, they were securing strategic locations, building forts, sending out scouting parties, and gauging the enemy. They were conducting warfare like a Varkuvian army would, and it mystified Trystan.

Finished relieving himself, Trystan tied his leggings and turned back toward his companions. The only person awake other than himself was Gavin who sat the last sentry duty. It was time to be up and about. Moving to Jaxon, he nudged him in the side with his boot.

"Come on you ox, it's time to get up. I'm surprised your snoring didn't alert the entire Khali horde by now."

Jaxon grumbled, rolling onto his side. "Just ten more minutes, mother Trystan."

"Ten more minutes and you will find out what my boot up your ass feels like."

"All right, all right. Five minutes it is then. No need to get touchy."

Trystan chuckled, moving away from him. Kaleb awakened at the sound of their conversation and was sitting up rubbing at his temples. His eyes look haggard, and even though he hadn't sat watch at all during the previous night, he looked like he barely got any sleep. Trystan let it pass. Kaleb clearly wasn't an early riser. It still shocked Trystan how easily Kaleb joined their party. Not even a day into their journey, the noble cantered his horse up to them and without a word fell in line. Trystan knew the noble was instructed by King Markos himself not to accompany them, and he wondered how he left the city without question.

Moving to Kole, Trystan bent down and shook his shoulder. His eyes flared open, his hand gripping Trystan's like an iron vice. Seeing there was no danger, he relaxed, his grip loosening. Sitting up, he swore, his hand moving to his right shoulder.

"Must've slept on a damn rock during the night. Gods, but that does not feel pleasant."

As everybody was rousing themselves, Gavin moved to Trystan's side. Despite being up for the past few hours, he looked like he received a full night's sleep, his eyes fresh and alert.

"I didn't see anything during the night. Is it me, or does it seem strange the Khali have not advanced upon Karalis? All we have seen is outriders, and no sign of the main body of their forces."

"I have been giving some thought into the matter myself. It makes no sense. They have a clear path to Karalis with minor opposition against them. The longer they wait, the more likely the chance reinforcements can be gathered and ride to King Markos's aid. From what Markos said, their leader, Timon, does not seem to be a fool. So why does he wait?"

"Maybe they did not expect to advance this far onto Varkuvian soil with such little resistance and are rethinking their strategy," speculated Gavin. "Or perhaps it is as Markos suspects, and they lack the siege equipment."

Trystan thought it over. It made sense, but he doubted it. "For the time being, it is immaterial. We have a mission at hand. Once we reach the river, how do you think we should proceed?"

"It will all depend on how many tribesmen are stationed at the mill. We won't be able to make the crossing while guards are still stationed on the other side. They will slaughter us. Markos has provided each of us with a bow and a full quiver of arrows. If there are only ten tribesmen guarding the mill, then we might have a chance. If there's more"—Gavin spread his hands—"then we will have to rethink our strategy. After we have taken out the guards, we will make the crossing on horseback. One of us will have to remain at the mill and stand watch in case more Khali show up. Then we will advance upon the Bale Fort with another one of us watching the horses. Assuming everything goes according to plan, which is asking for more luck than all of us have combined in our lifetimes, once we have Leon safely back at the mill, we cross the river and race back to Karalis."

"My thoughts exactly. My concern is the enemy will have more men than we can handle fortifying the bank. If there are more than ten tribesmen, then we will be hard pressed to kill all of them without one slipping away and alerting the others of our presence. Then this trip will be for nothing."

"We're asking for a lot of luck here, Trys."

"We will make our own luck. Let's go rescue a prince."

The group mounted and left the sanctuary of the woods, making for the blue ribbon that wound its way across the rugged landscape to the east. The ribbon expanded as they got closer, becoming the rushing Memure River. The land before the river was full of hills, and they hid their movements in the dips between the mounds of earth. The roaring of the river filled their ears as they approached. As they came to a ridge that overlooked the river, Trystan dismounted, handing the reins to Jaxon. Gavin did the same, and the two shimmied their way up the crest of the ridge. There was the mill. And nobody could be seen.

For some time, the two observed the mill. The building appeared abandoned, and Trystan was about to ease himself down from the ridge when Gavin gripped his arm. He was peering intently at the front door of the mill when it swung open. Five men emerged into the sunlight, each of them dressed in the goatskin and fur tunics of the Khali. All of them were armed to the teeth with dagger, ax, and sword though Trystan noted only one tribesman with a wispy blonde beard carried a bow. The guards moved off, stretching and groaning. It was apparent they had just awakened from slumber. Now was the opportune time to spring a trap while their reflexes were dulled from sleep. Trystan watched the group for several minutes, making sure they were alone. He expected more tribesmen to be securing the mill, and it seemed for the first time in an age, the gods were smiling down upon them.

"Gavin, stay here and continue observing them. I will go and inform the others of their position. Signal to me if the situation changes."

Trystan eased himself back from the edge of the ridge, keeping his movements slow. When he was safely out of sight from the opposite bank, he loped down to his waiting companions.

"It looks like we have finally found a bit of luck," he said, addressing the gathered warriors. "There's only a handful of Khali guarding the mill. I also spotted several bushes on our side of the river, a perfect place for coverage. We will traverse this ridge, hobble the horses, and then disguise our presence in the foliage. Once we are under cover, the guards will easily be within range of our bows. Then we will wait for Gavin's signal before releasing our arrows. Take your time in getting to cover and take your time aiming. We cannot afford any mistakes now. Any questions?"

There were none to be had. Putting his fingers to his lips, Trystan whistled like a bird. Within moments, Gavin came into sight, and Trystan signaled they were moving out. He gave a nod of his head and mounted smoothly without question. Another few short minutes saw the group around the ridge with the bank of the river in sight.

Dismounting, they made their way slowly down to the river's edge, their movements disguised by the many bushes sprouting along the bank.

Each knew their role, and there was no talking or banter amongst them. With their bows slung over their shoulders, they dropped to their stomachs and began crawling toward the safety of the bushes. The bank was slick with mud, and within a short span, the front of their clothing was filthy. None of them complained. Trystan moved to a bush as the others crawled past him. Gently, he eased back the branches, moving silently inside the confines. Through gaps in the intertwined branches, he could see the Khali across the river. He was close enough now that he could make out individual features. If it wasn't for the fact they were dressed in furs, and some had intricate blue war paint on their faces, they would look like any ordinary Varkuvian. The main difference between a Khali and a Varkuvian was the look in the tribesman's eyes, always appearing hostile. These men were reared on war since babes at their mother's breasts against the tribes of the Northern Woods. This was the first time in noted history that a single chieftain was banding together the warlike tribes.

He heard a badger call somewhere to his left and set his mind to the task at hand. Carefully unslinging his bow from around his shoulder, he withdrew an arrow and sighted it on a Khali who was standing casually by, his thumbs tucked into the belt of his leather pants. Suddenly, Gavin reared up from the bush he was hiding in like a demon covered in mud. The Khali stood rooted to his spot as his bow sang, the arrow taking the wispy bearded archer in his right eye. The others surged up from their hiding spots. The edge of a branch pierced Trystan's cheek as he emerged from the catacombs of the bush. He winced as he felt blood trickle down his face, but his mind remained cool. His arrow took the casual Khali in the back as he was turning to flee. His target stumbled several paces and then pitched to the ground. Glancing down the length of the other bank, he saw the others' arrows all found their marks.

Nobody moved, all their senses alert. Trystan smoothly drew another arrow to his string. Two Khali burst the door of the mill open. Three arrows immediately lodged into the chest of the first, his hand gripping the doorframe, willing his body forward. The second dove headlong onto the grass beyond, arrows slicing the air around him. The surviving Khali began ducking and weaving, running for safety. Arrows hit the ground all around him, missing him by inches. Gavin watched the elusive man with bow bent, observing the tribesman's patterns as he ran. Just as the Khali was almost out of range, he loosed the arrow. It hung in the air as the man cut to the right, directly into the path of the projectile. The arrow skewered his neck, pitching him to the ground without another sign of struggle.

Gavin immediately notched another arrow. His eagle eyes scanned the mill for further signs of trouble. The others stood anxiously by, all with their bows nocked. After several excruciating minutes, Gavin finally relaxed and returned the arrow to his quiver. Everyone else followed his lead. The group converged onto a spot to convene. It was Trystan who addressed the warriors. The others listened intently as he spoke, except for Kaleb. Trystan finally became accustomed to the role of leadership, but for some reason, Kaleb could just not accept the fact that a commoner was giving orders to a highborn noble. Since departing Karalis, he would constantly interrupt Trystan whenever he gave an order. It was starting to irritate Trystan, but he kept his thoughts to himself. They were on the same side, and there was no point in making the situation worse than it already was.

"The first step is done. From this point on, there is no turning back. Jaxon and Kole, go and gather the horses. We will stay here and watch the mill to make sure no other Khali are waiting inside for us to become lazy. We will wait for your arrival and make the crossing on horseback. Then we will check the rest of the property to make sure these were truly the only ones stationed here."

"And then Kole will stay behind at the mill and watch it while the rest of us proceed?" ventured Kaleb.

Trystan hid his annoyance. At least he had voiced it as a question and not as a fact. "Aye, I think Kole will be the best choice. I would say Gavin, but we will need his archery expertise once we reach the Bale Fort. When we reach the fort, Jax will remain behind with the horses. After that, Kaleb and I will assess the fort and find a way to infiltrate it. Once we have Prince Leon out of there, Jax will wait for our signal."

He gripped Jaxon's shoulder. "Stay in the saddle, my friend. We might need you sooner than we would like."

"We started this thing together, and I will be damned if a few thousand raving tribesmen will stop us from finishing it together. Whether you lads are safe or not, I will be there," promised Jaxon.

Trystan went to say something else when Kaleb cut him off. "I hate to cut the sentiments short, but we are killing daylight here. If we are to reach the fort by nightfall, we will need to start moving."

Turning to him, Trystan began to give a retort when he realized how awful Kaleb looked. The sunken eyes had remained from the morning, and the veins at his temples were jutting out like copper wire. His face wore a pale sheen, and he looked as though he was in immense pain. The others noticed it, as well.

"By the gods, are you all right Kaleb?" asked Kole. "You look like death."

"Of course, I am all right," snapped Kaleb. He took a deep, calming breath, rubbing the veins at his temples and forced a smile. "My apologies, Kole. I don't know why I reacted like that. This damn weather just doesn't agree with me. Let's get moving. Perhaps then I will feel better."

Trystan looked closely at Kaleb. It was much more than the weather that was affecting him. Kaleb was keeping something to himself. Trystan decided he didn't care as long as he was able to function well enough to see Leon safely rescued.

"Kaleb will be fine," he said. "Let's go find out what the Khali have in store for us."

After Kole and Jaxon brought the horses back, the group mounted once more. Even though Markos informed them that the river current would be weaker at this bend in the river, it was still much stronger than usual, and the horses struggled to get across. The water was still frigid, not yet warming up to the spring weather, and Trystan found his teeth chattering despite his best efforts to keep them still. His leggings were soaked through as his stallion's hooves sunk into the muddy bank. The stallion snorted, showing its distaste at being pushed so hard. Trystan bent over to rub his flanks with a shaking hand. He felt the horse tense underneath his touch. The horse was used to being beaten and treated poorly. Its first reaction at a touch was fear. The stallion began whinnying noisily, and Trystan talked to the horse in soothing words while continuing to rub the powerful flanks of the majestic animal. Eventually, the horse calmed down, its breathing coming more evenly. *Maybe we can become friends yet*, thought Trystan.

The group dismounted and drew their weapons, scanning the area for more tribesmen. After a thorough search, they brought the dead bodies inside the mill and laid them down. With luck, nobody would come to relieve these men before they returned. Then, once they spirited Leon away, the Khali would focus their attention on the Memure Bridge, thinking they had secured every other position along the river. If the gods were kind, they would buy close to a day's head start on the tribesmen while they figured out what happened. Then they might have a chance to return safely.

Kole set up a defensive position with his bow strung and at the ready as the others cantered their horses farther to the east. Several stands of pine trees spread downward from the Bale Mountains as they drew ever closer to the Bale Fort, and their movements went without notice. In fact, it seemed as though there were no Khali outriders at all. *Their entire force must be mustered at the Memure Bridge*, thought Trystan. As dusk fell across the land, the group dismounted in a grove of pines that overlooked the fort, which nestled against the mighty Bale Mountains.

Trystan observed the military fortification if one could call it that. The walls were in awful disrepair, and he noted that the wall facing them had a massive crack running down the center, the stone crumbling away. There were many handholds in the walls, and it appeared to be an easy climb. For just a moment Trystan was the orphan thief back in the massive city of Calydon, scaling buildings and cutting through alleyways to escape the city watch. Half of his life was spent stealing and escaping the watch while the other half was spent preserving the peace of these lands and establishing codes of honor stronger than the rare sword he wore at his side. *What a contradiction I am*, he reflected.

His mind was brought back to one of the many evenings he spent with Master Layne, years ago in the library at the Fortress of the Van. They were reviewing the charge the Legendary Arrturi led, which saw the might of the eastern lords of the time brought to their knees during the Sevilian Wars. Layne was pointing out the benefits and drawbacks to having the presence of such a charismatic figure like Arrturi on the battlefield. His courage and valor inspired everyone around him to acts of similar heroism, but if he were to fall in battle, then the morale of the fighting men would be crushed. It was during this time that Trystan voiced a question that was bothering him.

"Master Layne, do you think I am a good man?"

Layne's violet eyes dragged away from the parchment they were reviewing and studied his prized pupil. "Where is such a question coming from? You are a fine man, Trystan, and will be a valuable asset to the Order."

Trystan's shoulders sagged. "I do not feel like a good man. In my youth, I was forced to acts that shame me down to my very soul. I robbed, bribed officials, murdered, and lied just to survive. We read about noble men like Arrturi, and I do not think someone such as myself, being inducted into the Order would honor the memory of the man."

"Now, listen to me, Trystan. You are one of the most honorable men this Order has had the pleasure of accepting. Do not judge yourself on the boy you were but on the man you have become. You will do great things while here in the Order. I know these things."

He smiled at the memory. Whenever things seemed hopeless, he would recall the words from that night and hold on to them. Everyone had the ability to change their ways. Trystan knew he was a perfect example of such a person. He suddenly realized someone was speaking to him, and he looked up to see Jaxon repeating a question at him.

"Now what?" Jaxon asked Trystan.

Kaleb cut him off once again. "We will wait until the cover of nightfall, and see how many sentries are stationed upon the walls. Once we have assessed the situation properly, Trystan and I will scale one of the walls. They are in an awful state, and it will be an easy enough climb. Gavin will take out any sentries that spot us while you remain here with the horses."

Trystan tried to hide his rising irritation though he doubted he did a good job at it. "My thoughts exactly," he said testily.

Gavin ignored the power struggle for leadership, a talent he seemed to have with all problems, whether they were big or small. "Now we wait for nightfall. I recommend we change into the dark clothing that King Markos supplied us with."

There were no arguments on that account, and conversation was cut off as everyone changed into black leggings, dyed black leather breastplates over long-sleeved black shirts, and finally replaced their riding boots with dark moccasins. Trystan strapped on a long hunting knife, angling it toward his back so it wouldn't impede his climbing and relocated his sword to his back. He saw Kaleb resituating his dual short swords in a similar fashion. Darkness descended upon them, and Trystan moved to the edge of the trees, looking up toward the sky. The moon was becoming obscured behind heavy clouds moving in from the north. He threw up a silent prayer to the heavens that the rain hold off until after they scaled the walls. The climb would be precarious enough in the dead of night without adding the slickness of rain to the handholds.

Kaleb came up beside him, his eyes also looking up to the heavens. Trystan glanced at him and noticed the noble's blue eyes, usually containing an almost subtle arrogance and vitality for life, had a feverish look about them. His condition had not improved at all. In fact, it seemed worse.

"Listen, Kaleb, you don't have to do this," Trystan said, keeping his voice low so the others wouldn't overhear. "If necessary, I can do this by myself. There's no reason for you to put yourself through this."

The noble's face bunched up in anger. Instantly, he relaxed, his shoulders sagging. "I don't know what is happening to me," he admitted. "You know the feeling of insomnia? That restlessness your body experiences, and no matter how much you will yourself to go to sleep, you just cannot?" Trystan nodded. "Well, that is the way I have constantly felt since we left Karalis. I find myself becoming irritated all the time and over the simplest things. I have never before experienced an ailment like this, but you cannot go into that fort and rescue Leon by yourself. If the prince has been beaten or malnourished, I highly doubt you will be able to get him out of there by yourself."

Trystan had not even thought about the notion that Leon might have been tortured at the hands of the Khali. Kaleb was right. He would never be able to carry Leon by himself. Especially if he was merely dead weight. Glancing at Kaleb once more, he saw beads of sweat covering the noble's forehead despite the temperature dropping. Was the risk worth it?

"Are you sure about this, Kaleb? Nobody will think any less of you if you choose to remain behind."

"I will be fine," replied Kaleb, an air of false confidence surrounding the words.

"Everybody has their limits," Trystan said softly. "Maybe now is a good time to learn yours."

The noble gave him a withering glance. "This conversation is over, and my decision is final." With that, he turned and stormed back inside the sanctuary of pine trees.

Trystan sighed. Humility was never a virtue that Kaleb would accept. Glancing up to the skies once more, he saw the last sliver of moon disappear behind the approaching dark clouds. Throwing one final prayer to the gods, Trystan turned on his heel and merged into the shadows of the trees.

# CHAPTER SEVEN

The darkness was all-consuming as Gavin, Kaleb, and Trystan moved swiftly across the open plains before the Bale Fort. Glancing to his left, Trystan could scarcely make out the features of Gavin even though he was only two feet from him. Turning his attention forward once more, his vision fastened onto the rearing black wall that protruded from the dark landscape. His eyes scanned the top of the wall, expecting at any moment for archers to line the ramparts, their bristling arrows trained on the three defenseless men. He tried to push such thoughts from his mind, but the same image kept coming back unbidden.

Pressing his body against the base of the wall, Trystan took deep, calming breaths. Craning his neck upward, he made sure no sentries saw their approach. Satisfied, he began scanning the foundations for a good handhold to begin climbing. He did not have long to look.

Grabbing a jutting stone, he hoisted himself up and began the ascent to the ramparts above. Kaleb, with a coil of rope looped around his shoulder, moved up behind him, copying Trystan's every move as they inched up toward the battlements. Once they had Leon safely out of the dungeons, they would secure the rope to one of the crenellations above and grapple down to the ground.

Trystan froze just before they reached the ramparts as a head appeared over the wall to the right, scanning the horizon. The darkness was total, and the only feature Trystan could identify was the outline of the fur-lined helm the Khali wore. It was more than enough to terrify him. He hugged the wall tightly, his heart thudding in his throat as the Khali's head swiveled to look where Trystan and Kaleb hung from the wall. The head stopped moving, and Trystan saw the guard lean forward, peering intently at his position. Just as Trystan was on the border of sheer panic, a thrumming noise filled the air. The outline of an arrow merged into the fur-lined helm. With the sentry's weight leaning forward, he tumbled from the battlements, landing with a soft thud on the ground below.

It took Trystan a moment to realize it was Gavin who just saved them. Clinging to the wall, he found himself marveling anew at the archer's talents. Not only had he found his mark, but he had done so in the dead of night, aiming upward at a small target. To say the shot was incredible would be an understatement. Trystan mouthed a silent gratitude to the archer and began climbing once more.

Hooking his fingers over the crenellations, Trystan pulled his head up to examine the walls. Braziers dotted the ramparts, and looking to his right, he spotted the gatehouse. Nobody was in sight. Glancing to the left, he saw a sentry wearing a thick fur cloak, warming his hands at a lit brazier. The Khali's back was to him. Trystan looked down at Kaleb, held up one finger, and signaled to the left. Kaleb acknowledged him with an imperceptible nod of his head. Keeping his movements slow, Trystan levered himself up. He dropped lightly onto the ramparts, his moccasins disguising the sound. His eyes were fixed on the sentry as Kaleb pulled himself up and landed next to him. The noble's landing was awkward, the sound reverberating across the silence of the night. The sentry jerked at the noise, and they both stood statue still as he slowly turned his head toward the noise.

A raindrop fell from the clouds above to smack the Khali on the forehead. He started as if struck. Turning angrily back toward the brazier, the sentry huddled closer to the warmth of the fire, wrapping his cloak tightly around his frame. A soft pitter-patter sounded all around them as a light rain began to fall. Only then did Trystan allow himself to breathe once more. He gave a warning glance at Kaleb to be more careful. King Markos's information said that the dungeons were next to the gatehouse, and the two began moving stealthily toward the staircase. As they moved along the ramparts, Trystan saw the barracks of the Bale Fort nestled in the courtyard below where up to three hundred soldiers could be billeted. In his mind's eye, he imagined hundreds of Khali being awakened by the alarm bell and rushing toward him with weapons raised. Savagely, he quelled the image.

He moved to the door of the gatehouse, which would lead them to the courtyard below. He opened the door tentatively as lightning flashed in the distance. Glancing through a crack in the door, he saw two guards standing on a platform before the staircase, talking to one another. He signaled to Kaleb. Trystan pulled his hunting knife clear, and Kaleb followed his lead by drawing one of his short swords. They would have to be quick or the Khali might be able to scream a warning. The image of the Khali pouring out of the barracks building came flooding back in Trystan's memory. Calming his senses, he turned to Kaleb, made sure he was ready, and then flung the door open.

The first guard died as Trystan's knife plunged into the back of his neck. The second whirled around, grasping at his sheathed sword. Kaleb's short sword plunged into his temple before the guard could even draw iron. Trystan saw a shadow dance on the wall behind Kaleb. Ripping his hunting knife clear from the guard's neck, he flung it toward the corner of the gatehouse. A Khali emerged from the shadows with his dagger raised, aiming toward Kaleb's unprotected back. Trystan's knife hung in the air before plunging it into the Khali's chest. The guard fell backward as Kaleb spun around.

Trystan walked across the platform and tore the knife clear, wiping it clean on the Khali's tunic before returning it to its sheath at his side. He began to conceal the bodies when Kaleb gripped his shoulder, halting him. "I owe you for that one," said Kaleb softly.

"Think nothing of it. I am sure you would have done the same for me. Remain focused on the mission at hand."

They dragged the bodies into the corner of the platform where the torchlight inside the gatehouse did not penetrate. They could do nothing about the blood upon the floor, so they descended the stairs. The rain outside began to pour, and Trystan stopped often, straining to hear any sounds below them. There was nothing to hear. Coming to the base of the stairs, he gently pushed open the door that led to the courtyard beyond. Wind and rain stung his face as he narrowed his eyes to see if any guards were patrolling the area. Ignoring the discomfort, Trystan signaled to Kaleb, and the two moved into the courtyard, hugging the inner walls of the fort and sticking to the shadows. Lightning once more illuminated the sky, and in that brief moment, Trystan saw the outline of the dungeon door to his right.

Moving toward the gate, he heard muffled voices coming from underneath the gatehouse where a group of Khali hid from the lashing rain. Glancing around the corner, Trystan saw there were six guards all with their backs to him. They were facing toward the portcullis gate, which was opened. Trystan quickly dashed across the gap in between the gate and wall, Kaleb following his lead. Water was coursing down Trystan's face, his hair drenched, as he peered back around the corner, making sure they were unobserved. The guards hadn't even paused their conversation. Trystan began moving silently amongst the shadows of the fortifications toward the dark oak door reinforced with iron studs set into the wall.

He grabbed for the handle when the door began swinging outward. Reacting quickly, he dove in between a stack of barrels that were placed next to the door, his shoulder jarring as it pounded against a heavy barrel. Grimacing against the pain, he squatted down, hugging close to the barrel. Glancing around swiftly, he could not see Kaleb and hoped his companion reacted as quickly as he had. He froze to the spot as a group of Khali emerged from the dungeon below, mere feet from where he was hidden. They were chatting jovially amongst themselves. Two Khali were supporting their companion who was staggering heavily, his words slurring. Not one of them glanced his way. Trystan listened as their laughter and footsteps faded away.

Letting out a sigh of relief, he rested his forehead against the barrel he had hidden behind. He felt as though he were rubbing against sandpaper and looked up to see black powder trickling down the outside of the barrel where the wood had cracked. *That is odd*, he thought. Taking his forefinger, he dabbed at the powder and placed it upon his tongue. The taste was acrid, and he spit to the ground. What was in these barrels? *This is no time for curiosity*, he reminded himself.

Moving out from behind the barrels in a crouched position, he moved toward the door. A noise from behind caused him to whirl around. Kaleb emerged from among the barrels, smiling to reassure Trystan. *I am going to have a heart attack before we even reach Leon*, he thought. Opening the door, he saw the rain trickled underneath the doorframe and was steadily dripping down the staircase. Torches were set in brackets along the walls. The sudden wind buffeted the flames. He quickly closed the door and walked gingerly down the steps. A puddle began to form at the base of the stairs, and Trystan hugged the walls so he wouldn't step in it. Kaleb moved parallel to him as Trystan peered around the corner. Four guards were sitting around a table playing dice. Flagons were uncorked and set around the tabletop or at their feet. The smell of cheap mead filled Trystan's nostrils.

The sudden sound of thunder shook the ground beneath Trystan. He pulled clear his hunting knife as Kaleb drew a curved dagger from a hidden sheath inside his boot. Nodding to Kaleb, he spun from the corner, Kaleb just on his heels. Raising his knife, he flung it forward, drawing his sword within the same motion. Kaleb's dagger followed right behind his. Two of the guards went down, and then they were upon them. Kaleb, with short sword in hand, plunged it through the side of a Khali's neck. The last sentry staggered to his feet, his eyes blurry. Trystan's sword ripped through his lungs, exiting through his back. The guard's dark eyes met Trystan's, the dice still clutched in his hand. Ripping his sword clear, he heard the dice clatter to the ground, the owner falling beside them.

There was no time to hide the bodies. Quickly searching the guards, he found a set of keys attached to the one his hunting knife took in the eye. Bending down, he withdrew his knife. The Khali's eye came along with it. Fighting down a wave of revulsion, he quickly plucked the orb from the tip of the blade, letting it immediately drop to the dungeon floor. His eyes were drawn to the hollowness in the Khali's face where his eye and Trystan's knife were imbedded moments ago. Trystan began shaking like a leaf in wind. Taking deep, calming breaths, he forced himself to trembling feet. For once, it was Kaleb who looked at him, concerned.

"This is no time to get squeamish, Trystan."

"I will be fine," Trystan said through clenched teeth. He calmed down another wave of nausea. "Watch the staircase in case those Khali come back. I will search the cells for Prince Leon."

Shrugging, Kaleb moved off to the stairs. Taking another deep breath, Trystan felt the queasiness in his stomach passing. Composing himself, he moved off to the cells that dotted the walls. Coming to the first one, he slipped the key in and opened the door on creaking hinges. The sight within would horrify him until the end of his days. A man, or what once was a man, sat on the ground mewling. His hands and feet had been cut off and then cauterized in pitched oil. His eyes had been burned out, and his tongue had been ripped from his mouth. The sound that came from him wasn't even human. From the prisoner's matted blonde hair, Trystan knew it wasn't Leon. Bile rose like a tempest in his throat, and he turned from the sight before retching violently on the ground.

Hearing the commotion, Kaleb came over to see what had caused it. He reeled in horror when he saw the mewling man. Then he steeled himself and drew one of his swords before stepping into the cell. Trystan had no strength to stop him. Kaleb slammed the blade into the prisoner's throat. A gurgling sound replaced the mewling, and within moments, no sound at all came from the tortured man. Gently placing a hand on the prisoner's head, Kaleb withdrew the blade and replaced it into its sheath. Trystan was still bent over, sucking in deep breaths when the noble exited the cell.

"You killed that man," gasped Trystan.

"That is no way for someone to live. They tortured him beyond any concept of humanity. What I did for him was a blessing."

Trystan stood up. "You murdered a defenseless man, Kaleb."

Gripping Trystan's arms, Kaleb flung him into the wall. "Dammit, Trystan, get a hold of yourself! Yes, I murdered a defenseless man. But what future was there for someone like that? The amount of pain he was in was unbearable. The Khali did not even treat his wounds, except to cauterize them so he wouldn't bleed to death. Get it together, damn you! We still need to rescue Leon."

Trystan shook clear of Kaleb's grasp, his eyes angry, but his face set. "Go back and watch the stairs. My mind is set to the task now."

Giving him one last glance, Kaleb returned to the foot of the stairs. Trystan's head felt as though it were full of wool. His thoughts were not clear, but he forced himself to focus. Kaleb was right. He needed to pull himself together. Moving to the next cell, he opened it. A prisoner in threadbare clothing was asleep on a cot in the corner of the dark room. He turned toward the open door, his hand raised toward the blinding light. It wasn't Leon. Trystan moved off, and the prisoner rolled over and went back to sleep. Opening the next cell, the decaying stench of death hit Trystan like a blow. Nausea threatened to overwhelm him once again, but he forced himself to make sure the dead prisoner wasn't Leon before he slammed shut the door. The next three cells were empty, and Trystan was starting to feel a sense of hopelessness as he approached the final cell.

Opening the final door, he peered inside. Sitting in the corner of the room was a broad shouldered young man with short black hair, his head lowered into his chest. The prisoner looked up, and Trystan tried to hide the revulsion from his face. A thin cloth of linen was wrapped around the prisoner's head, covering the left side of his face. Not even the bandage could hide the angry red marks that spread from where his left eye had been. The prisoner's eye had been burned out. Much of the face was a mask of bruises as well, but the one remaining eye was open. It was the same color as King Markos's eyes. He found Prince Leon.

Leon raised his hand before his face, his one eye squinting against the harsh light from the hallway beyond. All he saw before him was a dark figure silhouetted in the open doorway. A sight he began to hate with every fiber of his being. All of the fight had been beaten out of him, and he sat meekly by as the dark figure walked inside of his jail cell.

"Prince Leon?" a voice asked.

He jerked at the name. The tribesmen did not call him by his title. The Scum of Varkuvia had become his nickname. They would gather around and snicker with their cruel laughs as they rained blows down upon him. Constantly, they would tell him that Karalis had already fallen and that no one was coming to liberate him. In his heart, he knew they were lying, but the lie had been repeated so many times that he began to believe it to be true. He had no conception of time, for there were no windows in his cell. It felt as if weeks had passed, possibly even months.

"Who's there?" his voice croaked.

"It is Trystan. King Markos has sent me, along with others from the Order of Acrium, to rescue you. Kaleb awaits us in the room beyond. We have to get moving."

The prince heard the words, but they did not register. Trystan was a name from another age. Was this some cruel dream he was having? Or perhaps some trap set up by the tribesmen? Narrowing his one eye, he peered intently at the dark figure before him. Had his mind finally snapped, and this was merely a figment of his imagination? *No, I will never break*, he told himself forcefully. *I did not break as the red tip of the dagger inexorably came toward my eye. I did not break as they murdered my friends in front of my eyes. These savages will not break me. Not now, not ever.*

"Prince Leon?" repeated Trystan.

He snapped his attention back toward Trystan. "Is this really happening?" asked Leon. There were no more tears to be shed, but his dry throat was thick with emotion.

"Yes, Your Highness. I can only imagine what you have been through, but we do not have time to stay here and talk. Are you able to walk?"

The prince took a calming breath and fought back the tears he was sure his body was devoid of. "Aye, I can walk. I don't know how much strength I have in me, but it will be enough to get me out of this place. How long have I been down here?"

"If everything I have heard is accurate, I would say around two weeks."

Leon had a bemused look on his face. "Two weeks? Is that all? It has felt like an eternity."

Trystan was growing impatient. It was only a matter of time before the guards they killed on the staircase were discovered or before someone else came down into the dungeons. "I will explain everything that has happened, but we need to get out of here. Now."

This time the words cut through Leon's delirium. He stood up, staggered, and then righted himself. He looked down in disgust at the dirty rags full of holes he was forced to wear. He was the son of a king, next in line to the throne, yet he was taken prisoner by savages and tortured, with his only company at night, the rats that scampered across the floor. Anger began to burn deep inside of him. For weeks, he was beaten and forced to be subservient to men lesser than himself. *They will pay for these acts of cruelty in blood*, he thought. *But first, I need to get out of here.*

"Lead the way, Trystan," said Leon. He tugged at his abysmal apparel. "But first I think I will be needing a change of clothing."

"I believe the Khali lying outside might be able to supply that for you."

They moved into the hallway beyond. Leon was barefooted and skidded around the pile of vomit that Trystan left behind. Kaleb approached them, a forced smile on his strained face. The smile froze when he saw Leon's condition, and he simply nodded. His thoughts echoed Leon's. The Khali would pay for this. The floor beneath the table where the guards were playing dice was slick with blood, and Leon had no choice but to step in it as they found a guard suitable to his height and size. As Leon waited, he took a swig from one of the flagons left on the table. Back in Karalis, this would have been considered worse than goat's piss, but after being held prisoner for weeks, he doubted if the gods themselves could have provided a finer tasting vintage.

A few short minutes later, Leon was dressed as a Khali. The boots were tight around his feet as was the blood-spattered goatskin tunic around his chest. The disguise would do for now unless under close inspection. Anybody would be able to see the bruises and the raw angry scar marks around where his eye had been. Hopefully, it wouldn't come to that.

They approached the bottom of the staircase where the puddle of water had become a small pool at the base of the stairs. Leon was already feeling sapped of strength, and they hadn't even left the dungeons. Rain was now flooding down the stairs, and as they treaded through the water up toward the courtyard, they could hear the full fury of the storm outside. Trystan opened the door and made sure there were no guards beyond before he signaled the others forward. The rain was coming down in a torrent outside as they hugged the walls once again, making for the staircase that would lead them to the ramparts above.

Coming to the gate once more, Trystan peered around the edge. This time there were only three guards, all huddled together tightly in a group. Their backs were facing him. He made the dash across to the opposite wall. Leon came next, his breathing ragged as he fell in beside Trystan. Kaleb soon followed. Trystan felt hope boiling up in his chest. They were so close.

Searing pain erupted inside Kaleb's head without warning. With a strangled cry, he stumbled and then fell to his knees as he was halfway to the next wall. The huddled Khali turned at the noise. They stared incongruously at the man on his knees, clutching his head with both hands. Then they noticed his dark attire and drew their weapons. The guard in the middle pointed his serrated sword at Kaleb as they advanced upon him, barking out a question. Kaleb didn't respond, his teeth gritting against the insistent pain. They surrounded the downed noble and began looking at one another unsure of what to do. A knife flew from the darkness, taking a Khali in the chest. The other two spun around as Trystan's sword sliced cleanly through the neck of the first. The final Khali brought up his serrated blade to block a ferocious downward cut from Trystan. The blade shattered. Trystan's sword carried on to smash his opponent's face to oblivion.

An arrow sparked off the cobblestones right next to Trystan's feet. He glanced up to see a sentry upon the walls, his cloak flapping in the storm, bow still in hand. As the guard shouted, the sound was whipped away by the wind. Trystan's gaze swept the ramparts. Even through the darkness and driving rain, he could see shadows moving along the walls. They were finished. The alarm bell began ringing.

He gripped Kaleb's arm and tried to drag him upward. The portcullis gate was open behind them with the dark plain beyond beckoning. They could try to make a run for it. Kaleb's eyes were squeezed shut, his face pale white. He refused to budge. Trystan didn't know what to do. He couldn't just leave him there and stood helplessly by as the steady tolling of the bell rang across the courtyard. He could hear the pounding of feet coming from the barracks building and knew his imagined fears were coming to life. Reverently, he held his sword before him. Now, there was nothing to do but stand his ground and take as many of the Khali with him on the journey after life as he could.

Kaleb's eyes suddenly flared open, his right hand coming away from his head. With a shaky hand, he pointed toward the dungeon door, his face a picture of pain. Trystan stood mystified. What was he doing? The clouds above them began to glow with a fierce light, gathering in strength. Kaleb uttered a single word that Trystan could not hear above the storm. A bolt of lightning raced down from the heavens, erupting in the midst of the barrels filled with black powder. The barrels erupted in a gout of flame and fire. The sound of crashing thunder filled Trystan's every sense, the ground beneath him trembling. For a moment, the whole world stood still as he watched the stone wall ripped asunder under the fury of the explosion. Kaleb was still upon the ground, his hand pointing at the fire that seemed to reach the sky itself.

And then the shockwave hit him. Trystan was flung backward, skidding across the ground before slamming into the wall. The air was crushed out of him, his sword blade clattering next to him. Ringing filled his ears. Nothing else. Not the alarm bell sounding or the rain pouring all around him. Only the ringing. He pushed himself unsteadily to his knees. Carefully, he placed a finger to his ear and brought it in front of his face. His vision blurred in and out, but he could still see the moist blood on his fingertip. With a force of will, he staggered to his feet and tried to walk. He stumbled backward into the wall and stood there propped against it. The ringing still pounded inside of his head.

His gaze swept the courtyard, expecting at any moment for a swarm of Khali to emerge from the darkness and end his life. Lightning lit up the sky once more, and Trystan cringed in fear. The courtyard was alight, if for only a heartbeat. Blackened corpses littered the ground, smoke rising from their smoldering remains. The stench of burning flesh filled his nostrils, as if the sight of the bodies gave him his sense of smell back. Where the barrels were, there was nothing but scorched ground with random pockets of flame despite the driving rain. The wall was nonexistent, the blocks of stone strewn all over the ground.

He stood there for several moments, a look of complete bewilderment upon his face. Leon entered his line of sight and saw for the first time he was trying to say something to him. Trystan merely stood there, not hearing a word the prince was saying. Leon gave him a worried look and then repeated his words, his movements more forceful this time. Sound came rushing back to Trystan all at once as Leon repeated himself a third time, screaming now.

"Trystan, we need to get the fuck out of here!"

Brushing past him, Trystan stumbled forward to see what happened to Kaleb. The noble was now standing, his back to him, completely oblivious to everything around him. Trystan grabbed the stunned man's arm, turning him around. He looked completely unaffected by the explosion or the shockwave that took place afterward. Kaleb's expression was blank, his face still a pale white. If what Trystan believed just happened then Kaleb had just controlled the weather. Something which was impossible. Something that had not occurred since the Verillions were wiped out nearly a millennium ago. Kaleb just performed magic. The mere thought of it was terrifying.

There were so many questions to be asked, but the sound of shouting from the darkness beyond cut through Trystan's gnawing curiosity. "Are you all right now, Kaleb?"

Kaleb's response was a slow nod of the head, his eyes and face still blank and devoid of emotion. He seemed utterly detached, a different person altogether. Trystan highly doubted it but had no choice at that point. It was only a matter of time before the Khali remembered why the alarm had been rung. Leaving Kaleb where he stood, he moved to his fallen sword and sheathed it. Glancing toward Leon, he saw the prince staring intently at Kaleb. He had also seen Kaleb point at the barrels before they exploded in the fire. Hiding in the shadows and up against the wall, Leon escaped the worst of the aftershock, but even still, he witnessed the same thing Trystan did.

"Let's go," commanded Trystan.

They turned and moved beneath the portcullis gate to the plains beyond. Trystan constantly glanced over his shoulder every time lightning lit up the sky, expecting to see arrows flying from the ramparts. Looking at Leon, he saw that the prince was close to the end of his strength, his face strained with exertion. Then he looked at Kaleb and saw his eyes were still devoid of emotion. They weren't even out of range of the Khali's bows, yet they would have to stop soon to rest. Even as he thought it, Leon staggered to his knees, crying out in pain as the force of the landing jarred his empty eye socket.

Trystan helped him to his feet, throwing his arm around his shoulder to support him. The sound of approaching horses forced Trystan to stop. Releasing Leon, he drew his sword and waited. Jaxon and Gavin came galloping out of the darkness, leading the horses. Trystan didn't waste a moment's time. Sheathing his sword, he helped Leon into his saddle. Kaleb went to his horse without a word. Trystan vaulted into his saddle as Jaxon leaned forward.

"You mind explaining what happened in there?" yelled Jaxon over the storm.

An arrow flew in between them. Trystan's horse reared in panic. Looking toward the ramparts, he saw a sentry pointing forcefully in their direction. Other archers could be seen moving into place.

"We will talk more once we are out of harm's way," Trystan yelled back, steering his horse toward the safety of the woods. Kicking the stallion into a gallop, he sped across the plain. The others followed his lead as arrows sailed harmlessly by them.

The rain was finally letting up when they entered the sanctuary of the pine trees. Trystan shivered as a fat raindrop dripped from the branches overhead, falling directly on the top of his head. A dense fog settled upon the land as the group reined in their horses, standing in a tight circle.

"So what happened back there?" Jaxon repeated. "I was waiting for the signal when the bell began ringing. I gathered the reins of the horses and moved with haste toward the fort believing the lot of you were in trouble when a tremor struck me. Then I saw fire rise from within the walls like I have never seen fire before. It was all I could do to keep the horses from panicking. Hell's teeth, it was all I could do from not panicking, myself. That was when I saw Gavin stumbling around. So I picked him up, and thankfully for you lads, Gavin caught a glimpse of the three of you when lightning struck." Jaxon shook his head. "What happened?" he asked again.

Trystan saw that Leon was staring at Kaleb once more. The Prince began to say something when Trystan cut him off. "It was a miracle, nothing more. A sentry upon the walls spotted us, and I was certain we were doomed. Then the gods themselves released a bolt of lightning from the heavens to save us. It exploded in the midst of barrels containing some kind of powder I have never seen before. We were certainly blessed."

Kaleb looked up and Trystan saw a look of pure relief in his eyes. Then pain caused his face to spasm, and he looked away. Jaxon was inspecting Trystan closely. He knew when his friend was lying, and now was one of those times. The distant tolling of a bell echoed through the fog. The search was on.

"Maybe we should count our blessings and get back to the mill," prompted Gavin.

They needed no more motivation and thundered through the trees to the Memure River. The horses were tiring fast as they approached the mill. Light clouds still hung in the sky as dawn heralded the beginning of a new day. Trystan felt bone weary as Kole emerged from the mill. He went to greet them when his eyes flickered to the horizon behind them. Trystan swiveled in his saddle following Kole's gaze. A large group of Khali riders emerged from the tree line. They were less than a mile away.

"Kole, mount up," yelled Trystan. "We are leaving."

The warriors urged their mounts forward, pushing the tired animals into the frigid waters of the Memure River. Trystan shivered violently. His clothing had been soaked through the entire night, and his body was not prepared for the coldness once again. The group pushed on into the swirling river. His personal discomforts were forgotten when an arrow splashed not even a foot from him. Turning around, he saw the Khali pounding toward the riverbank. He transferred his gaze forward. They were almost on the other side.

Gavin turned in his saddle with bow in hand. Nocking an arrow, he sighted it on the lead Khali. Releasing the arrow, it took the Khali in the chest at full gallop. He flew from his saddle, impeding the others behind him. Kole and Jaxon's mounts emerged onto the opposite riverbank. Immediately, they dismounted, drew their bows, and provided cover for the others still in the water. Gavin and Kaleb soon followed. Trystan looked around him, searching for Leon. The prince was just behind him bent over in his saddle. His lips were blue, and his mount was snorting heavily from the physical labor of crossing the river. An arrow fell dangerously close to the horse's head. The horse whinnied in fear, tossing its head.

Leon was dislodged from the saddle, slipping into the river. Trystan fully extended his body backward, his hands questing for something of Leon's to grab on to. His fingertips hooked into Leon's goatskin tunic. Then he too was dragged from his saddle. The water closed in on him like a vice, his head falling below the icy water. Leon was deadweight in his hands. Trystan kicked for the surface. Their heads bobbed above the flowing river. Drawing in deep, short breaths, his vision fastened to the shoreline where the others waited. Arrows splashed all around him. He was so damn close. The river pulled him back under once again. Fighting for control, Trystan wrapped both arms around Leon and drove toward the shore with everything he had. They barely moved. Air bubbles escaped from his lungs, and he felt the darkness of the river closing around him. Calming himself, he tried once more and felt his back slam into the riverbed, his head emerging from the water.

He spit water from his mouth as Jaxon hauled his body out from the river, Leon still clutched in his embrace. Jaxon took Leon and placed him down on the bank, ignoring the arrows that fell perilously close around him. He pounded his giant fist onto Leon's chest. The prince's eye flared open. Turning onto his side, his body convulsed as he vomited up water. Jaxon patted his back. Trystan drew himself up and looked to the opposite shore. The Khali's ponies were not nearly powerful enough to attempt the crossing, and they gathered on the other side loosing arrows. Behind the archers, Trystan saw a smaller group of Khali bustling with activity. Realization dawned and a new panic gripped him.

Kole suddenly reeled back, an arrow lodged in his shoulder, his bow falling from his hands. He fell to the ground, his good hand going to his shoulder, grimacing against the pain. Gavin answered by taking the culprit on the other bank in the neck with an arrow of his own. Jaxon went to help their fallen comrade.

"Leave him for now," Trystan shouted. "Mount up. We need to get out of here."

Jaxon fixed Trystan with a cold stare and then helped Kole to his feet. Crying out in pain, Kole mounted. Trystan grabbed the trailing reins of his own mount as the others hastily got into their saddles. As they powered along the riverbank, Trystan gave one last fleeting glance back toward the Khali. He saw smoke rising in puffs from the signal fire they were preparing. They were warning the other Khali that Prince Leon had escaped and were now making a run for Karalis. In Trystan's mind, he recalled the Khali outriders they spotted on the way to the Memure River. Even with their main force fortified at the Memure Bridge, there must have been hundreds of scouts and outriders that were now watching the only road that led to Karalis.

They would never make it.

# CHAPTER EIGHT

Hollow rings hung like halos beneath Trystan's eyes. He could barely keep them open, let alone focus. For three days now, the party caught glimpses of sleep in their saddles, falling blissfully into a pillow of dreams before being awakened back to harsh reality. Each of them was completely exhausted through down to their very souls. The food supply had run out the day before, and Trystan could hear his stomach grumbling in rhythm to the horse's hooves beneath him. He tried to push such discomforts from his mind, but when the gnawing thought of hunger was pushed away, it was replaced by the overpowering need to sleep.

He caught himself just as he was slipping from the saddle. *I must've dozed for a few moments,* he thought drowsily. Shaking his head, he forced himself to focus. Karalis could be seen just on the horizon, the colossal fortress city looking like a children's toy at this distance. *So close yet so far away.* Four times now, they were pursued by Khali outriders, the only thing saving them being Leon's and Gavin's extensive knowledge of the countryside and its terrain. In one of their encounters with the Khali, an arrow scraped past Jaxon's neck, only a hairbreadth away from ending his life. The wound, though shallow, was a reminder of the perils they still faced.

Leon's condition had gradually improved since they escaped the fort, the power of youth spurring his battered body to miraculous feats of healing. The young prince's bruises were becoming a thing of the past, and the angry raw marks around his empty eye socket were beginning to fade. Even Kole sat straighter in his saddle, the bandaged wound at his shoulder beginning to heal. Everyone's wounds were starting to heal. Except for Kaleb.

The young noble's condition had worsened over the past few days. It seemed the moments were rare indeed when he wasn't in a state of delirium. On the second night after the escape, they managed to steal a few hours of sleep among a group of boulders. Kaleb, fast asleep, began muttering in a language no one recognized. The ground beneath their sleeping bodies began to vibrate, the stones and boulders all around them shaking. At first, it was nothing, the ground only lightly vibrating. Then Kaleb's voice became louder, the words turning into a chant. The ground began to shake violently. A herd of deer, also seeking shelter among the rocks, began bolting for safety as soon as the ground shook, their fear of mankind overridden by their need for survival. Jaxon stumbled toward the chanting noble as boulders tumbled around him. Gripping Kaleb's shoulder, he shook him awake. The noble snapped awake, gasping as he did so, his eyes feverish. Immediately, the ground and boulders stopped moving. Kaleb looked around, utter confusion on his face, as the others stood warily by eyeing him. After that incident, everyone took notice to keep their distance from Kaleb. Something was happening to the young noble. And Kaleb was unable to control it.

Exhaustion fell upon Trystan once again. No matter how hard he fought against it, his weariness was overwhelming him. Taking a hand away from the reins, he rubbed at his eyes, yawning as he did so. They were yet to see any sign of the Khali today, and Trystan was becoming increasingly anxious. There was still only one road to Karalis, and no matter how carefully they tread, they would have to step upon that path. The Khali would be waiting for them. With their mounts exhausted near to death, they would never be able to outrun the tribesmen. A confrontation was inevitable.

Gavin broke off from the group and cantered his horse to scout ahead. They might not be able to avoid battle with the Khali, but they could still be prepared. Trystan watched Gavin until he merged with the woods they would have to travel through to get to the Green Ridge Road. Then it was less than half a day's ride to Karalis and safety. Trystan realized the odds of him surviving the ride through the great gates of Karalis were almost nonexistent, but while his body still drew breath, he would never give up hope.

Trystan's gaze flicked to the distant city of Karalis one last time before they blended into the woods. Not for the first time, he wished there was a way to signal the city of their approach. There were still close to two hundred cavalrymen stationed inside the fortress, and their assistance would be greatly appreciated at this moment. However, to signal reinforcements would surely alert the Khali lying in wait for them. Trystan had no doubts the Khali would surround them and slaughter them long before the cavalry from Karalis could ever hope to come to their aid. It was galling, in the extreme, to be within sight of the city, with Prince Leon in tow, yet know they were still doomed to failure.

Trystan's mind drifted, and he imagined the people of Karalis lining the streets, cheering as they walked their mounts triumphantly to the keep. King Markos would await them with arms wide open, heralding Trystan and the others as heroes of Varkuvia for rescuing his heir from the clutches of the Khali. The Order of Acrium would be reinstated with the surviving warriors flocking to Karalis. There they would smite the Khali, sending them back to the Northern Woods with their tails between their legs. Then with the gratitude of one of the Five Kings, Trystan would seek out Lord Drogos and kill him, toppling the Sons of Vikundo in the process. Jaxon would be allowed to return to his farm with Margaret and raise their child in peace.

Jaxon caught Trystan as he began to tumble from the saddle. They were at the edge of the woods, the Green Ridge Road just in sight. Trystan looked around confused. *When did I sleep?* Jaxon, his hand still holding Trystan to the saddle, leaned toward him. "Nap time is over, young princess," said Jaxon. "Gather your senses. We need you, Trys."

Trystan saw the smile Jaxon threw in with his words but also the fear behind his friend's tired eyes. They all knew what was awaiting them up the road. The sounds of the woods washed over him. The soft chirping of birds flittering among the tangled branches above them, the swaying of the trees as a gentle breeze came down from the mountains. He saw a pair of squirrels scampering up the trunk of a mighty pine tree only to be lost from sight among the catacomb of branches. Everything seemed more vibrant, so full of life. *It's funny how one never fully appreciates the miracle of life until their own existence hangs in the balance*, he reflected.

"We will wait until Gavin returns, and see what he has to report," Trystan said, addressing the group. "Everybody relax for the time being."

Everyone dismounted, attempting to act carefree. Despite saying the words, Trystan felt his own unease rising. Anxiety formed a pit in his stomach, alongside the emptiness in his belly. It was impossible to push the impending doom from his mind. He tried, unsuccessfully, to enjoy the beauty of the wildlife around him while he waited. Instead, he found his mind drifting to Arianna and the lingering kiss they shared. They had only spoken a few words to each other, yet Trystan could not help but think of her constantly. Now he would never know what kind of future they might have had.

Gavin's approach was sudden as he emerged from a thick bush to the left. The dark-haired young man looked completely at ease, and Trystan's mood lightened even without the archer saying a word. Nothing ever seemed to faze Gavin, and Trystan wished he could share the same sentiments.

The archer drew rein in the center of his waiting companions. "There are over a hundred Khali waiting to ambush us in a dip on the southern side of the Green Ridge Road. I looked for a way to outflank them, which is what took me so long. I finally found a way, but dust on the horizon heralded the approach of another large group of Khali. Both options will see us cross the enemies' path. I would've recommended we wait in the woods until the cover of darkness and attempt to make a dash for Karalis, but a third group is converging on us from behind. All around us the Khali move to cut off any avenue of escape."

Everyone stood still. Each of them had expected similar news but hoped against hope that they would live to see another day. That hope now vanished into thin air. There was nothing to be said, and everyone hung their heads, defeat hanging from their shoulders like a cloak. Finally, Jaxon stood up like an angry bear.

"So that's it, is it?" he roared. "We are all just going to just sit here and wait for the Khali's blades to end our lives? Well, not me! I will meet my end with ax in hand. The Khali will not find me sitting around like sheep for the slaughter. After all we have been through, all we have done, with Karalis just in sight; I will not allow the thought of defeat to enter my mind. So you can all sit here and wait to be killed if you want, but I will ride out to meet my fate."

"You will not be alone," said Trystan, moving forward. "I will be beside you as I have always been."

Kole also stepped forward. "As will I."

One by one, the others echoed agreement. Even Kaleb agreed though he looked delirious as he decided to ride to his doom. Only Leon remained. Finally, the prince moved to the center of the group. "Each of you risked your lives for me," said the wounded prince. "Regardless of what transpires by the end of this day, I will never forget that. You all have my gratitude and my friendship until the end of my days. As hollow a promise as that sounds, I mean it from the bottom of my heart. I would be honored to ride with you men, one last time."

Trystan joined him at the center, gripping Leon's shoulder. "We will meet our ends, as we lived our lives, defiant in the face of the impossible. Brothers 'til the very end."

"Brothers 'til the very end," echoed the others.

Honing their weapons one last time, everyone moved to their mounts, which were as exhausted as they were. Trystan adjusted the sword belt at his side. Then he drew his hunting knife, checking its edge. It was razor sharp. Sheathing the blade, he cantered his horse to the edge of the woods, awaiting the others. His mouth was dry, the pressure at his bladder insistent, a common occurrence before a fight. *That will pass soon enough*, he thought. One by one, his companions joined him. There was no fear on their faces, only a set determination. Each of them sat straight in their saddles, eyes set. The sound of approaching horses and shouts of the Khali filtered through the woods behind them. Trystan drew his sword, pointing it forward. A beam of sunlight glittered off the blade, making it shine a brilliant gold. The Khali waiting for them on the side of the road would not miss such a sign.

Trystan kicked his horse into a canter, his sword pointing before him like the arrow of a compass, directing him straight toward the awaiting Khali. The others followed his lead. He heard the rasp of metal as each of his comrades drew their weapons. Battle lust washed over Trystan. Spurring his horse into a gallop, he bellowed forth a battle cry. Gavin drew an arrow to his string. At full gallop, he loosed the arrow toward the dip where he knew the Khali were hiding. A cry of outrage echoed in response. The Khali swarmed forth from hiding, armed for battle, riding their war ponies.

Trystan's battle cry was swept aside as a hundred Khali answered in kind. Their hatred washed over him, and he felt fear rise like a storm deep inside of him. There was no way they could overcome such odds. And then he saw it, out of the corner of his eye. The Khali emerged from hiding too early, eager to kill the Varkuvians before them. The angle the Khali were taking opened a hole to the Green Ridge Road. And Karalis.

Thinking quickly, he veered his horse to the right. The others did not react at first. Then they saw it as well. Urging their mounts on, they followed Trystan's lead. The Khali saw the move and redirected their ponies to cut them off. But it was too late. Trystan and the others spurred their mounts on. And then they were past the Khali who screamed their hatred and frustration at their backs.

Trystan's stallion began breathing shallowly beneath him, its flanks glistening with sweat. The mounts were exhausted, close to death. He risked a glance over his shoulder. The distance between the pursuing Khali was increasing. Though exhausted, the Varkuvian horses were outpacing the smaller war ponies of the Khali. But they would not be able to keep it up for long not without killing them. Some minutes later, Trystan's fears came to life.

Kaleb's horse suddenly stumbled, whinnying in fear as its legs gave way underneath. Kaleb was pitched from the saddle, landing hard on the ground. His horse remained on the grass, panting frantically, with eyes wide. Trystan dragged on his reins. The others had not seen Kaleb's plight and were powering on toward Karalis. Kaleb was just coming to his senses, drawing himself to his knees. Trystan gave a longing look the other way toward Karalis and the sanctuary the fortress would provide. The sentries upon the walls would have seen their plight by now and would have alerted the cavalry. All he had to do was turn his mount back toward Karalis, and he would live. Cursing, he urged the stallion toward Kaleb who was still upon his knees staring incongruously at the approaching Khali.

Trystan jumped from the saddle, running toward the downed noble before his feet even touched the ground. A trickle of blood was streaming down Kaleb's forehead, his eyes glued on the charging Khali. The tribesmen, seeing their prey was within reach, urged their ponies on further. Trystan heard their cries of hatred thrown at him.

"Kaleb! Get up! We need to get the fuck out of here!" Trystan tried to keep the fear from his voice.

The noble didn't even react, his eyes still staring forward unblinking. Agony, unlike anything Kaleb ever experienced, erupted inside his head. A thousand needles pricked in and out of his brain. His hands flew to his head, trying desperately to suppress the pain. He screamed, hoping the cry would drown out the anguish that consumed his body. Tears streamed down his face, mingling with the blood. The pain was unbearable.

Trystan looked back to the Khali. Only a hundred paces separated them. He didn't have time for this. "Damn you, Kaleb! Get up, or we both are going to die!" He gripped Kaleb's arm and began dragging him.

Kaleb's hand came away from his head, his teeth gritting against the pain. His fingers lightly touched Trystan's chest. The force of a sledgehammer smashed into Trystan. The air left him in a whoosh as he was hurdled ten feet through the air, landing with bone-jarring force. His hands clutched his chest, and his breathing came in painful rasps. Forcing himself to his knees, his gaze flicked back and forth between Kaleb and the Khali who descended down upon them.

One Khali, bolder than the rest, drew an arrow, aiming it toward Kaleb. He knew from the moment he released it, his aim had been true. A smile crossed his face as he watched the arrow fall toward the defenseless Varkuvian. Kaleb suddenly stopped writhing in pain, his hands slowly falling away from his head as the projectile raced toward his blood-drenched forehead. His eyes snapped open. Trystan's own eye's widened in shock. No longer were Kaleb's pupils black, but instead, they shined like burnished gold while the irises remained a startling blue. An evil grin spread across Kaleb's face, splitting the blood that flowed down from his forehead.

The arrow stopped in midair, the point of the arrowhead landing lightly on Kaleb's brow. With a gesture of his hand, Kaleb turned the arrow in the air, pointing it back toward the Khali. With a flick of his wrist, the arrow sped off faster than the eye could follow right toward the Khali who released it. The Khali's mouth opened in astonishment just as the arrow ripped into the back of his throat. The force of it carried it through the back of the tribesman's neck, plunging it into the chest of the man behind him, propelling him from the saddle.

The Khali were only fifty paces away and closing the gap fast. Many seeing what just happened began releasing arrows at Kaleb. Every one of them veered off as it was about to strike home, bouncing off an invisible shield and hitting the ground harmlessly around him. Kaleb began laughing maniacally. Trystan remained rooted to the spot. The laughter sent a violent shiver up his spine. It was terrifying. Still laughing, Kaleb took his right hand and fully opened it in front of his face. Still kneeling, he smacked the ground before him with his open palm.

The ground shook violently. The Khali's ponies stumbled as the earthquake struck them, pitching several riders from their saddles. Kaleb stopped laughing, his brow furrowing in anger. Bunching his fists, he began pummeling the ground, screaming his fury before him. The landscape began to shift and tremble. The Khali's ponies whinnied in sheer terror. Both riders' and mounts' fears washed over Kaleb. He fed upon it.

The earth split open in the midst of the Khali. The tribesmen, unable to control their mounts, tumbled into the yawning chasm, falling into the depths of the underworld itself. Kaleb was forgotten as the Khali's fear overrode any option but flight. They directed their terrified mounts back toward the seeming sanctuary of the woods. But there was no escape. The earth split once more before the fleeing tribesmen. A roaring wall of fire erupted from the bowels of hell, engulfing the nearest Khali in flames. Flesh, muscle, and tendons were stripped away as the inferno ripped the screaming souls from the tribesmen's bodies. The fiery wall advanced upon the Khali, consuming everything in its path.

A dozen Khali, accepting their fates, vaulted from the saddles of their terrified ponies. Drawing their weapons, they rushed on quivering legs toward Kaleb, ignoring the shifting and shaking land all around and beneath them. Kaleb stopped striking the ground, causing the wall of flames to stall its advance. He looked up toward the feeble tribesmen charging toward him. At last he stood. In full stride, a scarred Khali wound back his arm and threw his dagger at the demon before him. Kaleb let the dagger come. The blade stopped just as the tip was right before his eye. With a shake of his head, the dagger began to dissolve into ash, flowing into the wind. Within moments, the blade was nonexistent.

He allowed the Khali to continue their charge toward him. The tribesmen raised their weapons, determined to kill this monster. The same Khali who'd thrown the dagger jumped in the air only paces away from Kaleb, his sword blade lancing toward the demon's neck. Kaleb raised his hand. The Khali stopped in midair as if he had struck a wall. Air wrapped around him, immobilizing any further movement. The other tribesmen froze in midstride with weapons raised as the same effect constricted them to the spot. Kaleb saw the hatred in the scarred man's eyes before him. He gave an evil grin to the trapped tribesman. And then he allowed the wall of flames to continue advancing.

Trapped though they were, the Khali could feel the approaching heat upon their backs. The tribesmen closest to the back of the group were defenseless as the flames licked at their clothing. Their screams washed over Kaleb. He heard them beg and pray to their god for deliverance. There was no mercy for them. Instead, he watched with a hint of insanity in his eyes as one by one the Khali were consumed by the flames. He halted the flames once more, right behind the scarred Khali. Kaleb stood, unaffected by the sweltering heat all around him. The glow of the fire reflected off of Kaleb's gold-and-blue eyes as he inspected the trapped tribesman, suspended before him.

The scarred Khali was the only survivor left of the hundred men that set out to pursue the Varkuvians. The man was terrified, any thoughts of hatred, long gone. Trystan, still upon the ground, watched as the front of the Khali's breeches darkened as his bladder gave way. Choking sobs ripped from the man. He begged Kaleb to let him live. He promised him anything. He told him he had a wife and children. Kaleb shook his head, and the flames began moving inexorably forward once more. The roaring red flames slowly took on a bright blue hue.

A scream that was more beast than human ripped through the Khali as the blue flames devoured his flesh. Kaleb stood and watched as the Khali's flesh melted away in strips before him. He watched as the helpless man's eyes turned to liquid, spilling down his face. There was no remorse in Kaleb's eyes. No pity. He merely stood and stared at the burning torch that used to be a man. The flames continued to burn long after the Khali's soul fled his body. In midair, before Kaleb's eyes, nothing was left but a blackened skeleton.

Kaleb suddenly faltered. In the blink of an eye, his gold pupils turned back to black. The wall of flames was extinguished in an instant. The yawning chasm that was opened began to slowly close. Nature began to revert back to normalcy. The charred skeleton before Kaleb fell at his feet. Kaleb swayed, looking down upon the remains of the man who tried to end his life. His body turned mechanically toward Trystan who still sat upon the ground. A look of both utter horror and relief at being alive was upon Trystan's face.

"I am redemption," said Kaleb. His eyes rolled into the back of his head. He collapsed to the ground beside the blackened skeleton.

Trystan did not move. He feared his body would not respond even if he tried to. For the longest time, he sat there, staring at Kaleb's unconscious body. He tore his gaze away, his eyes moving of their own accord, witnessing the horrific sight Kaleb just imprinted upon time. Charred bodies of both Khali and horses alike littered the ground. Most of the flesh was stripped away by the roaring flames that brought an end to their lives. He could see the bones of the corpses exposed in the harsh sunlight. The ground was scorched and lifeless. He was too shocked to feel revulsion, too dazed to feel alleviation at being alive. The chasm that dragged so many Khali to their deaths finally closed, belching a cloud of dust and debris into the air.

The dust spread to Trystan, filling his nostrils and stinging his eyes. Coughing, he stood to his feet. He did not bother looking for his horse. What was the point? The stallion would have bolted at the first opportunity. And who could blame him? Trystan wished he could have done the same. He walked over to Kaleb's body, ignoring the blackened corpses spread out before him. He knelt down, feeling for a pulse. The beat beneath his fingers was strong and rhythmic.

Standing once more, Trystan was unsure of what to do. The dust began to thin in the air around him, hanging like a light fog. The sound of approaching horses combined with the muffled sound of armor filtered through the screen of dust surrounding him.

"Trystan?" a voice called. The voice, though muted by the dust, sounded incredibly familiar. Trystan could not place who it belonged to.

"Over here," he shouted back. He waved his arm, hoping the newcomers would see him gesturing.

The shadows of riders upon their mounts entered Trystan's vision. A banner could be seen flapping in the breeze though he could not make it out. A rider emerged from the haze of dust, upon the back of a black stallion some sixteen hands high. He was wearing the armor of Acrium. The visor was down on his winged helmet, shielding his upper face. The dust slowly began to settle as more riders came forth. The black banner he could not make whipped around in the wind. It had the five interlocking silver circles of the Order of Acrium upon it. There were over fifty riders, and each one of them wore the armor of Acrium.

The first rider that emerged raised his visor. Trystan's heart lifted, recognizing the deep violet eyes.

"Always playing the part of hero, I see," said Layne, the Master of Sword, with just the tiniest of smirks upon his face.

"I had a fine teacher once who told me, 'You do not play the part of hero, you live it,'" responded Trystan with a wide smile.

Layne dismounted, handing the reins to the warrior beside him. Walking over, he gripped Trystan's wrist in the warrior fashion. "It is good to see you still remember some of my teachings. I hope they helped you in these trying times."

"Without your guidance, I would not have survived this long," said Trystan, his face solemn. "I owe you my life, Master Layne."

Patting his pupil's shoulder, Layne looked beyond him at the carnage. His eyes dropped to Kaleb who was still unconscious upon the ground. His gaze met Trystan's. "We have a bit of talking to do, I believe."

"That we do," Trystan agreed.

A tall rider came forth, holding the reins of a horse. It was Trystan's stallion. The rider raised his visor. Trystan smiled once more as he saw the freckled face. With a shock of red hair, Owen was six and a half feet tall and stick thin. Freckles dotted his face without a single strand of facial hair. Despite his appearance, Owen was one of the finest archers amongst the ranks of the Order of Acrium. The only peer said to be his better was Gavin, and that depended on whose opinion was being given. If it wasn't for the armor of Acrium, Owen would look anything but a warrior. However, wearing the armor, he sat straighter in his saddle, his light blue eyes, normally friendly, containing a hint of winter.

He handed Trystan the reins of his stallion. Trystan mounted smoothly. "It is a pleasant surprise to see you once again, Owen," he said.

Owen smiled, the freckles upon his face bunching close together. "The sentiments are reciprocated, Trystan."

One by one, the riders surrounding Trystan raised their visors. He knew each of them by name. Allyn, skilled with the spear and born in a small village in the lands of King Stefanos. Domenic, born in the same village and skilled with both sword and dagger. Bailey, whose favorite weapon was the Morningstar, a spiked mace. Kevan, an expert at throwing knives. Giles, skilled in all weapons but master of none. So many names washed over Trystan as he scanned each and every face. A sense of pride filled him. These were the finest fighting men in all of Varkuvia. He felt privileged to be in such company once again.

A wagon skirted around the riders, going straight to where Layne stood next to Kaleb. At Layne's command, Kevan and Bailey dismounted. Bringing a stretcher made of ox hides over to Kaleb's unconscious body, they gently lifted the body onto the stretcher. Then they carried Kaleb to the rear of the wagon where they carefully placed him down. The driver of the wagon snapped on the reins. The wagon lurched forward as it rumbled back toward the city. Layne vaulted back into his saddle and drew rein beside Trystan.

"We should start heading back. It's only a matter of time before the Khali grow bold enough to try an attack again." Layne held up his hand. "We're moving out," he yelled.

The warriors dropped their visors back into place in unison. The effect was chilling. They fell smoothly into disciplined ranks, their horses marching back to the gates of Karalis. Layne rode ahead of the main group, so he could talk in private with his former student. Trystan fell in beside him.

"How is it there are so many of you here?" asked Trystan. "There's no way my arrival in Karalis already reached so many ears. It's barely been a week."

Layne removed his helmet, placing it on the bridle of his saddle. His long dark hair was held in place by a leather strip. A light wind blew, ruffling his hair. "We have been here the whole time, Trystan. When the Order was disbanded, there were many of us who knew no other place in this world other than being a soldier. No king of Varkuvia would hire a disgraced member into the ranks of their army, so we have remained in Karalis. Underground and out of sight. At first, there were only fifteen of us. Then Owen arrived at the house all of us were staying. He was bloodied and mortally wounded, telling us of an assassination attempt on his life. That was when we learned of the Brotherhood attacks. I had no way of knowing how many warriors already lost their lives to the assassins working in the shadows, so I sent a message to all the realms of Varkuvia, telling any member seeking refuge they should make their way to Karalis. What you see here are those who answered the call. I requested several times to have an audience with King Markos and discuss matters with him. He refused, every single time. The affairs of the Order of Acrium were no longer his concern, it seemed. That was until his own life and that of his family were put in jeopardy."

Trystan was surprised by the news. "You were in Karalis when the others and I arrived? Why didn't you come forward? We could have used a Master of the Order to speak for us. To lead us."

"My intentions were just that," replied Layne. "Word reached Karalis of the bandit attack at Fursta and your triumph there long before you arrived. The city was divided when they discovered you and the others were making their way to the city. One-half wanted you imprisoned while the other half wanted to receive you back into their warm embraces. With the invasion under way, the men were unsure of what kind of reception a large force of disbanded members might receive. They were scared that if we went forth, King Markos would have us executed or at the very least imprisoned. By the time I talked them into seeking an audience with the king, you had already left the city. Nobody would tell us where you were except to say it was a vital mission. So we reluctantly sat and waited. Then the sentries upon wall one sounded the approach of riders. I reacted immediately, rousing the men, expecting us to ride forth with the Karalis cavalry to give you a proper escort. Yet when I arrived at the gate, all of King Markos's troops were upon the wall, looking toward the horizon. Moving alongside them, I watched from above as the land opened and fire blew forth from the bowels of the underworld to decimate the Khali. The Karalis cavalry was terrified and refused to leave the city. So I took it upon myself to lead the men under my command to come to your assistance." Layne glanced over his shoulder, making sure they were alone. "What happened back there?"

"I can honestly tell you I have no idea, Master Layne," said Trystan, running his hand through his hair. "One day Kaleb just started acting…strangely. At first, he just seemed overly tired and became easily irritated. And then, he slowly began to change. When we rescued Prince Leon, we were spotted by a sentry. I thought for sure we were doomed, but then Kaleb muttered a single word, and a bolt of lightning flew from the heavens to smite the Khali. Just now, it was as if a different person all together was controlling Kaleb. He was always arrogant, a trait common in most nobles, but he was never cruel. Yet he tortured defenseless Khali, reveling in the fear he showed. Even his eyes changed color."

Layne started at that. "What color did they change?"

"Only the pupils changed gold. The rest of the eye remained blue."

Layne looked off toward the wagon in front of him, carrying Kaleb, as it passed beneath the first gate of Karalis. His face was scrunched in deep thought. "You must not tell anyone what you saw. If what you just say is true, then Kaleb is the descendent of a Verillion *razeem*." Trystan gave him a quizzical look. "A sorcerer. The pupils confirm it. Kaleb would be considered a second-tier *razeem* since only the pupils turned gold. Only the strongest and most powerful of Verillions would have the full eye turn pure gold. Granted, the Verillions of old never used their powers with such destructive purpose. They were a peaceful people and would only use magic to benefit their communities. Because Kaleb had no training, his soul should have been burnt to ash by the raw, uncontrolled power surging through him. The fact he is still alive is nothing short of a miracle. Such power has not emerged in these realms since the Verillions themselves were exterminated over eight hundred years ago." Layne watched the wagon disappear from sight. "Kaleb's body must've fallen into a coma as a defense mechanism after using such unbridled power. It is the only reason he is still connected to this world. I fear, without someone to guide him and help him control these powers, he will not survive long once he awakens from the coma. The last man capable of helping him died around the same time the Verillion genocide took place."

Trystan gave Layne a questioning look. "If all this knowledge disappeared from this world centuries ago, how is it you know so much about the subject?"

"Years ago, before you were born, and after distinguishing myself in a battle against the Argarians, I was told I may have Verillion blood. As you might imagine, I was curious and visited the Great Library at the Fortress of the Van. For months, I spent all my free time sifting through old tomes that were dusty and forgotten. Some were in languages that disappeared from Varkuvia centuries ago. Others stated myths so outrageous, I could hardly believe they were even written. After thoroughly searching, I finally found several pages divulging the information I just shared with you. One section in particular focused on swordsmen who were descendants of the Verillions. It was said such a swordsman's pupils would reshape into the semblance of a cross. Their aging process also slowed, considerably more than that of a Varkuvian." He looked at Trystan. "How old would you say I am?"

The younger man thought his answer over. "Not a day passed forty."

"I am fifty-one, Trystan. Yet my reflexes are still the same as when I was in my early twenties. I can still march for an entire day or fight all afternoon if need be. And I have but a thimble's worth of Verillion blood in me. What Kaleb just displayed was a hundred times stronger than anything I will ever possess. If he were to learn to control what is raging inside of him and harness it, he would become not only the most powerful person in Varkuvia but in the entire world."

Trystan's mind was too tired to process such a thought. Giving the Kaleb he knew during their time together in the Order such power might not be problematic. But Trystan saw a new side of Kaleb unleashed. That Kaleb was merciless and reveled in the torment of others. Nobody would be able to stand against that side of Kaleb.

"What news of the war?" he asked, trying to change the subject.

Layne sighed. "The Argarians have pushed deeper into the Wood Realm. Now that they have a foothold, they are shipping in more supplies and more men. There have only been minor battles and skirmishes so far. King Ragnar will not commit his forces to a pitched battle against the Varkuvian armies. Instead, his men use hit-and-run tactics, severing Varkuvian supply lines or striking at the rear column of an advancing army before melting away. The only good news is that the Haraliam Wall in the north of King Markos's realm still holds. The Khali up there have only been attacking halfheartedly as if they are waiting for something."

"What of the other kings? Have King Lucan and King Alaric pledged their forces to the cause?"

"King Alaric's army arrived just the other day with the king himself leading the relief force. Two thousand infantry, well equipped, though poorly trained I am afraid. King Alaric has never been a military man. King Lucan, it seems, still remains in his lands, despite the growing concerns in his neighboring king's realms. It is rumored that Kaleb's father, Lord Rickart, is furious at his liege's decision and is railing upon him to come to our aid. For the time being, we have close to six thousand trained infantry, five hundred archers, two hundred cavalry, and two thousand conscripted militia, consisting mostly of farmers.

"Nearly nine thousand well-trained Varkuvian soldiers, manning one of the greatest fortresses in the known world and ranged against them will be a horde of ill-trained, poorly disciplined tribesmen who, despite giving themselves unity with the name Khali, are still a broken people consisting of multiple cultures and beliefs. I do not want to sound overly optimistic for fear of offending the gods, but I think our chances of winning this war are still quite good."

Momentary anger flashed in Layne's eyes. "Spoken like a true Varkuvian." He quickly looked around. "What I am about to tell you must not be repeated to anyone else. I need you to promise me." Trystan nodded. "Say it aloud."

"I promise, Master Layne."

The master took a deep breath. "I take it by now you have heard of this Khali leader, the one everyone calls Grand Chieftain Timon?" He sighed. "He is really Master Mason."

Trystan gave an incredulous look. "Master Mason? As in the Master of Spear, once a leader of the Order of Acrium? I cannot believe such a thing."

"Believe it, Trystan. When the masters of the Order went to Karalis to petition the disbandment, they were imprisoned moments after they were heard. All they wanted was an audience with the Five Kings, to reason with them and reconsider their decision. Instead, they were treated worse than scum. Then they were banished, never to set foot on Varkuvian soil while their bodies still drew breath. Master Roderic died within a month of the banishment, his heart and spirit broken by the loss of the only thing he held dear in his entire life. That was when the other masters took over the mantle of leadership in the

Northern Woods. Who better to tame the wild, volatile spirit of the tribesmen than the greatest living military instructors this world has to offer? Have you not thought it strange that the Khali have been deploying tactics they have never used before? Within a six-month span, the masters have molded a savage, warlike people into a cohesive nation able to make King Markos himself tremble."

The news was frightening. There had always been five masters in the Order to reflect the five kings. Master Roderic died of a broken heart, and Master Layne rode beside Trystan. That still left Mason, Master of Spear; Petros, Master of Bow; and Orrin, Master of Ax. The thought of such men leading the Khali was terrifying.

"We must tell King Markos of such news."

"Have you lost your senses? If Markos were to discover such a thing, he would execute all of us regardless of the fact you saved the heir to his throne. Do you truly believe a king of Varkuvia would allow any of us to live if he were to find out that the exiled masters of the Order were the ones leading the Khali? Use your head, Trystan. You would condemn us all to death."

A sudden thought occurred to Trystan. "Why didn't you join the other masters in leading the Khali? Next to Master Roderic, you were considered the most respected master. With you leading them, disbanded warriors of the Order would have come from all over Varkuvia to join you."

Layne looked away. "I spent most of my life defending these lands, Trystan. Men such as Master Roderic, and Master Aeolos before him, instilled upon me the codes I lived my adult life by. I would not only sully their names by working toward destroying everything they, and every member of the Order of Acrium who came before them, fought for. If I had been banished along with the other masters, my outlook would most likely be different. The very thought shames me."

"You are an honorable man, Master Layne. There should be no reason for you to feel any shame. I, for one, thank the gods you are here."

"You must not call me Master Layne anymore," Layne said with an edge of sadness. "That is a title I no longer have the privilege of being called. Now, I am simply Layne, an old mentor and friend." The open gate of Karalis loomed before them. "We will talk again later. For now, you and the others who rescued Leon are the toast of the city. I saw children play fighting in the marketplace just the other day with wooden sticks. They were arguing over which of them got to be Trystan of the Blade." He chuckled at Trystan's discomfort. "You have become a figure to be emulated and looked up to. Such a burden has always been your destiny. Let's go show the people of Karalis their hero."

# CHAPTER NINE

King Markos stood upon his balcony, which overlooked the city of Karalis below him. He wore a simple crown of gold. No gems or other fineries decorated the symbol of his sovereignty. A gray keep, the symbol of his house, was expertly stitched into the center of the finely woven blue cloak fringed with gold clasped at his shoulders. From his high vantage point, he could see the streets of Karalis choked with his subjects. The cheers of his people reached his ears upon the winds. Markos leaned forward, gripping the marble rail of the balcony, listening to the celebrations.

Verlos, the head of the Stone Guards, politely stepped onto the balcony behind the king, his helmet cradled in the nook of his arm. "Your Majesty," said the guard, "Trystan and the others approach."

"I am not senile, Verlos," responded the king. "I can hear my people's jubilation at their return. After I see Leon, I want Trystan brought in. I wish to speak to him privately."

The royal guard shifted his feet nervously. "My king, is such a thing seemly? He is nothing more than a peasant."

"I will decide what is seemly," said Markos, his gaze still glued to the streets of Karalis. "Trystan rescued the heir to my throne and has proven himself more than worthy of my time. He is now admired by the populace, both noble and commoner alike. I would rather have such a figure as an ally instead of an enemy. That is the end of the matter. Send Leon to me as soon as he arrives at the keep. I wish to see my son once more."

"Your will is my bidding," said Verlos. He bowe, and then exited the balcony.

Markos heard the door leading to his bedchambers click shut as Verlos exited, leaving the King to his own troubled thoughts. His gaze swept over the city of Karalis below him, moving to the landscape beyond. There the enemy waited while he sat in the comforts of his keep. Their approach was as evident as the coming of summer, and he was defenseless to prevent it. There was a power shift coming to these realms, and he feared the Five Kings would no longer be preeminent. The world was changing; it was in the very air around him.

The king's thoughts were somber, and he felt his mood falling toward depression. An anonymous letter arrived the same day as King Alaric and his army. The contents were short and to the point, the words themselves, written in blood. His reign would soon end. It was simply signed, SV. He wondered whose blood was used to write the letter and thought it merely to be a scare tactic. Later that day, he received a package containing the severed head of one of his Stone Guards. The incident was withheld from the populace, but he could not conceal the murder from his guards and soldiers. Markos could see the fear in their eyes. All of their thoughts were the same. Which of them would be next? The fear amongst his fighting men was palpable.

Every precaution possible was taken to prevent an attempt on Markos's life, but he still could not shake the feeling of dread that hung over his head like a pale shadow. He awakened in the dead of night in the midst of a dreadful nightmare in which an assassin's knife stabbed him to death. The dream was so lifelike that he felt for the wounds on his sweat-drenched body. He finally calmed down and went back to sleep. The dream plagued him once again. Markos was beginning to feel paranoid, and he no longer felt safe leaving the confines of his bedchambers. His paranoia was the only reason he was not greeting his son in front of the keep as originally planned.

The door opened quietly behind him. He turned to see his wife, Queen Lorain, enter their bedchambers. His spirits lifted merely from seeing her. Twenty years of marriage and the sight of her still made his heartbeat quicken. Despite being in her midforties, Lorain was still exceptionally beautiful. Her golden hair hung in curls past her shoulders, and her sparkling blue eyes were still as full of life as when they first met. She wore a gown of shimmering white and held herself like the queen she was. Markos moved to his wife, drawing her tightly into his embrace.

"Our son has returned to us, my queen," Markos said gently, stroking her back.

"It seems the gods have finally answered my countless prayers." Lorain's voice was strong, a woman's voice accustomed to others obeying her command.

Markos held his wife even tighter. Lorain spent almost every waking moment in the Temple of Crassos, the Divine Ruler of the Heavens, praying for the safe return of their son. The people of the city loved the queen for her kind nature and thus joined her in prayer. Day and night since the invasion of the Stone Realm, their subjects filled the temple, praying for Leon's deliverance from the hands of the foul Khali. The majority of the people believed that deliverance came in the form of Trystan. The young warrior was something close to a demigod amongst the commoners and a force to be reckoned with among the nobles.

"If only the gods would answer our other prayers," said the king. "Our people are suffering Lorain while our enemies grow stronger by the day. In the twenty years of my reign, I have never felt helpless. Until now."

Lorain looked up. She took her arms from around his waist, cupped her husband's chin in her soft hands, and looked into his gray eyes. "You are the finest man I have ever known, Markos. You have always put the needs of your own people before your personal desires. Since the beginning of your reign, you have constructed universities and built roads and hospitals, making life easier for the common people. You increased the city watch in the poorer districts of Karalis so your people could sleep more soundly at night. Many of your fellow kings and lords under your command criticized you for educating men below your station and protecting those considered too weak to defend themselves. Regardless, the people love you for it. They would die for you, Markos."

The king leaned forward, kissing his wife deeply upon the lips. He let the kiss linger for several heartbeats before pulling away. "I do not know what I did to deserve you in this life," said Markos while gently stroking her cheek. "But I thank the gods every single day that I have you in my life. Without you, I would be lost."

"I will always be by your side," promised Lorain. She leaned forward on the tips of her toes, kissing her husband once more.

A polite knocking came at the door. "Come in," commanded Markos.

Verlos opened the door, holding it open as Prince Leon entered. Markos's eyes narrowed when he saw the bandage around his son's empty eye socket. Lorain cried out, running to Leon. "Oh, my son, what have they done to you?" she asked, tears brimming her eyes.

Leon kissed his mother on the cheek, drawing her away from him. "I am alive, Mother. That is all that matters."

Lorain brushed the tears away. Markos stepped forward. "Father," Leon said, dipping his head.

"Enough of those formalities." The king embraced his son warmly. "I cannot tell you how good it is to see you. I feared for the worst."

"As did I, Father. Trystan, along with the others, truly proved to be men of worth."

The door suddenly swung open as Vasilis all but ran into the room. He stopped in midstride when he saw Leon. A smile split his handsome face. "Praise the gods above and below. The rumors are true."

Brother embraced brother in a warm hug. "It is good to see you, little brother," Leon said, thumping his sibling on the back. "I hope you haven't been getting into too much trouble without me."

Vasilis laughed good-heartedly. Lorain and Markos moved forward, and they enjoyed the moment as a family. Emotions threatened to overwhelm Markos. "This is the most important thing we have in life," he said. "Family over everything. I hope you remember everything your mother and I taught you, boys. One day we will not be here to guide you."

"We will not let you down, Father," guaranteed Leon. "What do you plan to do about the Khali?"

The king stepped back, thrown off by the question. "We have no choice but to wait, Leon. Our resources are spread thinner than you could possibly imagine. As long as the Argarians push deeper into King Eryk's realm, we cannot move against the Khali."

Anger flashed in Leon's gray eye. "Not moments ago you spoke of family coming first. Look at what those bastards did to me." He pointed to his ruined socket. "By the right of blood, I demand retribution."

"And you shall have it," said Markos, calmly, alarmed by the sudden change that took over the room. "But we must wait until all of our forces are gathered or face ruin ourselves."

"These savages stand no chance against a disciplined Varkuvian army," Leon responded arrogantly. "With the addition of King Alaric's forces, we can drive them back, Father. We must ride out to meet them."

"The last time I checked, I was the king," Markos said, suppressing his building anger. "I will not gamble my entire kingdom on the outcome of one decisive battle. The decision is already made."

"Then you are a coward," snapped Leon. "If you do not possess the courage to lead the charge, then I will."

"You forget your place!" the king roared. "I am the king, and you are the prince. You will take your orders from me, not the other way around. These are my soldiers, and they will obey my commands, not yours!"

Leon bunched up his shoulders, drawing himself upright. The look of thunder was in his eye. Lorain stepped in between the arguing father and son. "Come now," she said sweetly. "This is ridiculous. Leon and Vasilis, return to your rooms. It has obviously been a trying day." She stepped into Leon, kissing her son upon the cheek. Some of the fire went out of his eye. "It is good to have you home, my son."

Leon gave his father one final cold stare then spun on his heels to stalk out of the room. Vasilis shrugged his shoulders and then followed his older brother. After the door closed, Markos threw his crown across the room. It clattered against the wall before bouncing off the floor. He brusquely sat down upon the bed.

"The Khali took more than his eye," he said. "Vengeance rages inside of him like a winter storm, cold and deadly. It clouds any reason other than seeing the Khali wiped off the face of this world."

Lorain sat down beside her husband. "He has been through an awful ordeal, Markos. Maybe he just needs time to heal."

The king shook his head. "Did you not see the rage burning from him? He is a different man all together. And when has he ever raised his voice toward me in such a manner? I feel as though I have lost a son rather than gained one back." His voice was thick with gloom.

Before Lorain could say something to cheer her husband up, a knock came at the door. Markos's thoughts were elsewhere, and he did not respond. "Come in," Lorain shouted.

Verlos opened the door. "Trystan awaits your audience as requested, Your Majesty," the guard said, addressing Markos.

Lorain stood then Markos lightly gripped her arm. He took her hand in his, gently rubbing the back of it. "I love you, Lorain." He looked up into her blue eyes. "Let me speak to Trystan alone. We will talk more later." Markos looked around his wife. "Bring him in, Verlos."

"I love you too, my husband," said Lorain before moving toward the open doorway.

The queen stopped as Trystan entered the room. "So you are the one the city is buzzing about?" she asked sweetly. "You have my eternal gratitude for bringing my son safely back to me." As a sign of respect, the queen of Karalis slightly dipped her head toward Trystan. Then she left the room.

Verlos closed the door once more, leaving King Markos and Trystan alone. The young man dropped to one knee, bowing his head as Markos rose. "That is unnecessary, young Trystan," the king said. "Rise."

Trystan stood up as Markos moved closer to the young warrior. Trystan's eyes were sunken into his skull, his cheeks hollow. His skin, normally glowing with the power of youth, seemed drained. It looked like he could barely keep his eyes open. Markos also noted the travel-stained clothing he wore.

"You look dreadful," Markos said with a smile.

"It has been a tough journey, Your Majesty," responded Trystan with a tired smile. "It seems everything has changed since you first asked me to bring your son safely back to you."

"The world does seem to have changed," agreed Markos. "Please take a seat." He gestured to a table surrounded by cushioned chairs set against the wall. "You look all in."

Moving to one of the chairs, Trystan sank into it with a groan. "I did not think a chair could possibly feel so divine."

Chuckling, the king drew a seat opposite the swordsman. "You are quite the mystery, young Trystan. Everything I heard about you says that you were a shy and solitary man while a part of the Order of Acrium. You turned down positions of advancement and few knew little to nothing about you. Yet you have displayed acts of extreme heroism with both my son and Kaleb. The men you led from this city would now follow you into the depths of the underworld itself. They would do this not because you would command such a thing but because they see you as a brother and would willingly die for you. Even Leon, a prince destined to rule, speaks of you with reverence. So I ask you this, what is it that you desire?"

The younger man shifted uncomfortably. It was obvious such compliments left him uneasy. "My desires have not changed, Your Majesty. I merely wish for a place where disbanded warriors of the Order of Acrium can assemble peacefully. Then with your permission, after the Khali have been pushed back from the Stone Realm, I would have words with this Lord Drogos."

"Even as we speak, my scribes are writing the documents that will see the Order of Acrium reinstated," said the king, leaning back in his chair. "King Alaric himself gave his blessing at my decision. Such times call for drastic measures, it would seem. However, they will only be allowed to operate under my jurisdiction and will still fall under my laws and rules. I will not have anarchy reign in my lands. As for Lord Drogos, with recent events, I would gladly allow such a thing. Both of these things I have already promised were you to bring Leon safely back to me. My people and myself believe you deserve more. Is there nothing else I can give you? Lands? Titles? Wealth? Women? I could make you a lord in my lands, Trystan. All you have to do is voice your desires aloud, and I will see them brought to life."

He saw the prospect of such rewards piqued Trystan's interest. Who wouldn't be interested in such riches? Trystan lived half of his life in squalor and the other half training day in and day out to become the perfect warrior. How couldn't the prospect of a life of luxury sound appealing?

After several moments, Trystan looked up to meet the King's powerful gaze. "With respect, Your Majesty, I must decline. I would serve you better as a soldier, than as a lord. It is all that I know."

"You are an honorable man, Trystan," replied Markos, keeping the shock from his face. Who could refuse such an offer? "If you ever wish to claim it, then my offer stands. I want you to know you will always have my gratitude for what you have done."

Trystan chuckled. "Did I say something amusing?" asked a confused Markos.

"I had a teacher once who told me there are only two things that are certain when dealing with a king: their enmity will last a lifetime and their gratitude will last a heartbeat."

"Even still," Markos said, trying to keep the anger from his voice. *What is this world coming to when a peasant can speak to a king in such a way?* He kept his opinion to himself. "My offer remains."

An intrusive knocking came at the door. Markos's irritation flared. "Who is it?" he demanded.

Without so much as an answer, the door swung open. A messenger entered, appearing flustered. The messenger, a short man with a round honest face, looked extremely ill at ease. "My apologies, my king," he stuttered. "But an urgent message just arrived from wall one."

"Well, what is it?" Markos snapped, his impatience growing.

The man swallowed hard, his jutting Adam's apple rising and falling. "The enemy is advancing upon the city. The captain of the guard upon wall one reports they will be fully assembled in front of Karalis by dawn tomorrow." The messenger hesitated.

Tension rose in Markos's throat. "And?" he prompted.

The messenger swallowed once more, wiping his sweaty palms upon the front of his tunic. "It is not just the Khali, Your Majesty," he blurted. "The eastern lords ride with them as well. There are tens of thousands of them, filling the valley itself."

King Markos rose abruptly, scattering his chair to the floor. "This cannot be!" he exclaimed, utter disbelief in his voice.

"The captain saw Lord Randell's banner himself, the rearing golden horse with white clouds behind it. He also spotted the banner of Lord Drogos, the three-headed serpent. He did not see the banners of the other eastern lords, but he says if one of them is here, they are all here."

Markos stood rooted to the spot, his eyes shifting uncontrollably. Ignoring the messenger, he moved back outside to the balcony, looking to the horizon beyond. A black mass could be seen moving slowly toward the city like a never-ending shadow of death. The dust from the approaching army reached up to challenge the heavens.

"It all makes sense now," Trystan said, moving alongside Markos. The king had not even heard his approach.

"What are you talking about?" responded the king, his mind full of rattling thoughts.

"The eastern lords planned this from the beginning. They knew when the Argarians invaded the Wood Realm, you would send men to King Eryk's aid. With a majority of your forces committed to fighting the Argarians, the Khali invaded. Without the manpower, you had no choice but to let them advance into your lands. King Lucan refused to come to your aid because he thought you were only dealing with tribesmen. If he knew the eastern lords joined their forces with the Khali, he would have had no choice but to rush to your side. Their combined forces would have been a threat to all of the realms of Varkuvia. Everyone wondered why the Khali were waiting at the Memure Bridge and not advancing upon Karalis. Now we know. They were waiting for the eastern lords to arrive." Trystan turned to Markos. "By the time word reaches King Lucan, it will be too late. It would take over a month and a half for his army to reach us. King Stefanos and King Eryk have the Argarian threat to deal with. We are on our own. And there is no way we can hold out."

King Markos did not respond at first. All of the pieces were coming together now. He suddenly remembered a report he received some time ago. "One of my agents thought he spotted Lord Randell in the port city of Sura nearly two months ago. He described him perfectly, down to his fiery red beard, and even mentioned an extravagant stallion he rode. It is well known the eastern lords are not the closest of friends, so I was slightly concerned why he was in Lord Dorian's city. When the eastern lords did not join the Khali's invasion of my lands, I thought the report to be false. Now, I know otherwise. I should have had that treacherous cur killed when he visited Karalis years ago. All of my counselors advised me to do so, but I thought Randell was different. Now it seems I will pay for that mistake."

He turned around sharply, his blue cloak whipping behind him. The messenger still stood by the door, shifting nervously. "You will report back to wall one. Take as many men as you have to with you, but I want to be constantly updated on the enemies' position." He waved his hand, dismissing the messenger. The man turned on his heels and quickly exited the room.

Trystan entered the room from the balcony. Markos gestured for him to sit once more. "You once offered me strategic advice. At the time, I scoffed at the idea. Now I find myself much more receptive. If your advice proves sound, then I want you to attend the war council tonight."

"There are several things we must address," Trystan said, leaning forward in his chair. "News of the eastern lords' arrival will even now be spoken in every tavern, bakery, and blacksmith. Fear will be spreading like the plague through Karalis. The people need a victory, no matter how small. If the first wave can be repulsed, it will lift the spirits of the fighting men. They need to know they can stand their ground and stare their fears in the face. You will also need to form a reserve force, ready to plug any breeches that open up in the defenses. Right now, the most important thing is morale. All it will take is one man to turn and flee for the rest to follow his lead. The men must be lifted and believe they are fighting against an evil force that will see their brothers, sisters, wives, and children slaughtered. They need to believe they are heroes of Varkuvia and that they alone can shape history. Make them believe this, and they will fight until the last breath leaves their bodies."

The king stood, moving back onto the balcony. "The war council is meeting in three hours. I will have a servant bring you to your rooms. Rest up, and when you are ready, meet us in my study. We have a war to prepare for."

Trystan walked as if he were in a trance behind the shuffling elderly servant. Every soldier and servant he passed along the corridor looked at him as if he were the walking form of Crassos. Their eyes would widen, their jaws drop. Some called out to him, asking him to save them from the doom descending upon the city. They saw before them a king amongst men, a man that could overcome all odds set against him; a man who did not need sleep and feared no living thing. The reality was that Trystan was so tired he felt numb, and his own fears made his limbs weak. No longer could he voice his fears aloud or be seen as Trystan, a mere man. Now he was Trystan of the Blade, and as long as he remained so, the people would keep hope alive in their hearts.

The servant stopped before a thick door. So distracted was Trystan, he nearly collided with the elderly man. "Is there anything I can get you, m'lord?" asked the servant.

Trystan took a deep breath. It was not the first time since reentering the city that he heard someone address him as a lord. Was it such a wild concept that a thief of Calydon City could become a hero? Instead, he was transformed into a lord of Varkuvia, yet no one could say from which of the five realms he hailed. And a powerful one too, if the rumors were believed. He had already learned to ignore it.

"Thank you, but no," he answered. "I just need to get some rest."

The servant bowed before backing away. Trystan shook his head and then entered his new quarters. The room was elaborately furnished.

Stunning paintings hung from the walls, ones Trystan would not have been able to afford in a lifetime of hard labor. He kicked off his riding boots, his feet sinking into the finely woven rug. Moving to the bed, he pulled back the silk sheets. He quickly undressed, got under the covers, and his body melted into the goose down mattress. His last thoughts before he drifted off to sleep were, *So this is how the privileged live?*

A soft knocking reverberated through his dreams. He tried to push it away, but it came again. Groggily, he opened his eyes. Sunlight could still be seen peering through the drapes of the windows. The war council wasn't for another hour. *Why would someone be visiting me now?* The knocking came again. With a muttered curse, he forced himself into a sitting position, blinking sleepily. Pushing himself from the bed, he stumbled toward the door, rubbing grit from his eyes. Opening it, he found himself staring into Arianna's eyes.

She entered the room, bearing a tray of food. Her mouth opened to offer a greeting when her gaze drifted downwards, her eyes widening. Trystan followed her gaze, and only then realized he was still naked. His tiredness was forgotten in an instant. He swiftly shut the door so others would not see his nakedness. Arianna ignored his discomfort and moved into the room, placing the tray down. Trystan hastily put on a pair of pants. Such was his rush that he tripped over a pant leg, falling to the floor. Arianna giggled. Composing himself, Trystan finally pulled up his pants, tying the strings.

Arianna's gaze shifted to him as she set the food down. "The Savior of Karalis embarrassed by a serving woman seeing him naked? I had contemplated placing the food outside the door, for I figured you would have your bed filled with women ready to spread their legs for you."

Trystan cleared his throat, blushing. "I haven't exactly had time for such things. Even if I did, that is not the kind of person I am."

"Is that so? Well, every serving woman in the keep is taking bets on who gets to sleep with *Trystan of the Blade* first." She emphasized the title. "It seems being a hero has it perks."

Even Trystan could not miss the jealousy in her voice. "Why would you care about such a thing?"

"Who said I did?" she retorted.

"It was only a question," he replied, holding up his hands. "You just seem angry is all."

"I believe you are mistaking a hard day's worth of work for petty jealousy. I hold no such feelings toward you. Sleep with whomever you want. I care not."

"I think you are lying," he said with a slight smile.

This time it was Arianna that look flustered. She hurriedly set the remainder of the food down and then picked up the tray. "Well, it was nice seeing you again, Trystan. Each meeting becomes more memorable than the last." She moved briskly to the door, her hand resting on the handle.

"I missed you," Trystan blurted out. Arianna's hand fell away from the handle though she still faced the door. "There were several times when I thought I wasn't going to make it back alive. And whenever that happened, my thoughts turned to you. It was the thought of you that gave me the strength to carry on when all seemed lost. In my hour of desperation, I prayed to the gods that I be given just one more chance to see you, if only for a moment. I don't know what it is I am feeling, but if I had my choice of any woman in all of Varkuvia, I would choose you every time."

Arianna did not react, and Trystan was afraid that he'd made a complete fool of himself. Then she spun around and crossed the room toward him, dropping the empty tray to the carpeted floor. Her arms circled around his neck, drawing him into a deep kiss. Arianna's lips parted, her tongue darting into Trystan's mouth. The kiss was passionate and Trystan drew her closer, pressing her against him. Arousal flowed through his body, stiffening his manhood. Arianna felt it as well, rubbing against the inside of her leg. Her hand dropped down, stroking Trystan through the fabric of his pants. He groaned aloud. She pulled back from kissing him, still rubbing him.

"Does that hurt?" she asked, raising an eyebrow in mock humor.

Despite his rising ardor, Trystan chuckled. "You are a tease, my lady. Someone should teach you a lesson."

She took a step back, her eyebrow still raised. "A lesson, m'lord?" She unhooked her dress, letting it fall to the ground. Trystan's arousal became more intense as he drank in her full breasts, the tautness of her stomach, and the curves of her hips. She was the vision of perfection. "Come teach me then, Savior of Karalis."

He needed no further urging. Dropping his pants to the floor, he drew Arianna toward the silk-covered bed. She lay down upon the bed as Trystan moved on top of her. He guided himself inside of her. Arianna moaned, arching her back. Trystan's primal passion became a roaring flame. He dipped his head, kissing her intensely. Steadily, he increased the rhythm, the sound of flesh on flesh driving him on further. Arianna responded by wrapping her legs around him, drawing him deeper inside of her, her nails digging sharply into his back.

Trystan's passion consumed him. He wanted this moment to last forever. The world outside the bedroom walls melted away. He grabbed ahold of Arianna's shoulders, pounding into her. She screamed out in ecstasy. He covered her mouth with his hand, stifling the sound. She bit at his palm as an orgasm shook her body. Trystan reached his climax at the same time. Groaning in pleasure, he collapsed on top of her, their bodies intertwined, and drenched in sweat.

They lay there for several minutes, panting, unable to move. Finally, Trystan withdrew from her, lying beside her. Arianna snuggled close, resting her head on his chest, her leg draped over his. She was still catching her breath.

"That was…incredible," she managed to say.

He wanted to agree, but words escaped him. There were few instances in his life that left him breathless. This was the single most perfect moment he could recall. He wrapped his arm around Arianna, drawing her close to him. His limbs felt like water. Leaning forward, he kissed the top of her head before collapsing back onto the bed. They laid there for some time, cuddled close. Trystan became aware of Arianna's bare breasts pressed against him, her nipples resting against his side. Arousal stirred once more, and he drew her on top of him.

# CHAPTER TEN

Standing upon the first wall, Jaxon's massive hands gripped the haft of his ax tightly. He stared out upon the ocean of enemies preparing to assault Karalis. He saw the eastern lords riding in front of the first ranks, galvanizing the men. Jaxon looked up to the sky. The sun still had not cleared the mountain peaks to the east. Once it had, it would be in the eyes of the defenders, a clear disadvantage from the start. There was no point in worrying about it now. Soon the fighting would begin and Jaxon relaxed, sitting down with his back against the battlements.

He saw the men around him shifting nervously. They readjusted pieces of armor that had been adjusted a hundred times over. Many of them were honing their weapons that were already razor sharp. He knew each of them was wondering if today would be their last day on this world. Many were the doubts and regrets that would never be rectified. It was hard not to reflect on one's life in the calm before the storm. For Jaxon, his thoughts turned to Margaret. He wondered what she was doing at this exact moment and prayed he would be allowed to hold her in his arms once more.

He found his mind wandering to the previous night when Trystan asked him to accompany him to the war council. At first Trystan was nervous as the lords and generals of Karalis mapped out their plans for the siege. Trystan was no general and had never led men into battle. Jaxon could see it upon his friend's face; he did not know why he was there.

King Alaric was present at the war council. It was the first time Jaxon saw the monarch. He wore the black-and-gold striped insignia with a jeweled crown; on the chest of his tunic was the symbol of his house. King Alaric was in his early fifties and stoop-shouldered. Even with the ruby-studded golden crown upon the ruler's head, Jaxon could still see that Alaric's light hair was receding, giving him a sharp widow's peak. Jaxon looked into the king's soft brown eyes and saw a scholar, not a king. A king's eyes were supposed to be powerful and make a man cower before him. His opinions were mostly useless, and Jaxon saw the generals around the table exchange glances at his suggestions. They were polite enough, not wishing to offend the king, but nevertheless, not heeding his counsel.

Jaxon recalled the words of Orrin, the Master of Ax, years ago during a lecture regarding King Alaric. Orrin said that an army of lions commanded by a deer would never be an army of lions. King Alaric's men were the best-equipped troops in all of Varkuvia, but their king was a coward. Like all armies, the men reflected their leader, and just like King Alaric, his men looked like frightened rabbits. Jaxon had no doubts that once the tide of battle turned sour, King Alaric's men would be the first to turn tail and run.

It wasn't until halfway through the meeting, when Trystan spoke. Jaxon recalled one of the generals speaking though he could not remember the man's name. The only thing he remembered about the general was his beak of a nose, looking more bird than human.

"We should put every man upon wall one," the birdlike general had boasted, his voice haughty. "And show the enemy what it is like to face the might of Varkuvia." Others voiced their agreements.

"Such a move would be an act of sheer stupidity," stated Trystan.

The general was taken aback by the comment. His eyes blazed in anger. "And what would the mighty Trystan of the Blade suggest we do?" he asked with just a hint of derision.

"A force must be kept upon wall two," responded Trystan. "If the enemy breaks through with our entire force mustered upon wall one, they will have a clear path through the streets of Karalis. Then you will see how well discipline remains when the common soldiers know their children, wives, and homes are in jeopardy. There is great killing ground between the first and second wall. That is where the majority of the damage will be dealt to the enemy."

"Are you suggesting that wall one is going to fall?" the general asked, his voice hiding undercurrents of malice.

"The first wall will eventually be taken," answered Trystan. "It is the longest of the three, stretching between the Bale Mountains in the north, and the Amarro Mountains in the south, making it the hardest wall to man. Wall two also stretches in between the mountain ranges but is much shorter and easier to defend. As long as these walls hold, the enemy will be unable to encircle us, forcing them to assault us frontally. Wall three is not protected by the mountains. Instead, it surrounds the Keep of Karalis in a protective ring. If the second wall is to fall, the enemy could surround us and starve us into submission. Then they will burn the homes and businesses of Karalis while we helplessly watch from the wall. The soldiers will lose the will to fight, and all will be lost. At that point, the enemy will have free domain to move into the countryside to the west. Our main priority until reinforcements arrive is to hold the first two walls for as long as possible."

Jaxon looked at the generals and lords under King Markos's rule, expecting to see open scorn upon their faces at being told what to do by an untried commoner who never led a fighting force in his life. Instead, they were all leaning forward intently, hanging upon Trystan's every word. By the end of the meeting, Trystan had each and every one of them in the palm of his hand. A sudden itch at Jaxon's backside dragged his mind back to the present. With the armor of Acrium on, it was impossible to scratch. Cursing, he stood.

He heard booming laughter and looked to see where the sound originated from. Gabriel stood amongst a group of soldiers. He wore the armor of Acrium and was laughing good-heartedly. One look at the man, and one would think he was a stone-cold killer. Black tribal tattoos decorated his face and powerful arms. His head was bald, and he sported a braided forked goatee. He was tall and massively muscled with dark eyes. Gabriel's mother was of Argarian descent, and when she passed from this world, he honored her memory by getting the tattoos, a common tradition among the Argarian people. He wielded a giant sledgehammer with as deadly a purpose as Jaxon did with his ax. And just like Jaxon, he was easily liked. It was one of the main reasons many looked past his Argarian heritage.

A cheer went up to Jaxon's right. He turned to see Trystan walking through the ranks of soldiers, resplendent in the armor of Acrium. He left the winged helmet off, an idea suggested by King Markos. Trystan needed to be seen and raise the hopes and spirits of the men around him. Jaxon left his helmet behind also, for he found it always limited his field of vision in battle. Trystan came before Jaxon, smiling from ear to ear when he saw his friend. Jaxon returned the smile though not entirely from seeing Trystan. The men around them stood straighter, their eyes alert, hoping to impress the hero. Jaxon shook his head.

"What do you think they are saying?" he asked Trystan, gesturing to the eastern lords addressing their men.

"I would imagine it would have something to do with how evil we are," responded Trystan. "They will be symbolizing Karalis as a bastion of corruption, greed, and deceit. And when the city falls, they will install a new leadership and bring peace to these lands. Some bullshit like that."

Jaxon chuckled. "Let all bow before the mighty wisdom of Trystan of the Blade."

He saw Trystan blush. At least fame had not gone to his head, and he was still the same man Jaxon had grown to love as a brother. Blaring war horns sounded across the valley in a wave. All conversation died upon the wall as every soldier turned their attention forward. Both easterner and Khali alike began stamping their feet in unison. Jaxon heard armor rattle around him as the wall itself shook. A surge of hatred erupted from over sixty thousand throats at the same time, washing over the defenders. Jaxon looked at the soldier next to him. All color drained from the man's face, and he was blinking rapidly. Jaxon thumped him on the back.

"Don't worry, lad," he said. "They will be screaming a different tune soon enough. Now, if you don't mind clearing a little space for me, I am going to need some room to wield this ax here."

The soldier shuffled farther away from Jaxon. Others took the hint and left a small space around the giant axman. Jaxon loosened his shoulders. Trystan drew his sword of gold and green beside him.

"Stay close to me, Trystan," advised Jaxon. "We will send these puppies running back to their masters together."

The enemy surged forward, running toward the rearing walls of Karalis. Leon, standing toward the center of the wall, raised his arm. "Archers," he yelled.

The five hundred archers, standing on the open ground between walls one and two, loped up the stairs to take up their positions along the ramparts. The fifteen archers among the Order of Acrium joined them. Arrows were nocked to bows as the enemy raced toward the waiting archers. Gavin, his longbow stronger than the shorter bows of King Markos's troops, released his arrow first. It took an easterner in chain mail full in the throat. A ragged cheer went up along the wall as the man fell beneath the swarming mass.

"Draw bows," yelled Prince Leon. Over five hundred arrows were drawn back to cheeks. "Loose."

Hundreds of arrows sang from their bows toward the surging mass. The Khali, lacking conventional armor, fell by the scores. The easterners, protected by chainmail, fared much better. Even still, arrows found their way into unprotected legs, arms, and throats. The charge did not falter. Hundreds of arrows followed the first volley. And then hundreds more. Ladders clattered against the wall as the enemy milled around the base of the wall. "Archers, retire to safety," commanded Leon. The archers ran back down the stairs to the ground beyond.

Once there, they aimed their arrows over the wall where they fell with deadly purpose on the bunched together enemy.

Nervous soldiers began pushing the ladders from the wall with the butts of their spears. "Wait until there are men on them!" bellowed Jaxon. "We need to kill men, not ladders."

The first Khali died as Trystan's glittering sword lanced through his open mouth. All along the wall, Varkuvian blades and spears fought back the first attackers to reach the ramparts. Try as they might, the enemy could not gain a foothold. But it could not last. An easterner cresting the battlements grabbed hold of a soldier's wrist as he lunged toward him. Yanking on the Varkuvian's arm, he threw him from the ramparts, to plummet to the ground behind him. Slashing open the throat of another Varkuvian, he leapt to the ramparts, his comrades surging behind him.

Jaxon saw the breech open up and charged in amongst the enemy, his ax swinging in a murderous arc. The ax sheered the top of a Khali's head clean in half. Brushing aside a thrust, he plunged the tip of the butterfly blades into the gut of another foe. He savagely ripped the blades clear as the man fell writhing to the ground, desperately trying to hold his entrails in place. Varkuvians surged forward all around him. The enemy began to close in on themselves as they were cut down one by one.

One breech closed only for another to open. This time it was Gabriel who led the charge. His massive sledgehammer pulverized a man's face to oblivion, catapulting him into his comrades. Sidestepping a downward thrust, Gabriel spun, swinging his mighty weapon into his opponent's breastplate. Such was the force of the swing the man's armor was crushed, his shattered ribs piercing his lungs. He was dead before he hit the ramparts. A Khali ran at Gabriel with ax raised. Gabriel dropped his sledgehammer, dodging a wild hack. He grabbed a hold of the Khali's wrist as he tried another swing. Drawing back his head, the half-Argarian delivered a bone crushing head butt to his opponent's face. The Khali, stunned, dropped his ax. Gabriel gripped the man by his throat and, with a massive push, flung him back over the wall where he fell, screaming to his death. Picking up his sledgehammer once again, he lifted it over his head and brought it down with all of his force onto the head of an easterner who was just cresting the top of the ladder. The man's helmet crumpled into his brain, blood spraying everywhere. Without a sound, he fell from the ladder, dislodging two others beneath him. Another Khali ran at him from behind, his spear aiming toward Gabriel's back. An arrow took the spear wielder in the cheek, pitching him face first into the battlements.

Gabriel spun around, seeing Owen with bow still raised on the ground beyond. He nodded his gratitude and then surged into the enemy ranks once more. All along the wall, the Varkuvians held, pushing back the Khali and easterners. The attackers were relentless and would not pull back. The ramparts became slick with blood. A massive breach suddenly opened at the far end of the wall. Varkuvians were pushed back along that section of the wall. Prince Vasilis, leading the reserve force, immediately recognized the peril. Leading his five hundred men, he sprinted toward the breach.

Simultaneously, another breach opened at the other end of the wall. Varkuvians began streaming back. Wall one was in danger of being overrun. Trystan instantly read the situation. The reserve force was already committed to a breach; if the enemy reached the stairs, they would be able to flood onto the ground beyond and then encircle the defenders. Trystan pushed his way through the retreating ranks of Varkuvians, moving ever closer to the enemy. Jaxon saw the insane move Trystan was attempting. In a vain attempt, he tried to join him, but the fleeing Varkuvians impeded his way. The same sensation that came over Trystan in Fursta gripped his body. This time he welcomed it, as he would a long lost relative. Drawing his hunting knife, he twirled his sword.

He emerged from the ranks of withdrawing Varkuvians to see a member of the Order of Acrium cut down by an eastern swordsman. There were now no allies surrounding Trystan. He was alone, and before him were scores of enemies, their blades dripping with the blood of Varkuvian dead, their eyes gleaming at the heady prospects of victory. Single-handedly Trystan charged into the enemy.

He swayed back as a sword blade swept toward him. He opened kicked the wielder in the chest, flinging him backward, impeding his comrades. Ducking under another sweep, he dropped to his knee, slicing the Achilles tendon of his new foe. Rising up, he kneed the man in the face as he was reeling in pain. He swept past him like a wrath, his sword, and knife moving with blistering speed. Deflecting a dagger thrown at him, he tore into the enemy. His hunting knife took an opponent in the throat. Ripping it clear in one motion, he flung it toward the man who'd thrown the dagger, taking him in the eye.

Sidestepping a spear thrust, he grabbed the haft of the weapon, drawing the wielder toward him. His sword licked out, slicing open the man's jugular. Still holding the spear, he cut it in half, using the point as a weapon. Blocking a swinging ax to his right, he plunged the spear point upward through a Khali's jaw. Blood oozed over Trystan's hand. The enemy, though outnumbering Trystan greatly, was terrified to go against him. They slowly pulled back, leaving a gap between them and the blood-drenched silver warrior.

The Varkuvians, seeing Trystan attacking the enemy by himself, stopped retreating and ran to join him. A slow chant began as the Varkuvian troops witnessed the Savior of Karalis. "Trystan! Trystan! Trystan!" The chant took up along the entire length of the wall as soldiers fought more valiantly, pushing the enemy back.

Trystan let the chant roll over him. The longer he waited for reinforcements, the more the enemy would gain purchase at this end of the wall. He charged into them once again. A curved sword moved in slow motion toward him. Spinning around the lunge, his blade sliced through the back of the man's neck. The sensation gripping him grew stronger. The hairs on the back of his neck stood up. Spinning, he sliced open a Khali's face, spraying blood into the air. Feeling danger once again, he dropped to his knee as a double-headed ax sliced through the air where he was. Whirling around, he sliced the axman's leg in half. Even the man's screams seemed to be delayed, coming in slow reverberations.

Enemies converged all around Trystan. There was no fear. Surging to his feet, he plunged his blade through an easterner's ribs, cutting cleanly through the armor, his sword cleaved through the man's heart. He withdrew the blade, whipping it behind him to plunge deep into a charging Khali's gut. With his free hand, he pulled the dead man into the path of the men behind him. His opponents slipped on the blood-drenched ramparts, as they tried to avoid their dead comrade. Two of them fell from the ramparts, plunging to their deaths. Jaxon, finally making his way through the Varkuvians, ripped into the men facing Trystan. His ax crushed through a man's chest. Wrenching it clear, he joined Trystan; fighting back to back, they withstood the enemy onslaught.

The Varkuvian troops tore into the rear of the enemy surrounding Trystan and Jaxon. They were slowly pushed back. The men facing the silver warriors turned tail and ran for the ladders.

A giant Khali with braided hair, wearing a studded leather breastplate, ran at Trystan, the massive club in his hand swinging toward Trystan's head. Trystan easily swayed backward as the club whooshed by his head. His blade swept out, opening a cut in the Khali's midsection. He cried out in rage, throwing a right cross at Trystan. Spinning around the punch, Trystan's sword cleaved through the man's arm. The limb flopped to the ramparts. Screaming in rage and pain, the Khali dropped his club. His one good hand snaked out, attempting to crush Trystan's windpipe. Trystan's blade moved with stunning speed to plunge into the giant's chest. The giant fell to his knees, blood pooling from his mouth. His malevolent gaze bore into Trystan before his eyes glazed over, and he pitched sideways.

All along the wall, the enemy fought for their lives as they were forced back to the ladders. The signal to retreat echoed through the sounds of battle. A massive cheer rose from the defenders as the attackers fell back out of bow range. Varkuvians moved to surround the blood-soaked Trystan. The nearest soldier went to grasp him on the shoulder when he abruptly stopped. He peered closely at Trystan's eyes.

"What is the matter with your eyes?" the soldier asked.

Without warning, the sensation left Trystan. He staggered, exhaustion sweeping over him. Jaxon took his weight, thinking his friend injured. "Don't you worry, Trystan," the big man said. "I will get you to the hospital."

Trystan did not complain as Jaxon half carried him down the stairs to the makeshift hospital that had been erected. Soldiers cheered as they passed. Jaxon placed his friend gently down upon a cot. A bald-headed surgeon with tired eyes came over to them. He went to check

Trystan for wounds, but he waved him back. "None of the blood is mine," explained Trystan. "I am just exhausted."

The surgeon looked at him skeptically. The cries of the wounded and dying sounded all around them as more men were carried in. "I will come back and check on you in a few minutes." He handed Trystan a cup full of crisp water. "Stay here and sip this. When I come back, we will clean you of blood, and see if there is any worry for concern."

Jaxon looked up to see Master Layne walking toward them. Other than a few scratches and minor splashes of blood on his armor, the disbanded master didn't even look like he had just been in a battle. His dark hair was drawn tightly back, and as always, his violet eyes looked powerful and all knowing. Jaxon always felt uncomfortable under that gaze when he was a part of the Order. It seemed Layne could read an entire man's life just by looking at him. He stopped before his former students.

"It's good to see you two survived the first wave," said Layne. "Seven of your brothers cannot say the same."

The sounds of frenzied activity from the wall above filtered through the hospital. The enemy was amassing for another charge. Trystan rose unsteadily to his feet. "We have to get back to the wall," he said. His legs gave way underneath him.

Jaxon caught him, levering him back to the cot. "I think you ought to sit this one out, Trystan. Don't worry, I will go and deal with them. You just rest up."

Trystan did not look pleased about sitting around, but he grasped Jaxon's outstretched hand. "Try not to get yourself killed, big man."

Gathering his ax, Jaxon made for the wall once again. It wasn't until he was out of the hospital and onto open ground before he realized Layne was not with him. Glancing behind him, he saw his old master speaking intently to Trystan. It was obviously a conversation intended between student and teacher, and Jaxon kept walking. The sound of clashing steel came from above. A body suddenly plummeted directly in front of Jaxon, splattering blood all over. Everything but the face was mutilated. It was the soldier Jaxon first clasped upon the shoulder, and told him not to worry before the first charge. Sighing, Jaxon loped up the stairs to the action above.

Three more waves were repulsed before the enemy finally retired back to their camps, dejected and demoralized after a long day of fighting. Jaxon slumped to the ramparts. His entire body was exhausted, and he was afraid he would not be able to get back up. Dusk was just falling upon Karalis, the sky streaked red. To Jaxon, it seemed like a month had passed since he first thought the rising dawn sun would be a disadvantage for the Varkuvians. Kole approached, sitting alongside him. The former innkeeper grunted in pain as the wound at his shoulder jarred against the wall. He handed Jaxon a canteen of water. Without a word, Jaxon drank deeply.

All along the wall, the Varkuvian wounded were being tended to with the more seriously injured being carried down to the hospital. The enemy injured, easterner and Khali alike, were ruthlessly dispatched before their bodies were tossed unceremoniously back over the wall. The toll for the day was devastating. Over five hundred Varkuvians were dead with another two hundred carrying wounds too grievous to see them fight again. Over seven hundred fighting men were removed within the first day of fighting. If such casualties continued, Karalis would fall within two weeks.

Jaxon rubbed at his dirt-streaked face. "Thanks for the water, Kole," he said, handing the canteen back to his comrade. "I am going to grab something to eat, see how Trystan is doing, and ask about the condition of Kaleb. You want to come with me?"

"No thanks, Jax," responded Kole. "I have a lot on my mind and would rather be alone for a little."

With a huge effort of will, Jaxon pushed himself to his feet. Patting Kole on his good shoulder, he walked toward the stairs, groaning at the soreness in his joints. Campfires glowed all over the open ground between the walls. Only a couple hundred Varkuvians were left upon the first wall in case the enemy attempted a night attack. The rest of the men were sitting around the campfires, relaxing for the first time that day. Many would be mourning friends or brothers who were lost. Others would be wondering if tonight would be their last night upon this world. Even more would be thinking about their wives and sweethearts, hoping for the opportunity to hold them just one more time.

For Jaxon, he recalled Margaret's smile and the way she would hug him close after a hard day of working on the farm. Every day that passed found him missing her more and more. It felt as if his heart was being ripped from his chest. If it wasn't for Trystan and Gavin, he would've left after meeting with King Markos and returned to the partner of his soul, but he could not leave his friends to their fate. When he was eight years old, his two older brothers were killed during a raid while trying to protect their mother. She was slain regardless, and his two sisters were sold into slavery. Only Jaxon and his father survived the attack. To Jaxon, Gavin and Trystan were his second chance at having brothers. He would die to protect them.

The sound of raucous laughter came from a campfire close by. He looked over to see Gabriel, Gavin, Owen, and several other members of the Order sitting around a roaring fire, laughing amiably. The sound seemed out of place amongst the morbid Varkuvian soldiers all around. Jaxon had intentions of seeking out Trystan and inquiring about Kaleb's condition, but the smell of roasting meat hanging in the air swamped his senses. He made his way over to the others.

A wide smile crossed Gabriel's face when he saw Jaxon. Even without the armor of Acrium on, the half-Argarian was an imposing figure. The flames played off his tattooed face, and if it wasn't for the smile or the fact that Jaxon knew the man, he would've looked like a demon.

"Finally, a man who can hold his drink almost as well as I can," said Gabriel, his voice deep and resounding. He gestured to the men around him. "These girls are already drunk, and I've only just begun drinking!"

Jaxon unbuckled his armor, placing it down next to where the others stacked their own armor. Taking a seat next to Gabriel, he chuckled wholeheartedly. Gabriel shoved a flagon of wine into Jaxon's chest. "You have some catching up to do, I think."

Gavin handed Jaxon a platter with roasted beef topped with heavy gravy. Taking out his hunting knife, he reversed it, passing it to Jaxon. The beef was flavorful, the wine rich and sweet. Jokes and tall tales were told around the fire by the warriors. At the end of one joke, Gabriel spit out a mouthful of wine, which was immediately followed by gut-wrenching laughter. The camaraderie shared by the men spread to the other campfires, easing the tension of the stressed soldiers after a hard day of fighting. For a few blissful moments, the worries of tomorrow melted away.

A man, wearing a white-plumed black helmet and jaded black armor came to an abrupt halt right in front Jaxon and the others. He was leading close to twenty men, each one wearing similar armor. From the armor they wore, Jaxon recognized them as King Alaric's men. The leader, a grizzled veteran, was staring malevolently at Gabriel. Gabriel, who consumed a massive amount of alcohol and was in the middle of telling a ribald jest, was completely oblivious to the hostile stares the jaded soldiers were giving him. The leader moved around the campfire, standing directly behind Gabriel. Bending forward, he forcefully tapped the half-Argarian on the shoulder.

"Just one second. I am almost done with the story," Gabriel said, slurring his words. As an afterthought, he held up a finger, emphasizing to give him a moment.

The jaded leader's face turned red, causing a pale scar on his cheek to stand out. This time he shoved Gabriel. Any other man would've been sent sprawling to the ground, but Gabriel was a mountain of a man. Rocking forward, Gabriel blinked slowly and stopped telling the story. Groggily, he stood to his feet, turning unsteadily toward the rude display of manners. Gabriel dwarfed the man standing before him. King Alaric's soldiers spread out behind their leader. Other Varkuvians, sensing the tension, turned from their fires to see what was going on.

"How can I help you, my friend?" Gabriel asked merrily.

"I am no friend of yours, Argarian," the leader said vehemently. "My brother and his family live in the Wood Realm where your brethren are laying waste to the countryside. His village was burned to the ground, and I haven't heard from him since the invasion. Yet you dare sit here and laugh and jest while thousands are being slain."

Gabriel began to sober up at the intensity in the man's voice. Holding up his hands, he tried to de-escalate the situation. "Come now. I was born in Varkuvia, same as all of you. I got these tattoos many years ago out of respect for my departed mother. I fought and bled alongside all of you today. I have earned the right to be called a Varkuvian."

"You haven't earned shit." The leader spat in Gabriel's face.

The other members of the Order stood up, moving to stand behind Gabriel as the half-Argarian wiped the spittle from his face. King Alaric's men were armored and outnumbered the warriors two to one. With many of the members intoxicated, the odds seemed to heavily favor the jaded armored leader and his men. When Gabriel looked up, his eyes were angry, his jaw clenched.

He attempted one more time to calm the situation. "I am going to forget what you just did, for I know how it feels when a relative or loved one might be in harm's way. The enemy is outside of these walls, not in here amongst us. As I said before, I got these tattoos out of respect for my departed mother who even though was born on the Storm Islands, spent a majority of her life on this continent. Now, before things get worse than they already are, why don't we just shake hands and go our separate ways?" He extended his hand.

"I could give two shits about respecting your departed whore of a mother," said the leader, ignoring Gabriel's outstretched hand. "She was an Argarian bitch and—"

Gabriel delivered a powerful uppercut to the man's jaw. He spun through the air before landing face-first into the dirt. His leg twitched once and then he lay still. Gabriel looked up, his eyes thunderous. Many among King Alaric's men backed away before the gaze, but one soldier rushed forward, attempting to tackle Gabriel to the ground. The fool tried to tackle Gabriel by wrapping his arms around his midsection. He would've had better luck tackling a brick wall. Gabriel swung his hip, throwing the soldier off him. The rest of King Alaric's soldiers rushed forward. The Order of Acrium moved to meet them.

Ducking underneath a right cross, Gabriel grabbed the man by his groin, and the top of his breastplate. Surging upward, he lifted the helpless man into the air before throwing him into his comrades where they crashed to the ground. A haymaker connected with the side of his head. Staggering backward, he turned directly into a left jab. This time he rolled with the punch. Dodging the next blow, he threw a right jab, followed by a left cross. His opponent reeled backward, blood streaming from his broken nose. Gabriel moved in, delivering a mighty right that sent the man to his backside.

Soldiers from the surrounding fires rushed forward, trying to break up the fight. One of King Alaric's men threw a cheap punch as a member was being restrained, his arms pinned. The others, seeing the shameful blow, rushed forward once more. Prince Leon, walking among the soldiers to raise their spirits, heard the commotion. He ran forward as the situation was close to getting ugly, once again.

"What is this madness?" he thundered.

The fight slowly broke a part, each side glaring at the other with open hostility. Uncomfortable silence fell over the entire area. Leon moved to the center, looking back and forth between the two groups. "I bet the enemy would truly rejoice at the sight of this." The prince's voice was angry and disbelieving. "Here we stand, with everything we hold dear in the balance, and I see Varkuvians fighting amongst themselves! I still cannot believe it. What is the meaning of this?"

One of King Alaric's soldiers, holding his hand to a gash on his face, stepped forward. "That Argarian bastard struck Orthos. That's what you get for allowing an animal in our midst."

Arguments erupted once more as both sides threw insults at each other. "Silence!" bellowed Leon. "One more outburst out of any of you and I will throw all of you in the dungeons." The prince pointed at the soldier who spoke. "I didn't see any of you complaining today when Gabriel rescued three of your comrades as they were cornered on the wall. He didn't stop and think they were undeserving because they have Varkuvian blood. I will personally speak to King Alaric about this incident. He will deal with all of you accordingly. Go to the hospital, and see your wounds tended to."

King Alaric's men moved off, casting scornful glances over their shoulders at the members of the Order. Leon swung toward the gathered warriors, moving close to Gabriel. "Look, Gabriel, I don't know the full details of what just happened, but you can't be hitting King Alaric's men. He will most likely be furious when he hears about this and will demand you be locked up or at the very least whipped."

"That man flat out insulted the memory of my mother to my face," Gabriel said, taken back. "He spit at me and then spurned my handshake when I offered to let bygones be bygones. He was itching for a fight."

"That's probably true," said Leon. "But the report is going to show that an Argarian threw the first punch, and even though I do not hold your blood against you, I know many that will. These are troubled times, and there will be men here who will have lost loved ones to the Argarian invasion of the Wood Realm. I will defend you as much as possible, but you must lay low for a little bit. No more fights. Is that understood?"

"It is understood," Gabriel answered, his eyes and face angry.

"That goes for the rest of you as well," Leon said, his gaze sweeping the gathered men. "The Order of Acrium is already on thin ice as it is. I would hate to lock you men up. So please, just behave." With that, he turned and walked away.

Jaxon pushed his way through the angry warriors. Rubbing his bearded jaw where a solid left connected during the fight, he moved alongside the prince. Leon, seeing that Jaxon was alone, walked a few extra paces and then stopped.

"What can I do for you, Jaxon?" the prince asked.

"I was just wondering how Kaleb is doing," said Jaxon. "I have heard no news about him."

Leon scratched at his empty eye socket. "Funny how I can still feel it. I keep thinking I will just wake up the next day, and I will have my full eyesight back. Then all of this will turn out to be one bad dream." His hand fell away from the ruined socket. "Kaleb has been in a coma ever since we arrived back in Karalis. The doctors and apothecaries treating him have tried to get him to take in water and some form of food, but so far, it hasn't been necessary. Kaleb's body is providing sustenance on its own. Doctors who have been in the medical profession for the majority of their lives cannot explain the phenomenon. It's almost like his body is in a cocoon state." He looked around as if realizing for the first time what he just said. "I would appreciate it if you didn't mention this to anyone else, Jaxon."

"Why's that?" Jaxon asked bemused.

"Because a lot of people are scared, that's why. Nobody has any idea what is going on with Kaleb. They just know he somehow managed to defeat a large group of tribesmen by himself. Many inhabitants of the city think he might unleash that power on Karalis when he awakens. If it were to leak that his body is self-sustaining, without any water or food, then the people's fear would turn into paranoia. We already have enough problems on our hands without having to worry about the people clambering for us to burn a wizard or whatever it is that Kaleb has turned into."

"You make a pretty good point. All right, I will keep the news to myself."

"Good man. Get yourself some rest. We have a long day ahead of us tomorrow." Leon went to move off when he stumbled. He gathered himself, shaking his head as if trying to focus.

"Are you all right, Leon?" Jaxon asked, concerned. He rested his hand on Leon's shoulder.

The prince shrugged off the hand. "I am fine. It's just the opiates the doctors gave me for my eye. Some of them are fairly strong, and at times, I find it hard to concentrate. I just need to lie down. That's all. I will see you tomorrow."

Jaxon watched the prince walk away with an unsteady gait. Leon had changed drastically from the man he knew in the Order. The prince was always well-liked for his humor and easy familiarity. The Khali burned that out of him with the tip of a red-hot knife. Now, he always seemed so bitter, a constant scowl upon his face. Jaxon could not recall the last time he saw the prince laugh or even smile. Just now, when he asked if Leon was all right, his response was distant and cold. His thoughts were consumed with retribution toward the Khali and their allies.

A hooded, cloaked figure walking at the edge of the campfires suddenly caught Jaxon's attention. The graceful style of movement looked so familiar. Jaxon, his curiosity instantly piqued, weaved his way through the groups of soldiers, making his way toward the figure. As he got closer, he felt his heartbeat racing. He quickened his pace. Could it truly be who he thought it was? The figure suddenly stopped moving and began looking around. Jaxon halted just behind the cloaked figure.

"Margaret?" he asked, hope building inside of his chest.

The cloaked figure turned toward him. The hood fell out of place, exposing long, curly chestnut brown hair. Margaret looked at her husband, her eyes brimming with tears. For several moments, Jaxon was too shocked to move. They reacted at the same time, rushing forward to embrace one another tightly.

"Oh, Margaret, what are you doing here?" he asked, stroking her back. "It is not safe here."

"We heard everything in Modina," said his wife, burying her head into his chest. "The town was abuzz with news of the invasion and the arrival of the Order of Acrium. It was said you were imprisoned. When I didn't hear word from you, I feared for the worst. I had to come here and see for myself you still lived."

Jaxon hugged his wife close to him. He knew she shouldn't be there, and her life was in more peril here than it was when the Brotherhood attacked the farm, but he did not care. He was complete again. Margaret looked up, concern showing in her eyes when she saw the bruise spreading upward from his jaw.

"Where did you get that?"

"Oh, this is nothing," Jaxon said with a smile. "Just a minor disagreement with a man's fist." His hand strayed to Margaret's stomach where signs of her pregnancy were starting to show. "Our child has grown since I have been gone."

Margaret stroked her husband's thick beard. "Our baby will be a son, just for you, and he will grow up to be as fine of a man as his father."

Dipping his head, Jaxon kissed Margaret upon the lips. The kiss lingered for several moments. They walked hand in hand away from the noise of the soldiers to a small clearing of grass. It was a beautiful night. The moon shined brightly overhead, the stars twinkling in the sky. For the first time in over a month, Jaxon felt truly happy. Sitting down upon the grass, he held his wife close, talking to her long into the night.

# CHAPTER ELEVEN

rystan flexed his forearm. The muscle was extremely tight, and he kneaded the spot with his fingers. The tension slowly eased. He sagged back against the ramparts, sweat running down his face in rivulets. The second attack of the day was repulsed. This time the attackers had focused their efforts on the thick oak gates reinforced with bronze. A battering ram, protected by ox hides and resembling a giant tortoise, crept its way through the mass of attackers while they simultaneously assaulted the wall with grappling hooks and ladders.

Once the ram was under the gatehouse, Trystan heard the steady thumping as the iron head pounded against the gate. The defenders in the gatehouse poured boiling oil down through the murder holes above the ram. At first, this did nothing since the ox hides of the ram were soaked through time and time again with water, but the enemy missed a section of the hides. Once the oil was lit, the dry part of the hides went up in flames. Soon afterwards, the ram itself caught on fire. The enemy streamed back, coughing from the thick fumes.

It wasn't long after the ram went up in flames that the call to retreat was sounded. The enemy would have to rethink their strategy if they were to take the wall. Trystan leaned his head back against the crenellations. The doctor had advised him to stay in bed for another day, saying that his body was beyond exhausted and needed to rest. Trystan ignored his advice and was one of the first upon the wall, waiting for the enemy. Now he was regretting his decision. His energy for the day was already spent, and he wished he had listened to reason.

He recalled his conversation with Master Layne the previous day after Jaxon left. Layne sat down upon the cot next to Trystan. "You have Verillion blood," he stated.

"What are you talking about?" Trystan asked, caught off guard.

"I witnessed what you did upon the wall," Layne began to explain. "No ordinary man could have done such a thing. You moved faster than the human eye could follow. Even I had a hard time following your movements, and I am considered one of the most prestigious swordsmen of our age. That alone wouldn't confirm it for me, but a soldier who approached you after the attackers were beaten back told me your pupils were in the shape of a cross. That is why you are now so exhausted. Your body doesn't know how to control your Verillion blood when it takes over."

"This is a lot to take in right now," Trystan said, leaning backward. "But it would certainly explain a good deal. If what you say is true, then I need to learn to control it. Granted, whatever I unleashed certainly helped turned the tide, but I feel as weak as a newborn baby. How do I learn to control it?"

"You would need someone else that has Verillion blood to teach you." Layne gave a slight grin. "Luckily for you, I am on hand. I haven't felt the ancient blood in quite some time, but I do remember the sensation, and I did study the matter thoroughly. Unfortunately for me, I did not have anyone to teach me, and without proper guidance, I never learned to fully control it. Things are going to be different for you, Trystan. If we can teach you to control the ancient blood and how to use it, then you will become the greatest swordsman these lands have seen since the Legendary Arrturi."

"All right, where do we start?"

Layne chuckled. "Always so eager to learn. For the time being, your body is too exhausted to supply the results your heart desires. Rest up, Trystan. We will see if you are ready tomorrow. If you are, then we will begin sculpting you into the finest swordsman these people will see in their lifetimes."

"Master Layne, if you can teach me to control the ancient blood, maybe you can help Kaleb to control his when he wakes up."

"I'm afraid not, Trystan," Layne responded. "The power that Kaleb displayed is on a whole different level than what you and I have. We were born with only minor Verillion blood while he was born with pure, undiluted Verillion blood. If the odds of us being born with minor Verillion blood in today's world are one in a million, then Kaleb being born with that kind of power has to be in the billions. Most people are killed by the pure blood long before it can even manifest itself."

"Then his arrival at such a time is truly a miracle."

"A miracle or a curse, I can't help but wonder." Layne stood up. "We will talk more later. Rest up. Tomorrow I might get the opportunity to be your teacher once again."

A refreshing breeze brushed against Trystan's sweat-drenched face. His head swiveled to see Jaxon approaching him with two loaves of dark bread in his hands. There was an extra spring in the big man's step today. The arrival of Margaret revitalized him like nothing else possibly could. He handed Trystan one of the loaves, taking a seat next to him.

"What's the enemy up to now?" he asked Trystan.

"Right now they are assembling trebuchets," Trystan responded, ripping off a chunk of bread. "They are hoping to bombard us into submission. I have already spoken to Prince Leon, and we agreed we should only keep a token force upon the walls. The rest will stay out of range until the enemy advances. I will be staying with the men upon the walls and endure the barrage with them."

"Then I will stay, also," declared Jaxon.

"Don't be an idiot." Trystan admonished him. "Margaret would kill me if she learned I allowed you to go through with such foolishness. Speaking of your wife, where is she staying?"

"I booked a room for her at an inn between walls two and three," Jaxon said, devouring his loaf of bread. "She should be safe there for the time being."

"Nowhere is safe, Jax. It's only a matter of time before the walls fall. We just simply don't have the manpower to hold them indefinitely, and more enemy troops arrive every day. I saw a column of over two hundred Khali arrive this morning. The best we can do is hold out long enough for the other kings to come to our aid. Margaret will not be safe for long, and you know this. So why do you let her stay?"

Jaxon sighed. "Of course, I know, Trys, but you don't know what it was like for me to be separated from her. She's my wife and is going to be the mother of my child. There is no life for me without her. Even with peril all around us, it gladdens my heart just to know she is near. It gives me a reason to live."

A few weeks ago, what Jaxon just said would have sounded like complete gibberish to Trystan. He would've asked how it was possible that a person could feel so strongly toward another. Then Arianna came back into his life and his world changed. Trystan had seen gorgeous women before, but there was a quality to Arianna that made her seem so much more beautiful than her actual physical appearance. Instead of being intimidated by her good looks, he found he could open up to her and be himself. The more he thought of her, the more beautiful she became in his mind. Just summoning her image from his memory lifted his spirits. *Is this what love feels like?* he asked himself. He never experienced the emotion before, so he had no idea.

Arianna was helping out the surgeons in the hospital the day before by fetching water and cloth for wounds. When she saw Trystan, her face was a picture of worry. She rushed over to him, searching for injuries.

"I am fine, Arianna," he told her calmly. "My body is just exhausted."

She looked at him sternly. "I will be the judge of that. You look as though a child could lay you low right now. Now let me take a look at you."

"You sound just like a mother," he had muttered, but he allowed her to inspect him for injuries. Satisfied he was, in fact, only exhausted, she returned to her duties. Even still, she continued checking on him throughout the day.

Then when night fell, she came to his bed, crawling in beside him without a word. Trystan awakened as she approached him. There was no nervousness, no fear. They did not make love, just merely enjoyed each other's company long into the night. She cuddled close to him, falling asleep upon his chest. Trystan played with her hair, staying up long into the night, his thoughts many. This was the worst time imaginable to be falling in love, yet he could not help it. He could not shut off his emotions, and every passing day his feelings for Arianna grew.

He realized Jaxon was speaking to him and asked his friend to repeat his question. "Where have King Markos and King Alaric been?" repeated Jaxon. "Their men are starting to talk."

"According to rumor," began Trystan, "King Markos received a death threat the same day King Alaric arrived. He now refuses to leave the keep and has left the defense of the walls to his sons. As for King Alaric, I could not tell you. Maybe the man is a coward, or he is taking the lead of Markos and staying in the keep."

"Their presence would lift the men as we never could. The men fight for their kings, and the longer they stay at the keep, the more you are going to see morale worsen."

Trystan could not argue with that. The soldiers needed to see their kings and be lifted by them. By staying at the keep, doubt would start gnawing its way into the troops' minds. Are the kings staying in the keep because they believe the walls cannot be held? Do they not believe in us, or do they simply not care? Trystan decided he would request a meeting with King Markos and try to show the monarch the way to reason.

Pushing himself away from the wall, he peered in between the crenellations at the enemy's position. It was now obvious; they were constructing trebuchets. He could see the slings being hammered into place even now. The eastern lords must've brought the pieces in wagons from their respected city-states. A trebuchet could hurl stones weighing two hundred pounds up to three hundred yards. In Trystan's mind, he imagined the massive barrage the wall would sustain. The walls looked strong enough, but would they be able to withstand such a beating? *I guess we will find out soon enough,* he thought.

Prince Leon moved along the walls. "All right, everybody retire to the shadow of wall two. Only the men I spoke to remain behind."

Jaxon stood up. "Keep your head down, Trystan. I will see you shortly." He clasped Trystan in the warrior fashion and then followed the line of soldiers making their way down the stairs.

Thousands of Varkuvian soldiers began making their way to a safe distance. Prince Leon, remaining upon the first wall, moved alongside Trystan. Trystan looked at the one-eyed prince. "Is it really a wise thing for you to be here, Leon? If both of us were to fall, the blow to morale would be devastating."

"It would be," agreed the prince. "But when we both survive, the men will say, 'Look at that, not even an army of trebuchets could kill Trystan of the Blade or Leon the Demon Prince.' Our legends will grow, and the men will fight all the harder for it."

"Forget about the legends," said Trystan. "I pray that Leon the man survives, and I wouldn't mind if the gods deemed I was to see another sunrise."

The prince smiled genuinely for the first time since his capture. "I think the gods still have plans for you, Trystan. You still have some time upon this world, I believe." With that, the prince turned and moved farther down the wall, talking to the soldiers who were left to man the wall.

Trystan knelt down upon the ramparts. The trebuchets were now fully assembled, and he could see men struggling to move the massive stones into the slings. He watched as the arm of a trebuchet was lowered to the ground. His heart thudded in his chest. The siege engineer released the lever, and he watched as the boulder flew through the air. It crashed some twenty paces short of the wall in a shower of grass and dirt. The soldier next to him let out a sigh of relief.

"The idiots assembled them out of range," he said, laughing.

Trystan ignored the man. There was no point in crushing the soldier's hopes. He knew they were only getting the range down correctly. He watched as fifty trebuchet arms were drawn back. Fifty levers were released. Trystan did not react at first. The sky darkened as massive boulders flew through the air. He ducked down at the last second. The entire wall shook beneath the force of impact. A section of a tower was ripped off, showering the defenders in debris. The wall finally stopped shaking. Trystan looked up to see the action being repeated as the trebuchet arms were drawn back once more. The soldier who originally thought the enemy had misjudged the range was now cowering in fear.

And so the bombardment continued. For the next half hour, the enemy barraged the wall, trying to expose any weaknesses. Another tower was destroyed, a section careening off to hurdle towards three terrified Varkuvians. They were killed instantly. Another five were killed when a massive stone ripped through part of the ramparts, smashing anyone or anything in its path. The soldier next to Trystan stood up during the barrage, fear overriding his duty to stay upon the wall. Before Trystan could even say a word, a hurdling stone ripped the soldier's body in half. In front of Trystan, there was nothing but a lower torso, blood spraying from the mutilated body. He was too shocked to even react. The legs stood there for a few more seconds before convulsing and collapsing to the ramparts. Trystan closed his eyes and lowered his head as the barrage continued.

Try as they might, the enemy could find no flaws in the wall, and after what seemed like an age, the wall finally stopped shaking. Trystan risked a glance through the crenellations once more. The enemy was massing in front of the trebuchets, getting ready to assault the wall. They surged forward. This time there were no war cries as they tried to catch the defenders off guard. Prince Leon, his face and armor covered in the debris from one of the collapsed towers, looked up to see the mass of enemy swarming forward.

"Varkuvians!" he yelled. "Man the walls!"

The Varkuvian soldiers, waiting in relative safety, rushed forward. Ladders clattered against the wall and grappling hooks bit into the crenellations as they took up their positions. Jaxon jumped to the crenellations, his ax biting down to sever a grappling line with over twenty attackers climbing it. They fell to the ground screaming. An arrow flew perilously close to Jaxon's head as the archers below aimed at the easy target above them. He quickly jumped back down to the ramparts.

And so the bloody assault on Karalis continued. Men fell screaming to their deaths and writhed in pain upon the ramparts.

Almost an hour after the barrage, the enemy retired once more. A section of wall next to the gatehouse suddenly shifted and groaned. Soldiers were thrown to the ramparts as a massive crack shivered up the length of the wall. Varkuvians scrambled back, thinking the stone was going to crumble beneath their feet. It did not, and men began carefully inspecting the wall. Trystan looked at the massive crack with a look of defeat. *That part of the wall must've taken substantial damage from the barrage,* he thought. *The enemy will now focus their full attention on the damaged wall, and then it will only be a matter of time before it falls.*

As the wounded were being tended to, he sought out Prince Leon. The one-eyed prince was talking to a group of soldiers, assuring them the wall was fine. Trystan stood respectfully back as Leon finished addressing the men. From the looks on the soldier's face, they weren't buying anything Leon was telling them. When the prince was done, the Varkuvians shuffled away to attend other duties. Spinning on his heel, Leon strode toward Trystan.

"Walk with me," the prince instructed.

Trystan followed Prince Leon along the wall. A group of soldiers were attempting to clear away the debris from one of the fallen towers. Leon halted right before the rubble where no one could hear them.

"What do you think about the wall?" he asked, rubbing at his ruined eye socket, which was covered by a dark leather strip.

"I think the enemy has been waiting for this exact opportunity," answered Trystan. "The barrage was meant more to expose any flaws in the wall rather than to kill multiple defenders. Now that a crack has appeared in the foundation, the next trebuchet assault will be focused solely on that one spot. They are looking to bring the wall crashing down and then attack the breach when it opens. Simultaneously, they will attack the ramparts with ladders and grappling hooks as they have done before. Weight of numbers will see the first wall fall."

Leon nodded in agreement. "What do you suggest?"

"We need to immediately evacuate the wounded to wall two. It will take some time, and even though darkness is fast approaching, we cannot rely on the enemy to wait until dawn before they attempt another attack. Then I would make sure there are plenty of ropes upon wall two. The enemy might be right on the heels of our men when we call the sound to retreat. We cannot afford to keep the gate open in case of disaster. We will need some way of getting our men to the second wall without giving ground to the enemy."

"I will see it done," promised the prince. "If the wall comes crashing down, I will make sure there are soldiers ready with spear and shield to hold the tide. Seek out Master Layne and have him speak with the members of the Order. Spread them out along the wall during the next assault. We will need their fighting skills to bolster the resolve of the men."

Trystan dipped his head and then turned on his heel to walk down the stairs. It took several minutes to locate Master Layne amongst the bustling activity. The Varkuvian wounded made a procession towards wall two. Those with minor injuries, such as leg or arm cuts, were supported while the more seriously injured were carried by stretcher-bearers. He finally found Layne organizing a group of soldiers who were equipping themselves with heavy spears and round iron shields. These men would withstand the brunt of the assault if the wall fell. The idea was for the soldiers to form tight ranks and lock shields in front of the breach to replace a wall of stone with a wall of men. Trystan saw Kole amongst the men, hefting spears to find the one with perfect balance.

Seeing Trystan for the first time, Layne excused himself from the soldiers and made his way over to him. "Prince Leon has requested that you summon the members of the Order and speak to them about the next attack," Trystan said. "He thinks we should spread them out along the wall."

"I am already a step ahead of Prince Leon," said Layne. "The Order of Acrium is meeting after dark near wall two."

"Is it wise to wait to address the men?" asked Trystan, his brow scrunching. "What if the enemy attacks beforehand?"

"Did you not pay attention to any of my teachings? The enemy would have to attack under the cover of darkness. It would be as much of a hindrance to them as it would be to us. No, they will wait until there is light in the sky to ensure they take the wall. They will spend the night galvanizing their troops, and let fear seep its way into our ranks."

"We cannot be too overly confident," cautioned Trystan. "They might be thinking we would expect such a move and catch us unawares."

"I would normally agree with you, but I know the men who lead the Khali. They are not just the finest military instructors, they are also some of the greatest strategic minds of our generation. They will not unnecessarily risk the lives of the men under their command when they can ensure victory in the morning."

"I still cannot believe they would betray Varkuvia," said Trystan, disbelief in his voice.

"You would not believe the acts men and women are capable of when they are pushed to the brink. A starving mother, normally a kind and gentle soul, without the means to feed her children, would kill and steal to provide for them. The Masters of the Order were five of the most respected men in all of Varkuvia. We had everything stripped from us. Our lands, titles, and our very names were stolen. We lost our identities and, in the process, lost our ways in this selfish and greedy world."

"You sound so cynical, Master Layne. There is more to this world than selfishness and greed. People are capable of great acts of kindness as well as great acts of love. I have witnessed it here upon these walls in the midst of this horrible war. This morning, I saw a soldier knocked to the ground, an eastern sword poised above his defenseless body. Another soldier jumped in the path of the blade and dragged the swordsman from the ramparts. Such heroic deeds are performed all day long. I have seen men put their own lives on the line to save their countrymen. I have seen women moving amongst the wounded, tending to their injuries, and lifting their spirits. Not everyone is as you portray them."

Layne scoffed. "Now because everything they hold dear is in the balance, they act selflessly. Yet for centuries, the five realms of Varkuvia and its kings have stamped their civilization upon the ancestors of the Argarians, the easterners, and the tribes of the Northern Woods. The tribes of the Northern Woods were seen as sport for nobles. We raided their villages, murdered their men, enslaved their women, and left their children orphaned. If there was any kind of retribution, we would return with an army and stamp out the tribe responsible. We guarded technological advancements in agriculture and medicine that would've advanced other cultures, just so we could reign supreme. We have sowed the seeds of their hatred with our arrogance, and now we gather the harvest. That is the truth, Trystan."

"What happened to the Layne I knew who refused to join the other Masters of the Order because he believed in the teachings of Master Roderic?" asked Trystan, his voice suddenly angry. "I will not remain here and listen to you spout such pessimism. We are not responsible for the actions of our ancestors, only for our own lives and decisions. Right here and now, there is an army waiting outside of Karalis that will slaughter countless innocents if we allow these walls to fall. I, for one, will not allow that to happen while I still draw breath. When the Master Layne I knew as a teacher, and as a good man, decides to show up, I will be ready to talk to him." Trystan spun to stalk away. Layne grabbed his arm, stopping him.

"I apologize, Trystan," he said, his tone conciliatory. "I did not mean to sound so defeatist. It has been a long and trying day. And I did say, if you were up to it, we would begin training on controlling your Verillion blood. We might not get an opportunity tomorrow."

Taking a deep, calming breath, Trystan looked up into his mentor's eyes. How could he remain angry at the only man he had ever known as a father figure, and at the first man to show trust and inspire confidence in him? He would never voice aloud how much Layne actually meant to him, but it pained him to speak slightingly about his idol. There was genuine hurt in Layne's eyes, and Trystan saw his words struck home.

"Let us begin then," Trystan said, forcing a smile to try and ease the tension.

Returning the smile, Layne began walking toward a clearing away from all the frenzied activity. Drawing his sword, he began moving in a series of exercises to loosen his muscles. Trystan followed his lead.

"Whenever I felt the ancient blood beating in my veins," began Layne, "it was in the midst of battle. Each time it felt as though someone else had taken over my body. I was aware of my movements, yet I was never able to fully control them the way I wanted to. The trick to controlling your Verillion blood is when you first feel the sensation, do not embrace it as a brother, but welcome it inside yourself and make it part of you. When you and your Verillion blood are one, you will then have the ability to summon it whenever you want. When that happens, you will become faster and stronger than you can possibly imagine. You will become even more powerful than you already are, and your body will not be exhausted as it was when you used it last. Are you ready?" asked Layne, dropping into his fighting stance.

Slashing his blade through the air, Trystan nodded. Layne attacked. The sound of ringing steel clashed across the clearing. Soldiers walking by stared incongruously at the two men. Who in their right mind would be sparring when there was a massive army stationed outside the walls begging to kill and maim them? Ignoring the sparring partners, the soldiers continued with their duties. Trystan blocked a lunge from Layne, answering with a high slash. Layne parried the blow easily, agitation showing in his eyes.

The disbanded master took a step back. Holding up his blade, he halted the training. "Your movements are not nearly as fast as they were upon the wall. There were already three openings where I could've ended your life. Where is the skill I saw displayed when the wall was in danger of being overrun?"

Trystan shrugged his shoulders. "That was a completely different situation. My life, as well as the lives of thousands of my comrades, was at stake. Had I not acted as I did, then we would have been encircled with our avenue of retreat cut off. The sensation came out of nowhere, and I just embraced it."

"So your Verillion blood is only released under high pressure situations," Layne noted. "All right, let's go again."

Dropping into his stance once more, Trystan prepared to defend himself. Layne's blade moved with astonishing speed toward his face. Trystan was just in time to block the thrust. He backed up several paces, uncertainty in his movements. This was only supposed to be training, yet Layne had just tried a killing thrust. He began to say something, but Layne pressed forward, his sword licking out. Trystan defended desperately. Layne slowly backed him up toward the second wall. If Trystan gave up much more ground, he would have his back to the wall.

He was hopelessly outclassed, and he knew it. Layne was one of the most noted swordsmen in the Order's history, and even though Trystan was highly skilled, with or without his Verillion blood, he was not in the same class as Master Layne. The only armor Trystan wore was his breastplate. He removed the chain mail protecting his arms and the majority of his legs. If one of Layne's attacks got through his defenses, and cut deep, he could be crippled.

"Master Layne!" yelled Trystan while parrying a disemboweling move.

Layne ignored him. A thrust finally got past Trystan's defenses, opening up a cut on his upper arm, spraying blood into the air. The Verillion blood took over without warning. Layne's next attack, which moments before appeared lightning fast, moved toward him with an extreme lack of speed. Trystan easily blocked the blade. Such was the force of the block that Layne's sword arm was thrown to the side. Trystan kicked Layne in the chest, sending him sprawling backward. Layne recovered quickly, coming to his feet in a roll.

The Verillion blood pounded inside of Trystan. He moved on the offensive. Now it was Layne who frantically defended. Trystan contemptuously swatted Layne's sword from his hand. It clattered against the ground. Before Layne could react, the point of Trystan's sword pressed against his jugular. There they stood for several tense moments. Layne dared not breathe for fear the blade would cut him deep. Slowly bringing his hand up, he moved the point of the sword away from his throat.

"That was a good start," he said with a strained smile.

The sensation suddenly fled Trystan. He staggered back as weariness settled in on his already exhausted body. The sword fell from his shaking hand. Taking in deep breaths, he tried to remain standing. As he stood there, he realized with dread, he just almost killed Layne.

"I am so sorry, Master Layne," said Trystan. "I lost control."

"The fault is my own," Layne conceded. "I pushed you too hard. How many times must I tell you to not call me Master Layne anymore?"

Trystan smiled despite his exhaustion. "Old habits die hard."

"That they do," agreed Layne, bringing his hand up to his throat where a small trickle of blood ran freely from a small cut. "I think we are going to have to find a new way to tap into your Verillion blood. I might not survive the next time it is unleashed if we continue this way."

"I'm inclined to agree with you. I don't see how I can learn to control it. The feeling is so sudden and overpowering. How am I to learn to merge into it instead of embracing it? I only have a split second to react."

"I do not know, Trystan, but we will find a way. If your Verillion blood were to take over right now, you would pass out from sheer exhaustion. Your body cannot take much more strain. You should go and get some rest. You will need all the strength you can get for tomorrow's attack."

"What about the meeting tonight? I do not wish to miss it."

"Pah, it is a meaningless gathering, anyways. I will tell the men to fight hard tomorrow and to spread themselves out amongst the other soldiers. You do not need to concern yourself over such a trivial matter. Take some advice from your old teacher and get some rest. The men expect to see *Trystan of the Blade*." Layne's voice deepened as he dramatized the title.

It was hard for Trystan to argue, especially with exhaustion overtaking his body. Saying his farewells to Layne, he looked for a place where he could spend the night. Every soldier he passed either averted their gaze or stared at him with open admiration. No soldier, other than the warriors of the Order, would even speak to him. He had become a man apart. It was a massive burden to bear, and it was beginning to take its toll on him. He did not mind the fact they did not talk to him, for Trystan was never a social man, and he did not pretend to be otherwise. The thing that bothered him was the expectations in their eyes. The men expected him to perform acts that would rival the gods themselves.

Returning to where he left his chainmail and cloak, he bent down to gather his possessions, groaning at the soreness in his joints. Moving off once more, he looked for a place away from the soldiers to lie down and recuperate for the night. He saw Gabriel, Gavin, and many others of the Order gathered around a fire. Jaxon was with them, a flagon of wine in one hand, the other draped around Margaret's slender shoulders. They were all laughing and seemed to be in high spirits despite the horrors of war they had witnessed. Trystan thought about joining them and enjoying the companionship. Jaxon looked up as Margaret was kissing his bearded cheek. His eyes met Trystan's. Trystan returned the gaze for a moment and then moved off. Even through his peripheral vision, he could see Jaxon was both concerned and upset he did not join them. There were times, such as now, when Trystan needed his solitude. It was something Jaxon and Gavin never understood.

He found his thoughts slipping toward depression as he wound his way through the gathered soldiers. He lived his entire life without any real purpose. During his youth in Calydon city, he was merely one of many thieves the city watch wanted to catch. Trystan didn't want to be a thief his whole life, but knew nothing else, and was never given the opportunity to prove he could be more than just a common thief. Then he was given a new chance at life when he escaped execution and joined the Order of Acrium. This would've given direction and purpose to just about anyone. But not Trystan.

Looking back now, he knew he had been given several chances to rise through the ranks of his peers when he was part of the Order. Despite his common upbringing, he also knew he could lead men into battle. His grasp of strategy rivaled that of Master Roderic himself, and on the rare occasion when he opened himself up to others, he was genuinely well liked. Yet every time the opportunity arose for him to advance himself, he shied away from it and allowed less capable members to take positions of advancement. He could still see the disappointment in Layne's eyes at the lack of development in his prized pupil. Layne always believed Trystan was capable of greatness, and one day he would become a leader of men. The only problem was that Trystan could never see himself in this light.

The simple fact was that Trystan was scared to live and terrified of failure. As a child, he was given the awesome responsibility of caring for his sick and dying mother. No matter how hard he tried to cure her ailing body and pleaded with the gods for her to recover, he watched her wither and die before his eyes. She simply lost the will to live. Even now, he still felt a sense of hopelessness and despair that he could not inspire his mother, his own flesh and blood, to rejoin the world of the living once more. What sort of mother would not wish to recover so she may see her own son raised to become a man? For the longest time, Trystan saw himself as a failure, and without him knowing, that impression burrowed itself deep inside his heart and mind and remained lodged there. It was the main reason he turned down responsibility his entire life. He subconsciously lowered his own expectations of himself, just to make sure he would not fail.

During those troubled times, when his mother was in and out of states of delirium, her life hanging by a thread, he imagined his father riding through the streets of Calydon upon a golden horse. He would ride directly to the shack of a house that Trystan lived in, take his son in his arms, and heal his mother. At the age of eleven, Trystan learned life was not some fairy tale with a happy ending. His mother died in agony, her soul lost and dejected, and his father never showed up to be the hero he dreamt he would be. The sad truth was, he could not even remember what his mother looked like anymore, not even the color of her eyes. And he had no memories of his father to go back on since he left before Trystan was even born.

Unbuckling his breastplate and sword, Trystan placed them down upon the ground next to wall two. Draping his cloak around his tired frame, he lay down upon the ground. Locking his hands behind his head for support, he stared up at the night sky, watching the light clouds glide effortlessly in front of the glittering stars. Despite his exhaustion, the memories of his past and thoughts of what might have been made sleep impossible. He knew the power of the word *if* could haunt a man or woman. That one word could destroy someone's life if they allowed it to consume their every waking moment. When Trystan tried his hand at farming after the disbandment, he witnessed a prime example with one of the farmworkers.

The man, a loving husband and father of three, was out hunting one day when a group of bandits struck his farm. He returned home at the end of the day to find his crops burned, his wife brutally raped and murdered, and his children ruthlessly slain. The man never forgave himself. He could not stop wondering what would have happened if he had been there. *If* only he had been there, he could have fought back the bandits. *If* he had been there, he could have at least died beside his loved ones. The endless possibilities of *what-ifs* haunted the man. Trystan saw the lack of life in the man's eyes. The word *if,* along with the deaths of his family members, destroyed any kind of future he might have had.

Despite this knowledge, Trystan could not help but wonder what his life would have been like if his father had been present when his mother had fallen sick. Would his father have taken her in his arms and nursed her back to health? Would he have sat by her bedside day and night, holding her hand, and praying to the gods that he be given the chance to hold his wife once more? His mother might even now be alive and healthy, and Trystan never would have had to turn to a life of crime in order to survive. Instead, he would have learned the craft of his father as a blacksmith or a baker or a tailor. He could've grown up to become a successful and wealthy man with many friends. His entire life would be different if only his father was a presence in his life. This war he was dragged into would only have been idle conversation by paying customers in the taverns of Calydon while he shared a mug of ale with friends.

Yet if his father was a part of his life, then he never would have joined the Order of Acrium. He never would have met Jaxon and Gavin and forged friendships lasting a lifetime. Master Layne would not have instilled upon him the codes of honor he lived his life by or become the father figure he grew to become in Trystan's mind. Things started becoming clearer as he analyzed how different his life would have been. If Trystan had not been by Jaxon's side when the Brotherhood attacked the farm, then Jaxon and Margaret would have been killed. Gavin would have shared an equal fate if Trystan had not warned him of the Brotherhood attacks. Kole would've been slain along with the entire town of Fursta. Leon would still be rotting in a dungeon cell. All of these things would have happened if Trystan had never joined the Order of Acrium and lived a normal life instead. It was an overwhelming realization when he thought about all of the lives he unintentionally affected because of the way his life panned out.

The wise words of Master Roderic echoed from beyond the Halls of the Underworld. He spoke them on a night similar to this one many years ago. Trystan remembered the words as if they were spoken yesterday, *"The ultimate measure of a man is not defined how he stands in moments of comfort, but instead it is revealed how he stands in times of challenge and controversy."*

The truth of those words hit home more so now than they did years ago. Whether he liked it or not, responsibility was finally thrust upon him and at the most unexpected time. The people, both commoner and noble alike, looked up to him, and great things were expected of him. He wondered if it was the same for the Legendary Arrturi. Had the famous warrior desired such idolization and fame, or had he simply wanted a normal life as a soldier? Did Arrturi feel as though the weight of the world was upon his shoulders, or did he revel in his fate and embrace the legend he would one day forge? Had he enjoyed the songs the bards sang about him, or did he simply just want to be left alone? Centuries ago, Arrturi himself might even have stared longingly at the stars and wondered if past legends felt the same as he did. Trystan did not know the thoughts of the long dead hero, but his own fluttered around his mind like trapped moths.

It was one of those thoughts flittering around that made Trystan realize he promised Arianna he would seek her out at the end of the day. He started rousing himself and wondered where she might be. It wasn't until he was in a full sitting position he realized what he was doing. He had openly turned down joining in a night of jesting and drinking with men and friends he had known for a decade and sought a place away from the noise of the other soldiers so he could enjoy his own solitude. Yet he was willing to search through a camp full of thousands, to find a woman he barely knew but constantly thought about. Even now, he could not help but think about the way her eyes changed color as the light hit them or the way she tilted her head ever so slightly when she smiled. He knew looking for her when he was so overly exhausted was foolish, but even still, he could not help thinking about the woman who was slowly stealing his heart.

Finally, reason made its way through his thinking. As enjoyable as Arianna's company might be, he would need all the rest he could get for tomorrow's attack. After deciding he would seek Arianna out tomorrow and apologize to her, he wrapped his cloak tightly around himself and turned on his side. His first thoughts when he closed his eyes were of Arianna, and her smile was the last image on his mind before he drifted off into a blissful sleep. For once, his dreams stood out vividly. He and Arianna were wed, and living in a small cottage besides a flowing stream among verdant hills. The war he was part of was a thing of the past, and Varkuvia was at peace. Arianna was lying upon his chest in their bed, and she looked up at him, her curly auburn hair tumbling in front of her eyes. She smiled up at him and said something to him. The noise sounded like the clinking of armor. Trystan looked at her confused. The noise came again.

He slowly opened his eyes. He must've rolled in his sleep, for his gaze was once more looking up at the sky. The faintest of orange hues tinted the night sky. Dawn was fast approaching. Recalling the sound of armor that interrupted his dreams, he tilted his head to the left to see two men approaching. They were fully dressed in the jaded black armor of King Alaric's men. His groggy mind tried to process why they were there. Was the enemy already attacking? Stretching his body, he began rousing himself in case the enemy was in fact attacking. He froze in midstretch.

Something was not right. The two soldiers' faces, unprotected by helmets, were strained, and they seemed on edge. The atmosphere around them exuded tension. Trystan's gaze flickered lower. Their hands were resting on their sword hilts. The slightest of glints came from one of the soldier's fingers. He peered intently at the man's hand. The soldier wore a ring with a golden sun inset into it. The symbol of the Sons of Vikundo. Trystan's mind raced as the two assassins moved ever closer. His gaze flickered down to his armor and the sword at his feet. The assassins saw the move. Drawing their swords, they darted toward Trystan.

Flinging his cloak into the air, Trystan dove forward, his hand gripping around the hilt of his sheathed sword. One of the assassins angrily tore the cloak from the air before throwing it to the ground. Trystan rolled to his feet, drawing his sword from its sheath in the same motion. The assassins converged on him. Trystan threw his sheath at the face of the first and then blocked a savage thrust from the other. Even with the element of surprise lost to the assassins, Trystan was still outnumbered, and he wore no armor at all. The men before him wore the finely crafted armor from King Alaric's realm. Even his rare sword could not easily cleave such armor. Their only weakness lay at their faces where they wore no helmets.

Blocking another lunge, Trystan riposted, aiming for his opponent's face. The assassin blocked the attempt and then attacked once more. The other assassin, the one Trystan threw his sheath at, recovered quickly and joined his companion. Blood was streaming from the man's hooked nose. Now Trystan was slowly pushed back, defending himself against two highly skilled opponents. A thrust got past his defenses, opening a cut just below where Master Layne wounded him earlier. Trystan's Verillion blood began pounding inside of him. For a moment, he thought about embracing it. Even in the heat of battle, he knew if the ancient blood were to take over right now, his body might not be able to handle it. He could pass out from sheer exhaustion. His mind reacted to the Verillion blood as if it were a narcotic. All he needed to do was take it in, and everything would be all right. Fighting the overpowering sensation, he focused on the men in front of him.

The assassin on his right feigned a thrust while the one on the left tried a disemboweling move. Trystan read the move beautifully. He spun away from the slashing sword toward the assassin that feigned the thrust. The man brought up his sword to defend. Trystan's sword swept past his defenses, ripping open his face in a shower of crimson. The assassin stood still, his face in bloody ruins and, finally, pitched to the ground. Spinning around, Trystan barely deflected a powerful slash. His opponent's sword careened off to slice open a shallow cut in Trystan's thigh. Pushing the pain from his mind, Trystan warily circled the assassin.

His opponent was in no mood to wait. Varkuvian soldiers would have heard the clash of steel by now, and it was only a matter of time before men rushed to Trystan's aid. The assassin snarled and then hurled himself at Trystan. Their sword blades locked together. Trystan saw the pure hatred in the blue eyes of his bearded opponent. He quickly threw a left cross into his foe's unprotected face. Taken by surprise, the assassin reeled back. Trystan moved in too eagerly for the kill and was barely able to block a thrust intended for his head. Stepping back, he felt blood running down the side of his face where the assassin's blade got past his block. The loss of blood from his wounds, combined with his exhaustion, started to make Trystan feel dizzy. He swayed slightly, his vision blurred. His opponent saw the weakness and moved in for the kill, his sword arm pulling back to deliver the killing stroke.

Stepping in quickly, Trystan grabbed the assassin's sword wrist. His own blade swept toward the man's face. The assassin grabbed for Trystan's sword arm with his free hand. His grip slipped, and the blade plunged through his blue eye, and exited through the back of his skull. Trystan felt the strength seep away from his opponent and watched the life ebb away from the assassin's remaining eye. Withdrawing his sword, he watched the man crumple to the ground. Looking down at his sword blade, he saw it covered in bits of the man's brains and blood. He began shaking as the aftershock set in.

The Sons of Vikundo became an afterthought, and Trystan realized it was this complacency that almost cost him his life. They were waiting patiently for the moment when Trystan was away from loyal soldiers who would gladly give their lives to protect the Savior of Karalis. His need for solitude gave them just the opportunity they needed. He looked down at the bearded face of the man he just killed. He had never seen him before. Remembering the armor the assassins wore cut through Trystan's shock.

If it were to leak out that men wearing the armor of King Alaric attempted to take Trystan's life, it would mean dissention among the ranks of the Varkuvian coalition. It would not matter they wore the rings that distinguished them as Brothers from the Sons of Vikundo. The common soldier would not care about such a thing or would believe it to be a rumor spread to cover up the truth. The Order of Acrium was already at odds with King Alaric's men after their scuffle the other night. This would only make matters far worse.

Thoughts raced through Trystan's mind. How could he conceal these bodies without being discovered? He thought about waking Jaxon and Gavin to see if they could help him. But where would they hide the bodies? Even if they stripped the armor from the men, questions would arise if they were spotted. There was no fighting during the night, and all the enemy dead were thrown back over the wall. All of the Varkuvian wounded had already been carted back to the second wall, so the two dead men could not be Varkuvians.

Looking up, Trystan saw a group of soldiers approaching him. A look of caution and alertness was upon their faces. They must've heard the ring of steel. In the midst of a siege, it was the sensible thing to discover where the noise was coming from and find out if they were under attack. All thoughts of hiding the bodies vanished. Now it would not matter. The assassins won a small victory, even in death. The Order of Acrium and King Markos's men would now look with open skepticism upon their allies. The same questions would be asked by every soldier. What grudge did King Alaric hold against the Savior of Karalis that he would wish him slain? Can I trust the men fighting alongside me, or will they plunge their blades into my back when I'm not looking? Trystan pushed such thoughts from his mind and focused on the most important matter.

The Sons of Vikundo were in Karalis, and they were no longer waiting to make their move.

# CHAPTER TWELVE

ays of sunlight broke through the bunched up clouds of cotton white overhead, bathing the area in beams of golden light. Kole gazed longingly at the heavens. When his grandfather had passed away when he was little more than a boy, his mother told him the rays were departed souls watching over their loved ones. He cherished his grandfather above all others during his childhood and kept his memory close to heart. Always, when the sun's rays broke through the clouds, he would make a silent prayer to the memory of his grandfather and now added his departed father and mother to the list.

The soldier next to him hawked and spit. Kole glanced around him. Some two hundred heavily armored soldiers waited in the shadow of the second wall, separated from the main body of defenders. They were handpicked for their strength and courage to ensure they would stand firm if the weakened wall were to come crashing down. Each of them was equipped with a heavy spear, a round iron shield, and a short sword was sheathed at their sides. They would form tight ranks in the breach and fight in close quarters. Their goal was to hold off the tide of enemy attackers long enough for the defenders upon the ramparts to retreat back to the safety of wall two.

The previous night, Master Layne asked for volunteers from the Order to hold the breach. The only two who stepped forward were himself and Allyn, who stood beside him now. Allyn was one of the deadliest member with a spear. The weapon would snake out of his hand, as if it were an extension of his arm, plunging home, to be withdrawn before the enemy even knew what hit him. Allyn was a man of honor and knew his skills would be needed to allow the other soldiers an opportunity to withdraw safely to wall two. Kole held no such notions of honor.

Even a blind man could see, once the wall came crashing down, the odds of any of the two hundred men surviving were slim to none. Kole simply did not care anymore. He did a lot of thinking since Trystan and the others came back into his life. After weeks of reflection, he finally came to the conclusion that he was devoid of life and a narcissistic human being. Not even once could he remember a time when he helped others without some kind of gain for himself or felt any genuine happiness. He might never have realized this if the others had not come back into his life and would have continued with his life as he did.

The strange truth was, Kole could not think of a single reason why he went through life as he did. His parents always were a constant in his life. His father never drank nor did he beat his mother. He worked day in and day out to provide for his family, and not once did he complain. The only thing that got his father through a hard day of labor was the thought of coming home to his loving wife and son. He was truly a great man and touched many lives while he still drew breath.

His mother was the sweetest woman a son could ever ask for. She was always there to bandage his scrapes and bruises and whisper soothing words to the sobbing child he was. Kole could not remember a single time when she scolded him out of place or treated him poorly.

Every night she would cook a homemade meal, and everyone would sit down as a family to eat dinner. She was proud of everything Kole did, no matter how menial it might have been. When he won a foot race at the age of twelve, his parent's pride was a sight to behold. They reveled in their son's accomplishments and constantly spoke of him with parental affection.

Kole's mother passed away just before he joined the Order. One night she came in to say good night to her son and went to sleep, never to waken again. The community was shocked, for his mother always seemed so full of life and was a focal point from where people could draw strength. The doctor explained that his mother had a clot in her brain she was unaware of and passed away peacefully in her sleep. Her funeral was a time of great sadness. Hundreds came to pay their respects to one of the finest woman they ever knew. He never saw his father cry before, but on that day, he was a mess, tears streaming down his gruff face. Many a tear was shed by friends and loved ones alike. Except by her son whom she cherished most in her life.

Even at the time, Kole thought it strange he had not cried at all for his mother, who he would never see again in this life. He knew he loved her, and she had loved him. Just as he knew, he was sad at her passing. Kole simply could not express his grief in public as others did. He even tried to force himself to think of something sad, just so he might, at least, shed a tear for his mother and show others how much she meant to him. The idea was ridiculous, for he should have already been sad enough at her passing. It was around this time Kole realized he simply did not behave normally. He was different, and from that moment on, he would merely feign happiness or sadness when he felt it was necessary.

The following year, at age seventeen, Kole enlisted into the Order. His father, still reeling from the loss of his wife, was devastated by the thought of his only son leaving him as well. Kole knew now he should never have left his morbidly depressed father and should've stayed by his side. He had not cared at the time, and the thought had not crossed his mind again for another two decades. His only thoughts were about himself. *As they have always been*, he thought. In the Order, he believed he would finally become his own person and could stop pretending to be something he was not.

Looking back now, Kole knew he was never happy in the Order. Of course, he made friends and was considered popular, but his supposed friends formed a friendship with something he was not. He never acted like himself, and after years of pretending to be something he was not, he doubted he even knew how to be anything but a fake expectation. Not once had Kole thought about why he went through life that way. He rationalized in his mind that everyone was like that on the inside. All he was doing was acting as everyone else did. But as the years passed, he saw not everyone behaved as he did.

Jaxon was truly a good friend, and Trystan was truly an honorable man. The late First Master Roderic genuinely enjoyed teaching his pupils. They did not act that way because they thought it was expected of them. They did not even act at all. That was just the way they were. It was weird that Kole never realized this before.

Not once did it cross his mind it was strange he was in the Order longer than most. Most stayed in the Order until their early thirties and then retired, collected their pensions and their tracts of lands, before returning to their respected homelands. Some stayed on to lead as officers or, to the privileged few, to become a master. Kole had no thoughts of advancement and before the disbandment was considered one of the oldest members who was not a master or an officer.

Even after the disbandment, when he returned to his childhood town of Fursta, there was no joy. He arrived back home to find his father deathly ill. For months, he tended to his needs and cared for him as he once tended to Kole as an infant. His father was slowly weighed down, year by year by the loss of his wife. Without any immediate family on hand to raise his spirits, his health slowly slipped away. Toward the end, his father called out for Emily, his mother, time and time again. He would reminisce about times that happened decades ago as if they were just happening. This deterioration of the mind should have filled any son with a sense of hopelessness, but Kole endured his duties for his father almost mechanically. Every day turned into repetition until one dawn, his father ceased to wake up.

He remembered the day as if it were yesterday. Sitting next to his father's bed, Kole prayed his father would wake up, so he could have the opportunity to tell him, just once, how much he meant to him. Sunlight streamed through the window of his home, bathing his father in a golden glow. He looked upon his father's wrinkled face and saw a sense of peace surrounding him. Kole still wondered if his father saw his mother waiting for him in his final moments on this world and, at last, knew contentment. All alone, Kole cried for the memory of his father and mother. He prayed to Crassos, the Divine Ruler of the Heavens, that they be reunited in the afterlife.

Then, as a dutiful son, he arranged the funeral. As with his mother, hundreds showed up to pay their respects. Once again, Kole did not shed a tear in front of all of his father's friends and loved ones. He remained like a stone, still and devoid of emotion. It was the main reason why a woman never touched Kole's life. He was incapable of showing genuine sadness or any kind of raw emotion in front of others. His emotions were kept bottled up until he was all alone.

*What have I done with my life?* Kole asked himself. He had great parents that were always there for him yet abandoned his father when he needed him the most. It wasn't until after his father passed away he even felt any regrets for leaving him to join the Order. And then, once part of the Order, he had the greatest friends a man could ask for. They were friends who would willingly die for him. Yet he never did anything for them to show how much he appreciated their friendship. He was forced to face the fact that his whole life had been about himself and no one else. Even after Trystan saved him and the entire town of Fursta, he had to do some serious thinking before he agreed to join him. A true friend, and man, wouldn't have hesitated.

Kole sighed aloud, causing Allyn to turn toward him. "What's the matter, Kole?" asked Allyn while readjusting his greaves.

"I am just tired of this damn waiting," replied Kole. "The sun is some hours past dawn, and they still haven't attacked. It's starting to set my nerves on edge." *Yet another lie.* Kole had known Allyn for eight years, and he still couldn't tell him the truth.

"I know exactly what you mean," said Allyn. "Don't worry, Kole. Stay close to me once things start to get thick, and we will survive this together."

A blaring of trumpets from outside the wall caused every soldier to perk their heads up. "It seems the gods have heard you," observed Allyn, hefting his spear, and slipping his shield into place.

Kole felt a bead of sweat running down his spine under his chainmail. It was unpleasantly warm for this time of year, and the usual refreshing breeze blowing down from the Northern Bale Mountains was absent today. Pushing such discomfort from his mind, he watched as Prince Leon moved among the soldiers on the ramparts above, raising their hopes and morale. Something beyond the wall caught the Prince's attention. Kole saw him lean forward, peering intently at the enemy. The prince suddenly whipped around and began forcefully gesturing for the soldiers to pull back and to get off the wall. Kole's brow scrunched in confusion. Why would he give such a command?

The air became filled with a high-pitched whistling noise. *The enemy must be launching the trebuchets, and Leon wants to keep casualties to a minimum*, he thought. The whistling seemed strange though. It didn't sound like the boulders that hurtled through the air the day before. Kole heard something crack against the wall followed by the clap of thunder. The ground shook beneath him as soldiers were thrown to the ground all around him. Kole kept his footing and watched as the top half of the cracked section of the first wall was ripped apart in an explosion of fire. Before he could wonder what was happening, the rest of the wall erupted as a repeated explosion ripped it apart.

Transferring his gaze to the wall, he watched as soldiers were thrown through the air. Scores fell screaming to their deaths. Panic swept through the Varkuvian ranks like fire through brush. They were expecting the enemy to attack the cracked foundation with trebuchets. Instead, they watched as that section of wall was ripped asunder by what appeared to Kole, like magic. There was no other explanation as to what just happened. A massive section of the wall came crashing down, sending dust and debris showering into the air. No one reacted. The debris combined with the dark fumes from the fiery explosion. The mixed cloud hung thick in the air.

Kole could hear the sounds of trumpets reverberating through the newly formed, low-laying cloud, which was punctured by the golden rays from above. The enemy was attacking and still no one was reacting. He suddenly realized he was on his knees in a crawling position. The second explosion must have knocked him to the ground. Dust caked the inside of his nostrils, and choked the back of his throat. The combined fumes made it even more difficult to breathe. Wiping his hand across his nose, and spitting whatever dust he could from his mouth, Kole rose to his feet. Gripping his spear, he began jogging unsteadily toward the downed section of the wall where a mound of broken rubble formed a small hill. He did not know if any of the two hundred selected spearmen were following him. He didn't even know if the Varkuvians upon the wall still remained or if they were retreating in sheer panic. Kole did not care.

*Today will not be about me for once*, he thought. *Today, my friends and comrades are depending on me to stand strong and hold the tide.*

As he approached the top of the small hill made of rubble, he gripped the leather straps of his shield and raised it to protect his face from the incoming arrows. He could hear the pounding of feet coming from the direction of the hostile encampment. Narrowing his eyes, he looked for any indication of the enemy. His gaze could not pierce the obstructive man-made fog in front of him. Movement from behind caused him to turn his head ever so slightly. Allyn came alongside him, his armor of Acrium covered in dust and soot. One by one, every hand-picked soldier made their way to the gap that opened up.

Pride roared through Kole. These men followed his lead and showed more courage in overcoming their fear than any normal human had a right to. Turning his attention forward once more, he was just in time to deflect an arrow with the brim of his shield. The arrow ricocheted off, plunging into the throat of the soldier behind him. The soldier fell to the ground, his hands desperately trying to prevent the mortal wound from claiming his life. Kole watched as life slowly faded from his eyes. Anger coursed through him. The Khali and easterners would not find him such an easy target.

The cloud of obstruction slowly began to dissipate. Kole could see a horde of blurred images rushing directly toward him through the dust. The soldiers, still shaken by the explosion, shifted nervously all around him. Morale was a fragile beast at best, and even though these men were handpicked for their courage, they were weighing their options. Did they want to stand and die or run and survive?

"Lock shields," yelled Kole.

Discipline took over. The front rank of Varkuvian soldiers dropped their shields, creating a new wall of rounded iron.

"Spears!" bellowed Kole.

The first ranks of the enemy cleared the mixed cloud. Seeing the Varkuvians before them, they yelled their hatred, surging forward. Spears bristled over the tops of the iron shields, ready to plunge home. For better or worse, the Varkuvians were set on their path now. A volley of arrows came from beyond the dust. The Varkuvians brought their shields to bear, deflecting the projectiles. Still, some got through the defenses, piercing unprotected legs and arms.

Kole sighted his spear on a tall easterner in a conical helmet. The rubble from the downed wall caused a slight incline, giving the defenders an advantage. The easterner ran uphill directly toward Kole, bellowing a war cry, bringing his sword back, ready to cleave his way into the Varkuvian ranks. Kole's spear point entered his brain, stopping him dead in his tracks. The front rank of Varkuvian spearmen followed his lead, plunging their spears downward into the flesh of the men who sought to destroy everything they held dear.

The enemy charge faltered as the Varkuvian spears found their marks. The carnage rose as they pressed tightly together, eager to avoid the thrusting spears. Hope built up inside Kole's chest as his spear claimed another victim. A mound of enemy dead was beginning to build up at the base of the rubble. They could hold this breach all day if they must. With a wide smile set upon his face, Kole looked up. The smile fell from his face.

The dust from the ruined wall and dark fumes from the explosion finally dispersed. Spread out before Kole was an ocean of enemies. On each face, whether it was the painted faces of the Khali or the helmeted swarthy features of the easterners, was open hatred. They were not deterred by the losses sustained by their forces but instead looked eager to replace their fallen comrades and sweep the Varkuvians aside.

"Kole, watch out!" warned Allyn.

Distracted as he was, Kole had not seen a massively muscled easterner bull rushing toward him. The double-headed ax in his hands was moving in a murderous downward sweep. Kole dropped down to his knee, bringing his shield above his head to block the blow. The force of the ax connecting with the shield shivered up the length of Kole's arm. His arm and fingers went numb. He was thrown to the ground, the shield slipping from his grasp. The muscled easterner towered over him, battle lust gleaming in his dark eyes. He brought the ax over his head to extinguish Kole's life.

Allyn jumped in front of Kole, his shield crashing forward into the easterner's face. The muscled axman staggered back. Recovering quickly, he yelled in fury. He stepped directly into the path of Allyn's plunging spear. The iron point exited through the easterner's spine. Blood bubbling from his mouth, the easterner grabbed ahold of the haft of the spear, drawing Allyn toward him. Releasing the spear, Allyn drew his short sword. The easterner feebly brought his ax up. Allyn's sword plunged into the man's heart. Withdrawing the blade, the easterner crumpled to the ground before tumbling down the mound of rubble, crashing into his comrades.

Unable to reclaim his spear, Allyn locked his shield in front of Kole, allowing him a moment's respite. Shaking his head, Kole forced himself to stand. His fingertips were throbbing. With a grimace of pain, he tried to close his hand into a fist. The action sent fresh pain lancing up his arm. Holding down a scream of anguish, he took short breaths between clenched teeth. The bones in his arm were shattered. Sweat coursed down his face. In the brief lull he had, his eyes raked the lines of Varkuvian spearmen. The line was still holding firm and taking a deadly toll upon the enemy, but the Khali and easterners were taking their toll as well. Almost half of the Varkuvian spearmen were down, and it was only a matter of time before the line would splinter and then they would be surrounded.

The sound to retreat came from the wall above. The Varkuvians upon the ramparts were given the order to pull back. Kole wiped the sweat from his eyes with his good hand. The spearmen could pull back in a fighting retreat. Even as Kole thought about the possibility of survival, he knew it would not happen. If the spearmen gave up any ground right now, the enemy would pour around them. Then they would have free reign to attack the retreating Varkuvians. Even still, if they stayed here as they were, the enemy would gain purchase upon the ramparts and attack them from the rear. They would have to act soon or face utter annihilation. With a force of will, Kole drew the blade at his side.

Allyn plunged his blade into a bearded opponent's face. Hearing the rasp of steel behind him, he glanced backward at Kole. He noted the gray sheen on Kole's face. "How are you doing back there, Kole?" he asked.

Kole began to answer when his gaze flickered beyond Allyn. "Allyn, get down!" he shouted.

Turning around, Allyn was just in time to see the Khali archer release his arrow. Twisting his body at the last possible moment, he prevented the arrow from piercing his jugular. Instead, the arrow ripped through the side of his neck, spraying blood into the air. Screaming in pain, Allyn did not see another Khali rushing toward him with spear raised. Kole stumbled forward, attempting to move into the path of the spearman. The Khali screamed a war cry as he plunged his spear forward. Kole dove forward to intercept the spear and watched as the darting weapon moved within inches of his body. The spear plunged into Allyn's side.

In a gasp of pain, Allyn clutched the haft jutting from his body. Kole landed hard on the mound of rubble directly on his broken arm. He channeled his pain into pure rage. His sword blade lanced forward. The Khali spearman released his hold on the spear but was too slow. Kole's sword sheered into his side and then pulled it out in the same motion. The Khali fell to the ground, clutching the mortal wound. Rolling onto his side, grunting in agony the whole time, Kole looked hopelessly upon Allyn. As gently as he could, he pulled him back from the action as Varkuvian spearmen moved forward to take their place.

Grabbing ahold of the spear still jutting from Allyn's side, Kole tore it loose. Allyn cried out in pain, his hands trying to staunch the arterial blood pumping from the wound. His hands were drenched in blood and gore. Kole saw his face was deathly pale. Allyn saw the concern upon Kole's face.

"Never thought it would end quite like this," Allyn said, managing a smile.

"You saved my life, and I could not return the deed," answered Kole grievously. "I am so sorry, Allyn."

"It doesn't exactly matter, does it?" Allyn responded, gesturing to the thinning ranks of Varkuvians.

Kole gazed all around him. Allyn was right. It was only a matter of time before the attackers would break through. The sounds of battle came from his left. Peering through the ranks of the defenders, he saw the enemy had taken the wall and was now attacking their flanks. They were doomed. Kole lowered his head to his chest, closed his eyes, and prayed to the gods for deliverance. He felt the warmth of sunlight bathe him. Opening his eyes, he gazed up at the sky. The sun shone through a break in the clouds overhead, covering the area in a golden hue.

For the first time in his life, Kole knew peace. He had overridden his desire for self-preservation and looked certain death in the eye. His quick actions when the wall fell ensured there were men to hold the breach. He saved hundreds if not thousands of lives on this day. Kole could feel the presence of his grandfather, mother, and father smiling down on him. They would be proud of him as they always were.

With a smile upon his face, he looked down at Allyn. Dead eyes stared back at him. His hand moved forward to close his recently departed comrade's eyes. Closing his own eyes, Kole whispered a prayer for Allyn. When his eyes opened again, they gleamed with renewed vigor.

"I will see you soon, my friend." He looked down once more at Allyn. "We will walk the road together into the afterlife."

Drawing his legs underneath him, he stood with sword in hand. As he said his final farewells, the last remaining Varkuvians formed an ever-tightening circle around Kole. All pain from his broken arm vanished. He waited patiently as one by one the men around him began to fall. The soldier in front of him fell, gurgling on his own blood. Kole stepped forward into the hole that opened up. His sword lanced forward into his opponent's eye.

Withdrawing the blade, he was just in time to block a thrust from his right as the soldier next to him fell. An ax head slammed into his left side. Kole calmly turned to dispatch the bearer. He felt blood running down his side, but he did not care. Swiveling back to the right, he sliced open the face of a painted Khali. A sword clanged against the back of his breastplate. He heard a bone snap. Turning around, he sliced open the jugular of the wielder. It was then, he saw there were only a handful of Varkuvians alive at wall one. Surrounding him was nothing but the enemy.

He chuckled, blood spilling from his mouth. A young Khali rushed forward, eager to claim the kill. Kole's wounds made him too slow to dodge the sword entering his side. His vision misted over. The Khali before him gave an evil grin. With the last of his strength, Kole's powerful arm thrust his sword forward into the Khali's smiling face. The point of the blade shattered the young man's ruined teeth before punching upward into his brain. Kole spit out the blood filling his mouth, spraying the enemy all around him.

As he fell to his knees, the enemy rushed forward. Their swords and axes pierced his body. Kole did not feel any of it. Warmth spread through his body, and he felt a strange feeling take over. His last conscious thought was that he had somehow ended up on his side, his blood staining the broken mound of wall beneath him. His eyes looked towards the heavens, searching for the sun. As darkness entered the corners of his vision, the sun broke free of the clouds one last time. A single tear slipped from the edge of Kole's eye. Three blurred figures were walking toward him from the sun, their arms opened wide in warm embrace. A smile split Kole's face. It remained there even as the ax fell that separated his head from his shoulders.

# CHAPTER THIRTEEN

Lightning forked the sky in the distance. Thunder roared forth from the heavens, growing in strength as it drew closer to the besieged city of Karalis. The ground beneath Lord Randell's chair shook as the thunder moved overhead. Lanterns hanging on brackets around the war council tent shook from side to side, casting flickering lights off the canvas walls. All conversation died down as the leaders of the eastern coalition waited for the booming disturbance to pass.

The dark eyes of Lord Drogos flicked to the ceiling of the tent, listening to the sleeting rain outside and the dying rumbles of thunder. His gaze fell back down upon the waiting war council. "As I was saying, we have won a great victory today. We saw the mighty Varkuvians humbled, fleeing before us as if the sight of our soldiers would put them in their graves." He raised a goblet brimming with wine. "Let us toast to the victory of our forces. In a few days' time we will be feasting in the famed Keep of Karalis itself."

The leaders of the eastern coalition raised their various drinks of wine and ale. A feast was laid upon the trestle table. There was roasted mutton and venison along with trays of exotic fruits and delicious sweet cakes and pies. Servants walked around the tent, filling empty cups, making sure those present were content. A juggler performed in the corner, throwing several glittering knives spinning through the air while a bard sang a jaunty tune of the victor. *This is more of a banquet than a war council*, Randell thought. *We should be making preparations to claim Karalis, not sit here indulging ourselves.* While the lord of Cabalo sipped his wine, his sharp blue eyes scanned the faces of the men around the table. The major chieftains of the Northern Woods, the Khali, they now styled themselves as, sat on the opposite side of the table. *This is why we are feasting*, he told himself. *To hold this fragile alliance together.*

There were some thirty chieftains of the Northern Woods, but only the seven most powerful were present. Their hostility for one another was barely concealed. Randell's eyes flicked to Jarla, the sour hatchet-faced leader of the Tetron tribe. Jarla's pale gaze constantly darted at Rolan, the leader of the Bidai tribe, who sat at the far end of the table. Randell could see the daggers thrown in Rolan's direction with each and every look. Before the uniting of the tribes, the Bidai and Tetron had been at war with one another for so long, that no living soul could say who started it.

Randell's eyes drifted to Dusana, leader of the Kanza tribe, and the only woman chieftain present. Her features were lined from years living in the harsh environment of the north, yet there was an intelligence to her face and a look in her brown eyes that demanded respect. The tribes of the Northern Woods viewed women as not only their equals but in most cases far superior. With the men of the north generally learning to fight from birth, the women were raised to assess a situation from a far less physical aspect and, thus, make better judgments. Of the thirty tribes of the Northern Woods, twelve of them were led by women.

Even though they were allowed to lead, women of the tribes were forbidden to kill anyone in the heat of battle. All of the men could be slain in battle, yet the tribe's name would live on if all of the women were left intact, even if they had to merge with another tribe. Regardless of this rationalization, the women were trained in combat, and it was said that many could handle a blade as well as any man. One day Randell asked Dusana why the women were trained to fight if it was against their beliefs for a woman to kill. She responded, "It is far better to know how to defend oneself if the situation arises than to wait like a pig, ripe for slaughter."

How strange it was that the tribes of the Northern Woods, considered to be the most barbaric of civilizations, allowed their women the right of leadership and trusted in their ability to better their people; yet a women like Dusana, strong and proud like an untamed colt, would never be given that opportunity in the eastern city-states or the realms of the Five Kings. If she had been born in these civilized lands, she might have become an owner of a productive business or inn, but her accomplishments would always be overshadowed by men that were more than likely less competent than her. Her income would be substantially less as well, not because she was undeserving, but due to the simple fact she had been born without a second head dangling in between her legs.

It would be even worse if she was born into nobility. Her strong personality and daunting gaze would either drive any suitor away or give him the impression that he could break her strong will either with whip or harsh word. She would be sold off to the highest bidder, her personal happiness an afterthought to the lands and wealth that would be gained at her expense. That was all women were to the nobility, breeding cows for the right price. Yet in the Northern Woods, women not only had the right to choose whomever they wanted to marry but could also dissolve the marriage if they were unhappy. The chieftains did not inherit their title based on their blood, passed down from generation to generation, but instead were elected to position based on their merits. It was truly puzzling to Randell, and he found himself reassessing the word *civilized*.

The tension surrounding the chieftains of the Northern Woods was so tangible that it was starting to grind on Randell's nerves. Each of them had a bodyguard standing close by, their hands constantly on their weapons, ready to react at the first sign of danger. Even though they were a people who believed in equality, they were still brought up to hate one another and taught from their first steps, they must destroy their enemies. Randell's gaze swept over all of the chieftains until his eyes fell upon the man seated to Drogos's right at the head of the table.

Here was the man who held them all together. Grand Chieftain Timon, he called himself, though Randell knew him his as Mason, the exiled Master of Spear. Seated next to him were the other exiled masters, Petros and Orrin. These three once were the leaders of the Order of Acrium and were some of the most respected men in Varkuvia. Their very names lit the fires of fear into the hearts of their enemies.

Petros, the banished Master of Bow, was wolf lean with shoulder-length white hair and a well-trimmed beard. Despite being in his midfifties, his pale blue eyes had a sharpness to them that missed nothing, and he sat as straight in his chair as the arrows he loosed. Though he was a man of few words, when he spoke, his words were treated with respect. Many years ago, Petros was banned from participating in any archery tournament in all of the five reams. It was declared unanimously, he would hopelessly outclass any who went against him, making the contest unfair from the start. Few men in the known world came close to his skill.

Orrin, the exiled Master of Ax, sat beside him, looking like a miniature ox. The man was ripping through a hunk of roasted mutton, the hot grease running down his wide face. In between bites, he swilled down a large mug or, more accurately, a jug of ale. The woolen shirt he wore was sleeveless. His biceps were larger than most men's thighs. It wasn't just his sheer strength that made Orrin special though. The man could grab a fly in midflight, straight from the air. His reaction time and hand-eye coordination were astounding for a man of his size. Despite his massive physique, his light brown eyes and broad face wore a constant jovial expression. Even now, with the tension from the chieftains, Orrin's eyes sparkled and a subconscious grin spread across his greasy cheeks.

At last, Randell inspected Mason. Here, there was no joviality, no open friendliness. Mason's hooded eyes gleamed with feral intelligence, and his face was set in permanent seriousness. He rarely sipped the cup of wine set before him, his fierce eyes instead, observing the men set around the table. No one believed an outsider from the Northern Woods could unite the tribes, yet this man achieved the impossible in just six months. Randell saw Drogos lean toward Mason, whispering into his ear. Then Drogos laughed, grasping Mason on the shoulder wholeheartedly. Mason laughed politely, the false bravado unable to hide the distaste from his eyes. It was obvious the banished master did not like sitting amongst such company, but his need for revenge outweighed his desire for such companionship. *Bitterness can truly be a potent weapon*, Randell thought.

Randell knew Drogos was no fool. He would see the dangers that Mason posed. Even while he sat next to him jesting, Drogos would be planning in his mind how to eliminate the future threat. With Drogos, there were no friends, only temporary allies. Randell hid the loathing for the serpent from his expression. His contempt for the ruler of Yursa had increased tenfold since the siege of Karalis began. His men were always the last to join the fray, and Drogos was always sure to keep himself far from harm's way. Instead, he manipulated others to do his bidding as he watched from a safe distance. A true leader should stand side by side with his men and endure the same perils they do. Calming himself, Randell took another sip of his wine.

Drogos rose from his seat at the head of the table, lifting his hands for silence. Randell hated that he obeyed the man instantaneously as did everyone else present. The singing bard and juggler ceased their entertaining, standing awkwardly by. "My dear allies," began Drogos, "I am afraid the time for celebrations must be put off. Disturbing news arrived today even as our brave men were taking the wall. It seems that our Argarian allies were utterly crushed while besieging King Eryk's capital city of Varlos. Our ally and dear friend, King Ragnar, grew impatient waiting for our forces to combine with his and took it upon himself to tackle the two kings alone. The battle for the city that ensued was decisive, to say the least. Of the twelve thousand men King Ragnar had under his command, less than two thousand remain alive. Many of the survivors carry injuries, and a majority of his fleet was burned in the retreat. King Ragnar himself was slain in the battle and his son, Prince Logan, took what remains of their crippled fleet and battered army back to the Storm Islands with his tail between his legs. Prince Logan, now acting as king of the Storm Islands, has renounced us as his allies and has declared the Argarians will remain out of the war. We now have three weeks before King Eryk and King Stefanos will reinforce the defenders of Karalis. I do not think I need to point out the obvious. The city must be taken before they arrive."

"What of King Lucan?" asked Lord Nikolaos. "Has there been any word of him?"

"For the time being, it would seem that King Lucan is staying out of this war," said the lord of Yursa. "He is not a threat at present. King Stefanos and King Eryk will bring seven thousand cavalry, three thousand infantry, and over two thousand highly trained archers. Over eleven thousand vengeful men looking to bring the wrath of the gods down upon us."

Despite the devastating news, Randell could not help but feel an inner elation. King Stefanos, and the reason he even agreed to join this war, was now riding to him. He was finally being presented the opportunity to avenge the stain left on his ancestors' memory. For a moment, he imagined the usurper being slain by his own hand. *I will fight you face-to-face*, he thought, *even if it's the last thing I do in this world.* Focusing on the matter at hand, he observed the men sitting around the table and their reactions. Glancing to his left, he saw Lord Nikolaos leaning back in his chair, deep in thought, but offering nothing. Seated next to him, on his right, Lord Dorian was dabbing at his forehead with a scented handkerchief. The fat lord of Sura was sweating profusely and ill at ease.

He flicked his gaze across the table to see how the chieftains were taking the news. His blood froze. Not just the chieftains, but also their bodyguards, were staring intently at Mason, no expression evident on any of their faces. Their belief in their leader was absolute, and they knew, when he spoke, he would be speaking for all of them. Randell looked to Mason. The chieftain was leaning forward intently in his chair, his sharp gaze studying the frayed map spread out before him, seeming to read it all at a glance.

Mason looked up, the light from the lanterns catching in the globes of his eyes. "It seems we have little option presented to us." His voice was low but still managed to carry to every ear present. "As long as the defenders hold the second wall, we can only make a frontal assault. We must take this wall, and swiftly, before we can make any other plans. Once we have taken this wall, we can surround the city, and the final wall that surrounds the Keep of Karalis like a protective ring. Then we can attack the defenders from multiple angles, overwhelming them with sheer numbers. Once King Markos and King Alaric are defeated, we can focus on the other kings." He transferred his attention to Drogos. "How much of this black powder do we still possess?"

"Unfortunately, we used the last of it destroying the first wall," Drogos said with the slightest amount of irritation in his voice. The man was unaccustomed to unforeseen variables, such as Kaleb and the power he displayed. "Most of our precious stores were destroyed when Prince Leon was rescued from the Bale Fort and that cursed lightning bolt erupted among our cache of barrels."

For the first time since the war council feast started, Randell saw the chieftains shift uncomfortably. Many put their fists over their hearts, the tribal sign to ward off evil spirits. Dark stories were told around their campfires after the rescue of Prince Leon and the destruction of a large group of their outriders at the hands of a disbanded swordsman of the Order, Kaleb. Randell himself found the outrageous stories hard to believe, but the scorched earth and charred remains of the corpses left in the wake of the aftermath did not lie. Few people in recorded history in the Northern Woods or the eastern city-states possessed the ancient blood, but even still, they were told the stories as children of the all-but-extinct Verillion people. As implausible as it seemed, a man wielding magic emerged.

And he was on the opposing side.

The tribesmen believed Kaleb was a demon called Toraz summoned by Hastos, their Forest God, to wreak vengeance upon them for their sins. Toraz, according to their legends, had eyes that blazed like the sun and could not be defeated by any mortal man. And the legends surely matched the description they heard of Kaleb. The Khali were unafraid to face any foe with spear or blade, but they were a superstitious people. Three of the chieftains, believing the wrath of Hastos was being unleashed upon them, packed up their belongings and returned to the Northern Woods with all of their men in tow. Randell and the other eastern lords arrived several days before with the vanguard of their forces to a gathering of the chieftains in the middle of a heated discussion.

The chieftains were gathered in a tight circle around Mason with Orrin and Petros on either side of him. Mason stood with his arms across his chest, his demeanor calm. He listened patiently as the chieftains presented their arguments as to why they should abandon the cause and go home. After hearing each of them out, he raised a hand for silence. One by one, the chieftains obeyed. Randell, standing his horse close to the group, heard the speech that followed.

"I hear what each of you says," said Mason. "And I respect your words, but none of you know this man as I do. For years, it was I who trained Kaleb and instructed him. It was I who grew to know him, to understand him. I personally rejoice it is he who possesses these powers and not another more worthy. Kaleb is nothing more than a spoiled, arrogant young man who will never know his own limits. He is no demon. He is just a typical Varkuvian. We should not cower before him but strive to strike him from this world. Hastos is not punishing us for our sins. He is seeking to test our faith." Mason paused to let the words soak in, his eyes scanning the gathered men before him. "If we run now, after all we have accomplished, we will forever banish our souls to the Wood of Tears and bring disgrace upon our children and their children's children. Our shame will echo through the Halls of the Fallen. Let us stay and show Hastos our faith is strong."

The speech was not dramatic in its deliverance, but even Randell, lacking the beliefs and ideals of the tribesmen, found his heartbeat accelerating and felt his confidence soaring. The majority of the chieftains were won over, the tension easing, but Randell could see one, standing slightly in front of the others, his broad chest puffed out, his close set eyes blazing in anger. Later, Randell would learn this was Zurok, chieftain of the Chetco tribe and considered one of the most powerful chieftains in the Northern Woods. The man was ferocious with a sword and built a reputation as a brute. It was rumored he had beaten his own brother to death with his bare hands after a woman spurned him for his brother instead. Zurok took a step into the circle, towering above Mason.

"An outsider dares question our faith in Hastos?" asked Zurok, menacingly. "You speak to us as though you are one of us, but Zurok did not see your blessing beneath the Sacred Tree. Zurok did not see you learn to hunt the great elk with your father or drink from the Falls of Hastos to become a man. Zurok says Toraz will kill us all if we stay here. You are like an angry child who will get us all killed. Zurok says you are no leader." Stepping back, Zurok spit at Mason's feet. Drawing his sword, he slashed it through the air. The other chieftains moved back, creating a space between themselves and the challenger.

Orrin shook his huge head, chuckling. "Let me crush this man for you," he said amiably, stepping forward.

Mason's hand flashed out to stop him, his eyes drilling into Zurok's. The challenge was made public in front of everyone to see. To the tribesmen, strength was everything. If Mason allowed others to fight his battles for him, he would not last long as leader. Waving Orrin and Petros back from him, he drew his sword. He did not loosen up but merely stood there, his sword hanging casually at his side, staring at Zurok.

Screaming a battle cry, Zurok rushed at Mason. Holding his sword double-handed, he swung for Mason's head, seeking to end the duel in one mighty stroke. Mason ducked under the swing easily. Zurok's charge carried him past Mason for several paces. When he turned back around, there was a thin line of red running from his top shoulder down to his hip. A gasp echoed through the gathered chieftains. Randell blinked, focusing on the wound. He had not even seen Mason's sword move to deliver the blow. Zurok glanced down, touching his fingers to the blood streaming from the wound. When he looked up the anger was gone from his eyes. It was replaced by fear. Looking around the group, he saw no one, not even his own men, would come to his aid. He was utterly alone. Swallowing hard, he looked back at Mason, his face pale white.

This time it was Mason who advanced. He did not rush but merely walked toward Zurok, his eyes locked to the chieftain's the entire time. Zurok did not react at first as if he were in a trance. At the last possible moment, he brought his sword to bear, aiming for Mason's chest. Mason casually swatted the sword aside before stepping in to drive his own blade into Zurok's heart. Withdrawing the sword, Zurok fell to his knees, his eyes looking up at Mason as if begging for forgiveness. Without hesitation, Mason spun in a circle before bringing his sword into Zurok's neck, decapitating him. His body remained up for a few more moments before convulsing and collapsing to the ground.

Mason then thrust his sword into the ground, the blood dripping down the length of the blade soaking the grass. His eyes raked the circle of tribesmen. "Is there anyone else who wishes to question my faith? If so, make it known now."

Over a hundred tribesmen had gathered by the conclusion of the duel, including blood kin to Zurok. Not one of them said a word. The next day they marched upon Karalis.

Randell dragged his mind to the present. Mason did not rule the tribesmen because they loved him. They followed him because they knew he was a strong leader, and under his leadership, their people would flourish and their enemies would die. Most importantly though, they feared his retribution. If another chieftain were to come along who was stronger or more willful, Mason would be replaced in an instant. Randell saw a flash of annoyance cross Mason's eyes. Drogos could have simply said there was no more of the explosive powder; instead, he subtlety brought up a subject that recently put Mason's leadership in jeopardy.

"Well that is out of the question then," said Mason, keeping his voice neutral. "We must explore other options then. So far, our strategy of attacking the wall with grappling hooks and ladders has failed miserably. We must strike at the heart of the defenders while they are demoralized from the loss of their wall. The longer we give them, the more their resolve will strengthen." He turned to Drogos once more.

"What of the Legion of the Rising Sun? We have not used them yet, and now would be a perfect opportunity to break the defenders."

"Don't be ridiculous," Drogos said, waving his hand dismissively. "It is far too early in the war to be using the best our forces have to offer. We still have King Lucan to deal with eventually if you haven't forgotten. He alone can muster close to twenty-five thousand men. We will need the Legion then."

"I think it is the entire council that should be making that decision and not only you." Mason stared Drogos in the eye. Randell shivered. It was the same exact way he stared at Zurok right before he killed him. "If we do not take Karalis before reinforcements arrive, then this invasion will fail. I think we should vote on the matter instead of the final judgment being solely yours."

The silence that followed was unnerving. Everyone knew Drogos was the unspoken leader of the invasion force. No one questioned his right to lead, not to his face, at least; yet Mason had just done so in front of everyone. Thunder boomed overhead. Drogos gave a tight smile though his eyes showed no humor.

"Unfortunately, that vote must be put off," he said, "since the Legion was still gathering when we departed our respected city-states and left after we did. They will be here within a few days. I will be more than happy to put the matter to a vote once they arrive."

"Then it seems we have no choice but to proceed as we have been for the time being," Mason said though it was obvious he was not pleased by Drogos's answer.

Within that short span, the tent was divided in two. For one perilous moment, it seemed as though the delicate alliance between the Northern Woods and the eastern city-states would shatter. Randell felt uncomfortably warm, perspiration forming under his clothing. His hand itched, a subconscious reflex that he should draw the knife sheathed at his side in self-defense. He resisted the urge. For several seconds no one spoke. Then Dorian gave a nervous chuckle, his chins wobbling.

Drogos put back on his facade of generosity, his smile slipping back into place. "I think we have discussed enough of war for one evening. Let's bring in the night's entertainment and enjoy our first victory. All of you can be assured, there will be many more to follow."

The lord of Yursa picked up a miniature bell next to him on the table and rang it. The front flap of the tent was opened by a sentry waiting outside. A line of women made their way into the tent, soaked from head to toe from the pouring rain. They were all topless, their nipples hard. The silk red skirts they wore swished back and forth with the movement of their hips, flicking droplets of rain to the ground. They were all stunningly attractive with tanned skin, full lips, and sultry eyes. Everything about them promised a night that would not be forgotten.

Drogos gave a broad smile. "This is the entertainment. Enjoy."

The bard that was standing uncomfortably by cleared his throat and broke into song once more. The juggler began twirling his knives, and within seconds, they were a blur, flying through the air. The naked women spread out around the tent. A woman with large breasts slid onto Lord Nikolaos's lap, wrapped her hand around his neck, and drew him into a passionate kiss. Soon the wine was flowing freely, the singing and promiscuous women easing the tension in the tent. Two women of surpassing beauty fed Lord Dorian grapes while he sipped on his wine. The fat lord was overly pleased with himself, grabbing one of the women's breasts forcefully. She screamed playfully.

Randell let the festivities slide over him. He was in no mood for celebrations. Without his wife beside him, it just wasn't the same for him. Normally, after a hard day such as this, he would fall into her warm embrace and let the worries of the world slip away from him. He leaned back in his chair, sipping his wine, when a woman with dark curly hair and eyes the size of saucers slid onto his lap. Her pupils were dilated, and it was obvious she had partaken in narcotics. She pressed her bare breasts against Randell's body, the soft flesh pressing hard against his chest. He became aware of a stirring passion in his loins.

"You can do anything you'd like to me, m'lord," she whispered to him before nibbling on his earlobe.

The promise was enticing, and Randell found his thoughts slipping toward his sexual desires. Almost immediately, the image of his wife came into his mind. She was probably worried sick about him right now, wondering whether he was alive or dead, and here he was thinking about fornicating with a drugged-up whore. He hated himself for even been tempted in such a way. Guilt overwhelmed him. The woman on his lap slid her hand expertly down his pants. Randell's hand clamped down on her wrist, stopping her. She was unperturbed and began kissing his neck, moaning while she did so. Groaning, Randell picked her up off his lap. She immediately went over to another woman and began kissing her intensely, which caused raucous cheering from the chieftains. One of them got up from the table and went behind the woman, grabbed her hips, and bent her over. Randell looked away.

Taking a deep breath, Randell stood up, heading toward the tent entrance. He needed fresh air. Nikolaos pulled back from the woman on his lap who was fondling him while biting her lower lip. "Where are you going, Randell?" he called after the departing lord.

Ignoring him, Randell walked out into the torrential storm. Lighting lit up the night sky as he walked outside. For the merest moment, the entire encampment was illuminated. Thousands of tents spread out before him, seeming to stretch on forever. So many people willing to die for the ambitions of just a few. Randell was disgusted by it all. The stupidity of war, the hatreds it bred, the horrors it inflicted, all of the men and women who would be cut down in their prime. The negatives were countless while the positives were nonexistent. War contributed nothing but heartache and suffering to the world. *And you are one of the main people causing the pain and grief for future generations to come*, he told himself.

He needed to take a walk to take his mind off things. Taking another deep breath, he wrapped his cloak around his stocky frame, lowered his head into the lashing rain, and began walking. He had no immediate destination planned. A sentry standing guard recognized Randell. Noting his strange behavior, he called out to him. "Excuse me, m'lord, do you need any help?"

*None that you can provide*, thought Randell. Ignoring the sentry, he kept walking. The sentry, unsure of what to do, shifted nervously. "Do you need an escort, m'lord?" he called out to Randell.

Randell just kept walking. His path eventually took him to the first wall of Karalis. The storm made it impossible to clear out all of the bodies from when the wall was breached. Bloated corpses still littered the muddy ground and remained in the gap of the wall. The rain had not stopped the carrion birds from feasting, however, and Randell could see that the eyes of the corpses were pecked out, and strips of flesh were missing. Choosing his path carefully, he wound his way up the destroyed wall, trying to avoid his gaze from the mutilated corpses.

Coming to the top of the rubble, he looked back upon the eastern coalition encampment. Here the Varkuvians had made their final stand even when all seemed lost. To them, they were opposing the evil Khali and the treacherous easterners. They died believing they were defending their lands and protecting their loved ones. Looking down, he saw the decapitated corpse of a soldier. Peering intently, he saw the man was wearing the armor of Acrium and received many grievous wounds. He found himself wondering who the man was. What ambitions did he have? Was he a kind man, or was he a tormented soul? Was he respected, or was he just another solider caught up in the craziness of war?

Turning around, he focused his attention on the second wall of Karalis. Right here was either the stepping stone for his hopes and dreams or the destruction of them. *Are they your hopes and dreams or your father's?* he asked himself. Randell's father was consumed by his desire to exact revenge. Day in and day out, it was all the old man spoke of. He died a bitter man, and upon his deathbed made his only son promise, he would do everything within his power to kill King Stefanos and restore honor to their family name.

Randell wanted none of it. All he wanted was to raise horses, live happily with his wife, and watch his two children grow. It was all any man should ever ask for, but it was never enough. Over the years, his father's bitterness had rubbed off on him, and soon enough it began consuming his days and nights, same as it did for his father. And so he dedicated his life to seeing King Stefanos toppled. No matter the cost. His gaze drifted to the decapitated corpse once more. *No matter the cost*, he told himself again.

For several minutes he stood there, his head bowed, lost in thought. The rain poured down upon him, soaking him to the bone, water dripping from his fire-red beard. His thoughts buzzed around his mind like a swarm of flies. He heard a piece of rubble shift behind him. So consumed was he in his own thoughts, he barely acknowledged the approach of another person.

"Thank the gods I wasn't an assassin, eh?" a familiar voice asked.

Giving a tired smile, Randell looked up at Kleitos, his most trusted friend and advisor. Silver spread at the temples of his friend's shoulder-length light brown hair and a fork of silver ran through his goatee. Kleitos's deep brown eyes looked as though they contained a world of knowledge, yet Randell knew all it would take was a moment of immaturity for a childish sparkle to enter those orbs. Despite being in his midforties, Kleitos was still ruggedly handsome. They were childhood friends and had known each other for the majority of one another's lives. Randell's responsibilities and title allowed him precious few moments to drop his guard and be himself in his lifetime. There were only two people he opened his heart to. One of them was Myra, his loving wife, the other was Kleitos.

"How did you know where I was?" asked Randell.

"Normally when the lord of Cabalo goes for a stroll in the midst of a murderous thunderstorm, it's going to raise some suspicions," Kleitos responded. "The sentry who reported you wandered off looked as though he was about to shit himself. Your mind is a thousand miles away." He grasped Randell on the shoulder. "My father always used to say a burden shared with a friend will lessen the heartache on your soul. Granted, he was a drunken sot the majority of the time, but fuck it, it still sounds good."

"What makes you think something is wrong?" asked Randell drily.

"Well, let's see, besides the fact I have known you for over forty years"—Kleitos looked around him at the destruction of the wall and the corpses still strewn on the ground—"you're also standing on a burial ground with the stench of death all around you and look so depressed you could kill a newborn kitten. Did the meeting really go that badly?"

"It could not have gone any worse. King Ragnar has been utterly crushed, his army in tatters and his fleet destroyed. King Stefanos and King Eryk are now riding towards us with their full force behind them. And the division between Timon and Drogos is going to draw blood sooner or later. Most of us walk around with bodyguards, fearing that one of our so-called 'allies' will stab us in the back and think nothing of it. Other than that, everything is just fine."

His friend chuckled, the sound whipping away in the storm. "Oh please, do spare me your tales of woe next time. You can feed that bull-shit to someone who doesn't know you. Those are serious matters, but I know that is not what's bothering you. Are you going to tell me, or do I have to stand here with you all night, getting drenched, and praying we do not get pneumonia or that the enemy doesn't sally forth while we do not have the wall fully secured?"

The only answer was the tinkering of the rain off the armor of the corpses around them. Randell's eyes were downcast. Kleitos stared closely at him. "All night it is then," he declared, shuffling his feet and wrapping his drenched cloak tightly around his frame. "We haven't spent an entire night in the rain since we had to run away from that farmer when he caught us laying with his daughters."

A soft chuckle escaped Randell's throat. "That was a good time. How old were we when that happened? Sixteen? Seventeen?"

"Damned if I know. Seems like just yesterday if you ask me. What I do remember is the breasts on the one daughter. Needed two hands just to hold one. If I had any sense, I would've married that woman."

"If I recall correctly, you shoved me into a thorn bush that night. My mother was furious when I arrived back home, covered in mud, still reeking of alcohol, and my new leggings shredded. That was the worst beating I ever received."

Kleitos was taken back. "The way I remember it, I shoved you into that bush to save you from the farmer while I took him off our trail. I was like your guardian angel that night."

"Too bad you shoved me after we already escaped, you bastard!"

"Funny how alcohol can affect the memory like that, huh?" asked Kleitos with a wide grin.

The two burst out into laughter, the sound reverberating off the wall behind them. Some of the tension eased away from Randell. The laughter died down until only silence remained. Randell looked away from his friend. "I am scared, Kleitos. I am scared down to my very soul. For the first time in years, I have doubts that leave me awake at night. That is what is bothering me."

"You would be a fool if you weren't scared," the advisor responded. "This is no child's game we are playing at here. It is either us or them. There is no middle ground."

"It's not just this war." Randell threw up his hands in frustration. "It is everything. When we started plotting this campaign years ago, I envisioned the Five Kings as evil. It was black against white. Good against evil. They were greedy, selfish bastards who hoarded their advancements in technology and kept their resources to themselves. And we were attempting to rid the world of their tyranny, to make the world a better place. It was that simple. For years, I have dreamt of nothing other than killing King Stefanos and reclaiming my birthright. It is all I have thought about." His eyes took on a faraway look. "I hate that man with every fiber of my being, yet I know nothing of him. I know nothing of his dreams or ambitions, whether he is a good father or husband. He might die in this war because of a promise I made to my father on his deathbed, and not even for his own personal actions, but events perpetrated by his ancestors over a century ago. I have witnessed atrocities committed in this war that will stain my soul forever. Now I wonder if either side is black and white or if we are all just shades of gray." He lapsed into silence.

"Then why not take your men home?" asked Kleitos softly. "They would follow you into the lakes of hell if you asked them. You know this. All you have to do is give the command, and we will pack up and leave. Damn this war and damn our so-called allies."

"And then what? How long before Drogos turns his wrath on us? How many sleepless nights can I have before one of his assassin's knives finds its way into my throat? How long will I have to look over my shoulder?" Randell shook his head. "And if the Five Kings win, how long will it be before they bring their retribution down upon me? I couldn't possibly hope to withstand them on my own. Whether I like it or not, I am in far too deep now to ever consider turning around."

"Drogos," Kleitos spit the name. "That man is a snake if I ever saw one. For years, he was always so damn adamant about timing. We tiptoed around, making sure we would surprise the Varkuvians when the time came, yet we allowed the enemy weeks to fortify their position and send for aid. And if I recall, Drogos said the Order of

Acrium would not be an issue, yet here they are, defying our forces and killing countless numbers of our men. If everything went according to plan, as he promised it would, then our combined forces should have taken Karalis by now, and we should have linked up with King Ragnar. Now the Argarian king is dead, and our army has no support once we move further west. So far this invasion has gone to complete and utter shit."

There was no argument to be given. Kleitos was right, and Randell remained silent. "I say we see this thing out and kill Stefanos," Kleitos stated. "That way your relatives can rest peacefully in the afterlife, and you can finally find some peace of mind. You are far too good of a man to allow this to gnaw at your soul."

"And what of Stefanos's seven-year-old son, Hagan, or his sixteen-year-old daughter, Isabelle? His son, Kastor, has already been slain by assassins, so at least I do not have to allow that to trouble my mind. The vengeance I promised is not just against him but his entire bloodline. I would have to slay them as well. And what of his other relatives? Will I also have to kill his nephews, nieces, cousins, and siblings as well? Even if I wanted to, I could not allow them to live. I would be taking over a hostile kingdom. There would be no room for sympathy, or else I would risk the people rising against me. Do I have it in me to order the deaths of babes and women? I fear I am not strong enough for this."

"What nonsense are you talking about?" asked Kleitos outraged. "You would be a monster if you could so casually take away human life without feeling the tiniest bit of remorse. The guilt you feel at the weight of this decision only emphasizes your greatness, but you cannot allow it to consume you. Your men need you right now. How do you think it will look to them that you wandered off depressed and alone in the middle of a storm? They will lose heart once they hear of it."

Randell said nothing. "If there's one thing I remember your father saying," Kleitos continued, "it's that life is just like the weather. It is constantly shifting and changing. One moment, the sun can be shining, and life can seem utterly perfect. Then it could feel like a thunderstorm, relentless and hopeless, but all storms, no matter how bad, will eventually pass. You just have to ride this current storm out. And as always, I will be there beside you. We will weather this damn thing together, no matter how bad it gets. Together we will spit in the face of adversity."

Even as he spoke, the rain began to lessen until it was no more than a light drizzle. Randell looked up at the cloudy sky, his hair and clothing completely drenched. He looked over at Kleitos. "You truly are a good friend, Kleitos," he said. "I feel as though I don't tell you enough."

"There's no need to mention it. Now can we get out of this rain before you get even more maudlin on me? Before I know it, you will be propositioning me, and I do not think Myra would approve of such a thing, even if I do just so happen to be a dashingly good-looking man. I have a flagon of wine that has been calling my name all evening. I might even be inclined to share it."

"Did someone say wine?" Nikolaos asked, stumbling toward them. The lord of Seren's eyes were blurry, and each of his arms was draped over the shoulder of a woman, both of which were naked from head to toe.

Kleitos ran his eyes over the two women, noting their large breasts and the wetness of their skin from the rain. One of them winked at him while the other blew him a kiss. "I would be willing to share," Kleitos said with a wide grin. "That is, if you are."

Nikolaos gave a lopsided grin. Before he could give his answer, the sound of thrumming filled the air. An arrow landed with a soft thud in the muddy ground harmlessly away from the group. It came from the second wall of Karalis. Kleitos raised his hand toward the wall, gesturing inappropriately toward his privates.

"Go fuck your mothers!" he yelled.

In response, the defenders sent another arrow, which landed far away from the group. Nikolaos looked ponderously at the arrows as if he had forgotten where he was. Sniffing, he turned his attention back on Kleitos.

"Step into my office," he said, his words slurring. "And we will work out an agreement." He licked his dry lips. "But be sure to bring that wine with you."

Kleitos laughed before slapping the buttocks of one of the women who yelped in response. Then he clapped Randell on the back. "Will you be joining us, my friend? If not for the women, at least to share a cup or two of wine in good company."

Randell had no interest whatsoever. "Not tonight. You two go off and have your fun."

The smile slipped off Kleitos' face. "Do not stay here for long. Those bastards are getting a little too bold for my liking."

"Thank you, mother," responded Randell. "But I think I will be fine. Go and enjoy yourself, you rascal."

Nodding, Kleitos, and the others began walking back to the encampment. Once they were clear of the corpses, Randell saw Kleitos gestured to the two women. Nikolaos nodded in agreement to whatever Kleitos proposed. Then one of the women jumped onto Kleitos's back. The other went on Nikolaos's back. Randell faintly heard one of them yell "Go!" before they began racing back to camp, each with a naked woman bouncing on their backs. Almost immediately, Nikolaos slipped and fell face-first into a large tract of mud, the woman on his back sharing his fate. When he stood up, he was covered completely in mud as was the naked woman beside him.

Booming laughter reached Randell's ears. A grin split his face and a deep chuckle escaped his lips. The soft thud of another arrow landing in the ground behind him caused him to turn his attention back on the second wall. A flash of lightning lit up the sky, followed by the clapping of thunder, caused the rearing wall to seem even more imposing. *I will claim my vengeance against Stefanos,* he decided. *And then I will make my move against Drogos before he makes his move on me. One thing at a time,* he reminded himself. Karalis must fall before he could deal with the serpent lord. Looking at the monstrous wall, his doubts came rushing back. He pushed them away. *I will shatter this rock,* he promised himself, *even if I have to do it with my bare hands.*

Turning around, he whipped his drenched cloak behind him and began the walk back to his tent. Tomorrow would begin the real test. Win or lose, his mind was set. Karalis would fall, or Randell would die in the attempt.

# CHAPTER FOURTEEN

The dream was fragmented, coming in sharply one moment then hazy the next. A shadowy figure was walking toward him, the movements smooth but unrushed. The face, partially hooded, looked familiar yet not easily placed. The figure stopped directly before him, offering no danger. From the shrouds of darkness, at the edge of his dream emerged four other hooded figures, crowding behind the one standing before him. The five hooded figures merely stood there, not offering a single word.

"Who are you?" he finally asked the stranger in front of him.

"I am the hope of tomorrow," answered the hooded figure, the voice strangely distorted. A knife suddenly flashed forward, plunging into his side.

Trystan's eyes snapped open. He could see the sky was still dark outside, hours yet from dawn. His leg was cramped, the wounds upon his arm and leg itchy and uncomfortable. Looking down upon Arianna resting on his chest, he realized his arm wrapped tightly around her fell asleep. He gently flexed his hand, the motion sending pins and needles up his sleeping limb. Not wishing to disturb her, he ignored the discomfort and attempted to go back to sleep once more. He was half-asleep when the flashing knife from his dreams entered his mind. This time he jumped awake, dislodging Arianna's head.

She groaned softly, opening one eye sleepily. Stretching, she looked up at Trystan, her curly hair falling in front of her fair face. "A bad dream?" she asked, yawning.

"Unfortunately, yes," responded Trystan, his brow drenched in sweat. "I am sorry for waking you."

"Don't be ridiculous," she said, rubbing at her eyes. "What was it about?"

"I do not know," he answered truthfully. "Most of the time I do not even remember my dreams, yet this one was filled with hidden meaning I cannot discern."

"Maybe you are just stressed," she offered. "These past few days haven't been easy."

"That's putting it mildly." He threw the covers from his body. "I think I just need to get some air to help clear my mind."

"I will go with you then," said Arianna though her head was resting on the soft mattress, her eyes closed once more.

Bending down, Trystan kissed her forehead. "You go back to sleep. I will rejoin you shortly."

"Are you certain?" she mumbled drowsily. "I worry about you when I am not with you."

"I am positive."

"Promise me you will return shortly."

"I promise," he assured her.

Throwing on breeches, a loose-fitting tunic of faded evergreen, and a dark cloak, Trystan picked up his sword and left the room. In the hallway beyond, Gavin sat honing his hunting knife. Ever since the last assassination attempt, Trystan had a constant escort. Two other members of the Order were slain in their sleep the night before, and it appeared Trystan was not the only target of the Brotherhood. Being a warrior in the Order of Acrium was becoming increasingly perilous with the passing of the days. After it was obvious that the Sons of Vikundo were in Karalis, a majority of the members who resided in the city moved their belongings into the Crowned Steed, the inn where they were currently staying.

Gavin looked up when the door opened. "What are you doing up?" he asked.

"Couldn't sleep," Trystan answered. Pulling up a chair, he sat beside the archer. "Have you seen anything?"

"Nothing noteworthy." Gavin stowed his whetstone and sheathed his hunting knife. "It would seem our enemies will only strike at us when we are separated, not when we are united under the same roof. How are your wounds faring?"

"They itch abominably," said Trystan, "which is a good sign, but irritating nonetheless. But nothing pains me more than the fact I was unable to fight beside you when the wall fell."

"I am afraid your being there wouldn't have changed the outcome. I have never seen such fear overcome so many people in such a small amount of time. Even I have to admit, when the wall exploded, it felt almost surreal. I was frozen to the spot, and there was nothing I could do about it. If it wasn't for Kole, Allyn, and the others, most of us would've been killed before we were given an opportunity to retreat."

Trystan felt his mood dip as he panned the events of the previous day. He felt so hopeless, watching upon the ramparts of the second wall when the explosion ripped the foundations of the first wall apart. Even from a distance, he could see the immediate fear spread through the soldiers and watched as many of them pulled back long before the signal to retreat sounded. He scanned the many frantic faces, hoping Jaxon and Gavin would be among those who made it safely back to the second wall. His relief was momentary when he saw his two friends climb up the rope together, for then his gaze flicked back to the circle of spearmen manning the breach.

He leaned forward against the battlements, his hand gripping the stone so tightly, his wounds reopened. And he watched as one by one the spearmen were cut down, the eastern forces, and tribesmen falling upon them like a pack of wolves. Through it all, he held a tiny sliver of hope that Kole and Allyn would fight their way through the enemy ranks and make it to safety. It never happened, and it was only a matter of time before there wasn't a single Varkuvian alive at wall one. The enemy went into a frenzy, cutting the heads from the defenders, and placing them upon their spear points, shaking them back and forth, taunting the remaining defenders. Trystan scanned the faces of those around him and saw the utter fear and hopelessness, but below it all, there was rage. Rage at seeing his brothers and friends killed, yet unable to do anything about it. But which emotion would prevail in the end, rage or fear?

Through it all, Trystan couldn't help but feel a sense of responsibility. He held the wall when all seemed lost, yet the one day he wasn't there fighting, it had fallen. He knew in his heart the outcome wouldn't have been different, but he could not help but replay how the day would have unfolded if only he had been there. Would he have been able to save Kole? Or would he have died alongside him? He would never know.

"You wouldn't have been able to save him," said Gavin, reading Trystan's troubled thoughts. "I saw him running toward the breach with a determined purpose. I yelled for him, but he either ignored me or he did not hear me. And when the call to retreat was given, he could have pulled back, but in doing so would've given ground to the enemy and endangered countless lives. He died a hero, and we should remember him as such."

After a moment's pause, Trystan spoke. "Sometimes I truly think you can read minds. I will keep his memory in my heart, along with the thousands who have already perished. Is anyone still in the common room downstairs?"

"The last one to come up was Gabriel, but I do believe Layne is still down there."

"It is still odd for me to not refer to him as Master Layne. Back at the Fortress of the Van, if we didn't call any of the masters by their titles, we would be severely scolded. Repeated offenders would be caned or sometimes even whipped. I remember one time Jaxon received five lashes because he called Master Orrin 'Master Whorein.' They were always so strict about that. Becoming a master was considered one of the most prestigious honors in not just the Order of Acrium but in all of Varkuvia. Yet whenever I call our former mentor Master Layne, I can see the sadness and hurt in his eyes."

"Times have certainly changed," said Gavin. "The man had children daydreaming about growing up, becoming just like him, and women swooning at the sound of his name. He had riches and lands one could only dream of. And in an instant, it was all stripped from him. How would you feel if you were him and were constantly reminded of what once was?"

"I never really thought about it, to be honest with you. The last thing I would want to do is cause him grief, especially after all he has done for me. I can't even begin to tell you how happy I was when he emerged from the dust before Karalis with a troop of the Order of Acrium in tow. It all felt right somehow as if this is where we are all meant to be."

"It does all seem fitting," agreed Gavin. "Where else would the Order of Acrium be, but fighting overwhelming odds, holding back the tides of destruction? Whether we like it or not, this is what we have been trained for. This is what we are destined to do."

"That is true though I don't think any of us imagined odds quite like this." Trystan rose from his seat. "If you don't mind, I am going to go down and speak with Layne."

"I will go with you then," Gavin said, starting to rise.

"I mean no disrespect Gavin, especially never to you, but I would rather speak with him alone. Also, I would feel much safer if you were to stay and stand watch over Arianna. I would never forgive myself if anything happened to her."

"That would be no trouble at all," Gavin assured him, "but try not to take too long. I am starting to hear my bed calling my name."

"Thank you, my friend. I promise I will return shortly."

Trystan walked down the stairs to the common room below. Layne sat by himself at a table before a roaring fireplace, nursing a cup of wine. Nobody else was in the common room, which wasn't surprising, considering most of the populace fled the city after the first wall had fallen. Only some two thousand residents remained in Karalis. These were the people who planted their roots in the city and wouldn't budge for any reason. They would stay no matter the outcome of this war, whether it be a glorious victory or a bitter end. One such resident was busying herself by wiping down the tables, and cleaning up dishes and cups left by her few remaining customers.

Approaching the table Layne occupied, Trystan could immediately tell his mentor's mind was far away. His normally attentive gaze was fixed on the fireplace, his cup of wine forgotten on the table before him, and Trystan's approach went unnoticed. Stopping before the table, Trystan grew slightly concerned at Layne's lack of focus. With the recent attacks and murders on the warriors of the Order, Layne's senses should have been on high alert, especially when sitting alone. Yet if Trystan had been one of the Brotherhood, he could have just ended Layne's life with ease.

"Is this seat taken?" asked Trystan.

Layne finally came to, his violet eyes switching to his prized pupil. "Ah, Trystan," he said, the words slurring. "I apologize, my mind was drifting. Of course, take a seat." He vaguely gestured to the chair opposite him.

Taking a seat, Trystan leaned back, the motion brushing his injuries against the wood. Grunting in discomfort, he readjusted himself to avoid the wounds from reopening again. Looking across the table, he saw Layne was now holding his cup, his gaze locked on the contents within. Trystan sat for several moments, starting to feel uncomfortable in the awkward silence. He had never felt this strange atmosphere when in Layne's presence before, nor had he ever seen the man drink. Clearing his throat, he leaned forward, resting his arms on the table.

"So if you don't mind me asking," Trystan began. "What were you thinking about just before I sat down?"

For some time, he didn't think Layne even heard him. Then the disbanded master sighed, took a sip of his wine, and placed the cup back down on the table. "The only good thing there is to think about now, the past. In particular, I was remembering a battle from close to twenty-five years ago when Master Mason and I were still fresh to the ranks of the Order. A rogue Argarian noble by the name of Odolf, after being banished from the Storm Islands, sought to reclaim his title by raiding along the length of the northern coast of King Eryk's realm though his father, Edward, was king at the time. Within a short amount of time, he amassed several victories, and his ranks soon swelled with eager young Argarians. Seizing an open opportunity, the banished Argarian landed a massive raiding force close to King Edward's capital city of Varlos. Sensing the threat, the Order of Acrium was assembled, and we marched forth from the Fortress of the Van to aid in the defense of the city." He lapsed into silence.

"And then what?" prompted Trystan.

Layne took a deep breath. "And then we linked up with King Edward's forces and met the banished Argarian on the plains before Varlos. The battle that followed was one of the most vicious and brutal ones I have ever taken part in. Neither side was willing to give ground nor were they willing to show any mercy. With the battle at its climax, Odolf, or Odolf the Terrible as he was known by then, led his most elite warriors against King Edward's personal guard. They were all but overrun, and the king himself was brought into the middle of the action, his life, and thus the battle, hanging in the balance. In an insane move, Mason and I charged into the elite warriors by ourselves, cutting down five of them before coming face-to-face with the Argarian noble himself. In all of my years in the Order, he was the most skilled opponent I ever went against. His sword work was astonishing, his timing perfect. In my youth, before reaching the pinnacle of my talent, there was no way I could defeat him, and within moments I knew I was outclassed. Shortly after I began fighting him, his sword got past my defenses, plunging into my side." Layne tapped his ribs, pointing to the old wound.

"I was finished," he continued. "But as Odolf the Terrible went to deliver the killing blow, Mason stepped in and deflected it. Even though Mason was named the Master of Spear in his later years, he was, and still is, one of the most talented swordsman I have ever seen, perhaps better than Kaleb and yourself. After deflecting the stroke that would've ended my life, Mason attacked the noble himself. There seemed no way he could win on his own, but within minutes, Odolf was dead at his feet, Mason's sword dripping with his blood. The remainder of the banished Argarian's forces, seeing their leader was slain, soon broke, and the city was saved. It was deemed a glorious victory. King Edward himself awarded Mason and I with daggers, studded with gems to reward us for our outstanding heroism and bravery. He said we would now and forever be heroes and friends of the Five Kings," finished Layne, his hands once more cupping his wine.

Conflicting thoughts swarmed through Trystan's mind. Master Layne had over a dozen similar stories where he performed miraculous acts of heroism and valor. So why was he recalling this one particular battle? The question gnawed at him. "And what about this battle is causing you such stress?"

"Because, Trystan, there is going to come a point in this war where Mason and I are going to cross swords. I can't explain how I know, but I can just feel it. It claws at my mind and impedes upon my better judgment. A man, who over the years has saved my life numerous times, and I his, yet I might be forced to fight him to the death. And the thing that bothers me the most is I never once thanked him. In all of our years together in the Order, I never let the man know just how honored I was to fight beside him. I do not think I have it in me to end his life, not after all I have been through with him."

"You are concerning yourself with a problem that might not even come to fruition," reassured Trystan. "Mason could get killed by a stray arrow or spear, and if our forces prevail, he will be forced to retreat with the Khali. Then neither of you will have to fight or die." He could tell his words were not getting through to Layne, so he tried a different approach. "Besides, I still need your help in training. How are you to do that if you are so distracted?"

His mentor drew in another deep breath. "I suppose you are correct. I shouldn't be concerning myself over what might transpire tomorrow, but I can't seem to help it. Distractions aside, I have been trying to recall all I could about swordsmen who learned to control their Verillion powers in centuries past thus, unleashing it in full. Do you know what they all had in common?" Trystan shook his head. "Every one of them experienced extreme amounts of pain, grief, or in rare instances, of love which helped unlock their abilities. The Legendary Arrturi himself saw his own father slain in front of him before his talents were unleashed. And the Mighty Artaxias before him watched as his entire family was butchered by outlaws. It seems I might be able to help you tap into your Verillion blood whenever you desire, but I do not know how you will be able to unleash your full potential unless a personal tragedy befalls you or you experience an extreme depth of love."

The young man's first thoughts turned to Arianna, who was asleep one floor above him. Was it possible if he fell enough in love with her, his true powers could be awakened? Other than the few words the two of them had spoken in their youth, he truly knew little about her, even still, it was a possibility. "How exactly would I even know if love unleashed my powers?" he asked.

Layne's eyes snapped up to lock to Trystan's gaze. "I heard of this serving woman you have been seeing, and I must to be honest with you, I do not approve. She is beginning to cloud your judgment, and you cannot afford it at times such as these. There comes a point in every man's life when he needs to stop looking for a partner who pleases his eyes but instead search for the one who pleases his heart. Make sure this woman is worth more to you than just physical attraction, for it could mean the death of both of you if you get too close to her."

"Mas—Layne, it is so much more than that though. Of course, she is beautiful, and everything a man could possibly desire when imagining a woman, but there is a connection between she and I that no amount of reasoning could explain. I truly believe given time, our love for one another could rival the great loves of history. She could be the one for me, and I would be willing to sacrifice my life to prove it."

"Be careful what you say aloud, Trystan. The gods have a funny way of hearing such provocations and making them a reality." Layne suddenly went quiet, his gaze flicking to the front window of the inn where a lone figure in a dark cloak was walking by. A sword of blue steel was unsheathed and strapped to his back. Layne leaned forward intently, his eyes narrowing to study the blade. Shock registered on his face, and he stood quickly, knocking the chair to the hardwood floor.

Turning in his seat, Trystan followed Layne's gaze to the stranger walking by. He could not make out the person's facial features. "Do you know that person?" he asked, confused.

"Did you see the blade?" Layne asked, ignoring the question. "The markings upon it were written in the ancient symbols of the Verillions. I am certain of it. The few remaining objects left in the known world bearing such markings are either in museums or in the ruling house-holds of the nobility. And I have certainly never heard of a sword having them upon it. Something is not right here."

Layne stood rubbing his chin, lost in thought. Then he began walking toward the entrance of the inn, his face set and determined. "Master Layne!" Trystan called out, stopping his former teacher. "Our lives are in constant peril, and it is the dead of the night. You cannot possibly be thinking about going out there right now just because you think you saw something upon a sword. That is madness."

Whipping around, Layne fixed Trystan with an unrelenting stare. "Madness? Do you not think it a little mad that a man bearing such a sword should appear at a time like this? There are questions I need answered, and he could supply them for me. I do not ask you to go with me, but you will not stop me from going out there."

"You know I will not let you go by yourself." Trystan rose from his chair. Thoughts whirled inside of his head. What of the promises he made to Arianna and Gavin? Going out onto the streets of Karalis right now would be stupidity on a grand scale, but he knew Layne would not be swayed, and he had no time to gather more men from upstairs to join them. "Lead the way," he said with resignation.

Layne turned around, moving quickly to the main entrance before throwing the door open. Walking outside, his head whipped to the left and right looking for the stranger. He pointed to an alleyway to the right. "I saw the hooded figure go that way," he said and began jogging in that direction with Trystan just on his heels.

The two entered the mouth of the alleyway, the darkness all-consuming. The murky figure was nowhere in sight. They advanced cautiously into the alleyway, nothing but silence all around them. Trystan loosened his sword in its sheath, his nerves on edge. Even though he was recovering faster than he expected from his wounds, he was still in no shape for a real fight. This very well could be a trap, and Trystan found his gaze constantly darting amongst the shadows of the alley, looking for any signs of danger. He was beginning to feel uncomfortable as they approached a fork in the alley as it branched off to the left and right.

Moving ahead, Layne looked down both alleys while Trystan hung back, checking behind them to make sure they weren't being followed. Seeing no sign of the stranger, Layne threw his hands up in frustration.

"Damn it all, we lost the bastard!" he said vehemently.

Having never heard the master swear before, Trystan was taken aback by the raw display of emotions. Layne was always so calm and collected, yet within the course of a night, Trystan saw the man drink himself into depression and lose control at the first sign of a setback. This was a side he had never seen from his mentor before, and he felt at a loss to explain it.

Whirling around angrily, Layne checked the routes the stranger could have taken once more. As his head swiveled to the right, the heel of a boot connected with the side of his head, careening him sideways landing face-first into the wall of the alley. He slumped to the ground unconscious. Trystan's eyes opened wide in shock, his gaze locked to Layne's unmoving body. From the shadows in front of him emerged the darkly attired stranger they were following. A hood was drawn tightly over the face, hiding the upper facial features while a cloth of dark wool was looped around the lower part of the face. Trystan's mind dragged back to the dream he experienced earlier, and the premonitions that went along with the hooded figure. Could this mysterious person be the one he dreamt about? *Don't be foolish*, he told himself. *It was only a dream.*

The blue sword that so distinctly piqued Layne's interest remained strapped to the stranger's back. At first, Trystan did not react, his mind racing, wondering who exactly this person might be. Then his eyes were drawn to Layne's body, which remained motionless, and Trystan's curiosity was replaced by anger. His hand flew to the hilt of his sword. The stranger nimbly stepped forward, his foot moving with blinding quickness to kick Trystan's hand away, preventing him from drawing his sword. Trystan's hand flew wide, knocking him off balance.

Recovering quickly, Trystan spun around, his hand bunching into a fist. Coming around in a full circle, Trystan threw a right cross with everything he had at the hooded figure. The stranger swayed back easily, the punch flying harmlessly by their face. Dropping into a crouch, the hooded figure sprang forward, their fists moving with impossible speed toward Trystan's body. Moving on the defensive, he blocked each blow that came at him, his footwork perfect. Still, he found himself back pedaling furiously from the ferocity of the assault. Blocking a left jab, Trystan was just in time to see the right cross that connected with the side of his face.

His back slammed against the wall of the alley, stars dancing in front of his eyes. The hooded figure stood easily half a head shorter than Trystan, yet the force from the blow was astonishing. His mind reeling, he barely registered a fast approaching left cross that was coming directly toward his face. Instinctively, his hand moved upward to block the punch, throwing it wide. Moving on the offensive, Trystan stepped forward, delivering an uppercut at his unbalanced foe. Recovering immediately from the deflection, the hooded figure swayed backward once more, springing off his hands into a backward flip before landing perfectly on the balls of his feet.

Blinking in astonishment, Trystan was truly humbled by the skill displayed by this stranger. He had never felt so outclassed in his entire life. *Who the hell is this person?* Deep down, he felt his Verillion blood begin to pound in his veins. Trystan hesitated and then allowed his abilities to take over. It was time to even the playing field. He saw the hooded figure react as if struck as Trystan's pupils slowly changed. For the first time since their encounter, Trystan's opponent seemed unsure. Taking advantage of the stranger's momentary lapse of focus, Trystan leapt forward, his arm cocking back with all the strength his Verillion blood unleashed.

His fist moved with blistering speed to connect fully with his opponent's jaw. The hooded figure was lifted off his feet in a full spin. A grin crossed Trystan's face. His elation lasted mere heartbeats when his opponent controlled his body in midspin and managed to land shakily on his legs. Not wasting a moment, Trystan launched himself forward. The hooded figure moved to meet him, this time blocking a crushing right cross, following it with an uppercut that Trystan dodged.

Even with his Verillion blood swamping his senses, Trystan found his respect for this unknown adversary growing to new heights. Ever since discovering his new-found abilities during the raid of Fursta, he was yet to face an opponent that could stand toe to toe with him and possibly hope for victory. Even Master Layne, one of the most noted warriors of this age, was easily overwhelmed by Trystan once his powers were unleashed. Yet this stranger was not only holding their own but was able to move on the offensive.

The stranger took a step back, giving Trystan a brief respite to think about drawing his blade once more. His hand moved to do just that when he paused. Why hadn't the hooded figure drawn their own sword upon their back to attack him? That moment's pause was all his opponent needed before launching a flurry of punches once more. Even with the added advantage of his Verillion blood, Trystan found himself moving on the defensive from the blistering and unrelenting attack. He felt himself begin to waver and knew that his recent injuries were preventing him from prolonging the Verillion sensation for much longer. He must do something and do it fast.

Sidestepping a lightning fast jab intended for his face, Trystan's hand snaked out to clamp onto the stranger's wrist. The hooded figure's other hand snapped forward, grazing the top of Trystan's head, allowing him to free his trapped hand. In doing so, the hood fell from his face, even though the dark cloth wrapped around his mouth stayed firmly in place. Trystan froze on the spot as he stared into the face of his opponent, all thoughts of the fight vanishing from his mind. The stranger's pupils were in the shape of a cross. He was facing a descendent of the Verillion race.

His shock was just the opportunity the stranger was waiting for. A roundhouse kick connected squarely with the side of Trystan's head, sending him spinning through the air to land heavily on his chest. All air knocked out of him, his lungs searing with pain when he attempted to breathe. Gasping for breath, his face red from exertion, Trystan rolled to his back, determined he would be able to get back on his feet and continue the fight. The stranger had vanished. Trystan's pain was momentarily forgotten as he searched frantically for the revealed Verillion. He caught one last glimpse of a dark cloak whipping around the corner of the alley before the stranger was gone from sight.

As Trystan lay there in the alleyway, his Verillion blood slowly fading away, he took the time to collect his thoughts. He had just faced an opponent possessing the same strengths and abilities as himself, and he had lost. But that's not what bothered him as he lay there. Trystan should be dead right now, and he knew it. His opponent had the chance to end his life and could've done so easily, yet the stranger hadn't even drawn their weapon and only fought long enough to be given a chance to slip away into the night without being pursued.

Exhaustion settled on Trystan, a recurring theme after his Verillion abilities receded. Layne was right. Something was terribly wrong in the city of Karalis. Possessing Verillion blood was supposed to be one of the rarest gifts in the world, ranging in the millions just to be born with it, and even then, it was rarer for those born with the ancient blood to be able to unlock their powers. Yet within the course of a short span, three Verillion descendants were revealed, all within the same domain. First with Trystan, then Kaleb, and now with this cloaked stranger. How was such a thing possible?

Pushing such thoughts from his mind, Trystan forced himself into a sitting position. The motion caused his head to swim, both from exhaustion and from lack of oxygen. For several minutes, he sat there, collecting himself, and allowing his body to recover from the beating he just took. Finally he stood, noting how filthy his clothing was from being knocked to the alleyway ground. His hand reached up to his head where the stranger's boot connected with it and felt a lump already forming. His head throbbing with pain, Trystan stumbled over to Layne's body.

The former master was still unconscious, and Trystan could see a small trickle of blood on the side of his face where he smashed into the wall. Bending down Trystan gently shook Layne's shoulder, hoping to rouse him. His mentor did not react, and the young man found his thoughts turning to the worst. He began feeling for a pulse when Layne groaned, his eyes fluttering open. Almost immediately, he tried to sit up and then stopped, his brow creased in agony. Layne's hand rose shakily to his head where he pressed it against the open abrasion.

"What in the name of Crassos just happened?" he asked as he brought his hand in front of his face, seeing the blood.

"You met the stranger we were following," Trystan answered.

"I am going to guess it did not go well," said Layne drily.

Despite the situation, Trystan found himself chuckling. "That's a safe assessment. Come on now, let's get you on your feet. We need to get you back to the Crowned Steed and have that head looked at. And I am quite positive I am going to get more than an earful from both Gavin and Arianna."

Layne looked up, studying Trystan's face, seeing the bruises upon it for the first time. "I am also guessing you didn't fair any better than I."

"We will talk about it back at the inn."

Bending down, Trystan looped his arm around Layne's shoulder, helping him to stand on shaky legs. Together, the two supported each other down the length of the alley before emerging back onto the streets of Karalis once more. Dawn was beginning to tint the night sky, painting it a light orange. Trystan was starting to feel nauseous and could feel sweat forming on his scalp. It was quite possible he suffered a concussion and felt a sudden urge to sit down. *You're almost back at the inn*, he told himself and pushed on.

As they approached the entrance to the Crowned Steed, the marching of boots reverberated off the streets. Halting in the middle of the road, Trystan looked up to see a troop of soldiers marching through Karalis in formation toward them. They were wearing the blue cloaks fringed with gold and T-shaped helms of King Markos's Stone Guards. Each of them had a spear in one hand the other resting on the hilts of their swords. Sounds from behind caused both Layne and Trystan to look over their shoulders. A similar troop was marching from behind them as well. There were close to twenty guards all together. They fanned out before the two battered men.

A guard stepped forward, a rolled parchment in his hand rather than a spear. Trystan recognized him as Verlos, the head of King Markos's Stone Guards. Verlos unrolled the parchment, holding it before him.

"This is a document, written and signed by King Markos, ruler of the Stone Realm," said Verlos, addressing the teacher and student. "Demanding for the immediate arrest of Layne, the disbanded Master of Sword of the Order of Acrium. He is to be brought to the Keep of Karalis immediately where he will be detained until further notice."

Trystan let his arm fall away from Layne and walked toward Verlos. "What is the meaning of this?" he demanded.

"Guards, take him away," directed Verlos, ignoring Trystan.

Five guards rushed forward to restrain Layne. Outraged, Trystan grabbed Verlos's arm. "I demand answers. What right do you have to take him away?"

The butt of a spear connected with the back of Trystan's head, knocking him sideways. Furious, he whirled around as the guard attempted to hit him once more. Grabbing ahold of the shaft of the spear, Trystan ripped it from the guard's grip and stepped forward to deliver a bone-crushing right hook, dumping the guard to the ground. Multiple guards rushed forward, raining blows down upon the young swordsman. A blow to the gut forced Trystan down to his knees. Looking in between the legs of the guards attacking him, he saw Layne being subdued, his hands tied behind his back.

Frenzied, Trystan rose to his feet, scattering those closest to him. An uppercut sent another guard flying through the air. The haft of a spear connected with the side of his leg, buckling his knees. Fighting against the inevitable, Trystan turned around, grabbing the wielder by the top of his breastplate and hauling him into a head butt, crushing the man's nose. This time Trystan staggered, his injuries from the fight with the stranger overwhelming him. One punch from a gauntleted fist dropped him to the ground.

Futilely, he tried to get his hands underneath him. A kick to his ribcage ended his defiance, leaving him sprawled on the ground. His face pressed against the cold street before the Crowned Steed, his breath coming in quick, painful rasps. He watched the booted feet of King Markos's Stone Guards march back toward the Keep of Karalis, two guards dragging Layne away. Right before he lost consciousness, he heard someone yelling his name. And then darkness consumed him.

# CHAPTER FIFTEEN

Sunlight blazed from the armor of Acrium as Trystan strode beneath the great portcullis gate that led to the mighty Keep of Karalis. Jaxon and Gavin flanked him while Gabriel and Owen brought up the rear. Each of them was fully dressed in the armor of Acrium, the silver metal, standing out brilliantly as they walked past the stunned troops of King Markos. No one dared challenge the fearsome warriors, and their approach to the massive oak doors that led to the inner confines of the keep went unopposed.

Trystan's anger was almost at a boiling point. The bruises upon his face where he was struck by King Markos's Stone Guards turned ugly, and he could barely open his swollen right eye. His entire body was awash with bruises, but his fury drove the pain away. How could King Markos arrest Master Layne at a time such as this? The king already had a host of enemies outside of Karalis's walls with tens of thousands hounding for his blood, yet he had chosen now to arrest one of the most prominent members in the Order of Acrium, causing immediate strife between the warriors in the city and the king himself. Trystan would have his answers, and he would have them now.

Pushing open the grand entrance to the Keep of Karalis, Trystan and his escort strode into the main hall. He was not shocked to see King Markos's Stone Guards ringing the pillared hall, their hands resting on their sword hilts, their faces set. His gaze was glued to the king, who sat leisurely upon his throne upon a raised dais, his fingers thrumming the gilded armrest. Despite daylight being upon them, the lighting in the hall was poor, casting a gloomy ambience. When they were within fifty paces of the king, a group of Stone Guards stepped into their path, impeding their way. The group was headed by Verlos. Trystan fought savagely against the urge to attack the man.

"No one is allowed to be in the king's presence while armed," said the head of the guards, addressing Trystan. "I am going to have to ask you men to relinquish your weapons by request of King Markos himself. You will have your weapons returned to you once you have left the keep. This I promise you."

Jaxon leaned in toward Trystan. "I do not like this," he whispered to his friend. "This reeks of a trap."

"What choice do we have?" he responded, his eyes sweeping the hall filled with soldiers loyal to Markos. He turned his attention back to Verlos. "And what is a promise from you worth, Verlos?"

Verlos reeled back from the question, his face showing the hurt at being asked such a thing. Trystan felt instantly contrite, feeling regret for treating Verlos in such a way. From everything he heard about the man, his honor was never in doubt. He was only following orders from his king and was not to blame here. Before the head of the guard could respond, Trystan quickly unbuckled his sword and hunting knife, extending the weapons before him to be taken away. A guard to Verlos's left stepped forward, took the blades, and then walked away without a word. As much as Trystan did not like the idea of giving up his weapons, nothing would get accomplished if they were to start a fight here and now. Such a rash action would see Layne slain, along with Trystan, Jaxon, and the others.

The others reluctantly followed Trystan's lead, relinquishing their various weapons. Gabriel, with a look of disgust on his tattooed face, was the last to unsling his massive sledgehammer from his back, holding it before him. He snarled at the guard who stepped forward to take his weapon. The guard blanched and stumbled over his own feet as he hastily backed away. After a quick search, Verlos indicated it was safe for them to proceed. The group continued their approach toward the throne. To King Markos's left stood his two sons, Prince Vasilis, appearing ill at ease, and Prince Leon, his face unreadable. To the king's right stood his faithful wife, Queen Lorain, her back straight and her blue eyes not backing down from the formidable warriors as they drew near.

Trystan approached the base of the throne, the others standing close by for support. The outcome of this conversation could turn ugly, and they were prepared, no matter the conclusion. Stopping directly before the throne, Trystan did not bother to bow. King Markos said nothing about the slight though his eyes showed his distaste. The silence stretched as the monarch and swordsman stared at one another.

"You and your men should be at the wall preparing to defend against our enemies," Markos said, looking down upon Trystan.

"I think you know we have other matters to attend to," Trystan responded. "I demand to know why Master Layne was unlawfully arrested."

The thrumming of King Markos's fingers echoed throughout the silent main hall, his gray eyes studying the man beneath him. "A peasant dares to make a demand from one of the Five Kings?" His voice was strangely calm. His fist suddenly slammed down on the armrest, the throne chair quivering beneath the blow. "I will not tolerate such a thing! Especially not in my own throne room. The only reason you are not in chains beside Master Layne is because my son still draws breath because of you, and a debt must be repaid. Now, you will treat me with respect, or all of you shall join your former master."

From the corner of his vision, Trystan saw the guards that were ringing the perimeter of the main hall, now hemmed in on the five warriors. The others noticed as well and stood with fists clenched, their wary eyes watching the guards. Trystan remained silent, aware his straight forwardness just put their lives in jeopardy.

"How long, exactly, did you think it would escape my notice that the exiled masters of the Order of Acrium are the ones leading the tribesmen of the Northern Woods?" asked King Markos, his tone still remaining neutral. The question was asked casually, but even still, it sent a shiver up Trystan's spine, his face losing its color. The situation was worse than he thought. The others, standing behind Trystan, who were not privileged with the information, began talking in hushed whispers.

"What are you talking about?" asked an outraged Jaxon. "That is ridiculous. The masters would never do such a dishonorable thing."

The king quickly studied Trystan's reaction, noting the loss of color in the young man's face and then switched his focus on the big axman. "I can assure you, it is true. I have heard several rumors in the past weeks about such a possibility, but a report I received yesterday confirmed it for me. The one known as Grand Chieftain Timon is in fact Mason, the exiled Master of Spear. The other masters, Orrin and Petros, are his right-hand men. These are the men who now lead the tribesmen of the Northern Woods and have brought death and destruction to thousands of my people. And their presence outside of my walls has me seriously questioning my decision of allowing the Order of Acrium to reside peacefully within my city."

The silence in the hall that followed was unbearable. By all rights, Markos could imprison all of them, and there was nothing they could do about it. "What do you plan to do with the rest of us?" Trystan finally asked, echoing the thoughts of the others.

King Markos leaned back in his throne, fully aware of the power he possessed in this situation. "For the time being, I am going to allow the rest of the warriors in the city to remain free. King Alaric has argued vehemently that I should do the exact opposite." He pointed at Gabriel. "Especially regarding you. King Alaric told me that you are an uncivilized Argarian bastard who unjustly started a fight with several of his soldiers." Gabriel began to argue his case, but Markos held up his hand, silencing him. "My son Leon has already argued on your behalf, and I have agreed not to take any action regarding your situation. However, I cannot speak for Alaric, so if I were you, I would remain wary. Now, say nothing else before I change my mind."

The king continued, "Despite this recent news that has come to light, I cannot argue against the fact the reinstated Order of Acrium has been instrumental in holding these walls. Members of the Order have fallen alongside my own soldiers, and other than the fight with King Alaric's troops, there has been no reported suspicions of rising unrest. However, from his moment on, each of you will be monitored, and if I sense even an ounce of treachery, I will have all of you hanged. In regard to Layne, the disgraced Master of Sword, he will remain imprisoned and under careful watch. And as I just said, if there are any signs of treachery or unrest, I will have him executed without a moment's hesitation. You men have roughly three weeks until reinforcements arrive that could liberate this city. If I were you, I would use that time wisely to prove your intentions because the decision of your freedom, as well as the outcome of Layne's life, will most assuredly be addressed by the other kings once they arrive."

Trystan's mind reeled. He was wily enough to know that Layne would eventually face execution, no matter what Markos said. Even if Layne wasn't in league with the other masters, the king would never allow a potential enemy like him to live. How could Trystan stand idly by and not do anything for the man who had given him so much? Layne devoted so much of his time on the young man, bestowing his codes of honor and a new way of life upon him. He showed Trystan there was hope in redemption and showed faith in him when so many others had given up. Standing there in the main hall, King Markos's Stone Guards crowded all around him with the king himself awaiting a response, Trystan found himself recalling his first conversation with Master Layne.

He was just inducted into the Order of Acrium. Six months prior to being inducted, he pushed himself through various exercises presented to him, assuring he was physically fit enough to even be tested. He would be awakened every day before dawn and directed to run for miles on end. After that, he would be instructed to lift weights for hours, working out various parts of his body, pushing himself to the limit, day in and day out. Every night, he would collapse onto the small cot of a bed that was provided for him. And this was the way his life was for three months. The other recruits would constantly complain about their aches and pains as they went to their beds, but Trystan would say nothing instead counting his blessings. Despite the physical exhaustion, for the first time in years, he was guaranteed three square meals a day and a place to sleep at night. He did not have to sleep upon a cold alleyway floor with rats as his only company. It was the closest thing to normalcy he could recall.

It was during this extreme training many quit, realizing the aptitude it took just to be tested, but Trystan toughed it out and advanced to the testing. For another three months, the remaining recruits would practice daily with various weapons presented to them. Each of the weapons was made from wood and designed to be heavier than a normal sword or spear. Once again, Trystan would go to bed at night, his body not only exhausted but also covered in bruises from the earlier lessons. The only days he would find some leeway were when they practiced with the wooden swords. He never handled a sword in his young life and was deemed a freak of nature, besting both nobles and commoners alike who practiced with the blade since childhood. The ease with which he was able to perform with a sword left those training him baffled, for they had never been in the presence of someone with no past training who excelled as he did. And as the days turned into months, his skills grew.

It was this substantial ability with the sword that allowed him to be inducted along with a dozen qualified others. Of the sixty other recruits who made the trip from Calydon city with him, he was the only one to proceed through the arduous six months and come out a newly anointed member of the Order of Acrium. The Ceremony of Induction was held in the main hall at the Fortress of the Van. Master Roderic himself presented Trystan the black cloak with the silver circles expertly stitched upon it, officially establishing him as a member of the Order of Acrium. For the first time in his life, Trystan felt a real sense of pride. He succeeded where so many others failed, and his hard work paid off in the culmination of receiving the black cloak.

Yet he had no one to share his elation with, for he had not become friends with any of the other inductees. As the others chatted amiably amongst themselves, showing one another their cloaks, Trystan stood to the side alone. He looked up to see a man dressed in the gleaming armor of Acrium, his movements catlike, striding toward him. Trystan was cowed by the powerful gaze in the man's violet eyes and found himself staring at the granite floor, hoping the warrior would pass him by. Instead, the warrior stopped directly before him.

"Why do you not join in with the others?" he asked the young man.

Trystan looked up, recognizing the gold brooch at the man's shoulder, holding his cloak in place. It was emblazoned with a shining sword. This man was the Master of Sword, and one of the highest-ranking members in the Order of Acrium. Trystan was instantly intimidated.

"I do not know any of them," he answered sheepishly.

The master nodded, recognizing the same shy demeanor he himself once possessed. "Well, I'm sure that will change soon enough. I am Layne, Master of Sword." He extended his hand.

"I am Trystan." He grasped the outstretched hand, feeling the strength in the master's grip.

Master Layne's brow raised in interest. "The Trystan all of the instructors have been talking about? They say you handle a sword like a seasoned veteran, yet you say you have never picked up a blade in your life. How is that possible?"

Trystan could think of no reply and simply shrugged his shoulders. Layne chuckled. "I can see you are a man of few words," the master said. "I don't know what it is about you, Trystan, but I like you already. Something tells me you are going to do great things while a part of this Order."

"You know nothing about me," Trystan replied.

"Ah, this is true, but being a master of this Order, I have an uncanny ability at judging talent. With the right guidance and tutelage, I believe we could make a hero of you yet." The master then threw his arm around the young man's shoulders. "Now, let's go find something to eat and show you to your quarters. Tomorrow you begin your training."

From the beginning, Layne had shown confidence in him even when Trystan himself did not feel it. It was this instilled self-assurance that allowed him to become the man he was today. The thrumming of King Markos's fingers upon the throne chair brought Trystan's attention back to the present. He looked up at the king, seeing the agitation upon the monarch's face. How long had he been daydreaming?

"King Markos," said Trystan, "not too long ago, you told me that if I ever needed anything, all I had to do was ask, and you would grant it. At the time, I did not take you up on the offer. I call upon that debt now. I request the release of Layne from the dungeons."

"Do not push my limits right now, young man," the king replied. "Extenuating circumstances have changed that offer, and you very well know it. I understand you and the imprisoned Master of Sword were close, but I will not release him. Not for you or for any man. Do not push the matter any further."

Trystan was beaten, and he knew it. Any further protests would see him thrown in shackles and then he would truly be unable to help Layne. The only thing he could do now was smite the enemy upon the wall and prove to King Markos he was no traitor and, with luck, save the life of Master Layne in the process. He would have to fight as though not only his life depended on it, but that of Layne's as well. Karalis must hold until reinforcements arrived, and Trystan would do whatever it took to make that possible.

"Then I respectfully request to have an audience with Layne," Trystan said.

The king leaned back in his throne, musing the request over. "Fair enough," he answered, "but only you, may speak with him. The others will simply have to wait until you are finished, and Layne is to remain in his cell. I will not have any attempt of escape."

"Thank you, Your Majesty." Trystan hesitated for a moment. "And if I may be so bold as to make one more request."

Markos looked irritated. "Speak," he commanded.

"I ask that you join your men upon the wall and fight beside them."

The king's eyes narrowed. "I just told you to prove to me you are no traitor, yet you make a request which would see my life endangered. Explain yourself."

"I had no intentions of making it seem like a threat, Your Majesty," assured Trystan. "But your men need you right now. With the destruction of the first wall, morale is at an all-time low. Defeat is etched into every movement of your men. It is my belief that if something does not change drastically, the second wall will fall within days. If we are to have any hope of holding out until reinforcements arrive, then we need you now more than ever to make your presence known."

"Are you aware of the threat that has been made against my life?" responded Markos.

"I am aware of it, Your Majesty, as are your guards. They will protect you. You are a king of the people, and the soldiers under your command will fight more valiantly for you than they ever would for me or either of your sons. I understand the increased danger to your life if you leave the sanctuary of the keep but at least take this under consideration."

"Go and speak with Layne, and let me discuss the matter with my family. You shall have your answer when you return." Markos gestured to Verlos. The head of the Stone Guards stepped forward, awaiting his ruler's instructions. "Verlos, escort young Trystan to Layne's dungeon cell and keep a close watch on him to make sure he doesn't attempt anything rash," the king finished, staring Trystan in the face.

Trystan read the look in Markos's eyes. He had no doubts in his mind if he tried something foolish, his life would be forfeited. He turned to address the others who accompanied him. "I will be back shortly," he said. "Await me in the courtyard beyond."

"That's if you come back at all," grumbled Jaxon. "They could lock you in a cell right beside Layne, and we would be completely helpless to aid you. I say we turn around, walk right out those doors, and don't look back. We have been given a second chance, and we should take it while we can."

The thought was tempting, but Trystan shook his head. "I must at least let Layne know he is not forgotten. If I do not come back, then

I advise you to do what you think is best for yourselves, but I beg each of you, do not attempt to rescue me."

"You know damn well I will not allow you to rot in some godforsaken cell," Jaxon said. The others nodded in agreement. "For better or for worse, we're with ya, Trys."

"Then let us hope that it does not come down to that. I will return shortly." Trystan turned to Verlos. "Lead the way."

The two left the main hall, Trystan following in Verlos's shadow. The head of the Stone Guards wound his way through a warren of hallways, and before long, Trystan was lost in his surroundings. The Keep of Karalis was imposing enough from the outside, but the inside made the mighty structure seem like a giant maze. Trystan admired the many tapestries and paintings hung on the walls as he followed Verlos through the never-ending corridors. He suddenly slammed into the back of Verlos and foolishly realized the guard stopped before a thick door set at the end of a corridor. Verlos turned around, giving him a warning glance. Trystan muttered an apology while the guard pulled a set of keys from his pocket and unlocked the door.

The door swung outward to reveal a poorly lit circular staircase. The stairs wound around a corner, and Trystan could not see how far down they went. The Stone Guard gestured for Trystan to go down first. *He does not want his back to me*, thought Trystan. The young man boldly moved forward to descend the stairs that led to the dungeons. A steady dripping noise echoed throughout the narrow staircase though Trystan could see no signs of water leaking through the foundations of the stones. The noise gave him an eerie feeling.

After some minutes, the two emerged into a poorly lit, close-spaced room with a table set in the center of it. Two dungeon guards were seated around it, playing a game of dice. Noticing Trystan and Verlos for the first time, they hastily stood to their feet. One of the dungeon guards, a heavyset man whose belly stretched the fabric of his blue tunic to the breaking point, quickly tucked the dice into his pocket. Stepping forward, he extended a dirty hand with thick fingers towards Verlos.

"What brings you down here, Verlos?" the man asked, revealing yellow teeth.

Verlos ignored the hand before him. "King Markos has commanded me to bring this man to see Layne," he said. A look of confusion crossed the fat guard's face. "The one brought in this morning. Lead us to his cell, Jerrod."

"Right away," answer Jerrod, bobbing his head.

The fat guard moved toward another door, set behind the table, the keys on his belt jingling off of close-set walls around them. Unhooking the keys, Jerrod fumbled through them, mumbling to himself until he found the right one and slipped it into the keyhole. The door opened inward on creaky hinges to reveal a dim corridor lined with doors with only a single torch casting gloomy light. A revolting smell assaulted Trystan, and he fought down a wave of revulsion. The smell did not seem to affect Jerrod at all, and it was obvious he was accustomed to it. Jerrod strode down the corridor, the sounds of misery and forgotten souls coming from behind every locked door they passed. He stopped before a door with a window of iron bars set into the top of it. He went to unlock the door when Verlos stopped him.

"Leave it closed," the Stone Guard commanded. "King Markos instructed he is only permitted to speak with him and to leave the door shut." Jerrod shrugged his shoulders and moved back down the corridor, his bulk causing him to waddle. Verlos turned to Trystan. "I will give you some time alone with him."

The Stone Guard turned and followed Jerrod back toward the first room they entered, leaving Trystan by himself. Once the two guards were far enough down the corridor, Trystan stepped up to the cell that Layne occupied.

"Master Layne?" he asked, his voice echoing down the dungeon hallway. "Master Layne?" he repeated, this time lowering his voice.

He heard shuffling behind the door. Peering through the bars of the door, he could just make out a figure moving in the darkness beyond. "Trystan?" came the voice of Layne. "Is that you?"

"It is I," he answered, relieved to hear his mentor once more. "By the gods," said Layne, surprised, "what are you doing down here? Have they arrested you as well?"

"No, I have not been arrested," assured Trystan. "I sought a meeting with King Markos on your behalf. Listen, Master Layne,

King Markos discovered the other masters are the ones leading the tribesmen. I do not know how, but he has. That is why you have been arrested. He believes you are working with them."

Silence was the only answer Trystan received. Gazing intently through the bars of the door, Trystan saw Layne sit down heavily upon his cot, sending a cloud of dust and filth into the tightly spaced air of the cell. "They would not tell me why I was being arrested," said his mentor, "but I feared as much. You should not have come down here. That was quite foolish of you."

A new fear touched Trystan. "You are not actually in league with the other masters are you?" he asked. Looking down the corridor to where Verlos waited, he made sure he was not overheard. "Please tell me it is not so."

"I am not working with them, Trystan, though at this point it no longer matters. You were one of my most prized pupils while I had the privilege of being a master. Your strategic mind rivaled Master Roderic in his prime, and you are an extremely bright and intelligent young man. Do you truly believe the Five Kings will allow me to live? You know they will not. They will use me as leverage to ensure that you and the others hold the walls of Karalis. Once my usefulness has played its course, then they will have me executed. Maybe by some miracle you and the others will have your lives spared though I highly doubt it. You should never have come down here."

"I refuse to accept that. There must be something I can do to help. Just tell me what to do, and I will do it, Master Layne."

Layne sighed. "You must forget about me, Trystan. That is the only thing you can do, for I am already a corpse in walking form. You were always destined for greatness. Do not allow me to weigh you down from accomplishing what you were destined to be. Go forth from these dungeon cells and live your life to the fullest. Show the world what I always knew you were capable of."

Trystan cursed loudly, the words echoing off the dungeon walls, coming back at him in angry reverberations. Verlos slightly craned his head but remained where he was. "How can you talk like that?" Trystan fumed in between clenched teeth. "I refuse to give up on you. Do you hear me? When I was a child, I was unable to do anything to save my mother. I will not allow that to happen again. Not this time! I will find a way to get you out of this cell. I swear it upon all that is holy."

"There are some things in life that are beyond our control. You must accept that the Five Kings are the power in these lands. Their word is absolute. If they speak the words of my death, then it shall be so. Just do not make the same mistake I did throughout my life, Trystan. Do not trust in the words of kings, for they are just noise. Trust instead in your heart and try to remember all I have taught you."

The anger that raged inside of Trystan was a hard thing to bear, and he found he could not control it. His eyes darted back and forth, thinking, praying for an answer. As a child, he was unable to care for his sick and dying mother and felt a complete sense of hopelessness as she slipped into the afterlife. It was the same hopelessness that gripped his body now though this time it was somehow worse. He could reason with himself that as a child he could not have done anything more for his ailing mother. But now as an adult, the life of the man who was a father to him was hanging in the balance, and still he could do nothing. How could he, a mere peasant, possibly persuade the Five Kings to listen to reason?

As he stood there, a deep resolution formed inside of him stronger than anything he felt in his entire life. The citizens and soldiers of Karalis already looked up to him as a revered hero. They all averted their gaze when he walked by and prayed to him as if he were a living God. *Well if that is what I am to them,* he thought, *then that is what I will become. In the weeks to come, I will become so powerful, that not even the Five Kings will dare go against me. I will hold these walls, and save this city, and the people will worship me as they never have before. Then the Five Kings will have no choice but to release Layne.*

There had been many doubts in Trystan's life. Was he capable of redemption? Would he ever amount to anything? Could he ever possibly be a leader or an idol the people could look up to? This was not one of those doubts. He would not allow Layne to be executed. If he was ever certain of anything in his life, this was it. If he could not change the minds of the Five Kings, then he would rescue Layne from these cells even if he had to do it by himself. He would not stand by and watch as another person he loved died.

When Trystan looked up there was a look of fire in his eyes. "I will get you out of this cell, Master Layne. If the people wish to see the Savior of Karalis, then that is what I will give them. I promise you I will get you out from behind these bars. I will never forget about you. Not as long as I draw breath."

"Do not throw your life away for me, Trystan. I beg of you."

"Your time is up, young Trystan," called Verlos from the end of the corridor. "Say your farewells, and let us return to King Markos."

"I have to go, Master Layne," said Trystan. "We will meet again whether it is in this life or on the road to the underworld."

Turning on his heel, Trystan started walking toward the waiting Verlos when Layne's voice gave him pause. "This is only the beginning," his mentor said, the words echoing strangely throughout the dungeon corridor.

Perplexed, he turned around to ask what he meant. "Let's go," repeated Verlos more forcefully, cutting Trystan off.

Trystan fixed the Stone Guard with an angry stare. "I am coming," he said testily.

He gave one final look at Layne's cell and then walked down the corridor, falling in stride beside Verlos. He did not say a word to the Stone Guard as they headed back toward the main hall. Instead, his mind was trying to piece together what Layne said. He said this was only the beginning. But the beginning to what?

# CHAPTER SIXTEEN

rianna's eyes were fixed upon the front doors of the Crowned Steed. She was awaiting Trystan's return and was nervous though she could not say why. *You are nervous he will not return from his meeting with the K\king*, she told herself. *Why do you care?* her subconscious suddenly asked. The thought leapt unbidden to her mind, but even still, she contemplated the answer. Why did she care?

Her whole life she avoided the company of men. She learned early on they were all the same. Each offered up honeyed words and paid her compliments, attempting always to sound genuine; but through it all, she would see beyond the words and recognize the ravenous looks in their eyes. All any of them had ever wanted was to possess her body and not her heart. It disgusted her. She knew the exact moment when she had been treated differently.

She was twelve years old, and boys began acting strangely around her. Boys she had been friends with for years and played with since she was a child. She shared many a fond memory with several of the boys in her neighborhood, yet these same boys refused to wrestle with her or play games with her. At first, she thought it a jest they were playing upon her, but as the days passed and they still would not play with her, her playful nature turned into frustration. Looking back now, it was obvious that puberty created many boundaries between her and the opposite gender, but as an adolescent girl, she was confused. She brought the subject up with her mother.

"Why will none of the boys play games with me anymore?" she asked one afternoon.

Her mother gave a sweet smile. "Because, my little dove, you are becoming a beautiful young woman. The rules between boys and girls are going to change quite drastically for you soon."

Arianna crossed her arms stubbornly. "Well then I don't want to become a woman. I don't like the looks the boys give me now. They look as though they are scared of me."

Her mother laughed. "They are not scared of you, Ari. One day soon you will understand."

She always hated hearing that as a child. *One day she would understand.* She did not want to wait; she wanted to know now, and so she asked her father the same question, hoping he would divulge some information her mother missed. Looking back now, she recalled the loving look in her father's eyes, and the realization his little girl was growing up. She would remember until her dying day what he said to her.

"They are not scared of you, princess," he said. "They are intimidated by how beautiful you are. You can thank your mother for that. She will most likely scold me for what I am about to say, but I will deal with that later. You will learn later on in life that any boy can stare at a girl with his eyes, but it takes a man to look upon a woman and, just by gazing upon her, show her just how much she means to him. That is the man you should look to spend the rest of your life with." He then embraced her warmly. "And as for all those other boys, you just let me deal with them if there are any problems."

Arianna smiled at the memory, but let it slip from her face. The good memories were always coupled with the bad. Two years after that conversation, her mother and father succumbed to the red plague that swept through the Merchant's Quarter, killing one in six. The death toll was catastrophic, and the area had been quarantined off so it wouldn't spread to the other districts of Calydon. Her parents attempted to act carefree so as not to scare her, but she saw the fear in their eyes. And then she saw the beginning symptoms—they broke out in fever and the glands beneath their armpits began to swell.

Before she came down with the symptoms herself, she watched her parent's skin melt away, and their eyes take on a sunken look. For the next week, she was delirious, going in and out of states of consciousness. When she finally awakened, there was the kind face of an elderly woman above her.

"You are going to be all right, my dear," she had told Arianna.

She tried to talk, but her throat was so unbearably dry. The elderly woman handed her a ladle of water. Arianna drank sparingly, allowing a small trickle of water down her parched throat. "Where are my parents?" she asked, her dry lips cracking. "They must be worried sick about me."

The look in the elderly woman's eyes told it all, and Arianna knew the answer before she even confirmed it for her. "I am afraid they did not make it, my child. Before he collapsed, your father was able to carry your body to the streets. The death carts thought you both had been claimed by the plague, but they discovered you were still breathing. They then brought you here to be tended to. Unfortunately, we were unable to do anything for your mother or father, but it was because of your father's last action we were able to help you. I am so sorry."

There were no words, and Arianna began to weep. Just like that, her parents had been stripped from her. There were no final words of farewell. She would never see them again in her lifetime, and the knowledge ripped through her soul. The woman politely stood and left her to her grief. In the following weeks, the death toll slowly waned, and food carts were finally allowed through the barricades. It was during that time her uncle found her back at the bakery her parents owned.

He entered through the main entrance, his close-set eyes taking in the bakery shop. Arianna had only met him once many years ago and could only remember he had a sly, crooked smile. Her parents rarely spoke of him, and she realized she knew nothing of the man. He stopped directly before her, running his hands through his greasy black hair.

"Do you know who I am?" he asked her.

"You are my Uncle Mathis," she answered. "You are here to take care of me now."

The open palm of his hand connected sharply with the side of her face. Arianna reeled back, her hand flying to her stinging cheek. "You will address me as sir," her uncle said. "Do you understand?"

Still rubbing her cheek, Arianna stared sullenly back at her uncle. "I understand. Sir."

"Good," Mathis responded. "It looks like I will have to teach you some manners since my dreadful sister obviously did not. I am not here to take care of you. I am here to take over the business of this pathetic bakery. The moment you are no longer useful to me is the day you will no longer be welcome here."

In that moment, Arianna wanted nothing more than to fly at this man, at this person who was supposed to be her only living relative. She wanted to claw at his face and make him wish he had never said anything slighting about her mother. She wanted to make him pay for slapping her, for hurting her, but she was still recovering from the plague and was weak in both body and spirit. So she bided her time, waiting for the moment she would leave this piece of filth and this city far behind her.

Her moment came six months later. Six months of silent beatings and mistreatments that caused her to cry herself to sleep at night. All the while, she saved money where she could, knowing one day she would leave Uncle Mathis and never see him again. It happened when the two of them were closing down the bakery after a slow day of business. Arianna became aware of Mathis's lingering gaze upon her as she went about her duties and started wearing apparel that was less revealing. Her selection of clothing was limited, and despite her best efforts, it did not stop the looks he gave her.

She was placing a jar upon a shelf when her hold slipped, the jar falling from her grasp. The pottery shattered across the floor in a loud crash. Mathis went into a rage, saying she would pay for that. Arianna stood meekly by, hoping her silence would placate him. It did not. He suddenly lashed out at her, knocking her to the ground. In an instant, he was on top of her, straddling her. Arianna, her lip bleeding from the blow, looked up into Mathis's face and saw the glittering, almost bestial, look in his eyes.

"Maybe you need something else to teach you a lesson," he said. "Maybe then you will finally learn your place."

He began unbuckling his pants. Something deep inside of Arianna snapped. Her hand was resting on a broken piece of pottery. With a cry born of desperation, she clutched the jagged piece in her hand and slammed it into the side of his neck. Mathis stood up abruptly, a look of utter shock in his eyes. His hand flew to the piece of pottery jutting from his neck. Grabbing ahold of it, he tore it out, spraying his lifeblood into the air. His gaze switched to Arianna and he began to say something. Blood dribbled forth from his mouth. He took a step forward and then fell face-first to the floorboards.

Shaking uncontrollably, Arianna stood, rooted to the spot. She had just murdered her uncle. *He was a wretch*, her mind told her. *You must get moving.* She went to her room, collected her meager stash of coins from its hiding spot, and took what possessions she could carry. Then, she left the bakery, making sure to avoid the sprawled out body of the relative she just murdered. She didn't look back once not even after she walked beneath the Pontis Gate and left the massive city of Calydon behind her. For the first time since the plague struck, she felt truly free. It was an exhilarating feeling.

But that was only been the beginning. Her cache of coins lasted her mere days, and she was forced to take up employment at an inn. For the next few years of her life, she bounced back and forth between various towns and cities throughout Varkuvia, always looking, always searching for a place she could finally call home. It was during that time of traveling she had truly come to loath men.

No matter what job she was able to take on, whether it was as a waitress, cook, milkmaid, or baker, she was constantly haggled.

Everywhere she went, men would grope at her, make obscene gestures, and lurid comments. She soon lost count of the amount of times she was propositioned. They were all the same. Of course, some hid it better than others, but deep down they were all animals. Each only wanted to possess her, to dominate her, the same as her Uncle Mathis tried to do. She would never allow it. The fact she was stunningly attractive did nothing to help her cause. Even at the age of fifteen, she had men looking at her with wide, prying eyes, and grown women look upon her with open scorn and jealousy. She knew she could do nothing about her looks, but even still, it was difficult to make friends in those early days.

Finally, at the age of seventeen, she stumbled upon Karalis, short of coin, and bereft of hope. It was here she met Theresa, a kind maternal woman, who took pity on the malnourished teenager Arianna was. She found her employment at her husband's tavern and dealt harshly with any customers who treated her unfairly. For once, she finally found some semblance of hope in humanity. After working at the tavern for another two years, she was offered employment at the mighty Keep of Karalis by a representative of Queen Lorain herself. She was ecstatic, and with Theresa's blessing, accepted. It was here she was finally able to make a living for herself.

Even at the Keep of Karalis, she did not allow a single man to touch her heart. At the same time, she knew she was no delicate flower. She had her fair share of fun with the Stone Guards, and on occasion a noble, but it was never against her will. She always made the choice, and once any of them attempted to pursue her further, she would cut herself off, throwing up a wall to block her emotion. Not once had she experienced feelings for any of them. *So what was so different about Trystan?* her subconscious asked her once again. *You know he will turn out to be just like the rest.*

In her mind, she pictured Trystan, recalling those brilliant eyes of green, and his slow, shy smile. That he was attractive she could not deny, but there were hundreds, perhaps even thousands of other men who made advances upon her, she had spurned. So what was so different about him? The truth stood before her, yet she did not wish to reach out and grasp it. He did not boast as most others did but neither did she consider him a weak man. Others looked up to him, and revered him, yet Trystan did not ask it of them, and he did not allow the adulation to swell his head. He was a humble and honorable man. By all accounts, Trystan was the truest definition of a hero there was, yet he would never admit as much or see himself in that light. Maybe that, in its essence, is what truly makes him a hero.

*None of those virtues are the underlying reason why you have feelings for him*, she told herself. There was a connection between Trystan and herself she simply could not explain. Not with words at least. They met if only for a brief moment in their youth. It was a time of happiness before the death of her parents, before the pain and suffering she experienced, yet she connected with the young thief. She saw the sorrow in his eyes and understood. The two of them were tattered and lost souls who traveled across a continent searching for something unattainable. They each chose completely separate paths in life and miraculously, against all odds, managed to bump into one another. The chances of the two of them meeting again in this lifetime had to be astronomical, yet somehow they did.

Not usually a believer in supreme beings or forces guiding her life, Arianna could not help but ponder the definition of fate. There was no other way to explain the two of them meeting once again. It was as if there was some kind of divine purpose behind the whole thing. Just the thought of Trystan sent her heart fluttering. Breathing deeply, she calmed herself. *Do not fall for him*, she warned herself. *It will only end in heartache for you.*

The front door to the Crowned Steed swung open. Without even thinking, Arianna was on her feet, waiting with anticipation. The first one to walk through the door was Jaxon, the giant's bearded face appearing sour. His wife, Margaret, who was also waiting in the common room, leapt with joy upon seeing her husband. The grim expression fell from Jaxon's face, and he moved forward to embrace his wife. The next to follow was the hulking form of Gabriel, and then the tall one, Owen. Finally, stout Gavin entered. Arianna peered around the archer, wondering where Trystan was. The stirrings of panic began in her breast when Trystan strode through the door, the bruises upon his face looking ugly in the dim light of the inn.

Fighting down the urge to run to him, Arianna calmly walked toward the man she knew deep down was slowly stealing her heart yet simply would not accept the reality of it. As she drew near him, she took in the full scale of the beating he withstood. Strangely, she felt angry with him, yet it was an anger born of caring. She warned him to be careful when he left her the night before, and he still managed to get himself thrashed. Yet she also felt responsible. She should have roused herself out of bed and helped him relax his mind, but her duties at the keep, and the volunteer work at the hospital had begun to take their toll. With so many people fleeing the city, her responsibilities had grown tenfold. She was exhausted, numbingly so, and not thinking clearly. *I will not let him out of my sights again*, she told herself.

"How did it go?" she asked, trying to keep the concern from her voice.

Trystan gently probed his swollen right eye, grimacing as he did so. "Awful," he answered. "Let's go upstairs and discuss it. I'm not sure who is listening anymore." His gaze swept the common room. Other than members of the Order of Acrium, there were only two other customers seated at the tables, but even still, Arianna could not miss the hint.

Nodding, she turned on her heel and walked toward the staircase. With Trystan walking behind her, she suddenly felt the urge to run from the Crowned Steed. Her inner demons came clawing at her soul, and every instinct in her body told her to flee now before she allowed herself to fall for this man. *You are starting to care far too much for him,* her inner voice told her. *You don't need him. You don't need anybody. Turn around now, and do what you have always done.*

At the top of the staircase she stopped, panic gripping her. Turning around, she began to brush by Trystan and make a dash for the front door. She was going to do just that when her eyes locked with Trystan's, and any thoughts of fleeing vanished from her mind. The look in his eyes was the same one he gave her all those years ago in Calydon when he was escaping the city watch. His eyes told her he was lost, and she knew deep down if she left him right here and now, he would break down. She was torn. Her past, and her instincts, told her to leave, but her heart told her to remain.

"Are you all right?" Trystan asked, moving forward and gently caressing her arm.

And in that moment, she knew she would not leave him. For once in her life, she would not abandon someone who showed interest in her because for the first time in her life the feelings were mutual. "I am fine," she said. "I was just concerned for you, that's all."

"I am all right," he assured her. "I will tell you all about it in the room."

After closing the door behind them, Trystan turned toward Arianna. There was a depth of sorrow so profound in those green eyes, Arianna wanted to step forward and embrace him, just to let him know everything would be all right. She wanted to say something, anything that would put a smile on his face. Instead, she remained quiet, waiting for Trystan to speak.

"Despite my pleas on his behalf," he said, "King Markos has refused to release Layne from imprisonment. However, the king did allow me an audience with Layne before I left the keep. It is my belief, along with Layne's, that once the Five Kings are fully gathered at Karalis, he will be executed."

Arianna knew the torment Trystan was going through. He constantly brought up his former mentor, and it was obvious, he held him in high regard. She was unsure of what to say. "And what of you and the others?" she asked, trying to divert his attention from Layne.

"For the moment we are safe," he answered. "King Markos cannot afford to lose the Order of Acrium. Not yet, at least. He needs us to hold the second wall until reinforcements arrive. Then I am afraid once the eastern lords and the tribesmen are beaten back, my fate will be the same as Layne's."

A feeling of dread crept into Arianna's heart. The thought of losing Trystan was appalling. It was a feeling she was unaccustomed to. *Get ahold of yourself,* her mind said. *He has always been in danger. This is nothing new.*

"We must leave the city then," she said, trying unsuccessfully to keep the terror from her voice. "We should run now while the kings are caught up in their war. Why must you stay when you know your life is in danger? You owe the Five Kings nothing."

"The Five Kings have done nothing but cause me grief in the past year. That much is true. But what of Master Layne? What of Jaxon, Gavin, and all the others? There will be nowhere we can run to escape the retribution of the Five Kings. If I run now with you, then I might as well forfeit the lives of all the others as well. That I will never do. How would I be able to live with myself after such a shameful deed? I would never be able to look upon my reflection in the mirror for the rest of my life."

*Run*, Arianna's mind screamed once again. *He has sealed his fate already. You do not have to be brought down with him.* No, she told herself firmly. *I will not abandon him.*

"Was there no good news at all during this meeting?" she asked while fighting down her inner demons.

"There was a small silver lining. King Markos has decided to make his presence known upon the walls. He will walk among his men and strengthen their resolve. It is my hope that Markos's presence, along with the news reinforcements are on their way, will bolster the men. With a little bit of courage and a whole lot of luck, we just might be able to hold until the others kings arrive."

"What of you? What will you do about this whole situation?"

Trystan looked up. Arianna shivered. There was something in his eyes she had never seen before. It was a look that would make even the most powerful of men avert their gaze. "I will fight like I have never fought before," he said. "The Five Kings believe every warrior of the Order of Acrium is a traitor. I will prove to them that we are not, and I will prove to them that Layne is innocent. Then we will all know peace."

"Sometimes peace is not so easily attained," whispered Arianna.

"There will always be peace when those you care for are near," Trystan responded. He reached out, gently gripping Arianna's hand. "I cannot tell you how happy I am you are back in my life once more."

Normally, Arianna's first reaction would be to rip her hand away from Trystan. Instead, she found herself squeezing his hand, reassuring him. It was as if a gentle breeze blew across her soul, sending her inner doubts floating away.

"I will stand by you," she said. Then she leaned forward and kissed him upon the lips.

# CHAPTER SEVENTEEN

For over two weeks, the defenders of Karalis fought like men possessed. With the loss of the first wall, their hope was reduced to dying embers but with the news of reinforcements and their liege King Markos now fighting alongside them, their hope reignited into a roaring flame. The men fought for their homeland, for their loved ones, and for everything they held dear in this world. Wave upon wave of Khali and easterners were repulsed with fearful losses to their ranks. As the hard fought days slowly turned into bloody weeks, the defenders' necks constantly craned to the western horizon, hoping, praying to see the reinforcements they knew were riding to liberate them.

Courageous acts were performed daily upon the wall. Many of these deeds went unnoticed, but this did not stain the valor of the men involved. One bright afternoon, the battlements slick with the blood of the fallen, a massive easterner wielded a double-headed ax toward Trystan's exposed back. A young volunteer, a farmer by all accounts, jumped in front of the murderous ax, taking the brunt of the blow in his side, his ribcage collapsing. Choking on his own blood, his life fading away, the farmer grabbed the haft of the ax and drew the easterner directly onto the point of his sword. The two fell dead to the ramparts, and the battle continued to rage all around them. No one celebrated the farmer's deed or wrote a ballad about it, but this did not matter to the young volunteer. He witnessed the heroic deeds performed by men such as Trystan of the Blade, and he mirrored those actions.

Other acts of outstanding bravery occurred more often than not. One of King Alaric's men, a spear in his gut, killed the wielder and then threw himself forward, dragging two others screaming to their deaths on the ground below. A Stone Guard stood back to back with Jaxon, defending against a breach in the wall that opened up, his sword blade weaving a spell of death. It was only after the enemy was beaten back that he allowed his body to crash to the ramparts, his life drained away by several puncture wounds in his sides and arms. Another man, a simple soldier, had his arm severed in half yet still managed to kill two and wound another before he was carried away to be treated.

Domenic, a member of the Order, was supporting a wounded comrade to the field hospital, the same man who had his arm severed. As he was leaving, a group of tribesmen broke through the defenses, racing toward the unprotected medical facility. Owen was able to take down two with his bow but four others, their blades soaked in the blood of Varkuvians, charged on toward the hospital. What they were doing was suicidal, for they would be cut down within minutes, but their hatred was so deeply ingrained they did not care. Domenic stepped forth into their path, his long sword singing into the air. He decapitated one and buried his blade in another. Then a long dagger lodged into his side, piercing his lung. Spinning around, he drew his own knife sheathed at his side and ripped it into the tribesman's throat. Falling to his knees, his vision misting, he watched the final Khali rush into the hospital his ax made of bone, poised above a defenseless man lying in his bed. With the last of his strength, Domenic flung his knife, taking the Khali in the side of his bearded face, pitching him sideways. Then he toppled to the ground.

As the days of horror turned to night, such stories of heroism were told around the campfires, lifting the spirits of the men. And through it all, the Order of Acrium held the defenders together, binding them into one cohesive unit. Many amongst them began to forge their own legends. With the defeat of the Argarians, Gabriel saw his own stock rise substantially. His berserk style of fighting and brutal strength combined with his weapon of choice, the sledgehammer, soon gave him the nickname the *Hammer of Death*. Late at night, many of King Markos's men would swap tall tales and share a pitcher of ale with the half-Argarian though Gabriel was quick to note that King Alaric's men never joined them. He was wise enough to heed King Markos's warning and kept his eyes open to danger from within his own ranks.

Owen and Gavin also gained massive acclaim one day. King Markos was surrounded, his Stone Guards were being cut down one by one around him. Then Owen and Gavin saw the King's plight, and together they unleashed their combined skills upon those attacking the king. Each of their arrows thrummed through the air finding their marks, the mound of enemy dead piling up. This allowed for others to come to the king's aid, pushing the enemy back. They saved the king's life. After the action was over, King Markos himself presented the two of them with arrows made of pure gold and conveyed his undying gratitude.

Jaxon made a name for himself while fighting beside Gabriel. Together the two of them held a section of the wall for an entire day. Not a single enemy gained a foothold where they fought, and as dusk fell, the two big men left the ramparts, their armor bathed in the blood of their enemies. As night descended, word spread like wildfire through the ranks of Varkuvians of the two indestructible men. From that moment on, whenever the two giants fought side by side, they were known as the *Beasts of Varkuvia*.

Shining above all others was Trystan, always Trystan. His name was upon the lips of every single soldier and every citizen who remained. Wherever he fought upon the wall, men cheered his name and battled all the more gallantly. The fire and passion in his eyes as he slew enemy upon enemy inspired everyone around him. He fought as though he was not human, and to the people of Karalis it was as if the gods themselves delivered him into their warm embrace to protect them, to save them. His hero status was legendary, and no matter the time of day, he was the topic of conversation. Easterners and Khali alike turned tail and ran when they saw the silver figure advancing toward them with his dazzling sword and strange pupils, for they knew death was sure to follow. Songs were sung of his bravery and charisma. The famous poet, Percival, wrote the ballad "Trystan of the Blade," and it was told time and time again, spreading from ear to ear, bringing hope in a time of darkness. Nobles and affluent merchants showered the young swordsman with riches and gifts, bestowing upon him wealth he couldn't possibly imagine.

None of it fazed Trystan. His mind remained focused on one single driving purpose. Every day before dawn, he went to the various shrines and temples of the gods. He prayed to Crassos, the Divine Ruler of the Heavens, and to Aether, the God of Light, and to Rhea, the Goddess of Love, and even to Vikundo, the God of War. Each of his prayers was the same, no matter the shrine or temple, he paid homage. He prayed he be given the strength to vanquish his enemies, so he could see Master Layne to freedom once more. And every day he honed his skills upon the bloody ramparts of Karalis. After two weeks of constant battling, he was now able to tap into his Verillion powers whenever he deemed necessary, but once it passed, it still left him feeling exhausted and groggy. He was still not able to unleash his full potential, as Layne called it, and he still searched for a way he might finally reach the pinnacle of his power.

And through it all, through all of the blood and horror he witnessed, there was Arianna. Whereas the common folk of Karalis found hope in his presence, Trystan drew strength from Arianna's beauty and compassion. As the days passed, his feelings for her grew. He knew deep down in his heart he loved her, but he could not bring himself to express it to her. He was afraid of rejection, afraid of how she might respond. So he kept the three sacred words of "I love you" stowed away, waiting for the right moment when he could be certain she felt the same way for him. Truth be told, he did not know when that moment might be in the midst of a war; but if the opportunity arose, he would seize it.

Despite the new heights of inspiration Trystan and the others were able to instill in the defenders of Karalis, desperation was slowly beginning to creep through their ranks. The weeks of fighting had begun to take their toll. Of the nine thousand men that started out defending the city, little more than three thousand now remained to man the walls. Two-thirds of their force had been claimed by death or suffered wounds too grievous to see them fight again. There were now too few left to allow for fresh ranks to replenish the exhausted defenders. Those who remained fought for days on end without rest, their minds becoming detached, and their bodies moving mechanically. Every day messengers arrived bearing letters declaring help was on the way and begging those remaining to hold out as long as possible. The defenders knew they could not go on much longer, but still they fought on.

As the days passed, and news spread the Order of Acrium was being reformed, many more answered the call. Some days, one or two would trickle into the city, bearing the armor of Acrium and prepared to join the cause wherever they were needed. Other days no one would arrive. But then there were days when small groups of ten or twelve would wander into the fortress city. Trystan did not have the heart to tell those that answered the call they were being monitored and their lives might be in equal peril if they were able to prevail against the combined forces of their enemies. He saw the look of apprehension in both King Markos's and King Alaric's eyes, but he also saw the enemy dead, the reformed Order of Acrium left in their wake. By the twenty-fifth day of the siege of Karalis, one hundred and seven members answered the call and combined their strength with the twenty others that remained in the city. It was on this day everything changed.

The defenders, bone weary and drained, both physically and mentally, stood upon the wall, preparing for another day of slaughter. They went through their daily routines of tightening shield straps and checking edges of overused blades. The morning meal of stale dark bread with sharp cheese they had grown so accustomed to was being handed out and eaten with little enthusiasm but eaten nonetheless. It might be the only food they consumed that day, and they knew they would need to keep their strength up. The sun was obscured behind light gray clouds hanging in the air. In the distance, a dense fog could be seen slowly rolling toward the battered city. It was almost noon, and still the enemy hadn't attacked. There was something different in the atmosphere this day. It sent a ripple of anxiety through the men, leaving them on edge. Trystan felt it as well and, with Jaxon beside him, gazed out over the battlements toward the enemy position.

Gathering just out of bow range they could see a large group of darkly armored warriors moving smoothly into position. Even with the poor light nature provided, they could still see the dull golden sunburst that was imprinted on each of the black breastplates. The same emblem was upon the shields strapped to their arms. There were thousands of them.

"That would be the Legion of the Rising Sun," Trystan stated. "Lord Drogos recruited them a quarter of a century ago, using the Order of Acrium as a model. There are five thousand of them, and they are the most disciplined force the eastern lords have to offer. I've heard they shipped iron ore from King Alaric's realm at an exuberant cost to craft high quality swords. They will be seeking to kill us using blades we helped them forge. I'm afraid the word ironic would be far too tragic right now. This is definitely not good."

"There's a lot of the bastards," observed Jaxon. He squinted his eyes. "And look at that armor. I can see no weaknesses from here. I don't know about this, Trys. Our lads are doughty fighters but look at them. They can barely stand right now. I'm surprised it's taken the eastern lords this long to send the Legion against us."

"This is a move born of desperation. They know each day that passes draws our reinforcements closer. They will seek to break us in one fell swoop. If we can hold them, then I believe we have a chance. If not"—Trystan shook his head—"then I am afraid the city is doomed."

"What do you suggest we do?"

"Pray."

Word spread along the length of the wall about the nature of the enemy the defenders of Karalis were about to face. Murmurs began and Trystan saw the onset of fear. He saw King Markos, with his sons flanking him, attempting to calm their nerves. It was not working. He heard a soldier talk boldly and loudly of retreating. Many others voiced their agreements. Soon angry voices mixed in, and it was only a matter of time before a fight would break out. Trystan switched his gaze to the Legion of the Rising Sun, which still remained stationary. He looked beyond them to the wall of fog that was slowly but surely advancing upon Karalis. *They are waiting for the cover of the fog,* he reasoned. A soldier jostled into his back, and he turned to see some of the soldiers were shoving one another.

"The Legion is going to take the wall without a fight soon enough," yelled Jaxon over the commotion, pushing the soldier away from Trystan.

King Markos was being berated by several soldiers, and Trystan saw his Stone Guards grab the hilts of their swords menacingly. Trystan knew he had to say something, anything that would deescalate the situation or else bloodshed was sure to follow. Without thinking, he jumped to the crenellations, his mind racing. He had never addressed a large crowd before, let alone an angry one. He had no idea what to say, and his mind came up empty.

Soldiers standing nearby turned toward him and this strange behavior, staring at the man standing above them. One of the soldiers recognized the interlocking circles on the silver breastplate and the green eyes many saw ablaze in the heat of battle. He nudged his companion, and pointed. "That's Trystan of the Blade," he said.

The companion looked Trystan up and down. "I expected him to be taller," he responded, his voice gruff. "Quiet down, everyone," he bellowed. "Trystan's got something to say."

For some time, the angry mutterings along the wall continued but soon enough word spread that Trystan of the Blade, their hero, their savior was delivering a speech. The defenders of Karalis bunched tightly together, their attention focused solely on Trystan. Many in the crowd were too far back to even see him. Regardless, they stood on tippy toes, hoping to catch a glimpse of the hero. Trystan stared into the eager faces of thousands, his mind completely blank. He gained their attention, but now they expected him to say something awe-inspiring, and he had no inkling of what to say. Clearing his throat, he sought to buy more time, trying to recall some heroic speech he studied at the Fortress of the Van.

"Today is the day our enemies will learn who we really are," he said, his voice quavering.

"What is he babbling about?" one soldier called out.

"I can't hear him," another complained.

"He sounds like a mouse," yet another said. That one was closer and brought snickers from those around him. "Trystan the Timid more likely."

Anger replaced Trystan's fear of addressing the gathered men. And anger gave him courage. His finger snaked out, pointing at the soldier who made the last comment. "Who are you to say such a thing?" The tone of the question subdued all mockery. "Who are you to call me a mouse?"

The soldier shifted uncomfortably, those around him clearing space, not wishing to be the brunt of further questioning. He looked around nervously, his face turning a bright red. "I am Oglesby, m'lord." His voice was as shaky as Trystan's had been.

Ignoring the title of lordship, Trystan pressed the point. "And who are you, Oglesby, to judge me so?"

Oglesby had no answer, and his eyes remained firmly fixed on the grey stones of the ramparts, which had taken on a dull red hue from the weeks of constant battling. "Now who am I?" Trystan asked.

"Trystan of the Blade," Oglesby responded meekly.

"Louder. I do not believe those in the back heard you."

"Trystan of the Blade," the poor soldier repeated, somewhat louder this time.

Taking his focus off the unfortunate Oglesby, Trystan's emerald eyes of fire swept the ranks of defenders, seeming to look into each face of the thousands gathered. "For weeks now, I have wondered if this city could hold." The words echoed throughout the silent crowd. "I saw before me men who were untried and frightened. I saw an army of mice that would run at the first opportunity. Do you know what I see before me now?" The question hung in the air. "I see an army of lions, fearsome and undaunted. I see men who have fought tooth and nail beside their brothers-in-arms and have stared unblinkingly in the face of their fears. And I have seen death. I have seen death in its tens of thousands. But *we* are still *here!*" His eyes raked the gathered men once more. "Help is on the way. There are thousands of our countrymen riding to our aid, and they are waiting, begging to drive our enemies back. And they are so very close. They could be here on the morrow or even this very day. So I ask you this, why now, why, when our brethren are within sight of our prayers, do you men falter? I know none of you are cowards, so tell me, why now?"

"There are thousands of them," one yelled.

"There are too few of us left."

"Too many of us have already died," a soldier called from the back. "Why should more of us share the same fate?"

Many voiced their agreement to the answered question, and conversation started up once more. Trystan held up his hand for silence. And they obeyed him. "Aye, it is true, many have fallen," he said, the words full of sorrow. "Just as it is true, many more will follow. Each of us has lost friends or brothers or cousins. We have all felt heartache and pain. But each of those brave men did not die in vain. They died in the belief that what they were doing was just and righteous. And those men have passed the torch onto us. The eastern lords seek to send the Legion of the Rising Sun against us. They are hoping to break us, so their Legion will be able to murder our children, rape our wives, and burn our homes. But I say not on this day." His voice grew louder. "I say, while good and honorable men fight beside me I will never allow that to happen." Many in the crowd shouted encouragement. "And if the gods deem this to be my last day on this world, I say, I am honored to be in such company. I will fight these bastards until the last breath leaves my body."

"As will I," Jaxon chimed in, his voice booming out.

"Will we be alone?" roared Trystan.

"No!" the answered erupted as one from three thousand throats.

"Then by the gods, let us show them how the Lions of Varkuvia fight!" Trystan's blade of gold-green flashed into the air.

"Trystan! Trystan!" The chant rolled along the wall, the noise deafening. "Trystan! Trystan!"

Trystan jumped down from the crenellation, soldiers all around, clapping him on the back and cheering his name. They were pumping their fists, all of their fears forgotten. Jaxon leaned in close to his friend. "Where in the seven hells did that come from?" he yelled over the chanting and raucous cheers.

Even if he could think of a reply, Trystan doubted he could speak. His legs and hands were shaking. *Where had that come from?* he asked himself. He remembered something that Master Roderic often said during his lectures, *"Come the moment, come the man."* And the moment had certainly seized Trystan.

The chanting continued long after the fog slowly began to settle over the city. It thickened all around the galvanized men until they could no longer make out the Legion of the Rising Sun assembled before them. As time trickled away, the cheering began to dissipate and the men stood and waited, knowing battle was soon to follow.

The slow and steady sound of swords clashing against shields echoed through the fog, reaching the ears of the defenders. It started out as a small noise, barely piercing the dense mist. The sound grew in strength, the beat picking up until it was the only noise in the air. The battle cry of five thousand fearsome soldiers suddenly erupted in the midst of clashing swords and shields. The noise, combined with the limited visibility of the defenders, was chilling in the extreme. In an instant, the battle cries and clash of metal on metal died away. The only sound now was from the shifting of nervous soldiers upon the wall and the slight scraping of armor against stone as men leaned forward intently against the battlements to see beyond the natural obstruction.

Trystan's breastplate pressed hard against the stone as well, the chainmail beneath digging into his chest as he too tried to gauge what the Legion was doing. *Damn this fog,* he told himself. An arrow suddenly flew from the mist, ricocheting off the battlements, missing his face by the length of a grass blade. He heard the arrow whistle by his ear and the cry of an unfortunate soldier behind him as it plunged into his flesh. He did not have time to turn and see if the wound was fatal, for the clattering of ladders against the wall filled the air and the biting of grappling hooks as they dug into the crenellations. The Legion moved as silently as a wraith. Five thousand men advanced upon the second wall and not a single defender heard their approach. *Maybe they are truly as terrifying as the men believe them to be*, he thought.

Such foolish notions were short-lived when a gauntleted hand clamped onto the battlements. Trystan's blade sliced downward, the gold-green metal cutting cleanly through armor and flesh as knife would through butter, leaving the owner with one less limb. He heard the screams from the one-handed man and then heard him fall from the ladder, plunging to his death, screaming the entire way. Not even seconds later, another hand appeared, ready to replace the fallen comrade, and this one was prepared. This time Trystan's slashing blade was thrown wide by a parrying sword of black steel, the same the Brotherhood wielded. He was forced to take a step back and watch as the first soldier of the Legion jumped to the ramparts.

From a distance, he could not make out the full features of the darkly armored warriors, but now, standing in front of Trystan was a fully clad warrior in armor as black as pitch. The dull sunburst of pale gold upon the breastplate, and kite shield strapped to his arm were still the same, but much more intricate up close and somehow more terrifying. And the helmet of blackest night was far more chilling. From afar, it looked like any normal helmet would with a full-faced visor protecting the entire face. But now, Trystan could see the visor was shaped and molded into the face of a crying man with the only opening in the visor being slits at the eyes. The cruel eyes of the legionnaire stared through those slits, drilling into the man before him. Trystan thought he faced all kinds and shapes of opponents in his twenty-five years. He was wrong. The man dressed all in black armor before him exuded fear, and any normal man would find his legs growing weak and his bowels loosen in the presence of such terror.

But Trystan was no normal man. Knocking aside a powerful thrust, he nimbly stepped forward, his own blade lancing forth in reply. The dark shield of the legionnaire blocked the attempt, and Trystan took a step back, reassessing his opponent. *His armor is well made*, he noted, *but cumbersome, limiting his mobility. And his shield hangs from his left arm.* With a new plan formulated, Trystan stepped forward, his sword thrusting at the legionnaire once more. The shield went up to block the blow, but this time Trystan drew his sword arm back at the last possible moment and spun to his right, bringing him to the legionnaire's exposed left flank. The shock registered in his opponent's eyes long enough for Trystan's blade to plunge through the slits of the visor, slicing through cruel eye and soft brain, alike.

Withdrawing his blade, Trystan looked up to see how the flow of battle was going along the length of the wall. He could barely see anything. His visibility was limited to three feet in front of him from the fog. The sounds of clashing steel and the screams of the dying were the only knowledge he had battle was still joined all around him. His thoughts turned to the three-foot bubble surrounding him when another legionnaire jumped to the ramparts, his shield held up before him, exposing no weaknesses. Trystan held his blade before him, planning in his mind how he would tackle this fresh foe. Jaxon's ax swung through the air, cleaving into the back of the legionnaire's helmet, crumpling the metal into the top of his spine. The darkly armored warrior pitched face-first into the ramparts.

Before Trystan could nod his head in gratitude, Jaxon turned back toward the ladders where another legionnaire was just reaching the top, his shield held above his head. The ax in Jaxon's hands rose above his head, and he brought it down with bone-crushing force. The shield splintered in two as the ax connected, continuing on to smash into the crying-face visor, obliterating the man's face. The legionnaire fell without a sound, dislodging another climbing below him.

Three of the Legion suddenly burst from the fog to the left. The first thing they saw was Jaxon's exposed back, and like hounds thirsting for blood, they prowled toward their prey. A common soldier stepped into their path but was cut down with ease, his brains dashed against the rampart stones. Sensing his friend's peril, Trystan did not hesitate. Drawing deep inside of himself, he tapped into his Verillion blood and felt it surge through his veins. He felt invigorated. He felt powerful. And he felt unstoppable.

Taking two quick steps, he launched himself forward feet first. The first of the Legion turned just as the boot connected sharply with his helmet. He was catapulted backward, knocking into the crenellations before flipping over spinning to his death. Trystan fell to the ramparts but surged to his feet just as dark steel clashed off the stone where he fell. His blade lanced forward, connecting with the visor of a second legionnaire. Such was the force of the blow, his foe's head snapped back, knocking his visor completely out of place, exposing his face. Even as his sword arm arched back to deliver the killing blow, Trystan had time to notice the sharp beak of a nose on the legionnaire, with his unshaven face, and the fear in his dark eyes. Trystan's sword cut the nose, along with half of the legionnaire's face cleanly off in a shower of crimson and broken bone.

Turning around, he faced the third of the Legion and was just in time to leap backward from a slashing blade. The legionnaire stepped forward too boldly, confident he could slay his distracted opponent. His boldness and overeager slashing put him off balance, exposing his breastplate. Stepping forward, Trystan kicked the dark warrior square in the chest, propelling him backward. He disappeared into the fog, but Trystan still heard the screams as he flew from the ramparts. Spinning around, he looked for fresh foes to face. Seeing this section of the wall was holding firm, he turned to Jaxon.

"Hold the wall, big man, and be safe."

Before Jaxon could respond, he turned and flew into the fog, determined the Legion would not claim the second wall. Wherever he went along the ramparts, his sword weaved a spell of death, legionnaires crumpling in his wake. The Legion of the Rising Sun heard the rumors about Trystan of the Blade and the notorious fighting skills he and others of the Order of Acrium possessed. They believed the rumors were spread by men they considered weak in both body and mind and arrogantly believed they would sweep the defenders aside. Now they knew differently. Any who faced the men wearing the silver armor of Acrium soon learned they were fighting against warriors beyond peer, their skills unquestionable. And soon enough they learned everything they heard about Trystan was true, and just like their comrades-in-arms, they were soon terrified to face him.

Despite Trystan and the Order of Acrium's best efforts, the fighting was still bloody and brutal. For a time, it seemed as though the second wall would fall regardless of their heroics. But as Trystan fought and raged along the wall, he slowly became aware of how the ebb and flow of the battle was transpiring. The defenders of Karalis were terrified when they first beheld the Legion of the Rising Sun, but as they saw they could die just as easily as any other could, their resolve bolstered, their courage returning. Not only were they holding their own, but they were also pushing the enemy back. The Legion felt it as well, and no matter how hard they fought, fewer and fewer were able to gain purchase on the wall.

The sound to retreat echoed through the fog from the eastern encampment, ringing like sweet music in the ears of the defenders. The Legion of the Rising Sun sulked out of bow range, the deafening cheers of thousands following them every step of the way. Not only were the defenders alive, but they fought the best the eastern lords provided and emerged triumphant. They pushed vacant ladders from the wall and cut tight grappling hooks, laughing all the while. Heady victory pounded like rich wine in their veins. They drank it in, feeling invincible. Nothing would stop them now. They would hold out until reinforcements arrived, and they would all live to see another day.

Minutes later another trumpet sounded, and even though he could not see, Trystan knew the enemy was forming up once more. His beliefs were confirmed when ladders once more smacked against the wall and fresh grappling hooks dug deep into the battlements. There was no noise from the Legion this time, no cocky swagger. From the moment the first legionnaire crested the ramparts, Trystan sensed a new aura surrounding the enemy. They underestimated the skills of the Order of Acrium and were proven wrong. They fed upon the unaccustomed ash of defeat and found the taste not to their liking. Now they would brush aside the defenders as an angry giant would swat a child from its path. The regular troops of the eastern city-states and the painted Khali mixed into the Legion's ranks. It seemed as though all of the east and its northern allies swarmed forth from their encampment, seeking to finally end the siege.

Despite his blade moving in a blistering series of dazzling sword work, Trystan found himself giving ground to the enemy. As soon as he dispatched an opponent, another would immediately step forward. Whether it was a legionnaire or tribesman or armored easterner, they were all eager to replace their fallen comrades. Even with the power of the ancient Verillion race unleashed, he watched helplessly as more and more of the Legion, easterners, and Khali poured over the wall like so many ants swarming forth from their home beneath the earth. The line still held but for how much longer Trystan could not say. His blade, dripping blood and gore claimed another legionnaire and then swung mightily, biting into the neck of a tribesman.

The sudden sound of frenzied noise to his right caused him to turn his head to see what was going on. Try as he might, his gaze could not pierce the fog that clung to the air. And then he heard it. A bugle was sounding, this time from within the city of Karalis. It echoed like some deep bullfrog, reverberating throughout the fog, rising above the discordant noises of battle. The sound to retreat was given. He fought his way with so many other defenders to the stairs closest to him, despair growing in his heart. He heard pounding feet and screams of triumph from his right. No, not to his right he suddenly realized. It was behind him. And then he knew what the noise was he could not identify. The right flank of defenders on the wall splintered and shattered. The enemy poured around them and now had a clear path throughout Karalis.

The wall was lost. And so was the city.

# CHAPTER EIGHTEEN

rrin, the exiled Master of Ax, rumbled through the paved streets of Karalis, his trademark laughter of battle roaring before him. A peasant in an ill-fitting tunic stepped into his path, frantically waving a pitted sword before him. He was no more than fifteen and paler than a ghost. Orrin's war ax shattered the useless blade, smashing the boy's face open in one mighty stroke. He continued past the body without as much as a backward glance. A mere peasant would not deny him his glory on this day.

Vengeance. The word itself was the only thought consuming his days and nights for months now. Another peasant stepped into his path, this one holding a butcher's cleaver, older and heavier than the frightened boy. There was no fear in the butcher's face. He died just the same, his guts spilled out on the steps of what was probably his home.

Orrin's laughter thundered forth once more. There were no barricades or set traps in the streets to impede his way. There were no armored soldiers, charging cavalry, or flying arrows to halt his advance through Karalis. The city had fallen, and the only opposition now was inexperienced boys and old cripples. The laughter bubbled from his lips.

For over eight months now, he was forced to wait and bide his time. And patience was never a virtue he possessed. A tribesman with black paint and blood upon his face raced past him to his right. To his left he saw, the Blade of Five Kings, owned by Balin, who was considered one of the finest armorers and sword crafters in the five realms of Varkuvia. Even with the heavy fog all around him, Orrin knew he and the thousands of tribesmen and easterners that had broken through the defenses were passing through Blacksmiths Way.

He summoned the layout of the city in his mind. After Blacksmiths Way would be Bakers Row and then the Jewelers District followed by the Houses of Merchants. The wealthiest and most powerful traders would be positioned near the Jewelers District with the less fortunate located near Old Town more frequently called Thieves Alley. Old Town was the lowest and poorest quadrant of the city where the gutter rats, thieves, and cutthroats dwelled. It was where waste was thrown from windows and a dead body wasn't given a second glance. It was also the largest part of the city before it tapered off onto the Plains of Karalis. Mason instructed his tribesmen, once the second wall fell, that they secure Thieves Alley before doing anything else. *Once Thieves Alley is under control, then the city will truly be ours,* Orrin thought. The few defenders who somehow managed to make it back to the third wall will be but a minor inconvenience. They wouldn't even have enough troops to man the ring wall with the Keep of Karalis at its center like an island.

Orrin's mood darkened as his thoughts turned to the Keep of Karalis. In the days of his youth, the keep had been a symbol of justice and honor. The keep had not fallen in the three hundred years since its construction. It was a source of Varkuvian might and one any child would look upon with a sense of pride. Now all he could think of was the cold floor and filth he was forced to eat while he was held captive in the keep's dungeons.

He sallied forth from the Fortress of the Van on that fated day when the Order was disbanded. First Master Roderic, Master Mason, Master Petros, and a dozen under officers were beside him, and he didn't have a care in the world. They were all heroes of Varkuvia, and awarded for their bravery a hundred times over. The five realms were safe because of the battles they fought, and the pains they endured. The Five Kings would surely see they made a mistake and listen to reason. And indeed, they agreed to listen to them. He could still remember the noble Roderic shuffling toward the assembled kings seated upon their thrones and the dignified bow his arthritic arm and bent back offered. The speech he delivered was powerful and moving, and Orrin felt certain the kings would reconsider their decision.

Instead, they arrested all of them, throwing him in a dungeon cell. For over a month, he lived in squalor, the stench of his own body filling his nostrils and senses. No matter how much he pleaded, the guards would tell him nothing. They would not tell him the fate of the other masters or why he had been arrested or what was to become of him. And then one day they barged open the door to his meager cell and beat him to the ground with wooden poles and fists. He fought back, but the month of poor nourishment and loss of hope sapped his strength worse than he could have imagined. Then they threw a sack over his battered face, bound his hands, and forced him to mount atop a horse. For days, he traveled as such, never once being told where they were taking him or what was going on.

One bright afternoon, he was forced to dismount. He was certain this was to be his end. Without warning, they had ripped the sack from his head. The sudden and harsh sunlight made his eyes stream, and he was forced to blink rapidly. He looked around with one eye open to see the other masters in just as bad a state as he must've looked. Master Layne was not present, and for that, he was at least grateful. Gathered before him was a troop of armored cavalry, and he could see the various banners of the Five Kings flapping in the breeze. Even with them hiding his face, he still recognized the soldier pines around him, and the mighty Bale Mountains to the north whose snowcapped peaks disappeared among the clouds. They were at the border of the Stone Realm. It was the beginning of winter, and it was cold.

A man dressed in a fine purple tunic wheeled his horse forward. Upon his chest were the five sigils of the ruling houses of Varkuvia. He looked down in disgust at the tattered men beneath him. "I speak with the voice of the Five Kings, and each of you has been brought here to be told your fates," he said, the words misting in the icy air. "In their generosity, the benevolent kings have decided you all may keep your lives. However, from this day forth, you are to be banished from these lands. Your titles and estates have already been forfeited. If any of you attempt to set foot on Varkuvian soil again, you will be considered a traitor of the realm and executed wherever you are found. Is this clear?"

In that moment, Orrin wanted nothing more than to break this man's neck who looked so smug seated upon his mount. He heard the taut sound of bowstrings and looked around to see archers training their arrows upon him. The masters voiced their complaints, but they fell on deaf ears. Eventually, they left the lands they'd defended for decades with heads bowed and with heavy hearts. With no money and no food, they wandered aimlessly. Even the weapons and armor they carried into so many battles was denied them. Four of the most respected men in all of Varkuvia were reduced to beggars simply because they sought a meeting with the Five Kings. And if they ever tried to return to the place they called home, they would be executed, their bodies left on display for all others to see.

The soft hue of orange punctuated the fog around Orrin, shifting and changing. The soldiers of the east and the savage tribesmen were setting the homes and establishments of Karalis ablaze. The exiled masters had returned home, and they had returned with a vengeance. A host, unlike any other, was now at their backs, and the Five Kings no longer had the Order of Acrium to stop them. Sadness crept into Orrin's soul, slow and deadly like an assassin's blade. For decades, he defended Karalis and countless cities just like it from all forms of invasion. He put his own life on the line, time and time again to protect the people of Varkuvia. Now, once again, he found himself leading the charge, except this time he wasn't liberating the city. He was conquering it.

*This is justice*, he forcefully told himself. *The Five Kings brought this upon themselves with their arrogance and their callousness. They made a decision, and now they will learn that every decision has a consequence.* The piercing scream of a woman ripped through the air though from which direction Orrin could not tell. It was followed by piteous sobbing and the hooting laughter of men. *The rapes and murders will be the worst part,* he thought. Though he himself had never committed such acts, he witnessed the demons of mankind unleashed during the heat of battle. The blood would run hot, and the surge of power could easily dominate a man. Men who were loving husbands and fathers would turn into base animals, all reason washed away in a wave of blood. It was worse during a drawn-out siege as if the prolonged anticipation made the rapes and murders of these women all the more worthwhile.

He was passing by the burning estate of a wealthy merchant when a mother and her son stumbled into his path. The mother screamed. Falling to her knees, she clutched her son tightly. Orrin's first reaction was to assure the frightened woman and child that everything would be okay. His massive arms spread wide in a friendly gesture, a smile falling easily into place. The boy, no more than four, looked up at Orrin with bright blue eyes. He burst into tears, burying his head into his mother's chest. That was when it hit Orrin. He was no longer the shining hero sent to save them. He was the invading monster, setting their homes on fire and killing their neighbors and relatives. His gaze switched to his arms, which were still held wide, and looked in horror at the blood that bathed his body. The ax in his hand dripped with blood, the shining steel of the crescent blade barely visible. *What have I become?* he asked himself. *Have I truly fallen this far?*

Letting his arms drop, he walked toward the fallen mother. She stroked her son's golden locks, whispering soft words in his ears. Her eyes met Orrin's, and he could see the tears spilling down her cheeks. She did not beg for mercy or attempt to flee. She merely sat there, holding her son close, shielding him from what was about to come. Orrin hefted his ax before him and, in doing so, found himself gazing upon the reflection in the bloody blade. The broad face that stared back at him was streaked with blood, and the once jovial eyes had taken on a haunted look. *No wonder the child is terrified of me,* he thought sullenly.

He let the ax fall to his side. "Get up, woman," he told the mother. "Take your child away from this madness and get him to safety."

She looked at him for a moment, disbelief in those teary eyes. "Did you not hear me?" asked Orrin. "Go on now. Run as fast as you can toward Old Town. We have not yet advanced upon the Plains of Karalis, and you should be safe there."

Finally the mother stood, clutching her crying son in her arms. "And where will I go to find my murdered sister and loving husband?" The question was asked with accusation. "You have taken them from me, and nowhere in the entire world will be safe again. I pray when your time comes, the gods are not merciful."

Before Orrin could reply, the mother turned and fled into the fog, disappearing from sight. He spared her life and that of her son yet received only scorn in return. *What did you expect?* he asked himself. *That she would embrace you with loving arms when you stood before her covered in the blood of those she knew and cared for?* Sighing, Orrin loped off toward Old Town. This time as he advanced through the streets there was no laughter bubbling forth from his lips. The elation he felt at the fall of the city was ephemeral, and now it was replaced with a depression so deep, he feared it would scar his soul forever. He just wanted this bloody business to be done with.

Any semblance of order was nonexistent as he lumbered toward Thieves Alley. The men had turned into a pack of hungry wolves in the conquered city, prowling through the streets, their lust insatiable. *It will be like this until dawn*, he realized. *Once they had their fill of looting, burning, and raping, discipline would once more take over.* He passed the front of an inn as a chair exploded through the front window, shattering glass all over the street. The front door was hurled open, and Orrin saw a tribesman grappling with the owner of the inn. The innkeeper had a large kitchen knife in one hand and blood streaming from a wound to his scalp. Another tribesman stepped behind him and plunged a dagger into the innkeeper's back, severing his spine. Orrin saw the stabbed man's eyes glaze into the back of his head before he collapsed to the streets. The tribesmen fell upon the innkeeper and began hacking his body parts off, waving them in the air like glorified trophies. *Dawn cannot come soon enough*, Orrin thought.

Just as he reached the outskirts of the Houses of Merchants, he saw a large group of easterners huddled around a tribesman, vigorously cheering him on. The man they cheered on was thrusting his hips frantically, the only sight of the unfortunate woman beneath him was her spread-out skirts. The tribesman suddenly thrust forward, his exposed buttocks flexing. Orrin heard him howl as he climaxed, the easterners around him exploding into raucous cheers. Even as the tribesman took his manhood out of the spoils of war, Orrin saw an easterner untying his breeches, ready to have his go at the downed woman. The whole scene disgusted Orrin, but it was none of his business. He began to move on, hoping at least some of the men remembered their orders to secure Old Town.

But then, something out of the corner of his eye caught his attention. As the tribesman stood from the woman he just raped, his face flushed with pleasure, Orrin caught sight of a body sprawled out behind the group of men. The bright blue eyes of the little boy Orrin had terrified stared back at him. They looked just as frightened even in death. He could see the hilt of the knife still imbedded in the boy's chest and the blood pooling beneath his tiny body. He now had a full view of the woman who was being made sport of. The mother he let go was staring at the dead body of her son. Her face was bruised and bloodied, her eyes vacant and devoid of life.

Orrin found himself walking toward the group, all thoughts of securing the remainder of the city lost to him. The mother did not even blink as the next man entered her. She did not react to the lewd comments being thrown all around her or to the sweating, grunting man above her. Her sole attention was on the body of her son who had been cruelly ripped from her. Her hand extended on the streets, falling just short of her little boy's hand. Without thinking, Orrin threw the easterner who was enjoying himself from the woman. He landed hard and then got up angrily, furious at being denied his prize. The others shouted their distaste, some saying they were to be next.

The easterner Orrin threw to the ground drew the dagger at his side and advanced upon the disbanded Master of Ax with murderous intent in his eyes. Orrin turned and swatted aside the thrusting dagger as he would have swatted the backside of an unruly child. Stepping forward, he casually backhanded the man across the face, sending him sprawling to the ground. There were no more arguments after that. He brought his attention back to the mother that still lay, staring at her murdered son. Finally, her head swiveled, those vacant eyes staring up at Orrin at the man who gave her a second chance. Her lip quivered as tears once more slipped down her beaten face. Sickened to the core of his soul, Orrin raised his bloody ax and ended the tormented woman's life. It was the first time in all of his many years as a warrior he ever harmed a woman. And it was the first time he ever recalled being close to tears when claiming another's life.

The arguments started up once more when the men saw he killed the woman instead of allowing them to enjoy her. Orrin was furious and sick to his stomach. He raised his ax to challenge any who felt strongly about the matter. Several looked as though they might rush him. An arrow suddenly flew from the heavy mist, plunging into the leg of an easterner. The man cried out in pain, clutching the shaft. Orrin whirled around angry.

"Who loosed that?" he bellowed.

The men looked around confused, unsure of who released the arrow. Another arrow emerged from the fog, bouncing off the street right by Orrin's feet. He narrowed his eyes, his anger at the men forgotten. The arrows came from Old Town. The blaring of horns echoed through the fog followed by the faint but distinct sound of pounding feet. Dread crept into Orrin's heart. That signal was one he heard dozens of times in his life. It heralded the arrival of reinforcements.

A single rider emerged from the fog, seated upon a magnificent black stallion, his full beard framing a face which radiated power and purpose. Seeing Orrin and the gathered men, he drew a sword of brilliant steel, a bright ruby set into the pommel.

"Who in the seven hells is that?" an easterner asked.

The rider pointed his sword before him and bellowed a command. Armored soldiers burst from the fog behind him, their swords raised high, and their battle cries trumpeting before them. Orrin could not believe his eyes. He saw banners rippling in the breeze, trailing behind the charging men. There was a griffin with wings spread wide upon one and a rearing black stallion upon another. The rearing stallion was nearly identical to the one that the rider was seated upon. And then Orrin knew. King Stefanos and King Eryk had finally arrived with their armies. The tribesmen and their allies were too preoccupied with plundering the city, their lines spread thin. There was no organized force to halt this fresh opposition.

Reacting quickly, Orrin grabbed the man closest to him, hauling him close. "Run back through the city and warn all those you pass. King Stefanos and King Eryk have arrived. We need all the men we can muster, or we will lose the city as quickly as we claimed it."

The man looked at him with a blank expression. "Do you understand me?" roared Orrin. "Run like the wind and raise the alarm. I better hear you screaming all the way through the city, or I will skin you alive myself!"

Orrin threw the man from him and watched him stumble off into the fog. Sure enough, moments later he heard the warning cries as the man heralded the arrival of reinforcements. Hefting his ax, Orrin turned toward the charging soldiers. There were hundreds, if not thousands of them. Gathered around him now were close to fifty men, consisting of assorted easterners and tribesmen. Every one of them appeared terrified.

"At them, lads!" he yelled.

Without waiting for the others to follow, he charged toward the armored soldiers that arrived to liberate Karalis. *Nothing will deny me my vengeance*, he told himself. *Not even an army.* Pounding feet behind him told him he was not alone. *The raving maniacs have finally come to their senses.* He sighted his ax on a thick soldier wearing a black-and-yellow checkered surcoat over dull chain mail. Ducking under flashing iron, he buried his ax into the checkered soldier's midsection, the blow parting the chainmail beneath like a lance through a boil.

The two lines clashed together, the thin ranks of the east and their allies almost completely washed away by the charge of the Varkuvians. Orrin stood his ground, sweeping aside a thrusting sword before bringing his ax into the bearer's neck. The few men that followed him into battle were falling one by one, and it was only a matter of time before the Varkuvians would completely overwhelm them and continue on into the city. If they were to somehow regain the wall, then the war would be lost. A tribesman fell to his right, a knife embedded in his eye socket.

334

Orrin bellowed his frustration, his ax swinging in a murderous arc to cut a soldier's arm off at the shoulder. The man fell back, blood pumping from the severed limb. After killing another, the Varkuvians took a step back from the maddened axman. The remnants of Orrin's meager force charged back into the fray with renewed vigor. *We will not hold out much longer*, Orrin told himself.

From all over the burning city, men who were enjoying themselves so blissfully upon the soft skin of women and the deaths of the innocent rushed to join the fight. Orrin's ranks swelled as more fighters took up arms against the reinforcements, and the lines slowly began to stabilize. The east and its allies might have been taken unawares by the arrival of the two kings, but they brought with them tens of thousands. Now that the second wall was completely overrun, the combined weight of their armies marched to the battle taking place before Old Town.

As the day wore on, the heavy fog that helped conceal the advance of King Stefanos's and King Eryk's troops finally began to dissipate. The streets became littered with the bodies of the slain, and the ground itself bled the tears of the fallen, the red liquid flowing beneath the combatants. Arrows flew overhead as both sides loosed shafts at one another. The clashing of steel and the cries of the wounded became one noise that was all consuming. Old Town soon became a charnel house, the corpses of both sides piling up.

To his left, Orrin could see the rider upon the black stallion, who he presumed to be King Stefanos, attempting to lead a cavalry charge against the left flank. The close confines of the city combined with the choked mass of the embattled armies made it impossible for him to gain any type of momentum. The king himself was soon brought into the thick of battle, his sword hacking left and right as he cut ever deeper into the ranks of his enemies. As the battle raged on, Orrin found himself being drawn ever closer to the king.

Blocking a downward stroke with the haft of his ax, Orrin pushed the blade wide and then brought his ax into the soldier's leg. The man's cries were washed away under the feet of the clashing armies. Blood ran into Orrin's eye. He wiped it away with the back of his hand, leaving a massive smear of red across his forehead, blinking rapidly so he could see again. He did not even remember being cut. Now that his mind became aware of the injury to his head, he could feel a throbbing in his leg and looked down to see the broken shaft of an arrow jutting from his calf. *When did that get there?* Such questions were pushed aside when he saw King Stefanos claim the life of a tribesman, his sword leaving a bloody trail in the air. The king was only a few yards away from him. If he could kill him, Orrin could change the tide of battle.

Shouldering a Varkuvian out of his way, Orrin limped toward one of the Five Kings, determined he would not only change the course of battle but kill one of the men who wronged him so. One of the mounted soldiers surrounding King Stefanos saw the axman approaching and kicked his horse toward the new danger, confident he would protect his liege. Orrin sidestepped a thrusting spear, gritting his teeth against the agony of his injured leg. His ax moved in response, burying into the cavalryman's chest, flinging him from the saddle. He turned and was just in time to bring the haft of his ax up to block a downward cut. Throwing aside the blade, he found himself face-to-face with King Stefanos, Ruler of the Horse Realm.

The king's dark beard was speckled with blood, and his armor of bright steel enameled with burnished gold was dented in more than one spot. The gold cloak fringed with black fur clasped to his shoulders was tattered and dirty. Even with the battered armor and less than splendid cloak, everything about the man radiated confidence, and there was no fear in his eyes at the swarm of clashing steel and screaming men surrounding him. Backstepping another attempt, Orrin rushed forward. His ax swung, aiming for the king's unprotected leg in the stirrup. Stefanos pulled hard on the stallion's reins. The horse reared in response, and Orrin was forced to halt his attack, taking a step back from the flailing hooves. The stallion came down hard, its hooves spattering the blood covering the streets of Old Town into the air. The king's sword flashed through the air. Orrin was too slow to evade the swing and felt the blade bite deep into his shoulder. He staggered back, needles of pain threading through the wound. His allies surged around him, and the king was forced to retreat into his own ranks, his guards forming up in front of him.

Orrin felt blood flowing freely down his leg, pooling into his boot. His breathing came in quick rasps, his shoulder throbbing and bleeding profusely. He had his chance at vengeance and let it slip away. There would never be another opportunity as perfect as that one. Composing himself, he looked along the lines of the combatants and judged with his warrior's mind how the battle was developing. The two king's element of surprise was lost to them, but even still, their armies were far more disciplined than the eastern lord's forces and their allies to the north. Only the Legion seemed to be holding its own, and the death toll was rising substantially. However, the eastern coalition still outnumbered the Varkuvian reinforcements by four to one. If they continued pushing, King Stefanos and King Eryk would eventually break.

A tribesman behind Orrin screamed out in pain, an arrow jutting from his shoulder. Another fell, the arrow driving so deep into his sternum that only the fletchings were visible. Orrin glanced up and had to duck as a shaft whistled by his face. The defenders that made it back to the third wall were releasing arrows down upon the tightly packed ranks of the Eastern coalition. The huddled mass of men made for easy targets and an arrow found its mark more often than not. A loud roar to Orrin's right caught his attention.

He swung to see Lord Randell upon a massive stallion, his face the same color as his fire-red beard, a vein jutting angrily from his neck. His sword pointing before him, aiming directly at King Stefanos. He was vehemently urging his mount on, but with men pressing all around him, he barely budged.

"Usurper!" Orrin heard Randell yell even over the clamber of battle.

The sound to retreat bounced off the crumbling buildings of Old Town. The sound came from the eastern encampment. The lines slowly pulled back from one another as the front ranks of both armies locked shields before them. A space slowly opened up between the two forces, the reinforcements of the two kings holding Old Town, and the eastern coalition holding the Houses of Merchants, along with the remainder of the city. Orrin heard Randell curse long and hard and turned to see the lord of Cabalo being restrained by his own men. Randell was furious, his face a deep red as he struggled mightily to be released. He screamed he would not be denied and told those holding him they would lose their hands if they did not release him.

Ignoring him, Orrin turned back toward the battle that just took place. The occasional ring of steel could still be heard, but for the most part, the two armies stared sullenly back at each other. Biting back the pain from his wounds, he assessed the situation through a strategic view. Without Old Town secured, they could not advance upon the Plains of Karalis. However, since the Houses of Merchants was secured by Orrin's allies, their army still encircled the third wall of Karalis. If they moved against the wall, King Stefanos and King Eryk would surely attack their flanks. Yet if they moved against the Varkuvian reinforcements, the defenders upon the wall would sally forth from behind and attack their rear or loose arrows down upon them as they still continued to do.

"It is a stalemate," Mason said behind him.

Orrin had not heard the exiled Master of Spear's approach. "We still have the numbers," continued Mason. "So they are reluctant to attack. That will change soon enough. See your wounds tended to. Tonight we will hold a meeting with the eastern lords and devise a new plan. I expect to see you there."

Mason turned and walked back through the ranks, stopping occasionally to say a word or two to his tribesmen. Soon he was lost to sight. Taking his old companion's advice, Orrin began hobbling back toward their camp which was set up beyond the second wall. His leg all but dragged behind him. Now that he was no longer in the throng of battle, he could see the arrow had cut cleanly through the meat of his calf, the arrowhead jutting out of his leg. He cursed under his breath. *That is going to hurt like the devil when they pull that out*, he thought miserably. Pushing such unpleasant thoughts from his mind, he focused on the truth of Mason's words. *This is in fact a stalemate.* Once both sides drew up new plans, the war would begin anew. *Come tomorrow, the siege of Karalis will continue*, he thought. Cursing once more, he limped as fast as his leg would allow, falling in line with the procession of other injured men.

# CHAPTER NINETEEN

"We had him!" raged Lord Randell. "The bastard had his back against the wall. All we needed was one more push, and the city would have been ours!"

His fist slammed into the dark oak desk dominating the center of the study, the legs quivering beneath the blow. Kleitos held up his hands. "You need to calm yourself, Randell," he said, the words containing a sense of urgency. "The others will be here soon enough. How do you think it will look if they see you behaving in such a way? Stefanos has earned a respite, nothing more. He sits in the shit and piss that is Old Town with nowhere to run. His time will come soon enough."

Randell would not be placated. "The others can go dine in the bowels of the underworld for all I care! We had the numbers, and they were about to break. Now King Stefanos, King Eryk, and their armies will be fortifying Thieves Way. I can picture them even now ramming their sharpened stakes into the streets, turning Old Town into a death trap. We will have to fight for every single blood-soaked inch to claim those decrepit buildings. And what do you think the archers standing upon the third wall will be doing while we advance? I'll tell you what they will be doing. They will be raining arrows upon us every damn step of the way. Who in the bloody seven hells sounded the retreat?"

"It was Lord Dorian who issued the order," Kleitos responded. "Everyone knows he is a cowardly man, yet it is said it was not his idea. I have heard rumors that it was Lord Drogos who whispered in his ear. It was his whispers that persuaded the fat lord to sound the retreat."

"Pah! The lord of Snakes strikes again. Does that man have any semblance of honor? He has no soul of that I am certain."

The lord of Cabalo whirled around, his fury pulsating throughout his body. Karalis was theirs, and King Stefanos was but a stone's throw away. He was so close to his vengeance, he could feel its sweet taste upon his tongue. He gripped the sill of the study's window tightly, a vein jutting from his temple. Randell had taken up residence in the illustrious manor General Corbin once occupied. The cavalry general was slain by Mason and his tribesmen at the Memure Bridge in the early stages of the war, and Randell highly doubted the late general would object to him staying a night or two in his bed. *At least the general had good taste*, Randell observed through his anger.

The study he was standing in was huge, the walls lined with bookcases, each shelf filled to the brim. Some of the tomes on the shelves were dusty and forgotten. Others looked as though they were falling apart, the pages crusty and yellowed with age. For the most part though, the books upon their shelves were neatly organized, arranged in alphabetical order. There were only three pieces of furniture in the room: the desk Randell struck, an elegantly crafted chair before it, and an old worn-out armchair of red leather in the corner. The only window in the study Randell now leaned against had a panel of stained glass set in its frame depicting a battle scene between the gods Crassos and his son Vikundo when Crassos cast the God of War from the heavens. The glass in the battle scene was made up of different colors of blue, yellow, green, purple, and red. With the setting sun hitting the glass just right, it made the whole scene stand out brilliantly.

Taking deep breaths, Randell turned from the battle of the gods and felt some of his rage melting away though he knew it waited below the surface of his skin like an angry volcano waiting to erupt. The oak desk in the study stood upon a rich carpet of bright red, the edges fringed with gold, standing out in stark contrast to the lifeless gray stones of granite beneath. There were still many pieces of parchment spread out upon the top of the desk, covering the surface. It was obvious the recently departed General Corbin spent much of his free time in here. *Maybe if he spent more time studying the subtleties of war and less time reading foolishness, he wouldn't be carrion right now,* reflected Randell. He thought about how fitting it was the lords of the east would be using this room the general used so frequently to relax, to conduct their war, and to devise new strategies to conquer the city.

The door of the study swung inward. Randell could feel his blood start to boil once more at the prospect of seeing Lord Drogos. He feared that he would not be able to guard his tongue this time and might have more than a few choice words for the devious lord of Yursa. Instead, it was Lord Nikolaos who walked through the door. The lord of Seren was resplendent in a doublet of dark olive green with a long-sleeved shirt of cotton white underneath. Thick rings of gold studded his fingers, and he wore knee-length boots of soft doeskin. The grime and filth of battle had been washed from him, and his short-cropped hair appeared freshly groomed. Randell saw Lord Nikolaos's advisors crowding behind him, seeking to enter the room, but Nikolaos waved them back and ordered the door be shut.

It clicked quietly behind him, and he moved to stand before Randell. His brown eyes inspected the lord of Cabalo. Randell hadn't bothered to wash or change from the battle for Old Town, and he knew that Nikolaos would see the dirt deeply ingrained into his face mixed with spots of blood. His armor was dented, and he was certain he looked like anything other than a lord of the east.

"You look horrible," Nikolaos stated, slight humor showing in his eyes. "Did General Corbin not supply you with a bathhouse so you might be able to cleanse yourself?"

With any other person at that time Randell might have found his anger unleashed, but there was something about the wiry lord of Seren which made such japes acceptable. He found himself chuckling softly. "I had more pressing matters on my mind other than a warm bath." He looked Nikolaos up and down. "You on the other hand seem to have had enough time to bathe for the both us. And what are you wearing? You look like you're about to attend a ball instead of a war council."

Nikolaos tugged at his puffy white sleeve and then smiled. "Dress to impress, I always say. You never know who you might meet." The smile faded away. "We need to talk."

"I figured as much when you left your men outside," Randell replied, waving toward the closed door. He turned to Kleitos, hating he had to ask the question, but knowing it needed to be asked. "Should Kleitos wait outside for this?"

"That will not be necessary." Nikolaos rubbed at his chin. "It seems you two are the only ones I can entrust with this information. I fear there is no one among my own men I can rely upon. Disturbing news has just reached my ears."

When the eastern lord remained silent, Randell pressed him. "Well, what is it?"

"Two tragic deaths have been reported since the battle for Old Town. The exiled masters, Orrin and Petros, have both passed onto the afterlife. It appears, Orrin bled to death from the wounds he suffered, and Petros fell from the second wall when we overran it. Now Mason refuses to leave the manor he is residing in and has surrounded himself with countless tribesmen."

Randell found his tongue stuck to the roof of his mouth. He saw the injuries Orrin sustained. An arrow through his leg and a sword cut to his shoulder hardly seemed life threatening. He saw the banished master limping away to be treated. Orrin was dragging his leg and bleeding profusely from his shoulder, but he still stood tall, and it appeared after a few stitches he would be right as rain. *Perhaps his wounds were more severe than they looked*, he thought. *Don't be a fool*, he told himself. At least Petros's death seemed more reasonable. He remembered all too well the cloying fog, and the tricks it played on the mind. The exiled Master of Bow was not the only victim the fog claimed upon the wall.

"Quite an unlucky turn of events," muttered Kleitos.

Nikolaos's gaze met Randell's. "I do not believe luck had a hand in this." He hesitated. "Randell, I witnessed Petros's death with my own eyes. It was not a chance of fate that claimed his life. I saw one of our men shove him from the wall. It was one of the Legion."

Silence descended upon the study. Each of them knew who commanded the Legion. Drogos. Randell's mind turned to the argument between Drogos and Mason those weeks ago and the tension that surrounded them. That's when it dawned on him it was far more than coincidence both Petros and Orrin should perish at this time. This was something Drogos had been waiting for, planning for. In one fell swoop, he killed Mason's two right-hand men, instantly leaving the Grand Chieftain of the tribesmen vulnerable. Mason would be far easier to manipulate without his most staunch supporters by his side. Drogos was no longer waiting to eliminate his future rivals. He was acting now.

"You are certain of this?" asked Randell. He needed to be sure. "It was a legionnaire that shoved him?"

"I am confident in what I saw, Randell, just as I am positive it was no coincidence. We both know who is responsible for this."

Running his hand through his thick beard, Randell sat down heavily upon the cushioned desk chair. His eyes scanned the scattered parchments, searching for some answer he knew he would not find. He looked up and met Nikolaos's worried expression. Randell knew what the lord of Seren would be thinking. Which of us will be next?

"What do we do?" asked Kleitos.

Randell leaned back in the chair. As always, when his mind was troubled, his thoughts turned to Myra. For once, thinking of his wife did nothing to soothe him. There was no turning back from what he was about to say.

"We kill Lord Drogos." The words were spoken with a calm Randell did not feel.

"Have you lost your senses?" blurted Kleitos, disbelieving. "One does not simply kill the lord of Snakes."

"And why not?" responded Randell. "He is a man, same as you and I. If he can bleed, he can die. I've yet to see any man or woman, live with a knife though their heart." He turned his focus on Nikolaos. "What do you think?"

The lord of Seren remained quiet, lost in thought. "Do you think we can do it?" he asked at last.

"I do."

"Then I am with you. It is only a matter of time before Drogos turns those black eyes on us, and then we will end up just like Orrin and Petros. Better we make our own preparations."

"Are you with us, Kleitos?" Randell asked his friend.

The advisor looked back and forth between the two as though they were deranged. "Both of you have lost your minds," he said, exasperated. "You are talking about killing one of the most dangerous men I have ever heard of. He probably has spies listening to this very conversation."

"Are you with us?" Randell repeated.

Kleitos sighed. "Aye, I am with you though I think this is folly."

"When do we do this?" asked Nikolaos, his expression serious. "And how?"

The door to the study suddenly swung open. Lord Drogos entered. The pasty lord of Yursa's black robe flowed on the stone floor as he walked, giving him the appearance, he was gliding toward the startled men. Another man entered behind Drogos, wearing the sinister armor of the Legion of the Rising Sun, the black helmet cradled in the nook of his arm. Randell had never seen him before. The newcomer turned and, despite the objections from the hallway beyond, slammed the door in the faces of the advisors waiting outside the room.

The legionnaire swiveled and followed on the heels of his master toward the others. *The man does not walk*, Randell noted. *He prowls like a wolf circling its prey.* Even with the heavy armor of the Legion, his movements were smooth and confident. His hand rested lightly on the hilt of his sword, his fingers subconsciously tapping the dark leather grip. The pommel of the blade was shaped into the head of a snarling wolf, giving more meaning to Randell's assessment of the newcomer. The legionnaire's blue eyes, resting beneath bushy eyebrows, had an arrogance to them as he surveyed the men gathered around the desk. *We are nothing to him*, Randell realized. *He looks at us as if he could kill us all with one swing of his sword.* The man's nose was scarred at the bridge, giving it a crooked appearance, and another scar ran horizontally from his cheek to his left ear, leaving a permanent pale streak across his face.

Drogos and the newcomer stopped before the conspiring trio. "I hope you three haven't been doing much scheming without me," the lord of Yursa said. The slightest of smiles split his pale lips. "Before we catch up on events, let me introduce Paxtos, my appointed general of the Legion of the Rising Sun."

Paxtos inclined his head ever so slightly, those arrogant eyes drilling into the men before him. Randell saw all kinds of soldiers and fighters in his days. Some were loyal, steadfast, and strong. Others were merciless, deadly, and fast. Everything about Paxtos said he was warrior born and utterly dangerous. No wonder the man was given command of the most brutal force the east had to offer. He appeared to be a stone-cold killer, and Randell had no doubts in his mind the general possessed great skill with the blade sheathed at his side.

"To continue with the formalities," continued Drogos, "this man, my general Paxtos, is Lord Nikolaos, ruler of the always summer city-state of Seren. And this is Lord Randell, ruler of the horse-raising city-state of Cabalo. And this—" Drogos frowned as he came to Kleitos. "My apologies, good sir, but I am embarrassed to say I do not remember your name."

"I am Kleitos," the advisor answered testily. Drogos had met him a dozen times in the past, and Randell was unsure of whether or not he was trying to goad Kleitos or he simply forgot his name.

"Ah, yes, and this is Kleitos, Lord Randell's trusted friend and advisor." Drogos's sly smile attempted to take away some of the sting of misplacing the name from memory. "I am sad to inform you, Lord Dorian, the robust ruler of the wealthy port city-state of Sura was called away on other pressing matters. Now that we are all introduced, what may I ask were you men discussing before I entered? You look as though you have seen a ghost."

No one reacted at first. Was the cunning lord playing his own game right now? Could he possibly know what they were discussing or what they were planning? "Lord Nikolaos just delivered the unfortunate news of Petros and Orrin's demise," replied Randell, not wishing to offer a complete lie. "We were dismayed to hear of it. Their losses will surely be a blow to morale."

Drogos took on an expression of genuine sadness. Randell didn't buy it for a second. "Such untimely deaths, that is true enough. I pray their paths in the afterlife lead them to a paradise with untold pleasures."

"The whole thing seems strange to me," Randell continued warily. "I witnessed Orrin's wounds myself. They did not seem to be life threatening. How is it he died from them?"

"A terrible twist of fate," explained Drogos, an edge of sorrow in the words. "The arrow caused his leg to go bad, and the physicians had to cut it off. Orrin died from the blood loss long before they were able to stop the bleeding. Terrible, really quite terrible. I am afraid the gods were not with him this day."

Kleitos's and Randell's eyes met, if only for a heartbeat. The lord of Yursa was lying. "I am afraid the tragic losses of these two noblemen must be put to the side," said Drogos, all signs of sympathy extinguished. And with those simple words, he resigned the two deceased masters to the vaults of his memory, never to be spoken of again. "Troubling news has arrived on the wings of one of our ravens. The contents of the message are worrisome to say the least." He picked up one of the scattered pieces of parchment on the desk, glanced at it briefly, and then let it float back to the desktop. "King Lucan has finally pledged his army to aid in the liberation of Karalis. He is now marching toward the city with twenty-five thousand men."

Stunned silence followed the news. If King Lucan were to arrive before the city was taken, they would not only be hard pressed to claim Karalis but would be lucky to escape with their lives intact. "How did such a thing happen?" gasped Nikolaos. "I thought the king was staying as far away from this war as possible."

"As did I," replied Drogos. "We can thank the recently departed King Ragnar and his unruly Argarians for this debacle. Even from beyond the grave, our old ally troubles us. King Lucan was good and far away from meddling with us, just how we wanted it. But King Ragnar, with one of his last commands, ordered five of his longboats to raid along the coast of King Lucan's realm, seeking to gain extra plunder and riches. Against all odds, one of the towns they chose to raid housed King Lucan's wife, Queen Jocelyn, and his seven-year-old son, Prince Lucius. The queen and young prince were only stopping by on their journey back to Calydon. The town was razed to the ground, Lucan's queen and son murdered. I do not wish to go into detail, but I've read the Argarians did unspeakable things to Queen Jocelyn before they slit her throat. Needless to say, the king himself is beyond furious. The moment he heard the news, he flew into a rage and sent out orders for his full army to assemble. His force of twenty-five thousand will consist of heavy horse, crossbowmen, pikemen, and armored swordsmen. This is what we have dreaded since we began planning this war so many years ago. We cannot hope to contend with the combined might of the Five Kings."

A sudden thought occurred to Randell. "Even if it took over a week to receive this news, it would still take close to a month and a half for King Lucan to assemble his full strength and travel from Calydon to Karalis. We still have time yet to deal with the other kings."

Drogos shook his head gravely. "I am afraid even that has been denied to us. The raven with its dark news arrived late. Whether it was my agent's fault who wrote the message or the raven itself, I do not know, but time is now against us. King Lucan, with his entire force behind him, will arrive within the week."

Randell's fury came back all at once with the news. He was so utterly close to King Stefanos and claiming his vengeance but was forced to swallow his frustration. The two were destined to meet on the field of battle. That much was written in the stones of history. Now the walls of the study, lined with their many bookshelves, seemed to be crumbling down around him as was this war. Their forces were bloodied, their losses substantial. King Lucan would be bringing with him over twenty-five thousand fresh troops, their swords sharpened, and their eyes full of battle lust. King Eryk and King Stefanos held Old Town and did not seem as though they were going anywhere anytime soon. And finally, King Markos and King Alaric held the third wall with the remnants of their armies and would fight unto the last man.

The Five Kings would all be gathered at Karalis. The mere thought angered him further. None of this was supposed to have happened. The Order of Acrium was to have been completely eliminated, their name not even mentioned in this war. The fortress city was supposed to have been taken swiftly with King Markos's head left upon the top of his precious keep for all to see. Then the lords of the east, with their tribal allies beside them, were supposed to march with their full strength, linking with King Ragnar and his Argarians. With all of the allies behind them, they would crush King Eryk, King Stefanos, and King Alaric. Lastly, they would have dealt with the mighty King Lucan who, without his fellow kings' backing, would have been destroyed. Varkuvia would be theirs, and the tyrants who were the Five Kings would have been overthrown. Every last part of the plan had completely fallen apart.

King Markos, with the less than capable King Alaric, held Karalis against all odds. The Order of Acrium reemerged and, even with their ranks substantially thinned, was defying any force set against them. King Ragnar's army and his longboats were utterly crushed; the king himself slain in the process. The only advantage the east and its allies now had was their overwhelming numbers, and even those would be denied them soon enough. King Lucan's army would be the hammer that pulverized the eastern lords against the anvil that was the walls of Karalis.

*The only option now is to beg the Five Kings for peace,* Randell thought. *We will just have to deal with the consequences.*

*No,* his warrior's spirit screamed savagely. *Peace is not an option with King Stefanos camped half a city away.*

*There is no other choice,* he told himself somberly. *My vengeance will have to wait for another opportunity.*

*There will never be another opportunity like this again,* his warrior spirit spat back.

*If the Five Kings are to kill me, then there truly will never be another chance,* he argued. *Better to return to Cabalo with my tail between my legs than to have my head removed and sent to Myra.* His warrior spirit remained silent on that last thought. With a heavy heart, he made up his mind. He would make his peace with the Five Kings and take his men back home. But there was still an issue needing to be addressed. He looked up and stared into the pasty face of Lord Drogos. The lord of Yursa still had to be dealt with.

No longer would he worry about when the poisoned dagger would be plunged into his back. It was time for him to make his move and then he would beg an audience with the Five Kings. His hand slipped to the sharp dagger sheathed at his side. He would end it now if he could. His gaze flicked to Paxtos. The general had not noticed his movements. Randell wrapped his hand around the hilt. He was an arm's length from Drogos. All he had to do was draw the dagger, step forward, and plunge it into the serpent's heart. His hand tensed. Nikolaos's voice cut through his concentration.

"What do we do now?" the lord of Seren asked.

Drogos gave a smile full of hidden deceit. "I have a plan of my own I was hoping would not be needed. However, it would seem as though desperate times call for desperate measures. Today's trials seem to have drained all of us. Let us convene for the time being and, once we have rested up, meet back here tonight to discuss what we shall do. This war shall end soon enough, of that I can assure you."

Randell's hand was still wrapped tightly around the hilt of his dagger. He caught Paxtos staring at him out of the corner of his eye. The general wrapped his own fingers around the hilt of his dark sword. Randell let his hand drop reluctantly to his side.

"Aye, we shall meet again tonight," agreed Randell.

He briefly exchanged glances with Nikolaos and Kleitos. Understanding flowed among the three of them. Tonight it would end. Tonight Lord Drogos would die.

# CHAPTER TWENTY

He was unsure of what it was that awakened him from slumber. It might have been the howling of the wind outside or the rain as it lashed against the thick walls of the keep. Perhaps it was the cold that guttered the flames in its fireplace sometime in the night, for not even springtime could prevent the icy tendrils from seeping through the gray lifeless stones. Or maybe, it was the pressure at his bladder. Regardless of what it was, his eyes fluttered open. His mind felt wide awake, his body anxious.

Trystan threw the covers from his bed-warmed body. He groaned as he sat upon the edge of the goose down mattress, the ugly bruise spreading at his ribcage, causing him discomfort. The rain beating against the thick walls was persistent and reminded him of the brutal storm, which broke over the Bale Fort the night he rescued Prince

Leon. *An event that took place a lifetime ago*, he thought. He looked behind him, hoping his stirrings had not awakened Arianna. She was not lying beside him. Confused, he searched the room, seeing if she was suffering from the same insomnia he was. Though the room was bedecked with expensive rugs and silk draperies, it was still tiny with the only furniture being the massive bed he sat upon. Feeling foolish, he wondered where she might be. Deciding he would seek her out himself, he tugged on a pair of breeches and threw on a tight-fitting tunic. *Where could she possibly be at this hour?* he asked himself.

He would get his answer moments later as he was pulling his boots on. The door gingerly opened, light spilling in from the hallway beyond. Arianna stepped tenderly into the room. She was wearing a simple nightgown of freshest snow. *Even in such a modest outfit she looks stunning*, admired Trystan. Passion stirred in his loins. He thought about taking her to bed when he saw the worried expression on her face, tears brimming in those ever-changing beautiful eyes. Stepping forward he held her tightly.

"What is the matter?" he asked gently, running his hand through her curly hair.

She pulled back from his embrace. "I have just heard grievous news," she said, her voice shaky. "I do not know how to tell you this."

Talons fastened onto Trystan's heart. "What is it?" he asked, afraid to hear the answer.

"Gabriel was set upon by a group of King Alaric's men while he was returning to his room," said Arianna. "He was drunk but still managed to fend them off. However, one man fell down a flight of stairs during the fight, breaking his neck in the fall. King Alaric is furious and has demanded Gabriel be chained in the dungeons below. His fate is yet to be determined."

Trystan took a slow, calming breath. That news wasn't as devastating as what he feared it might be. Layne's name was not mentioned, and for the time being, Gabriel was still alive. He felt a tenseness in Arianna of words unspoken.

"Is that all?" he asked.

She took a deep shuddering breath. "I am afraid not. Upon the insistence of his ally, King Markos declared that Layne will be executed at dawn. He is going to use him as an example to keep the rest of you in line. I am so sorry, Trystan. I know how much he means to you."

Trystan took a step back from her, his brow scrunching in confusion. He shook his head, seeking to get rid of the cobwebs lodged there. Was he still dreaming? "Who did you hear this from?" he heard himself ask.

"The serving woman Justina," she answered. "She overheard Verlos himself, talking about it. At the break of dawn, Layne will die. She swore it upon the lives of her daughters."

*At the break of dawn, Layne will die.* The words echoed inside of Trystan's mind. He felt the room sway. This was not possible.

"I'm afraid it is possible," said Arianna. He did not remember saying the words aloud. She stepped forward, caressing his arm with her soft hand. "I am so sorry. If there is anything I can do, all you have to do is ask. I am here for you."

Trystan tore his arm away from her touch, pretending not to see the hurt in her eyes. He stormed over to the fireplace with its stack of smoldering wood. Leaning heavily against the frame, he felt sweat beading on his forehead. Nausea and dizziness threatened to overwhelm him. For some time now, he held to the tiniest sliver of hope he would see Layne released from imprisonment. He was instrumental in holding the walls, and the kings would acknowledge his heroism when the war was over. The shackles chaining Layne would be struck from his wrists, and his mentor would bask in the sunlight once more.

When the second wall was overrun, Trystan barely made it back to the protective ring wall with less than a thousand others. The massive bruise at his side was testament to how close he came to not making it. Two thousand brave men fought and died valiantly during the retreat. Those who made it back to the ramparts of the third wall watched the fires spread through the fog until the mist itself took on a hue of shifting red and orange. They heard the screams of the innocent and the howling victory cries of their enemies. And when all seemed lost, they heard the blaring trumpets that heralded the arrival of King Stefanos and King Eryk. Hope, moments ago appearing lifeless, was reanimated into a roaring giant. The men who made it back to the wall rained arrows down upon those who sought to ransack their city and watched the stalemate develop that saw their reinforcements claim Old Town and the eastern lords take the remainder of the city.

Trystan was one of the loudest, leading the cheers. Jaxon, Margaret, Gavin, and so many others he had the privilege of knowing made it safely back to the third wall. King Stefanos and King Eryk had their enemies pinned against the wall. Things were finally looking up for the first time in an age, and now Arianna delivered the heartbreaking news of Gabriel's fight and Layne's execution scheduled at dawn. He felt all of his hoping and reasoning washed away by the rain lashing against the keep. His eyes were glued to the pile of blackened wood in the fireplace. As he stood there, he recalled the promise he made to Layne in the dungeons beneath the Keep of Karalis. He would not let his mentor die while he still drew breath.

The room he was assigned was on one of the uppermost levels of the keep, generally reserved for nobility. He was granted this room for his outstanding courage in the face of adversity. King Markos's personal bedchambers were but a few corridors over. Whirling away from the fireplace, he picked up his sheathed sword of gold-green steel off of the carpeted floor and marched toward the door. Arianna stepped into his path.

"Where exactly do you think you are going?" she asked, her tone suggesting she would not allow him to do anything foolish.

"I am going to speak to King Markos," he responded. "He will listen to what I have to say, or I will make him."

"By the gods, you will not! You are going to stay right here. Do you truly believe I will just let you walk out that door and throw your life away?"

Trystan gently placed his hands on Arianna's shoulders, feeling the warmth in the woman he was in love with. In that moment, he wanted nothing more than to tell her how he truly felt, but he knew he could not supply the words Arianna so desperately wanted to hear.

"I appreciate you wanting to protect me, I truly do, but I cannot stand idly by and watch as Layne is executed. You must understand this is something I would never be able to live with." He paused. "Please do not get in my way or try to stop me, Arianna. I beg of you to let me do this."

Tears spilled down Arianna's cheeks. "Oh yes, and I will just wait here for the King's Stone Guards to bring your head back to me. If I let you go, then that is something I will have to live with."

Despite the conviction in her words, she crossed her arms and moved out of his way, giving him a clear path to the door.

He stepped in close and kissed her full upon the lips. Despite the gloom surrounding her, Arianna found her lips parting. Her arms wrapped tightly around his neck, drawing him to her. After several moments, Trystan pulled back, his face inches away from the woman he loved.

"I will return," he said huskily.

"You better, you stupid bastard."

Before his resolve could weaken, Trystan spun from her embrace and wrenched the door open. He did not look back as he moved into the corridor beyond. Advancing toward King Markos's bedchambers, he looped on his sword belt, pulling it tight. He had no idea what he would say to the king or had any set plan. All he knew was he would not allow Layne to be executed. And he would do whatever it took for that not to happen. If need be, he would hold the king himself at sword point. *Do not be stupid*, he told himself. *The only thing that would be achieved by killing the king would be earning a spot right next to Layne come sunrise.*

He wound his way around a bend in the corridor, his hands clenching and unclenching. The king's room would be at the end of this hallway and to the left. The hallway itself was faintly illuminated, and he could see the torches in their sconces were snuffed out. Only a single torch cast dim, flickering shadows on the walls. At the end of the corridor, he turned left with a set determination in his stride.

And froze.

There were no guards standing watch outside of the king's bedchambers. His feet remained planted firmly to the gray stones of the corridor floor. The king always had six Stone Guards stationed outside of the dual doors even if he was not present. There were only two corridors that led to King Markos's room. The one he just walked down and a long passageway directly behind him. Glancing over his shoulder, his gaze met only blackness. The only light offered was from the high arched windows with their panels of glass. With night fully descended, and the storm raging outside, the entire hallway behind him was shrouded in darkness. He turned his focus back on the dual doors. *Where are the guards?* he asked himself.

The distant sound of a tolling bell reverberated lightly throughout the massive Keep of Karalis, filling the corridors and hallways. The sound was soon taken up by the steady ringing of a dozen other bells, the noise vibrating from the walls themselves, mixing with the sound of pounding rain. Trystan's blood ran cold. He knew what the call meant. The gate was breached.

"Trystan of the Blade," a voice echoed down the corridor, "we meet at last."

Trystan turned slowly. A man dressed all in black emerged from the darkened hallway, his mouth quirked upward in a smug grin, his eyes of ice blue sparkling. From the shroud behind him emerged five others dressed in similar fashion, their greedy eyes staring at the man set firmly in their path. On each of their hands glistened the ring that identified them as the Sons of Vikundo. Hearing movement to his right, Trystan's head swiveled ever so slightly to see three others stealthily prowling down the adjacent corridor. They circled around him, cutting off any means of escape. Lightning lit up the sky through the windows, casting the hallway in an ominous white light. In a heartbeat, it was extinguished, leaving Trystan surrounded by wolves dressed all in black.

The blue-eyed man moved forward until he stood but a few feet from Trystan. Those cold eyes burrowed into the lone man before him. "You do not know who I am, do you?" he asked casually.

Trystan heard the rasping of steel being drawn all around him. He slowly shook his head. "I am Paxtos." The blue-eyed man gave an elaborate bow, a smug grin still held in place. "I believe you had the pleasure of meeting my younger brother, Orpheus. You did kill him after all. It was quite some time ago on a small farm. He always was a little cocky whoreson, but he was still my blood. And for that, I am going to cut out your eyes and tongue. I will slice off your ears and make your torment last a lifetime. You will walk the underworld blind and deaf as my brother's servant for all eternity."

"King Markos!" Trystan suddenly yelled. "Run!"

The words echoed off the walls, bouncing back at him. Paxtos cupped his hand to his ear, listening intently for several moments. He let his hand drop. His smug grin transformed into a devilish smile. "Yell all you want, little Trystan. The king and his precious queen have been slipped a powerful sleeping draught that will not see them wake until morning, and as you can see, his loyal guards seem to have abandoned him." He drew a curved dagger of bright steel, the hilt intertwined with gold and silver. Trystan recognized it as King Alaric's ceremonial dagger. Paxtos ran his finger along the sharp edge. "I'm afraid it will not matter. You see, even if our attack on the gate somehow fails, this dagger will be proof King Markos and his lovely Queen Lorain were slain in their sleep by their dear ally. His son, Prince Leon, who I have heard is quite volatile will undoubtedly kill King Alaric in retaliation. Any way this night plays out, it will be a victory for our forces. I am afraid I am taking up your time though. This is the last night the king draws breath. Tonight King Markos dies, and you shall join him."

Paxtos placed the curved dagger back in its sheath and reverently drew the sword that matched the color of his soul. A steel ring of blackest sin surrounded Trystan. Panic engulfed him. Even if he unleashed his Verillion powers, he could not hope to defeat nine skilled opponents on his own. He was going to die. The knowledge caused him to tremble. Closing his eyes, he bowed his head and prayed. Snickering laughter reached his ears.

"The sheep waits to be slaughtered," taunted Paxtos. Cruel laughter sang down the hallway. "Come along, sheep. I will put an end to your suffering."

Trystan heard the blue-eyed leader's boot echo down the hallway as he advanced a step. Time froze. Through Trystan's mind erupted an endless stream of random images and memories. He remembered First Master Roderic inducting him into the Order of Acrium, a kindly smile on his old face. He recalled his first time meeting Jaxon with his booming laughter and cheerful persona. The first time he set eyes upon Arianna's beauty in the days of their youth. And then there was Master Layne, and the first time the two sparred together at the Fortress of the Van. The image of Gavin's bearded face jumped into the banks of his memory, and he reminisced on the battle with the tribesmen years ago when the archer stood firm beside him. A whole myriad of images collided together in his mind, coalescing into one massive sequence that was Trystan's life. Through it all, through all of the memories and remembrances, there remained one constant theme. His whole life he was a fighter. He fought for those he loved and for those who were unable to, and he fought day and night to make himself a better person. And he would continue to fight until the pale shadow of death claimed his soul.

Another booted step echoed throughout the hallway. Trystan's eyes snapped open. His head slowly rose. *I will fight until the bitter end.* He unleashed the power of the ancient Verillion race, feeling it surge through his veins, swelling his muscles, and eroding his fears. His pupils dissected, forming into crosses. Paxtos faltered momentarily and then his sword lunged forward. Sidestepping the dark blade, Trystan grabbed ahold of the leader's wrist, dragging him forward. His elbow rose swiftly, connecting sharply with Paxtos's nose. The leader stumbled backward, blood spouting into the air. He held a hand to his shattered nose, blood dribbling between his fingers.

"Kill him!" he roared.

The eight other Brothers rushed forward. Trystan's blade sang from its sheath. Spinning in a circle, he ripped open the jugular of one. Taking two quick steps forward, he blocked the swift lunge of a blade and rolled his wrist to plunge his sword deep into the assassin's stomach. Savagely wrenching the blade loose, the man's guts flopped to the floor, filling the corridor with an overpowering stench. Black steel rang against gold-green. Trystan threw the blade wide, and sent a riposte slashing open the wielder's face, sending flesh and bone into the air.

A blade opened up a shallow wound in his shoulder blade. Absorbing the pain, he spun as the Brother attempted another lunge. Trystan's sword cut deep into the man's wrist, cutting off his hand. The limb didn't even have time to reach the floor before his blade entered the assassin's screaming mouth, plunging upward into his soft brain. Ripping the blade loose, he dropped to one knee quickly as a black sword slashed through the air. His hand grasped around the hilt of one of the fallen Brother's discarded swords. Rearing up, he wielded two swords, one of green-gold, the other of raven's black.

The remaining Brothers charged. Trystan leapt to meet them. He spun, lunged, blocked, and parried. His movements were blinding fast, his dual swords an unrelenting blur of steel. The tip of a Brother's sword opened up a wound in his brow. Blood coursed down his face, flowing into his eye. He blinked back the blood, ignoring the discomfort. The green-gold sword in his right hand plunged into one of the assassin's shoulders. The black blade in his left blocked a downward thrust. A boot connected with his open chest, flinging him backward.

He slammed hard against the corridor wall, the breath driving from his lungs. The black sword slipped from his grasp, clattering against the floor. Regaining his senses, he saw the flames from the single torch play off black steel as it flashed upward toward his face. He swayed at the last possible moment, feeling the blade bite into the flesh next to his ear before careening up through his hair, leaving a jagged line of crimson. Strands of his hair flew into the air along with droplets of his blood. He was able to duck under the next attempt, the dark blade sparking off the wall. His own sword flashed forward in response, slicing into the wielder's kneecap. The man's legs buckled underneath him, his one leg hanging on by mere ligaments.

Another sword lashed toward him. Caught off balance, Trystan dove over the body of one of the slain Brothers. Coming to his knees in a tumbler's roll, he caught the edge of steel with his own blade. Rising to his feet, he sidestepped a murderous lunge. Knocking aside another slashing sword, he felt the hairs on the back of his neck stand up. Bringing his sword behind his head, he deflected a powerful over-hand stroke that would've left his brains upon the floor. Spinning on his heel, he opened the Brother's chest in a shower of blood. The man fell without a sound.

Trystan hastily took a step back, his breathing shallow, his sword held up defensively before him. The remaining assassins circled warily in front of him. The one assassin whose leg he nearly cut off was lying upon the floor, his bestial screams bouncing off the wall, and his hands clutching the ruined limb. Propped up against one of the walls was the Brother whose bowels he had opened up, dark blood staining his mouth, a soft mewling whispering from his lips. Only three of the Brotherhood remained, one of which was holding a hand to their blood-drenched shoulder. Slick blood caked the side of Trystan's face. Other minor wounds and cuts covered his body as well.

The three assassins spread themselves around Trystan, their movements far more wary than before. Sweat mingled into the wound upon Trystan's brow, leaving nothing but needles of pain. Paxtos stood before him. He could see white bone partially showing from the leader's crushed nose, the lower half of his face covered in dripping blood. Before there was nothing but sparkling humor in those icy eyes. Now there was only rage.

"It seems I underestimated you," said Paxtos, the words horribly mangled by his ruined nose. "That mistake is mine alone, but this farce must be put to an end. We do not need any others rushing to ruin the fun we have in store for King Markos."

He gestured to the others. The three assassins advanced as one. Trystan's eyes narrowed. This is what he feared. No longer were they thinking with singular minds but finally decided to combine their skills. He decided to focus on Paxtos. *Cut the head from the snake, and the others will flee.* That's what Layne always taught him. He went to charge the leader when the wounded Brother suddenly lunged forward.

Trystan swiveled, deflecting the blade. Rushing feet behind him brought his attention around. He blocked a lunge intended for his back and then plunged his sword into the man's face. The steel cut cleanly through the Brother's cheek, shattering teeth, and cleaving his tongue in two before entering out the other side. Trystan ripped his sword sideways, pulverizing the man's jaw, leaving the assassin's face in a mass of blood and horror. Black steel slid into his exposed side.

He gasped in pain, his one hand moving instinctively to the wound. Gritting his teeth against the pain, he spun, his sword moving in a fast moving arc, determined to kill the culprit who stabbed him. Paxtos swayed backward from the glittering blade, but his wounded companion was not so fortunate. Trystan's momentum carried him on, his sword burying into the skull of the other Brother. He wrenched the blade loose. All of his strength fled him at once. He fell to his knees, his sword slipping from sweat-drenched hands.

Trystan remained there for a moment, wondering how he ended up on the floor. Seeing his green-gold sword laid out before him, his shaky hand quested forward to grasp the hilt. Paxtos's boot connected squarely with his jaw, sending him flying backward. He landed heavily on his back. He feebly attempted to rise when the tip of a black sword pressed against his throat. Trystan could feel blood trickling beneath the steel, flowing down his neck. Paxtos loomed over him. Some of the previous humor was restored to his eyes.

"Gods, but you are a pathetic creature," he leered. "To come so close and fail anyway. That will be your legacy. The poets will write, 'Trystan of the Blade fought valiantly to save the king, but could not defeat Paxtos the Great.' Maybe they will even call me Paxtos the Magnificent. Yes, that does seem to have a better ring to it." Laughter peeled from his lips. "For now though I will be content with your death. Enjoy serving my brother in the afterlife."

Paxtos's hand tensed, his eyes gleaming triumphantly. Trystan held his chin up defiantly, determined he would die with courage. A high-pitched scream suddenly split the air. Black steel slammed into the side of Paxtos' neck. The blue-eyed leader reeled back in horror, his hand flying to the gaping wound. He fell to his knees, his sword slipping from nerveless fingers. His hand desperately tried to halt the blood that spewed forth.

The wielder stepped into Paxtos's view. The leader looked up into the face of the person who delivered the mortal blow, his eyes opening wide in shock. When he opened his mouth, blood tumbled out. "This cannot be. You're a…you're a—"

"A woman," Arianna finished for him. "In your next life, try to remember if you want to kill someone, kill them."

She clutched the hilt of the black sword with two hands and brought it over her head. With a mighty scream, she brought the blade crashing into Paxtos's skull. The general of the Legion of the Rising Sun fell dead to the corridor floor, black steel lodged into his temple. Arianna stared at the man she just killed. Then, her eyes of changing hazel and soft brown swept over the carnage in the hallway. Turning from the sight, she knelt beside Trystan, taking his hand in hers.

"Are you all right, my love?" she asked, her face pale.

She was still wearing the white nightgown he left her in. Only now, the fabric was speckled with droplets of fresh blood, the hem drenched in the red that covered the corridor floor. Forcing a smile, Trystan squeezed Arianna's hand. "I did not think it was possible for me to be happier to see you," he said weakly. "I will be fine, thanks to you. Help me sit up."

Arianna gently pulled him into a sitting position. Grunting the entire way, Trystan propped his hand underneath him to prevent falling over. He lightly probed the wound at his side. Paxtos's blade had not penetrated deep, and it did not seem as if any organs were punctured. A smile spread across his face. He just saved the king from certain death. If that was not a good enough reason to spare Layne's life, then he did not know what was. Arianna stood up, half her face hidden in shadow, the other bathed in the light of the single torch. Trystan could not remember her looking more beautiful than in that moment. He smiled up at her. Arianna returned the smile with teeth of pearly white. It was the most breathtaking moment Trystan ever witnessed.

She was still smiling as the point of the black sword erupted from her breast. Blood gushed from the wound, showering Trystan.

"Nooo!" he screamed.

With his Verillion powers still in full effect, he watched in slow motion as Arianna looked down in utter disbelief at the blood-covered steel that jutted from her body. Her eyes moved up to meet Trystan's, tears welling in the corners of those pools of ever shifting hazel and soft brown. The blade was viciously ripped from her. Her body went limp like a rag doll. She tumbled to the blood-drenched corridor floor, her head bouncing off one of the legs of the slain Brothers. Her eyes locked to Trystan's. Tears fell, flowing down her face. She opened her mouth to say something but only blood spilled forth. Her eyes slowly closed. And then, there was only stillness.

Trystan stared in a shock so deep and overwhelming at the fallen body of the woman he loved, his whole body began to shake. A rage unlike anything he ever experienced consumed him. It roared through his body, extinguishing all pain, smothering all reason. Arianna's unmoving leg rested lightly on the steel of his sword. His hand curled tightly around the hilt. He drew his legs underneath him, determined to hurl himself at whoever just robbed him of the only true joy he had ever known in his life. Angry eyes looked to the shrouded darkness from which the murderer stabbed Arianna.

The killer stepped forward, their blade dripping crimson with the blood of Arianna. Tattered and filthy clothing adorned their body, but it was not the grimy attire which drew Trystan's attention. It was the powerful eyes that stared down at him.

Violet eyes.

Master Layne looked down upon his prized pupil. All of Trystan's anger, all of his reasoning abandoned him. He rocked back on his haunches, his mind unable to process the figure standing before him. *This is not possible*, he told himself. *Layne would never do something like this*. His gaze was drawn once more to Arianna and the gaping wound in her chest, and then he saw the sword still clutched in Layne's hand. Tears welled in Trystan's eyes, blurring his vision. He tried to blink them back, but they fell regardless, leaving hot streaks coursing down his cheeks.

"Why?" he managed to say.

Layne stared down upon Trystan, his expression unreadable. Lighting flashed outside. Master and student stared back at one another in the hallway lit with the dead. Only silence greeted Trystan.

"Why?" he repeated forcefully.

Those violet eyes glared down at their prized pupil, devoid of emotion, devoid of life. "I warned you about the follies of falling in love," he said at last. "You did not heed my warning, and this is the result."

Trystan could not believe his ears. This was the man he looked up to as a father his whole life. This was the man who taught him everything he knew, who changed him into the man he was today. And he was also the one that murdered the only woman he cared for.

"How could you side with scum such as this?" he demanded, anger edging into his voice. "How could you do this to me? I came here to argue your case before the king. I almost died for you. And now you stand before me with the blood of Arianna on your hands."

Layne shook his head as if he were dealing with a child. "You still do not see the big picture, do you?" He lightly shook his head again. "It is of no consequence. King Markos must die."

He walked past Trystan without another word, striding toward the dual doors. Trystan found himself staring into the still face of Arianna. Fury, cold and unbridled, swept through him.

"Master Layne!" he bellowed. With a massive will of force, he brought himself to shaky legs. They almost gave way beneath him. "I will not allow you to do this."

His mentor stopped midstride. "You cannot possibly hope to stop me. Look at you. You can barely stand right now. I do not wish to kill you, Trystan. But if I must, I will." He slowly turned to face his student. "These last few months have opened my eyes to things I could never possibly imagine. I have rediscovered myself." Trystan watched as Layne's pupils slowly transformed into the telltale crosses of the Verillion race. "Join me, and together we will right the wrongs in this world. We can accomplish so much together."

"I once had a wise teacher who bestowed upon me words I will never forget." Trystan advanced a step, lifting his sword blade. "He told me you do not play the part of hero. You live it. In honor of that man, I must oppose you."

He halted before Layne, extending his blade before him. Layne slowly nodded. "So be it," he said. "Let us see how well this teacher taught you."

The two circled one another. They did not need to gauge one another's strengths and weaknesses, for they had sparred countless times. Layne's powerful gaze studied his decade-long trained pupil. His blade whipped out. Trystan barely deflected the blur and then hurled himself forward. All of his pain, all of his grief was pushed aside. The blades clashed together time and time again, the song of discordant steel on steel floating down the hallway. Their swords moved at an impossible tempo. Trystan blocked and riposte, his sword work infallible. As soon as the blades met, they were already moving again, seeking to plunge into flesh.

Lightning flashed once more outside. Trystan dropped to one knee as Layne slashed high. He lunged toward Layne's midsection. Rolling his wrist, Layne brought his sword crashing down into the questing steel, careening the sword wide. Spinning the blade, he cut downward toward his kneeling pupil. Trystan rolled to the side, the sword crashing off the blood-covered floor. Coming to his feet, he spun, blocking a fast-moving lunge. His vision misted, and he felt his body beginning to move sluggishly. The loss of blood from his wounds was sapping his strength. He could not maintain the impossible speed of the duel for much longer.

Layne knocked aside a clumsy attempt and then quickly moved forward. His sword hilt crashed into Trystan's injured temple. Trystan fell to his knees, barely conscious, his hands supporting him. Sweat and blood dripped from his face, the droplets plopping off the floor. His shallow breathing brought painful sears to his burning lungs. Layne took a step back. There was no evidence of exhaustion anywhere on his features.

"You fought valiantly, Trystan, but this is foolishness. Why should you die to protect King Markos? What has he ever done for you but brought heartache and pain? I have trained and taught you for years. You have always been destined to lead, not to follow. Take my hand and join me. Let me help put your foot back on the right path."

His hand extended, halting inches from Trystan's face. Trystan had no strength to respond. He looked up at the open hand before him and was then drawn to the unmoving form of Arianna. His eyes locked to the woman who he cared for and, in turn, cared for him. He stared longingly upon the woman who saved his life twice, yet he was unable to return the favor. The two of them were destined to be together until old age claimed them. Now Arianna's soul was sent to the afterlife without him to walk beside her. He looked once more at the hand open before him in a sign of unity. It was Arianna who was meant to be his destiny, not as a leader of men, and it was that hand before him that robbed him of his destiny.

Something deep inside of Trystan stirred. It started out as the small flickering flame of a candle and then the winds of grief and anguish fanned the flames into an inferno, spreading to every corner of his body. A white burning sensation exploded inside of his mind. His entire body tingled. He screamed out at the unaccustomed feeling, and only then realized his eyes were squeezed shut. He opened his eyes and saw the hallway was illuminated in a soft white glow. The light was not coming from the storm outside but emanating from his body, knelt upon the floor.

In an instant, the soft glow and burning sensation fled like darkness before the rising sun. Strength flooded through him, feeding his weary muscles, and easing his aching body. The pain from his wounds lessened dramatically and itched as they rapidly began to heal themselves. Trystan's breathing steadied, and he found he was upon his hands and knees staring intently at the floor. He brought himself slowly to his feet, marveling at the surge of new energy pulsating throughout him. When he looked up, he was amazed at how clear and distinct everything appeared.

His improved eyesight soared upward to meet Layne's startled expression. "Your eyes...," Layne whispered astonished. "You've unlocked your full potential..."

Trystan flexed his arm. Never in his life had he felt more powerful than in that moment. Even the sword held loftily in his hand felt lighter than a feather. He twirled the blade, watching the shadows from the torch play off of the metal.

"This is not possible," screamed Layne. "They told me this could not happen."

The disbanded Master of Sword leapt forward, his blade lancing before him. Trystan easily swatted aside the attempt. His eyes locked with Layne's. Layne backed away, frightened by the pure white crosses that glowed at the center of Trystan's emerald eyes. Screaming, he charged once more. Their blades screeched together in a shower of sparks. And the duel began anew.

They danced down the corridor, their blades questing for flesh, inching ever closer to the king's doors. Such was the force of each deflected blow that it would've cut a man clean in two. Trystan blocked a cut an inch away from opening him from neck to groin and answered with a murderous riposte. Layne swayed from the attempt and brought his sword crashing into Trystan's. Both of their swords were thrown wide, leaving a gap in their defenses. They both leapt upon the opportunity and drove their swords forward at the same time.

Steel entered flesh, and Trystan found himself nose to nose with Layne. Sweat coursed down both of their faces. Lightning cracked outside, the jagged bolt leaving a white streak in the black sky. The thunder that followed was instantaneous, shaking the foundations of the keep. Trystan stared into the face of the man who trained him for a decade, remembering all of their times together at the Fortress of the Van and the codes of honor he bestowed upon him.

Pain suddenly caused Layne's face to spasm. Trystan looked down to see his sword half buried in Layne's chest. He felt agony roar through his side and saw that Layne's sword had raked his ribs. Trystan ripped his blade out. His old mentor gave a shuddering breath and let his sword clatter to the corridor floor. His limbs turned to water, and he began to collapse. Trystan dropped his own sword and caught his falling idol, gently placing him on the ground.

Layne's face had taken on a deathly pallor. "Your teacher taught you too well," he managed, forcing a smile. His teeth were stained with blood.

"Not well enough," responded Trystan. "There were at least three openings where you could have ended my life. What stayed your hand?"

"There are some tasks I am given I do not delight in." Layne looked down at the blood flowing steadily from his chest. His head sagged against the floor. "Gods, but this hurts. There are powerful men hunting you, Trystan. Men of great influence and stronger than any of the Five Kings. And I am not talking about Lord Drogos and his ragtag Brotherhood of assassins. They are but pawns in a much grander scheme. You must oppose them. I'm ashamed to say I was not strong enough to refuse them. May the Gods forgive me." His voice was barely above a whisper. "I do not know if it matters, but I am sorry about Arianna. There are so many things I cannot take back."

He lapsed into silence, and Trystan thought he passed into the afterlife, but then Layne whispered something else. It was so soft, he had to lean forward to hear it.

"Your father still lives."

Layne gave one last shuddering breath. And then he was gone. There were so many emotions and thoughts whirling through Trystan's head; he was afraid he might pass out from it all. Layne had been like a father to him. Arianna was the partner of his soul. Now they were both dead. The woman he loved was slain by his mentor, and that mentor was in turn slain by his own hand. It was too much to take in.

He rose to his feet in a daze. Hot tears streamed down his face though he could not remember when he had begun to cry. His gaze swept the corridor and the corpses that littered it. *So much death*, he thought. *So much despair and anguish and grief.* He suddenly realized that he was staring at the still form of Arianna. *She is so beautiful even in death.* He stumbled over to her, collapsing to his knees beside her.

He cradled her head to his chest, pulling her tight against him. Choking sobs ripped through him, his whole body shaking. "Come back to me," he sobbed. "I love you. I love you so much. Please, Arianna, don't leave. I will do anything." His cries of anguish reverberated down the hallway. Only the dead were there to hear him, and the dead could not respond.

The rain lashed against the windows, bouncing off the glass. Trystan wrapped his arms around Arianna, and wept into her soft auburn hair. Through his cries and grief came the floating sounds of triumphant battle screams and the blaring of victory trumpets. The enemy was beaten back from the gate, and the king had been saved; but for Trystan of the Blade, his own battle was lost, and his world was in ruins.

# CHAPTER TWENTY-ONE

"By the balls of Crassos, is rain the only weather this damn continent knows?" Lord Nikolaos spun away from the windowed battle scene of the gods.

His words were accompanied by the crashing of thunder, the books shaking violently on their shelves. Nikolaos rolled his eyes. "What I wouldn't give to be back in Seren with the sun beating down on my back, a nice cup of red wine in one hand, and the other placed firmly on the breasts of one of my wives." He sat down roughly upon the study chair, the wood groaning beneath his weight.

"Well since none of your wives are on hand, I suppose we can content ourselves with some wine," Kleitos said, pouring himself a cup.

"This whole business has put both of our nerves on edge." He picked up an empty cup, gesturing toward Nikolaos.

"Aye, I will take a cup," replied the lord of Seren. He graciously accepted the proffered cup, sipping it lightly. "A little sweet for my taste, but it will do for now. Now, if only we could get some women in here, all of my fears would melt away. Where in the seven hells is Randell? The lord of Snakes will be here any moment, and we don't even have a definite plan."

"King Stefanos has been spotted massing his forces on the border of Old Town, hoping to take us by surprise under the cover of darkness," explained Kleitos. "Randell is summoning what men he can to quell the attempt. He should be here soon enough, and if he isn't, these sharp daggers should do the trick." He patted his arm where the dagger was hidden up his sleeve.

Nikolaos could feel the cold steel of his own dagger brushing against his arm. It all sounded so simple. They would wait until they plied Lord Drogos with enough wine to dull his senses and then they would sneak up nice and close to the drunken lord of Yursa, their hands moving up their sleeves to curl around the hilts of their daggers. Then with one quick thrust, they would send Drogos screaming to the afterlife. But it was one thing to plan such a thing, talking casually about it over a glass of wine by candlelight, quite another to actually go through with it. Nikolaos was growing increasingly anxious, and he continuously found himself touching the hidden dagger, making sure it was securely in place.

"Do you think we should wait for Randell before we make our move?" he asked.

"If the opportunity presents itself, then it should not matter whether he is here or not. We have all committed to this, and Randell would do what needed to be done even if we were not present."

"What if Drogos has Paxtos accompanying him again?" pressed Nikolaos. "You saw how much armor the man was wearing last time. He was bedecked for war. Our daggers will do nothing but scratch that monstrous breastplate and then he will leave our heads upon the floor."

"You were standing right there when Drogos told us he would be arriving alone. He has a special assignment for Paxtos. Now, you must calm down. You're starting to make my teeth grind."

But Nikolaos could not calm his nerves. His fingers tapped the side of his cup. More than half the contents were gone already even though he could remember taking only one sip. He drained the rest in a single swallow and then immediately poured himself another cup. The wine sloshed over the edges, drenching the polished wood of the desk. *Nothing is simple when it comes to Drogos*, he told himself. *The man knows everything. What if he has guards marching to apprehend us even as we speak?* His bowels rumbled in tune to his anxiety.

Pushing such thoughts from his mind, he wondered what was happening back at his city-state of Seren. He left the duties of the city in the hands of his eldest son, Landon. The boy was fast approaching his seventeenth name day, and it was time he learned some responsibility. He hoped his son was not overwhelmed by the burdens of rule. *Don't be ridiculous*, he assured himself. *He will have his own small council of advisors to help him along the way.* Nikolaos snorted. *The boy is lucky I can even remember his name.*

With six wives, eight sons, and seven daughters, he was beginning to lose track of the many names and ages. He knew his daughter Elania was his favorite of them all. She was delivered to him by his third wife or was it his fourth? It did not matter. She was turning six soon and had big brown eyes that mirrored his own. He was helpless against any request she made of him and had promised her a pony for her upcoming name day. Sitting there, waiting for Drogos to make his entrance, Nikolaos suddenly realized how much he missed his family, even his nagging wives and scheming cousins.

To the south of Seren was the Eternal Desert with its miles of endless dunes and scorching sands, but the landscape surrounding the city itself was beautiful. He would even now be strolling through his orange groves and rows of olive trees, for which his city-state was renowned. His newest and youngest wife, Lady Aaliyah, would be by his side. It was not that he disliked the company of his five other wives, but seeing the years pass them by only reminded him of the wrinkles that were creeping into the corners of his eyes and the fat that was slowly spreading along his midsection. His eldest wife, Lady Jacinda, inflamed such passion in him when they were first wed that entire days would sometimes pass before they would leave the slippery embrace of their bedchambers. He thought he was so in love with her, but it was not her spirit he had fallen for but her body instead. Now, he could only look in pity at her sagging breasts and crow's feet that plagued her once beautiful face. Aaliyah, on the other hand, had skin that was darkened nutmeg brown by the beating sun, sultry lips, and perky, full-sized breasts. One look upon her perfection would set his heart racing and instantly make him erect. *You will get sick of her, just like all the rest.* He wished he could tell himself otherwise as he tried five times before, but he now knew that intelligence was not always accompanied by the strength of flesh.

He suddenly wondered what it was he was doing here. Seren produced more than enough coin in ways of trade and commerce to content himself with for ten lifetimes over. His was the only city-state that produced exotic citrus fruits, and next to the port city of Sura was the wealthiest of the eastern city-states. He did not have just one wife, but six wives so beautiful that lesser men would spend their entire fortunes for a single night of pleasure with them. *So why not leave this war to the young men, their thoughts filled with righteous glory and idiotic heroics?* He asked himself. *Because I am bored*, he answered. The tediousness of ruling, marriage, and raising children had taken their own toll on him, weighing him down day by day, year by year. *I will take war over the simple burdens of life any day of the year.* Or so he thought, before the full devious nature of Drogos was revealed.

He started to take another sip of wine, when he realized his cup was empty once more. His vision was blurring at the edges, and he wondered how much he consumed. *I drank too much, too quickly.* He could feel the heady wine spreading through his veins. He shook his head and placed the empty cup down upon the desk top, which by now, had been cleared of its many pieces of parchment. In their place were trays of red and green grapes, ripe strawberries, and a dark loaf of sliced bread. Nikolaos ripped off a slice of bread and tore into it. He needed a clear mind for what needed to be done.

"Do you have any children, Kleitos?" he asked, hoping conversation would help him focus.

"I am lucky to say I have been blessed with four children," replied the advisor. "My three daughters are the eldest, and even though I love them dearly, I always wanted a boy. Five summers ago, the gods heard my prayers and delivered Kadin into my life. I promised him I would teach him how to ride when I returned home."

"I can almost remember what it was like to have only four children." Nikolaos chuckled. "I promised my daughter Elania something very similar. Is it not crazy what we would do for our children?"

"Indeed, it is."

Nikolaos refilled his cup and held it high. "To our children," he toasted. "May they learn from the mistakes of their sires and, gods willing, be far wiser."

"May the gods hear our toast and make it so," Kleitos responded, holding his own goblet up.

The two sat in companionable silence for a time, the only sound coming from the howling wind and persistent rain of the storm raging outside. It was during that stretch of silence, the distant sound of a bell ringing reached their ears. Nikolaos craned his neck.

"Did you hear that?" he asked.

There was no need for Kleitos to respond. The tolling of a dozen other bells was soon carried forth on the wings of the storm. Nikolaos stood up, moving to the paneled window. "That sounds like it's coming from the Keep of Karalis." His eyes narrowed as he tried to pierce the darkness of the night. "Did you know anything about this?" he asked, turning to Kleitos.

The advisor shook his head, obviously just as confused as Nikolaos. Just then, the door of the study thrust open. The flames of the tallow candles upon the desk flickered as if buffeted by a gust of wind. Lord Drogos entered, his arms spread wide, a false smile held in place. He changed his outfit from their earlier meeting. Now he wore a black silk tunic, slashed with dark grey at the sleeves, and breeches of shifting black and grey. His hair, waxed back over his ears, was held in place by a circlet of jaded black, a purple amethyst set in its center. The dark circlet merged almost perfectly with his hair, the amethyst looking as though it was part of him, rather than an adornment.

Nikolaos quickly snap shut his open jaw. Even with the knowledge of Drogos's arrival, the lord of Snakes always seemed to find a way to sneak up on a man. Composing himself, Nikolaos pointed to the window where the sound of tolling bells still filtered through.

"What is the meaning of this, Drogos?" he asked angrily.

"Be at ease, my lord," responded Drogos calmly. "I simply moved a plan into action."

Heat flushed Nikolaos's cheeks. "And you did not think to include me in these plans?" He fumed. "Was Lord Randell made aware of them or Lord Dorian? Perhaps Mason and his tribesmen were told. Were none of us important enough to divulge your secrets to?"

The humor left Drogos's face. "Only those who were needed were made aware. Some things are better done in secrecy. Otherwise a loose tongue might have set everything to ruin. I had no intention of upsetting you, of that I can assure you."

"Aye, and you have been doing everything in secrecy from the very beginning." The wine made him bold. "What other secrets do you keep from us? And what exactly is this grand plan of yours?"

"Since you insist on the matter," said Drogos, "the Keep of Karalis will be ours by morning, and King Markos will be dead. That is all that should matter. It will be a great victory for us. Now calm yourself before you say something you might regret."

But Nikolaos was beyond the point of caring. "And who will get the credit for taking the mighty Keep of Karalis?" He saw Kleitos slowly inching his way behind Drogos. The lord of Yursa was so distracted by the sudden argument he did not see the advisor. "Will they say Lord Nikolaos had a hand in it, or will they say one of the lords of the Eastwwas not privileged to the information because it needed to be carried out in secrecy?"

Drogos's face hardened. "If my victories are met with such scorn, then maybe it is time for a change in leadership."

"And what will you do?" Nikolaos's fury was beyond control. Kleitos advanced another step. "Will you dispose of us like you did with Petros and Orrin?" Kleitos's hand inched up his sleeve. One more step and he would be in striking range. "Will we meet our ends by falling from a rooftop or drowning in some godforsaken river? Or will it be by some other well-designed accident? Or will you be a man for once and face us with a blade in your hands?"

Kleitos's hand curled around the hilt of his dagger. He slowly drew the small blade, the bright steel detaching from the folds of his sleeve. A gleam of triumph flashed in Nikolaos's eyes. The door suddenly flung open. It slammed against the wall with a loud bang. Startled, Kleitos jumped, driving the dagger back up his sleeve, nicking his skin. He bit his tongue as blood oozed from the shallow cut. A guard entered the room, bowing low.

"Apologies, m'lords," the guard said, his voice muffled by his thick helm. "I tried knocking, but I do not think you heard me over this cursed storm. A rider just arrived from Seren, his horse all but dead beneath him. He insists it is quite urgent. Begging your pardons, m'lords, but he seems quite spooked. Shall I send him in or have him wait outside?"

Snapping his jaw shut once more, Nikolaos tried unsuccessfully to keep the annoyance from his face. If they were granted but a single more heartbeat, Drogos would have been sprawled across the red carpet, a dagger jutting from his back. What news could possibly have arrived from Seren that could not wait until morning, and so rankled the messenger?

"Send him in," he commanded.

The guard bowed once more and then turned from sight. Moments later, the messenger stumbled into the room, his soaked clothing dripping in a stream to the floor. He was trembling and his narrow face was devoid of all color. Nikolaos recognized him as a servant from his palace back in Seren though he could not recall the man's name.

"M'lord Nikolaos, I bring awful tidings." The messenger's voice was shaking. "I rode day and night to deliver it to you and have barely eaten or slept since. M'lord, Seren has fallen. The entire city was in flames the last I saw of it."

Nikolaos blinked and then shook his head. "Seren has fallen? What are you talking about? There isn't a force strong enough to take the city within a hundred miles of it. Who could possibly have taken the city?"

"They arrived from the Eternal Desert, m'lord." The messenger licked his lips nervously. "Thousands upon thousands of them, as far as the eye could see, like some ocean of death." The dam broke and the words came out in a flood. "They rained fire and lightning down on the city from the tips of their fingers. I saw it with my own eyes, m'lord. I swear it upon all of the gods, above and below. The walls crumbled and the remaining soldiers fled before their wrath. The city fell within a day, no, within an hour. There was no force in the world that could have opposed them."

Fear seized the lord of Seren. "What of my wives and my children? What has become of them?"

The messenger shook his head gravely. "I cannot say, m'lord. I barely made it through the Sun's Gate myself, the flames beating at my back. One of them walked past me, m'lord. The ones that made the fire and lightning with their hands. I will never forget his eyes, not even when old age claims my wits and mind, and I can scarcely remember my own name. They were gold all the way through. He looked at me as I mounted my horse with those golden eyes, holding me frozen in place. I'm ashamed to say my bladder gave loose beneath his stare, but he did not harm me or try to stop me. He simply told me to deliver a message for him. He said to tell everyone I came across they returned and that a new age had begun. And then he just let me go. What did he mean, m'lord?"

Lord Nikolaos stared blankly at the messenger. Were the man's brains completely addled? The servant appeared thoroughly shaken, that much was obvious, but his mind did not seem broken. Could such a thing be true? Had Seren truly fallen to an army mysteriously appearing from the Eternal Desert?

"I do not know," he responded warily, "but we will find out the full truth of this matter. Until then, get yourself some food to fill your belly, and I will provide you with a warm bed. Once I have heard the full account of these events, I will decide what needs to be done."

"But, m'lord—"

"We will discuss more on the morrow." He waved his hand, dismissing the messenger. The man walked out of the room in a daze. Nikolaos waited until the door shut behind him and then turned to Kleitos. "What do you think?"

The advisor held his chin in his hand, pondering over the fresh events. "It seems like quite a fanciful tale, but why ride countless miles to deliver such devastating news? And did you smell the stench coming off him? Even with his clothing soaked through, he reeked of piss and stale sweat. I wouldn't be surprised if he stayed in that saddle for days on end. Unless the man is a notable actor, then he has me convinced. As horrible as it sounds, I believe he is telling the truth."

"I would have to agree," said Nikolaos. "We will need to send out riders immediately and recall our men. We must march back to deal with this new threat whether it is imagined or not. I must help my people and my family. The gods alone know what has become of them. The invasion of Varkuvia will have to be put on hold. What do you think Drogos...Drogos?"

The lord of Yursa's back was to them, and his shoulders were lightly shaking up and down. Nikolaos thought at first he was crying but then hollow laughter echoed throughout the study, the sound like nails scraping against glass. It sent a shiver up his spine and helped restore his previous anger.

"I'm glad to see the destruction of Seren has put you in such high spirits," he said stormily. "That the deaths of my family members and people should send you into a fit of laughter."

Drogos turned toward them, brushing a tear away with the tip of his finger. His laughter slowly died away. "I apologize for my rude display of manners, truly I do, but you cannot even begin to comprehend how long I have been waiting for this moment."

"What are you talking about?" Kleitos asked.

"Ah, Kleitos," said Drogos, "forever the faithful hound, but not the brightest I can see. You still do not understand, do you? The Verillion nation has finally reemerged, and they are stronger than you could possibly imagine."

Nikolaos stared at Drogos as if he were a madman. "The Verillion nation was wiped out over seven hundred years ago by the early Varkuvians. They no longer exist. Everybody knows that."

"Do you know I have never liked you, Nikolaos?" Drogos laughed once more. "You are quite correct. The Verillions were hounded and slaughtered wherever they were found. That much can be agreed upon, but there is a part of the story most do not know. A small knot of survivors fled the bloodthirsty Varkuvians, seeking sanctuary in the barbaric lands of the east. The Varkuvian hunters found them even there and pushed them ever further south, killing off any stragglers until the Verillions eventually came before the vast emptiness that was the Eternal Desert. They had two options. They could remain and be butchered or attempt to cross the desert. They chose the latter.

"For over a month they endured the blistering sun, freezing nights, and endless dunes. Hundreds died from heat exhaustion and food deprivation, but most withered away from dehydration. When all seemed lost, the few remaining survivors stumbled upon a land of plenty, filled with verdant hills, bountiful game, and roaring rivers, brimming with fish. They tried to settle down once more and put their past horrors behind them, but another people had already settled these lands. And these people, just like the Varkuvians, feared them for their unique abilities. They attempted to slay the last of the survivors." A glimmer appeared in Drogos's dark eyes. "That was when Tytos the Chosen rose up and took over leadership of the remaining Verillion people. He taught them how to fight back and to no longer be subjugated by lesser beings. Though small in number, their powers, combined with their incredible speed, allowed them to vanquish any force set against them until all of the lands beyond the Eternal Desert bent the knee. For centuries now they have ruled, bringing peace and stability to these new lands and repopulating their ravaged ranks, but they never forgot the butchery suffered by their people. So they sent their own agents back across the Eternal Desert, sending them to every corner of their old world, infiltrating the powerful houses of the nobility, awaiting their moment to return home. After seven hundred and thirty-two years, their time has finally arrived. The fall of Seren is only the beginning of the Age of Verillia. Soon this whole pathetic world will follow until all are under their control."

Lightning cracked outside, casting the study in a fierce white glow. The thunder that followed was so powerful, it knocked an empty wine cup from the desk top, tumbling through the air to land with a soft thud. The lord of Seren licked his dry lips. *No*, he told himself. *None of that is possible. The Verillions are gone from this world.*

"How do you know all of this?" he forced the question.

"You still do not see?" Drogos asked merrily. "Oh, but I am enjoying this so. The greatest fortress the Five Kings have to offer is in ruins, their armies bloodied, and their lands ravaged by war. The armies of the eastern lords have been devastated and are hundreds of miles from their precious city-states. The Argarian fleet is crippled, their king slain, and their army nonexistent. Once Mason has been dealt with, then his tribesmen will return to their Northern Woods and squabble amongst themselves as they have always done. There is no one left to deal with any fresh opposition. All of the major armies and cities in these lands have been bled dry by this war. Do you think all of this was by a random twist of fate? My people and I have been paving the way for this moment for decades. There is no force in the world which can stand against the might of the new Verillion nation. There are no armies in the east to oppose them. The city-states will fall one by one and the Five Kings will soon follow." He turned to Kleitos, looking down at the advisor's sleeve. Blood stained the fabric where Kleitos cut himself. "Do you still plan on using that dagger, or have you two changed your minds about killing me?"

Kleitos looked sharply at Nikolaos. In the blink of an eye, his dagger was drawn. He thrust it quickly toward Drogos's face. His arm abruptly halted as the point was inches away. He strained with every muscle in his body, trying desperately to drive the bright steel into Drogos's temple, his face turning purple from the exertion. Drogos's lips parted, revealing a smile of tombstones. The helpless Kleitos watched as the blacks of Drogos's pupils poured out like spilled ink, slowly spreading to the whites of his eyes and beyond until the lord of Yursa's eyes were transformed into the darkness of the pit.

"There is such fight in you," Drogos said. "It is truly a shame you have to die."

His hand reached out, his fingertips brushing against the front of Kleitos's tunic. The advisor's heart exploded inside his chest like an overripe tomato. Blood spewed from his mouth, erupted from his ears, and fell in red streams from his eyes. Drogos lightly poked Kleitos's chest. The advisor's limp body flew through the air, colliding mightily with one of the bookcases. Books tumbled from their shelves before the case itself collapsed onto the lifeless form of Kleitos.

Ripping his dagger clear, Nikolaos vaulted to the desk, scattering trays of food, and knocking candles to the floor. Flipping the dagger, he jumped into the air, aiming for the lord of Snakes's backside. Drogos turned casually, gesturing with his hand. A gust of dark wind blasted Nikolaos full in the chest. He cartwheeled backward through the air, connecting forcefully with the paneled glass that depicted the battle of the gods. The window exploded under the impact, shattering multicolored glass across the room. Wind and rain howled through the opening. Nikolaos landed heavily on the stone floor, his back somehow propped against the wall.

Vaguely, he heard the pounding of fists on the study door and the shouting of the guards stationed in the hallway beyond. His hand rested on something sharp. A jagged shard of blue glass jutted from his side, with the distinct face of the God of War upon it. He tore it loose and let it fall to the floor where it shattered into a thousand pieces. His head swayed upwards until he found himself gazing into the beetle black eyes of Drogos.

"I wish no one had to die in this transition of power," Drogos said, "but sadly this is how empires are forged. Only through blood and anguish can peace be attained. If only my ancestors had realized the true extent of their powers centuries ago, then there would be no need for this conversation."

He picked up one of the candles that had fallen to the carpet. His black eyes studied the flame flickering lazily on its wick. "Do you find fire just as beautiful as I do?" He lifted his hand. The flame flowed from the candle to his outstretched hand, forming into a tiny, fiery ball that danced along his fingertips. "This is how all civilization began. Without fire, we would be nothing. It is really quite humbling when you think about it." His hand closed around the ball of flame, his fist aglow with orange. "All it needs is a little nourishment to grow, but like most things, too much nourishment can cause it to grow wild and out of control."

His hand opened. The ball of fire sped from his palm, striking one of the bookcases. Not even the rain driving in through the broken window could prevent the flames from licking at the dry pages. Within a matter of moments, the entire bookcase was turned into one massive, burning torch, spreading along the wall to the other shelves.

Drogos strode forward until he towered over Nikolaos. "I wish I could tell you that you will live, and at least allow you that small comfort. I know I told you earlier, I have never liked you, and I meant it, but we will still need to form new alliances to reclaim what is rightfully ours. Unfortunately for you, your city is already in ruins, and soon enough your name will be forgotten. It pains me to say we will be seeking our allies elsewhere."

He spun away, moving gracefully toward the barred door. With a gesture of his hand, the door flew off its hinges into the hallway beyond. Drogos advanced into the corridor. The agonizing screams of the guards that followed were abruptly cut off in gurgles of blood. The only sound now was from the flames as they devoured the many books and scrolled parchments. The sweltering heat spread to every inch of the room, the thick fumes blackening the ceiling.

Sweat and grime bathed Nikolaos's face. He could not move. It was not that he was held in place by some spell, but more so, his legs would not obey him. He watched as the flames slowly ate at the fallen body of Kleitos. Even then, he did not react. His earlier thoughts came back to plague him. *Nothing is simple when it comes to Drogos.* Maniacal laughter erupted from his throat. Everything and everyone he loved or cared for was now gone because he was too greedy and selfish to be content with what he had. It was only when the flames began to eat at his leggings, his mad laughter turned into screams. Soon enough, screaming was all he could do to stem the tide of unrelenting pain. The flames paid him no mind and continued to feast.

# CHAPTER TWENTY-TWO

he woeful cries of the grieving floated on the cool morning breeze. There were hundreds upon hundreds of mourners, each gathered around freshly dug graves that housed their loved ones. Many placed personal trinkets or handpicked flowers on the surface of the dark dirt, while others simply cried their grief away. The newly erected cemetery of the Triumphant Fallen housed all manner of people. There were soldiers and bakers. Poets and blacksmiths. Cutthroats and priests. Men and women. Children and the elderly. It did not matter the dead's occupation, age, or gender, for all came to pay their respects to the thousands who had fallen during the siege of Karalis.

Trystan leaned heavily against the crutch that supported him, his side all but numb from the hours of standing thus. He stood in between two graves. The one to his left had a garland of fresh white roses placed upon it while the other had the black cloak of the Order of Acrium folded neatly upon the hard packed dirt. The flowers held the body of Arianna; the cloak Master Layne. Two people he held dearly in this world were now buried in the ground beneath him. No longer would Arianna's sweet kisses or Layne's words of wisdom be a part of his life. Now they were just a memory, only to be remembered until he, himself, was placed in the ground. Soon enough, worms and other crawlers of the dirt would find a way into their graves and feast upon their decaying flesh.

For several hours now, Trystan stood in-between those two graves. In that time he had not moved to eat, drink, or even to relieve himself. When he first came here, the moon was shining brightly overhead, but now the sun could be seen inching up the eastern horizon. No matter the time of day, there was a constant stream of grievers. Many stood as motionless as he, unable to comprehend their loss. Others were there even before him. Even more dropped to the ground in hopelessness, their grief overwhelming. His gaze drifted lazily upward.

At the edge of the cemetery, he could see the gravediggers still hard at work. Five days had passed since the eastern armies and the Khali departed, and the carts full of the dead were still being trundled from the city. Some were blackened from the city being put to the torched while others showed the pallid signs of extreme decay. Many of the graves were filled with only the personal belongings of those who perished since the bodies either could not be found or were so far gone, they could not be identified. The ever-expanding cemetery formed a giant circle on the Plains of Karalis. At its center, Trystan could see masons and sculptors erecting a massive statue. He heard their chisels as they chipped away at the marbled stone and the grinding of saws as carpenters cut off fresh pieces of wood for scaffolding. King Markos promised the statue would be over thirty feet tall when completed and wasted nothing in the way of expenses to ensure all remembered the brave souls who fell during the siege of Karalis.

His eyes were drawn back to the two graves. The medicine the doctors provided him wore off hours ago, and he could feel blood seeping from the wound at his side where Layne cut him. His vision misted as tears formed unbidden. He awakened the previous night with a shuddered cry, his frantic eyes searching the darkened ceiling of his room. His arm instinctively reached out for Arianna, but his questing hand closed only on emptiness. It was only then that harsh reality rushed back at him. The vivid image of red steel jutting from Arianna's breast consumed his mind. It was instantly followed by his own blade buried in Master Layne's chest. He groaned aloud, and the tears fell. The doctor found him so and misconstrued his tears as caused by his injuries.

It was then he learned from the doctor he had been in a coma for days. While he was unconscious, the eastern armies and the tribesmen pulled back. The Five Kings were triumphant. Karalis was liberated, and the continent of Varkuvia was safe once again. Trystan didn't care. The doctor advised him to remain in bed and get some sleep to allow his wounds to heal. Sleep was the last thing Trystan wanted, for his dreams were filled with death and despair. Despite the doctor's insistent objections, he left his bed and aimlessly wandered the Keep of Karalis. No one recognized the shining Savior of Karalis with his head heavily bandaged and needing a crutch to prevent himself from collapsing. It was the first time in weeks he was able to walk carefree without the prying eye of the common people watching his every step. He was descending the steps of the keep, when he heard a soldier passing by speak of the massive cemetery being constructed.

He moved painfully, slowly through the city, passing through Thieves Alley before shuffling onto the Plains of Karalis. He did not know how he ended up before the two graves. It was as if the gods themselves had drawn him there. There were no names marked on either of the graves, but Trystan somehow knew he stood before the buried bodies of Arianna and Master Layne. The day slowly began to creep by. Mourners came and went, but Trystan remained. His throat became unbearably dry, his side on fire, and his head throbbing. Still he did not care. Jaxon and Gavin found him there around noon. They were dressed in simple woolen tunics, their weapons discarded.

The two stood a respectful distance back, knowing the inner struggle their friend was experiencing. The fading signs of a massive bruise spread along the right side of Jaxon's face where the hilt of a sword had struck. The blood vessels in his eye had exploded under the impact, the whites of his eye submerged in red spots. Gavin's arm hung in a sling, and an angry line of stitched skin could be seen at his neck where the point of a spear ripped at his flesh. The three stood in silence for some time, listening to the cries of the mourning and the frenzied activity of the masons and carpenters hard at work.

Trystan shifted the weight of his crutch. His focus remained on the graves. "Do either of you remember the lecture Master Layne gave on darkest valor?" he asked. The two remained silent to the question. "He said the concept of darkest valor was to do the right thing, no matter the sacrifices needed to be made. 'Through darkest valor we must remind ourselves we will always uphold the peace, protect the weak, and vanquish the wicked.' It's been seven years since he told us that, and I can still remember exactly what he said." His eyes took on a faraway look. "Until this moment, I never fully understood the meaning of darkest valor."

A giant hand gently squeezed his shoulder. "I can only imagine what you are going through," Jaxon said. "If I were to lose Margaret, I would never be able to appreciate the beauty of life again. A part of me would die with her. To lose both Arianna and Layne in the same night must be terrible for you, but because of your heroics, the king was saved. The three of you saved the entire realm."

Trystan had to bite his tongue to stop himself from answering. He was the only one who knew the awful truth of what transpired that night. It was Layne who murdered Arianna, and it was Layne who would've cut the king's throat in his sleep. As far as everyone else was concerned, both Layne and Arianna died while protecting the king. The lie sat like acid on his soul, but as long as Layne's legacy remained intact, the remaining members of the Order of Acrium would be safe from the wrath of the Five Kings. If they were to ever find out the actual truth, then their lives would be forfeited.

Layne's escape from his prison cell was easily believed once the rumors spread that his gaoler, Jerrod, was in league with the Sons of Vikundo. According to rumor, Jerrod attempted to slay Layne while he lay imprisoned. Layne managed to fend the jail keeper off and rip the sword from his grasp. After slaying Jerrod, he rushed to defend the king and died valiantly in the attempt. Since Jerrod himself was dead, there was no one to dispute the fabricated story. Trystan himself still did not know how his mentor escaped captivity.

"I've never known pain like this before," Trystan said instead. "I keep imagining this is all some terrible dream, and eventually, I must wake from it." He pinched himself, wincing in pain. "But it is not a dream. This is reality, and the more I allow it to sink in, the harder it gets for me. I do not know if I will ever be the same again."

"I thought the same exact thing when I lost my family members to a raiding party," Jaxon replied. "For years, I had nightmares about it. Until this day, I can still hear my sisters screaming as the raiders descended upon them and the valiant death cries of my elder brothers as they tried desperately to defend them. I was little more than a child when it happened, and I was utterly defenseless to help my family. For a long time I thought things would never be the same. And they never truly were, but as time passed, the pain slowly began to lessen day by day. I will never have my mother or brothers or sisters in my life again, but they are still a part of me." He tapped his chest. "In here they are still alive. As long as they remain in my heart they will never die, and that is where you need to keep Arianna and Layne. Do not despair at their deaths, but cherish their memories, and honor them in your life."

"Thank you for that, big man." Trystan wiped the tears from his cheek. "Tell me all that has happened since I have been asleep."

"Much and more." Gavin stepped forward. "The eastern armies have pulled back, mostly in disarray, and the Khali have scurried back to the vast Northern Woods. The estate of the late General Corbin has burned to the ground in a freak fire. The body of Lord Nikolaos was found in the wreckage along with a dozen others. Lord Randell retreated to Cabalo with a majority of his forces, and Lord Dorian fled back to Sura with the few who would follow him. There has been no sign of Lord Drogos since the fires consumed the estate. Most of the soldiers that made up the eastern armies wander the countryside with no organization."

"Lord Nikolaos is dead? How did such a thing happen?"

"No one seems to know," replied Gavin. "One eyewitness claims he saw Lord Drogos walking from the estate, unaffected by the flames that consumed the building. That account seems to be mostly discredited since the man who reported it is a known drunkard. As of right now, the lord of Seren's death remains a mystery."

"Before I lost consciousness, I heard the ringing of victory bells. How were you able to prevail once the gates were breached?"

"We were hard pressed, that is for sure," Jaxon answered. "The gates were opened from within, and we were taken almost completely unawares. Our forces fought for every inch of ground we gave up, but our men were still reeling from the surprise attack and weight of numbers were sure to win in the end. But just as our lines were about to splinter, he appeared."

"Who did?" Trystan asked, perplexed.

"Kaleb," the big man continued. "He stumbled from the main entrance of the keep, battle joined all around him. The storm whipped at him, a short sword clutched in each hand. He looked as though a powerful wind could bring him low, but when lightning lit up the sky, the golden glow in his eyes was unmistakable. Just as our forces were about to break, he thrust both swords high into the air. Lightning flew from the heavens and struck the raised steel with a flash so bright you could not gaze upon it. And when the lightning finally dispersed, Kaleb advanced with both swords aglow with fierce light. Then he pointed those glowing swords at the massed ranks of the Khali and easterners. Blue lightning sprouted from the tips and erupted in the midst of our foes. Blackened bodies flew through the air, their charred flesh filling the nostrils. It only took another bolt of lightning before their forces were retreating with a speed I could not have imagined."

Trystan did not try to hide the shock from his face. Kaleb had been in a coma for nearly a month, his name all but forgotten. Had the young noble learned to control his powers while he was in a coma? Trystan highly doubted it. So much happened in the last month Trystan needed to take a deep breath; otherwise it would be too overwhelming.

"Where is Kaleb now? I think it is time him and I sat down and had a word."

"He hasn't left his chambers in the keep since the night he reemerged," said Gavin. "His door remains locked, but no one dares disturb him. Many are terrified of him."

A new thought occurred to Trystan, and he recalled a story he overheard. "Are these rumors about Seren true? Has a new Verillion nation truly emerged from the Eternal Desert? Surely the city could not have fallen within a day."

Jaxon and Gavin exchanged looks. They seemed tentative to answer. "They are true," Gavin finally responded. "Seren was utterly burned to the ground, the death toll catastrophic. Messages arrive daily from the few who escaped, but not all of the details are fully accounted for. However, all seem to be in agreement a large force has emerged from the Eternal Desert and are styling themselves as the new Verillion nation. One message claims the city fell within an hour. Another says the Verillions had sorcerers amongst their ranks, and it was their magic that conquered Seren."

"They claim to be descended from the gods themselves," added Jaxon, "and they have arrived once more to lead us. More and more emerge every day from the Eternal Desert, swarming around the ruined city of Seren. King Lucan and his army arrived the other day. The Five Kings have shut themselves in the Keep of Karalis since his arrival and are discussing how they will handle this new threat."

"That is not all," said Gavin. "The Five Kings have decreed that the Order of Acrium will be reinstated. Carpenters and builders have already been dispatched to make the Fortress of the Van habitable once more. We are told it should be ready to move into within a few weeks. Messengers are riding to every corner of Varkuvia, seeking suitable men to replace our fallen comrades." He gave a slight grin. "The five kings have already announced the new first master. They have picked you, Trystan. You will be our new leader."

"And I am to be the Master of Ax," said Jaxon merrily. He thumped Gavin hard on the back. The archer winced in pain. "And this rascal is to be the Master of Bow. Not too bad for three upstart commoners if I don't say so myself. The remaining two masters are yet to be named."

The big man was happy with the new title he was given, but Trystan was still assessing the new information. In centuries past, the Order of Acrium always elected their leaders from amongst their own ranks, and the first master was generally of royal birth with rare exceptions. With a majority of the disbanded members either assassinated or too afraid to come forward, it made sense for the Five Kings to elect whomever they deemed fit to lead. But why would they pick peasants to lead when they could easily elect nobles they could manipulate? That was when it dawned on Trystan. If the newly reformed Order of Acrium were to fail, it would be far easier to place the blame on the shoulders of untried commoners than on powerful nobles. The three of them did not have friends in high places to protect them if such events transpired. What seemed like a blessing to Jaxon suddenly seemed liked a poison-edged blade to Trystan. If they did not tread warily, then they would be consigned to death.

"This is surely unexpected news." Trystan forced a smile. "I am happy for you Jaxon and for you Gavin. I cannot think of two people more deserving of such an honor."

"Aye, Margaret has been in such high spirits since we were told the news. Our child will be given a life that I could have never dreamed. Who would have thought that a simple farmer could climb to such heights? This is the start of something great. I can feel it in my bones. Together, the three of us could finally make a difference. Gods, but this is a great day." He threw his arms around the shoulders of Trystan and Gavin. "Brothers 'til the very end."

"Brothers 'til the very end," the other two echoed.

Jaxon spun away and started chatting with Gavin about the potential warriors that would be inducted into their ranks. Trystan turned his focus back onto the two graves. He did not feel his friends' elation. All he felt was emptiness. As his two friends debated amiably about who would be a better master, he found himself recalling all that transpired since the disbandment of the Order of Acrium. He remembered the discovery of the Sons of Vikundo and his belief they would march to Karalis and seek the aid of the honorable King Markos. Then there was the defeat of the bandits at Fursta, and the dual invasions which consumed the peaceful continent of Varkuvia. There was the rescuing of Prince Leon from the Bale Fort, and the emergence of Kaleb's dormant powers. And then there was the betrayal of the lords of the east, and the bloody siege of Karalis. Then when the city seemed doom, there was the arrival of King Stefanos and King Eryk. Finally, there was the attempted assassination attempt on King Markos, which led to the combined deaths of Arianna and Master Layne.

His vision misted once more. Arianna. He had the courage to face any foe in battle yet could not find the strength to tell her how he truly felt. Little more than a month was all the gods deemed to grant them. In the midst of a terrible war, with death all around him and his life hanging in the balance, it was the happiest Trystan had ever been. She was the partner of his soul and stood by his side through thick and thin. She was there when he needed her the most, saving his life in the process. Yet when she needed him, he was as helpless as a newborn infant. He watched helplessly as her life was ripped from her. His eyes transferred from the garland of white roses to the folded black cloak.

A man of unquestionable honor had stripped him of his one true happiness. Not once in Master Layne's life had he ever struck a woman or harmed an innocent. But in the course of a single night he murdered an innocent woman, sought to butcher a man in his sleep, and fought a duel to the death with a pupil he held in the highest regard. None of it made sense. Had Layne truly fallen that far, and Trystan was blinded to it? He suddenly recalled the hooded stranger he fought in the alleyways of Karalis, and Layne's intense interest in the lone Verillion. Now there was the emergence of a new nation claiming to be descendants of the Gods. Layne's words came back to him. *Men of great influence and stronger than any of the Five Kings.*

His gaze drifted upward, looking toward the rising dawn sun. The two events went hand in hand of that he was certain. The people who destroyed Seren must have influenced Layne and turned him against everything he stood for. Trystan's face hardened. It was those people who converted Layne to their cause that led to the death of Arianna and forced him to slay his mentor. The true enemy was pouring in from the Eternal Desert, and they played everyone for a fool. *Your father still lives.* Those were the words Layne said with his dying breath. Trystan had no idea who his father was. Could he be a part of this new nation flooding in from the Eternal Desert? He had no way of knowing. There were so many things Trystan was uncertain of in the past few days. His head throbbed as he attempted to process everything. He was rubbing at his temple when something else Layne said came back to haunt him.

His emerald eyes looked to the eastern horizon. "This is only the beginning," he whispered. The words were whipped away by the cries of the mourning.

# EPILOGUE

Landon, the eldest son of Lord Nikolaos, stood behind curtains of orange silk, his entire body trembling, and his feet planted firmly into the marble floor. Even through his closed eyelids, he could still see the swirling flames of purple, gold, and green that devoured the city-state of Seren outside of his father's palace. The token force of soldiers Lord Nikolaos left behind were slaughtered to the last man, and two of the four walls were completely blown asunder. Landon shivered violently, his bladder giving out, leaking in a stream on the floor around him. He dare not move not even to drop the knife still clutched tightly in his hand.

That morning started out like any other since Lord Nikolaos departed. He slowly rose from slumber as the dawn sun streamed in through his father's balcony. The soft golden glow landed lightly on the sleeping face of Aaliyah, instantly making her more beautiful than she already was. She rolled in her sleep, the silk sheets of the bed tumbling from her bronze shoulders, revealing her full-sized breasts. Arousal coursed through Landon, and he took her breast in his mouth, slowly sucking on her nipple. It did not cause him any concern he was laying with one of his father's wives for weeks now, for Nikolaos had five others and no man should be that greedy. Aaliyah moaned softly in her sleep, biting her lower lip. Her eyes fluttered open and without a word began fondling Landon beneath the covers.

Just as he moved on top of her, the slow pounding of a bell echoed through the dawn morning. His head quirked up in curiosity. The intrusive knocking at his door that followed caused him to jump startled. Cursing, he rolled off Aaliyah. "What is it?" he demanded.

A soldier opened the door, his eyes averted from the naked couple lying in bed. "Apologies, but a scout upon the wall has raised the alarm. He claims to have spotted a force on the horizon."

Landon rolled from bed, fear seizing ahold of him. "From which direction?" he asked, hastily pulling on a pair of breeches.

"The scout says they are emerging from the dunes of the Eternal Desert," responded the soldier.

Landon's face took on a perplexed look. "That cannot be possible." He sighed heavily. "Have a servant fetch me my armor and then have the scout who raised the alarm brought to me. I want him flogged once this turns out to be a fabricated story." He transferred his attention to Aaliyah who was starting to gather her clothing. "Did I tell you to get dressed? I will return momentarily, and we will finish what we started."

He marched up the steps of the Dune Wall, his freshly polished armor shining brightly. Adjusting his greaves, he shouldered his way through the gathering soldiers and gazed out over the battlements. A host of an army filled his vision. He blinked rapidly, rubbed at his eyes, and looked again. The same image met his gaze. *This is not possible*, he thought.

The same soldier who knocked on his door stepped up beside him. "What do we do?" he asked.

Landon could think of no reply, his mouth as dry as the Eternal Desert stretched out before him. Lord Nikolaos had only left behind a small force of some two hundred soldiers, mostly old veterans and untried recruits. They were meant to deal with any unruly populace or bandits in the countryside, but stretched out before Landon was an army of tens of thousands. There was no way two hundred could stop a force such as this. *The walls are strong*, he told himself. *We can hold out.* He looked at the wall constructed of giant blocks of sandstone, feeling more confident. No army has ever breached the walls of Seren, and today would be no different.

Three figures detached themselves from the main body of the mysterious army and began walking casually toward the defenders stationed upon the Dune Wall. There was no hostility in their movements, but fear crept into Landon's heart nonetheless. "Archers!" he yelled shakily.

The fifty archers moved to the front of the battlements, nocking arrows to their bows. The soldier beside Landon gripped his arm. "Wait," he cautioned. "We should hear them out and listen to what they have to say."

Landon tore his arm loose. "Do not touch me," he said angrily. "They have brought an army to my walls. The defense of Seren was placed in my hands and these fools will learn only death will greet those who trifle with us. Archers," he commanded, "fill those dogs with arrows."

Fifty arrows were drawn, and fifty arrows were loosed, sailing toward the three walking figures. Every arrow veered off as it was about to strike home. The walking trio stopped and raised their hands to the sky. Dark clouds suddenly formed in the clear blue sky, spreading until they blotted out the unyielding sun. Thunder rumbled noisily from the clouds, bolts of lightning dancing amongst them. The defenders looked up with a sense of awe at the clouds forming from thin air. Unrelenting wind whipped at the defenders as the clouds above them glowed ominously. Jagged bolts of lightning raced down from the heavens and erupted amongst the defenders of Seren.

Blackened bodies flew through the air as repeated lightning bolts struck again and again. Landon was flung to the ramparts, the hair upon his arms and neck standing on edge. The electric air around him was filled with the charred flesh of the burned. He rolled onto his side and stared into the face of the soldier who cautioned him moments before. Half of the man's face was melted away, his armor twisted at a terrible angle, and his blackened tongue hanging slack from his mouth. Landon pushed himself shakily to his knees before vomiting violently upon the ramparts. He forced himself to stand and looked out over the battlements once more.

The trio still had their hands raised to the heavens even though the bolts of lightning ceased to flow. Shimmers of heat surrounded the three as pebbles and stones slowly rose from the ground all around them. Landon was too terrified to look away and watched as tiny spheres of flame coalesced in the raised palms of each of the trio. The flames gradually grew in size and strength, forming into torrents of flame. Each of the massive orbs of flame took on their own color. There was one of deep purple, another of verdant green, and the last of bright gold. Landon became so mystified by the dazzling colors that for one blissful moment he forgot he was in such peril.

And then the trio unleashed the flames toward Seren. Landon watched horrified as they drew toward the city, growing ever larger. The huge spheres of flame struck the Dune Wall mightily, ripping off entire sections as an ocean wave would to a wall of sand. The sandstone blocks were shattered into pieces. Many of the remaining defenders were blasted by the flames, their skin and armor catching fire. Burning torches of purple, green, and gold fell from the ramparts, plunging to their deaths and stumbling into their comrades. The few soldiers who remained alive sprinted from the wall as a repeated explosion of fire completed the devastation of the Dune Wall, turning it into a smoldering ruin.

Landon raced through the streets of Seren, his arms and legs pumping. There was no organized retreat, no plan of action other than flight. Massive orbs of multicolored flame rained down upon the city all around him. A ball of purple fire struck Seren's watchtower, sending it crashing down in a fit of smoke and flame. The watchtower collapsed on the street adjacent to Landon, cascading dust and smoke into the air. Landon continued his head-on race, even as the dust caked his nostrils and choked the back of his throat.

Lightning erupted from the dark clouds above, adding to the horror of the flying spheres of flame. High-pitched screams filtered through the air as Seren became an inferno. Landon stumbled before his father's palace, which was mostly unaffected by the barrage the city was under. He did not know how he ended up there or realize the immense traumatic shock his body was experiencing, but some insane childish notion told him all he had to do was get to his father's bedchamber, and everything would be all right once more. His father would arrive and deal with this new threat and make right the mistakes he made.

He threw open the door of his father's personal chambers. Part of the ceiling had collapsed from one of the many bolts of lightning erupting all over the city. Crushed beneath a pile of broken rubble was the body of Aaliyah, blood spilling across the floor. A shard of broken stone jutted from the top of her skull, her open eyes staring blankly up at Landon. All reasoning fled from the son of Lord Nikolaos. He meekly closed the door behind him and walked slowly toward the silk curtains set against the wall. Then, just as he had done as a child, he hid behind them, closing his eyes against the horror he saw.

For hours now, he remained hidden. He didn't even move when he heard the deaths of the few servants who remained in the palace. Their screams pierced his soul, and their pitiful pleas for mercy caused choking sobs to rip through him. It was then he drew the knife that was still clutched in his hand though he could not remember doing so. He wouldn't be able to use it even if he wanted. *I failed you father*, he thought miserably. The responsibilities of Seren had been left to him, and he allowed the city to be utterly destroyed, its people slaughtered, and its buildings ruined. All of his many siblings and cousins were now dead.

The noise of the bedchamber door opening suddenly filtered through the curtains. Landon's head shot up, his eyes snapping open for the first time in hours. The steady sound of boots walking across marble echoed in Landon's ears. The sound abruptly cut off. Landon stood frozen for several minutes, his body shaking. After finally building up enough courage, he gripped the edge of the curtains and slowly moved them to see who entered.

A man was knelt upon the floor, his attention on the still form of Aaliyah, his back to Landon. He wore a dark blue robe with a high collar, golden designs of weaving circles stitched along the length of the sleeves. The hem of the robe was drenched in blood as were his boots of soft brown. The man looked up, turning his head to inspect the remainder of the room. It was then Landon noticed for the first time, night had descended outside while he was hidden, for countless stars shined in a cloudless sky through the collapsed corner of the ceiling. Bright flames of purple, gold, and green still glowed through the balcony entrance, and Landon doubted anything could extinguish the fires. It was in the bright glow of those flames he was able to see the deep sorrow etched into the powerful face of the kneeling man.

Black soot lightly covered the man's features though it could not disguise his closely trimmed golden beard, which matched the color of his tightly curled hair. The eyes that inspected the room were a deep blue, which could have rivaled the depths of the ocean. Anger slowly replaced Landon's fear as he realized this man was one of the three he saw before the Dune Wall. It was this man who burned Seren to the ground. The grip on the hilt of his knife tightened. The kneeling man turned his focus back on Aaliyah, his shoulders sagging at the sight.

Landon carefully moved from behind the silk curtains, his eyes fixed on the man's back. *I will at least kill this monster*, he told himself. *I will avenge those he killed.* He gingerly took a step forward and then another. His arm drew back, the knife in his hand aiming toward the kneeling man's back. As he advanced another step, his foot brushed against a piece of rubble on the floor. The kneeling man was on his feet in an instant, whirling toward Landon. Landon thrust his knife forward. A powerful hand clamped onto his wrist, twisting it savagely.

Crying out in pain, Landon fell to his knees, the knife slipping from his grasp. He looked up into the face of the man that lit Seren in flames. The deep sorrow mirrored in the man's eyes moments ago was replaced by a burning anger.

"No" was the all the man said.

Landon watched helplessly as golden swirls emerged at the center of the man's pupils. The gold suddenly erupted into every part of the man's eyes until Landon found himself staring into two blazing suns.

The room began to lightly vibrate, the pool of blood on the floor shaking, and the mound of rubble tumbling broken stones to the floor. Warmth emanated from Landon's wrist where the man still gripped him tightly. It began to spread up the length of his arm, creeping to every inch of his body. Landon tried desperately to pull his hand away, but all of his strength evaporated into smoke. He looked in horror as liver spots sprouted along the length of his arm, his flesh melting away before his eyes. Blue veins jutted out all along his arm, and the powerful muscles of his youth disintegrated. His vision blurred into a rheumy film, and his bones withered into sheets of papyrus. He felt his face press into the floor and heard his skin crack and break. *I let you down, Father*, he thought.

Siras, the Minister of Verillia, let the dried-out husk of an arm slip from his grasp. It struck the marble floor before breaking into several pieces. He spun from the wretched sight and walked toward the open balcony, his long robe dragging across the blood-soaked floor. His movements were always fluid even when merely walking. His vision missed nothing, and his senses were constantly alert. *A child with a knife almost put to ruin everything I have planned*, he chided himself.

He strode onto the balcony, drinking in the flames still consuming the once peaceful city-state of Seren. For over sixty years, he envisioned the triumphant return of the Verillion nation. Never had he imagined it quite like this. As he walked toward the city walls hours earlier, he planned to give Seren an ultimatum. They could bend the knee or they could die. Drogos, one of his most loyal supporters, followed his instructions down to the last letter. The east and all of its city-states were the most vulnerable they had ever been, its armies far away. It was Siras's desire to draw as much support from the east as he possibly could. But then the arrogant fool who lay dead in the room behind him decided to attack instead of listen to his proposal.

Years of bitterness and resentment surfaced like a storm inside of Siras. Without thinking, he used his considerable power in an extreme display of might. Seren fell within the hour without a single one of his warriors perishing. *Then why do I feel such guilt?* he asked himself. *Because the beginning of your reign should not have begun in a river of blood*, his subconscious told him. *Those are the words of my father speaking,* he told himself.

Tytos, second of his name, was the exact opposite of the long deceased Tytos the Chosen. His father was a peaceful man, trying desperately to reestablish the old customs of the once-proud Verillion nation. *He never saw the futility of his actions,* thought Siras. It was the ridiculous notions of peace over everything which saw countless thousands slaughtered, all those centuries ago. It wasn't until Tytos the Chosen took over leadership of the devastated Verillion people the true extent of their powers were realized. No longer did they use their powers for the betterment of the community but instead used them to force others to bend the knee and pay homage to their betters. It was Tytos the Chosen who finally understood the Verillions were descended from the gods themselves and were destined to rule.

"If only I was alive to be by your side, ancestor," Siras said aloud, looking toward the night sky.

Siras was one of the last remaining direct descendants from the bloodline of Tytos the Chosen, and so it fell on his shoulders to rule one day. He had such grand plans for when the time came, he was bestowed the role of minister, but his father tried to set everything to ruin. Tytos, approaching his one hundredth and thirty-second name day, refused to listen to any council other than his own. His stubborn belief that the Verillion people should use their gifts to better those around them was seen as a weakness by their vassals. And so it was the many nations and tribes beyond the Eternal Desert rose in the thousands, seeking to overthrow the tyrannical Verillions.

"I loved you, Father," whispered Siras. "I truly did, but you refused to listen to reason. Our subjects only follow us because they fear us, not because they love us. If you had it your way, then our people would have been butchered once more."

Siras just turned fifty and was considered in his prime for a Verillion when the reports flooded in about a joint attack from the nations under their rule. Even then, his father refused to meet them on the field of battle, and so it was Siras took action into his own hands. He still remembered the warm smile on his father's face followed by the look of utter shock as he slid the dagger into Tytos's still beating heart.

The following day, Siras marched at the head of the army and quelled the uprisings. All of the leaders were burned alive, and Siras finally set in motion the plans he housed for so many years. Every waking moment of his existence from that moment on was devoted to restoring the power behind the name Verillia with the knowledge he would one day bring his people back across the Eternal Desert.

Now, sixty years later, he gazed out over the burning homes of Seren. The many nations beyond the Eternal Desert were united under Verillia's banner with thousands more flooding in from the sandy dunes. The proud Saratians, the noble Kuzai, and the warrior-like Yatari. All swore oaths of fealty to him and paid him homage. *And it is all because of me*, he thought. *I made this possible.* He heard the soft scraping of slippers behind him and turned with a smile on his face as his sister Giselle walked onto the balcony beside him. Her blue eyes mirrored his own, her golden spun hair hanging in curls to the small of her back. The purple dress she wore molded perfectly to the curves her body, her breasts pressing against the tight fabric. She was without a doubt the most gorgeous woman Siras ever laid eyes on.

"Is it ever possible to sneak up on you, brother?" asked Giselle, her sweet voice attuned to birds singing.

"You can never be too careful, dear sister," responded Siras. "This is the moment we have waited so many years for."

Giselle tried to hide the distaste from her heart-shaped face. It might have worked with anyone else, but Siras knew her better than any living person did. *There is too much of Father in her*, he thought. *One day soon, I will break her of that, and she will finally understand my reasoning.* He knew she did not approve of the brutal tactics he employed, just as he knew she would never confront him directly, for not only were they two of the last full-blooded Verillions alive, but Siras was more powerful than his sister was. It was one of the main reasons that kept her in line.

Siras leaned forward on the railing of the balcony, the flames catching in his hungry eyes. "Soon this world will learn to respect the name Verillia," he said eagerly. "This is the dawn of a new age, sister. And we will be the ones writing the pages of history."

The two gazed out over the burning city of Seren. The flames roared, reflecting off the star struck night sky. Beyond the ruined city walls, a constant line of dark shapes could be seen making a procession from the Eternal Desert, forming around the smoldering Seren. The line stretched as far as the eye could see. And so it was, the Age of Verillia began.

# About the Author

Tom Cifichiello was born in Suffern, New York in the spring of 1990. At an early age, he developed a love for reading and writing, sometimes spending entire days with his nose in a book. He began writing his first novel, Of Darkest Valor, in 2012, and it has become his passion ever since. The second novel in the series, The Blood of the Gods, is already under way, and he plans to continue writing for many more years to come. Always hopeful, Tom has remained a loyal fan of the New York Knicks and Giants throughout his life.